By Lynne Shelby

Standalones

French Kissing
Love on Location

The Theatreland series

There She Goes
The One That I Want
The Summer of Taking Chances

Love
on
Location

LYNNE SHELBY

ACCENT

First published in 2021
by HEADLINE ACCENT
An imprint of HEADLINE PUBLISHING GROUP

Cataloguing in Publication Data is available from the British Library

ISBN 978 1 4722 8931 5

Typeset in 10.5/13pt Bembo Std by Jouve (UK), Milton Keynes

Printed and bound in Great Britain by Clays Ltd, Elcograf S.p.A.

Headline's policy is to use papers that are natural, renewable and recyclable
products and made from wood grown in well-managed forests and other
controlled sources. The logging and manufacturing processes are expected to
conform to the environmental regulations of the country of origin.

HEADLINE PUBLISHING GROUP
An Hachette UK Company
Carmelite House
50 Victoria Embankment
London EC4Y 0DZ

www.headline.co.uk
www.hachette.co.uk

Love
on
Location

Chapter One

The sun is high overhead and fierce. I sit on the rock, gazing out over the impossibly blue Aegean to the horizon where sea and sky meet in a shimmering haze of heat. A yacht sails across the bay and vanishes around the headland. I hear the faint lap of water on the shore, and the cry of a gull overhead. London seems very far away . . .

Two years earlier

Walking as fast as my high heels and Soho's crowded streets would allow, I arrived at Silver Screen, the restaurant where I was meeting Marcus Farley, with minutes to spare. I took a moment to catch my breath, smoothed my wind-blown hair, and went inside.

As always, the restaurant was bursting with tourists having a break from sightseeing and hand-holding couples stealing a romantic interlude from their working day. My gaze travelled over the old black and white movie posters on the walls – the Hollywood-inspired décor was the reason Silver Screen was Marcus's favourite place to eat out in the whole of London – and spotted the producer himself deep in conversation with a companion who was hidden from my view by a pillar covered in film stars' headshots. Adrenaline surged through me, and I began edging my way past the other lunchtime diners to Marcus's table. He saw me just as I rounded the pillar, breaking off whatever he was saying to get to his feet and air-kiss each side of my face.

'Good to see you, Laurel,' he said. 'Meet Jason – Professor Jason Harding – your collaborator on *Swords and Sandals*.'

I turned to face the other man at the table, who had also risen to his feet.

'Hi, I'm Laurel Martin . . .' My voice trailed off. When Marcus had called me to offer me the job of rewriting the screenplay of his production company's latest movie – a time-slip story in which a girl holidaying on a Greek island travelled back through time to ancient Greece – he'd told me that the director was very keen to ensure the scenes set in the past were authentic and therefore I'd be provided with a historical advisor, a university professor no less. I'd pictured my new collaborator as a bespectacled old man, wearing a tweed jacket and smoking a pipe, reminding me in a quavering voice that the ancient Greeks didn't have mobile phones. Now, instead of the elderly academic of my imaginings, I found myself looking up at a guy who couldn't be more than a couple of years older than my own twenty-nine, wearing a plaid shirt and jeans. He was quite good looking in a rugged sort of way, with tousled dark blond hair, stubble just long enough to be called a beard, and blue eyes. Not my type, but I could see how other women might find him attractive. Realising that I was staring, I hastened to shake his hand and shrug off my coat, and we all sat down.

The next few minutes were taken up with ordering lunch. I asked after Marcus's wife and co-producer, Shannon, and their two little girls, and, beaming with parental pride, Marcus told me of his talented children's latest achievements. He asked if I was 'still seeing that actor you brought to my fortieth' and I was able to tell him that I was indeed still with Conor. There was, I decided, no need to mention that since Marcus had last met my boyfriend, we'd twice broken up and got back together again. When our lunch arrived, the conversation moved on to industry gossip – whose films were in pre-production, which star had turned up drunk on set – and it was only when we reached the coffee stage that Marcus opened his leather messenger bag and drew out two copies of the script that was the reason for our meeting, passing one to Jason and one to me – in my eagerness to have it, I almost snatched it out of his hands. I read the title on the front page: *Swords and Sandals – Draft Twenty-seven*.

Jason, who'd taken very little part in the conversation until then, said, 'Twenty-seven drafts? Is that usual?'

'It's more than I'd generally expect,' Marcus said, 'but it's not *un*usual for a script to go through any number of rewrites – and screenwriters.'

'I see,' Jason said. 'I didn't know that.'

'Yeah, we've already had five writers come and go,' Marcus said. 'It happens.'

'Was it *creative differences* that made them leave?' I said.

Marcus laughed. 'Something like that. Let's just say that Drew Brightman, our director, felt that their screenplays didn't reflect his vision for the movie.' He tapped my copy of *Swords and Sandals*. 'This script lacks sparkle – which is where you come in, Laurel, to iron out the issues with the dialogue and pacing. In other words, work your magic. And now we also have Jason on board to make sure the historical details are right. You guys are going to make a fab team.'

I glanced across the table at Jason. He gave a brief nod of his head.

'Everyone at Farley Productions is very excited about *Swords and Sandals*,' Marcus went on. 'It's a great concept – a feisty modern heroine falling through time, lovers born centuries apart – but right now it's a hot mess. We don't even know if it has a happy-ever-after ending, or if it's a tear-jerker with the heroine returning to her own time and the lovers parted for ever. The final scene has changed with every writer.'

'What do *you* want to happen at the end?' I asked.

Marcus shrugged. 'That's down to you and Jason. If you can't come up with a definitive ending, we'll just have to shoot more than one version and have our market research people check out which is likely to do better at the box office.'

'Cynic,' I said.

'I'm hurt you'd ever think that of me,' Marcus said, with a grin. 'Seriously, though, it's called the film *industry* for a reason. There's no point in making a movie that no audience wants to watch.'

'I won't argue with you about that,' I said. 'By the way, who's playing the leads? If I'm writing a character for a particular actor, I'd like to know who it is.'

'I can't tell you.'

I arched my eyebrows. 'It's OK, Marcus. I won't go running to the media before Farley Productions makes an official announcement.'

'It's not *that*,' Marcus said. 'The thing is, we're still in negotiations with a number of actors for the main roles. We haven't got very far with casting the minor roles either.'

I gaped at him. 'The film starts shooting in six weeks. You don't have a final script, you don't have a cast . . . Aren't you just a little worried?' If I was the film's producer, I wouldn't be able to sleep at night.

'I'll get it sorted before the first day of filming,' Marcus said. 'It's what I do.' His face broke into a broad smile. 'Have I ever told you how much I love what I do?'

'You may have mentioned it once or twice.' A thought struck me, a way for me to do a friend a favour. 'If I happened to know of someone who might be right for a role in *Swords and Sandals*, may I suggest they send Farley Productions their CV?'

Marcus gave me a long look. 'You after a part for your boyfriend?'

'No, not at all. Conor's got two plays lined up back-to-back over the summer. But I do have this friend – actually, she's my flatmate – who's an actress. Her name's Amber Wallace and she's really talented.'

'Doesn't everyone in this business have a really talented actress friend?' Marcus sighed. 'Oh, all right, have her send her showreel to my PA, and I'll take a look at it. Not that I'm promising I'll call her in for an audition.'

'No, of course not,' I said. 'Thanks, Marcus. I appreciate it.'

With a smile, Marcus checked his watch, raised his hand to catch the waitress's attention, and indicated that she should bring the bill.

'I have to get back to base,' he said. 'I've a conference call with New York. I'll leave you two to have another coffee and plan out how you're going to work together. If you could arrange to bring the revised script into the office by the beginning of next week?'

Before I could answer, Jason said, 'Not a problem.'

Hey, I'm the writer here, I thought, taken aback. I'm the one who agrees a deadline. Aloud, I said, 'That's fine with me.' The waitress arrived at our table. Marcus settled the bill, and got his feet.

'Bye for now, Laurel,' he said. 'Professor. Anything you need, call the office.' He made as if to leave, but then turned back to us. 'There's a lot riding on this movie. Just so you know.' With that, weaving his way swiftly through the other diners, he left.

'I'm not a professor,' Jason said.

'I'm sorry?' I said. 'What?'

'I teach at a university,' he said, 'but that doesn't make me a professor. I don't use the title outside work, but officially I'm Dr Harding. I've tried explaining this to Marcus, but he can't seem to grasp the difference between a doctorate and a professorship.'

I wasn't entirely sure I understood the difference either. 'But you are a historian, right?'

'No, I'm an archaeologist.'

'Please tell me that still makes you an expert in all things ancient Greek.'

Jason raised one eyebrow. 'Near enough for our present purposes, I should think.'

'Good to know,' I said. 'So, how do you want to do this? I'd like some time to work on the script on my own, so I suggest we meet up in a few days – let's say Friday – to compare notes.'

'Is that your usual modus operandi?'

'My what?' I'd heard the phrase before, but I wasn't quite sure what it meant.

'Your usual way of working,' Jason said.

'Er, yes.' Recovering my train of thought, I went on, 'I'm sure Marcus could find us some desk space at Farley Productions, but his offices are always chaotic – ringing phones, frazzled production assistants – so it's better if we meet somewhere else. I know a good coffee shop just round the corner from here.'

'We can use my office for our meeting, if you like,' Jason said. 'It's a little cramped, but it's quiet and conducive to study. The university campus is only a short walk from Aldgate station.'

Not an area of London I was familiar with, but one I could get to easily enough. I pictured the scene: an old rambling building of sand-coloured stone, a venerable seat of learning . . .

Becoming aware that Jason was staring at me quizzically, I said, 'OK. What time?'

'Can we make it nine a.m.?' Jason said.

'Sure.' I'd have to battle through the rush hour crowds to get across London by nine o'clock, but at least it would get the meeting over early in the day. 'Let me give you my number. And if I could have yours?'

'But of course.' Jason reached into his shirt pocket and brought out his phone.

'I guess that's all for now,' I said, once we'd exchanged contact details, and he nodded his agreement. I stood up, put on my outdoor coat, and stashed my copy of *Swords and Sandals* in my bag – Jason, I noticed, having donned a scruffy parka, placed his script in a worn canvas rucksack, such as a hiker might carry – and we went out into the street.

'See you later, Prof—I mean, Jason,' I said.

'Goodbye, Laurel,' he said. We both started walking – coming to an abrupt halt when we realised we were going in the same direction.

'Where are you heading?' I said.

'Piccadilly Circus,' Jason said. 'The station.'

'So am I.' I resumed walking along the pavement. Jason fell into step beside me.

'Have you known Marcus long?' I said.

'I met him for the first time today,' Jason said.

'So you've not worked for Farley Productions before?'

'No,' Jason said. I waited for him to say something more, but he seemed disinclined to talk, and as we walked through Soho and along Shaftesbury Avenue, our conversation became somewhat one sided, with me telling him about some of the scripts I'd worked on for Farley Productions – I'd been one of a team of writers on several well-known TV shows, but he hadn't seen any of them. We'd crossed over the road to the pedestrianised area in the centre of Piccadilly Circus, and were wending our way through the hordes of tourists who, even on this cold, overcast March day, were milling around the famous statue of Eros, when a stray thought drifted into my mind.

'Eros was the Greek god of love, wasn't he?' I said, gesturing towards the bronze figure of the winged archer with his quiver and his bow.

'He was the god of romantic love and desire,' Jason said, standing next to me, and looking up at the statue. 'His arrows had the power to make anyone, god or mortal, fall in love. Just one scratch was all it took—' He broke off. 'Another time, I'd be happy to stand here discussing Greek mythology, but I need to get back to Aldgate.'

I tore my gaze away from the statue. 'So do I. That is, I need to get home to Hammersmith.'

'I'll say goodbye, then,' Jason said, 'as we're travelling in opposite directions.'

'Bye,' I said. I was about to add that I'd see him on Friday, but he'd already plunged into the crowd swarming towards the entrance to the tube, and was lost to my sight. Well, he's a man of few words, I thought.

I took one more look at the statue and . . .

Eros draws back the string of his bow and lets fly an arrow. It streaks towards me, straight towards my heart . . .

Enough, Laurel, I told myself firmly, turning my back on the god of love.

Now was not the time to start running a movie in my head.

Chapter Two

Taking *Swords and Sandals* out of my bag, I sat down at the small desk in the corner of my bedroom and started to read. After a few pages, I was asking myself how a script could possibly go through twenty-seven rewrites and still be so dull. And yet, I liked the basic plot, the main characters definitely had possibilities – and bringing the story to life was what I was being paid to do. I picked up a pen, ready to jot down some preliminary notes.

The sound of the front door opening and crashing shut made me start. I heard the sound of my flatmate Amber's footsteps trudging up the stairs.

Her voice came to me from the landing, 'Laurel? Are you there?' Before I could reply, my bedroom door swung open to reveal her standing in the doorway. 'I was called in to audition for a TV series today,' she said, by way of greeting. 'It did not go well.'

'You didn't get the part?' I asked, although I was fairly certain I already knew the answer.

'I didn't even get a recall.' To my surprise and concern, for she usually got over a failed audition very quickly, Amber sounded as though she was about to cry.

'I'm sorry,' I said. 'I guess being cut at an audition never gets any easier.'

'No, it doesn't.' She came into my room and slumped down on the bed. 'You'd think I'd be used to it after ten years in the business, but it's still a rejection and it still hurts.'

'Hey, this isn't like you,' I said. 'Don't upset yourself. None of the actors I know get every part they audition for.'

Amber's eyes narrowed. 'Except for Conor.'

'He does seem to be on a roll at the moment.' It occurred to me to wonder if Amber's inability to utter my boyfriend's name without scowling might be due less to her disapproval of my taking him back after our last break-up and more to her being just the tiniest bit jealous of his long list of credits.

'I've not had any acting work in six months,' Amber went on, 'and my last job was only a voiceover.' She sighed heavily. 'So, I get cut, and I'm feeling down, and then, on my way home, I get a phone call from Tom to tell me that he's getting married. And he wants me to be his groom's girl.'

'But that's great news!' I said. 'You must be thrilled for him.'

'I should be, shouldn't I?' Amber said. 'My best friend has just announced his engagement. I should be ecstatic. But I'm not.' She bit her bottom lip.

'I don't see why,' I said. 'You get on all right with – what's her name? Tom's girlfriend?'

'Her name is Freya,' Amber said. 'She's OK, I guess. I don't really know her. I don't want to know her. I've seen little enough of Tom since he got with her, and I'll see even less of him once he's married her.' Her voice grew shrill. 'Tom and I have been friends since we were in primary school – I don't want to lose him.'

I stared at her, aghast. Where was this coming from? 'Just because the guy's getting married, it doesn't mean he's going to cut you out of his life.'

'But if he has a wife to go home to, he won't be crashing on our sofa after a Saturday night out, or calling round after work with a takeaway, will he?'

'No, he won't,' I said. 'Not if he wants his marriage to be a happy one.'

Amber fell silent and looked down at her hands. When she looked up again, she said, 'I'm being ridiculous, aren't I? I must be channelling my inner five year old. The one that says he's *my* friend, not *hers*.'

'You so need to stop doing that,' I said, relieved to hear her sounding more like her usual self.

'I so do,' Amber said. 'Tom is marrying Freya, and I need to get over myself and be glad for him.' Tucking her hair firmly behind her ears, she got to her feet. 'Right now, though, I have to let my agent know that yet again I didn't get a job she put me up for. And hope she doesn't decide to drop me and make this day even worse.'

'Wait a sec,' I said, recalling that Marcus had agreed she could send him her showreel. 'Your agent won't drop you when you tell her that the head of Farley Productions is considering you for a role in his next feature film.'

Amber's mouth actually fell open. 'You're joking.'

'I'd never joke about something that important,' I said. 'Remember I told you that I was meeting Marcus Farley today?'

'I do,' Amber said. 'Marcus — and some professor who's collaborating with you on the *Swords and Sandals'* screenplay?'

I nodded. 'Well, I mentioned you to Marcus, and he said he'll take a look at your showreel.'

'Oh, Laurel—' Amber sank back down on the duvet. 'That's . . . that's amazing. Thank you. Thank you *so* much.'

'Don't get too excited,' I said, quickly. 'He hasn't promised you a job.'

'I understand that,' Amber said. 'But it's still the best news I've had all day.' She clapped her hands. 'So, apart from *hopefully* rescuing my acting career, how did your meeting go? Did you get on with your professor? What's he like?'

'He isn't a professor,' I said. 'Marcus got that wrong. His name's Dr Jason Harding, he's younger than I expected, and he's an archaeologist.' I thought back over the meeting. 'I don't really know what to make of him. He didn't say much.'

'The strong, silent type. I once dated a guy like that. I thought he had hidden depths. Turned out he didn't have anything worth saying.'

10

I laughed. 'Jason did get a bit more communicative after we left the restaurant. He told me that Eros was the ancient Greek god of love and desire.'

'You've only just met the man and already you're talking about love?' Amber fanned her face with her hand.

'Ha, ha, very amusing,' I said. 'We were in Piccadilly Circus—'

'The romantic atmosphere of a crowded tourist attraction,' Amber said. 'That explains it.' She sprang up from the bed. 'Now, I really do have to call my agent, but then can we get my show-reel sent over to your producer friend?'

'For sure,' I said.

'Thanks again. For talking to Marcus. And for listening to me rant about Tom.'

'No worries,' I said. After all, she'd listened to me ranting about Conor often enough.

Amber went to the doorway. Looking back over her shoulder, she said, 'I hope you like your historical advisor when you get to know him better.'

'I don't have to like him to work with him,' I said.

'Really?' Amber said. 'I find it hard to act with someone I don't have a rapport with off set. I'd have thought it would be very difficult to work creatively with a guy unless you were . . . on the same page.'

I rolled my eyes. 'Stick to acting, Amber. Leave the one-liners to me.'

Jason sat at his desk in his home office, and set his copy of *Swords and Sandals* down in front of him, together with a notebook and pen. He turned to the first page of the script, but before he started reading, his mind drifted back to the meeting with Marcus Farley and Laurel Martin. The producer had an easy charm, the scurrilous stories he'd told over lunch amusing even to Jason – who'd had no idea who he was talking about – but before Laurel had arrived, he'd asked enough insightful questions about ancient Greece to convince Jason that he had a keen intelligence. As for his new collaborator, Jason found it difficult to believe that the woman ever stopped talking long enough to write anything – and yet, she'd reeled off the names of any number of TV shows she'd worked on. There must be something going on in that butterfly mind of hers, Jason thought, even if it wasn't immediately apparent.

With a shrug, he returned his attention to the screenplay, skimming quickly through a scene set in a Greek village. Memories surfaced of the first time he'd worked on a dig in Greece, staying in a village of whitewashed houses . . . He rarely thought about those days, but now he found himself smiling as he recalled how he and his fellow archaeologists had risen with the dawn to walk down to the beach where the fishermen were waiting with their brightly painted boats to ferry them to the small uninhabited island . . . the excavation of the ruined sanctuary . . . how it felt to make his first-ever archaeological find, to hold an artefact in his hand and know he was the first person to set eyes on it in three thousand years . . .

Those were good times, Jason thought. I'll always have those memories of Greece, despite what came after . . .

Chapter Three

'The man's impossible,' I said, pacing around my bedroom and coming to a halt in front of my boyfriend, who was lounging on the bed. 'Conor! Are you listening to what I'm saying?'

Conor looked up from his phone. 'Yeah, I hear you. But I don't understand why you're getting yourself in such a state.'

'I'm not *in a state*,' I said, 'but if I was, I'd have every right to be. *Swords and Sandals* is a larger-scale production than any film I've ever worked on. It could be the start of a whole new phase in my career – and Jason Harding is sabotaging it. He knows nothing about film making, yet he thinks he can tell me how to write a screenplay.'

'What does it matter?' Conor said. 'You're the writer, not him. He's only there to advise you.'

'That's what I thought,' I said, 'but nobody seems to have told Jason . . .'

I'd known on my first read-through of *Swords and Sandals* that it wasn't going to be the easiest rewrite I'd ever done, but that morning, as I negotiated the underground, twice changing trains, standing in over-heated, over-crowded carriages, finally reaching Aldgate East station and the escalators that took me up to the street, I was satisfied I'd done a good job. I'd have Jason glance over my new draft to make sure I hadn't left in any blatant historical errors, and on Monday I'd hand it to Marcus, confident that he'd sign it off as a shooting script.

I turned left out of the station, shivering in a sudden gust of wind and, following the directions I'd brought up on my phone, walked through the unfamiliar streets, catching the occasional glimpse of towering City skyscrapers as I passed old brick buildings that might once have been warehouses or factories but were now offices, and traditional pubs rubbing shoulders with modern coffee shops. After about ten minutes, I found myself walking alongside a stretch of iron railings, beyond which I could see a cluster of what appeared to be low-rise office blocks. It was only when my route turned into an entrance way where a sign informed me I'd arrived at London Aldgate University that I realised I had – as my phone confirmed – reached my destination.

I walked on past a car park and a sports hall, following a tarmac road that brought me to a windswept paved square. A few young men and women – presumably they were students – shoulders hunched against the cold, were hurrying into one or other of the surrounding buildings. I wondered if they were late for a lecture, were determined to bag the best seat in the library or simply wanted to get out of the biting wind. So this, I thought, is what an urban university campus looks like. I much preferred the sunlit hallowed halls of my imagination.

Jason's instructions for finding him on campus had been limited to a text saying that his office was '*in the Humanities building, fourth floor,*' but fortunately, on the far side of the square, I spotted a billboard-sized map which showed me the way I needed to go. Heading out of the square, I followed a concrete path that wound between a tower block – a sign by the door told me it was the Faculty of Science and Engineering – and a low-rise building that was, apparently, the Students' Union. I passed the School of Psychology, went down a flight of steps and across another square, and finally arrived outside the building that housed the Faculty of Arts and Humanities. Sliding glass doors opened on to a lobby, where a lift carried me up to the fourth floor, and the School of Archaeology.

Stepping out of the lift, I found myself in a narrow corridor, with no idea where to go next. Seeing a knot of denim-clad students, boys and girls, standing a short distance away engaged in a lively conversation, I walked up to them. They fell silent as I approached, and I noticed how young and fresh faced they were. It was something of a shock to realise that in their eyes I must seem quite old – almost a different generation.

'Would you be able to point me in the right direction for Jason Harding's office?' I asked.

'Turn right at the end of the corridor,' one of the girls said. 'Dr Harding's office is the first on the left.'

'Thank you,' I said, but they'd already resumed their conversation.

I walked further along the corridor. Rounding the corner, I stopped outside the first door I came to, read the words *Dr J. Harding* on the nameplate, and raised my hand to knock.

A woman's voice came to me from the other side of the door: 'What do you mean, you're not coming? I was counting on you being there.'

I lowered my hand and took a step back. I heard Jason's raised voice as clearly as if I was in a cinema with a state-of-the-art sound system.

'I've no interest in being paraded in front of your female friends,' he said.

'But – I've told them you'll be there,' the woman said. 'They're looking forward to meeting you.'

'That's your problem, not mine,' Jason said.

'For goodness' sake, Jason, you can't keep doing this to me.' The woman's voice was a shriek now.

Oh my days, I thought. Is this the scene in the movie where the girl tells the boy she never wants to see him again?

Jason said: 'You need to leave. I have an appointment at nine.'

'Fine, I'm going!'

And cut! I flattened myself against the wall on the opposite side of the corridor, just as the door to Jason's office was flung open and a thin, red-haired woman in her early thirties burst out. She started when she saw me, before stalking off down the corridor.

'Laurel.' Jason Harding, dressed like the students in a sweat-shirt and jeans, was standing just inside the doorway. He didn't look particularly pleased to see me, which I supposed was hardly surprising, considering the heated conversation he'd just had. Which he must know I'd overheard. Awkward, I thought, but more for him than me.

'Morning, Jason,' I said brightly.

He muttered something that might have been 'good morning' before moving aside so I could enter his office, and shutting the door.

I looked round the room, which was barely large enough to contain the desk — empty except for a phone and a laptop — positioned in front of a window that took up one wall, a filing cabinet, and a stack of chairs. Another wall was lined with book-shelves filled with box files and hardback books. There were no photos or any other pictures, but on the windowsill there was a small white figurine, about six inches high, of a woman loosely draped in a flowing robe with a crested helmet on her head — an odd choice of headwear to go with her dress, it seemed to me — and a bird perched on her shoulder.

'Can I take your coat?' Jason asked.

I handed him my coat, which he hung on the back of the door. He removed one of the chairs from the stack and set it down, gesturing for me to sit, before squeezing around his desk and sitting in the chair opposite.

'Let's get started, shall we?' He opened one of the desk drawers and brought out his copy of *Swords and Sandals*, a spiral notebook, and a pen.

'Absolutely,' I said, although after the train journey I'd had that morning and the walk from the station, I'd been hoping that, before we started work, he'd offer me a restorative coffee. I retrieved my copy of the script, now annotated in three different colours and covered in Post-it notes, from my bag. 'Right. First impressions. From an archaeologist's POV, was there anything that grated as soon as you read it?'

'I don't think much of the title,' Jason said. 'I wondered if it was meant to be ironic?'

'I don't think so,' I said, not having given the matter any thought at all. 'In any case, it's not part of my brief to change it.' Or yours, I thought.

Jason drew a line through something written in his notebook.

'So,' I said. 'Moving on. Anything that immediately leaps out as unrealistic, historically speaking?'

Jason leant forward, resting his elbows on the desk. 'Before we get to the numerous historical inaccuracies, I think we should talk about the plot.'

'OK,' I said, resisting the temptation to explain to him that whatever else he might have to tell me, as far as fixing the plot was concerned, I did *not* need his advice.

'I have issues with the time-travel element,' he said.

'Don't worry about it,' I said. 'Obviously, that part of the story doesn't have to be authentic.'

'I'm aware of that,' Jason said, 'but I still think there should be a rationale behind the fantasy – a reason why the heroine ends up in ancient Greece.'

'She's on holiday on a *Greek* island,' I said, wondering how someone clever enough to teach in a university couldn't understand something so blindingly obvious.

Jason drummed his fingers on the arm of his chair. 'Maybe I'm not explaining myself clearly. I'm asking what it is that draws the heroine back through time to the distant past.'

'It doesn't matter,' I said. 'She just has to get there and fall in love with the hero.'

'Wouldn't the story make more sense if rather than being a holidaymaker who spends her days sunbathing and her nights dancing in a beach bar, she has some sort of affinity with the ancient world?'

'Like what?' I said. It came out more sharply than I intended, but Jason gave no sign he'd noticed.

'She and her friend could visit a Greek temple.' He took a few loose papers out of his desk drawer and slid them over to me. 'Here, I've written a new scene—'

'So you have,' I said. I tried and failed to come up with a polite way of reminding him that *I* was the writer here. Instead, I bent my head over his typescript and quickly read through what he'd written, inwardly groaning when I saw it consisted of the heroine, Chloe, and her friend swapping endless facts that no one could possibly want to know about some ancient ruins. I thought, I don't have time for this.

'Jason, have you ever written a screenplay?' I said.

'No, I haven't,' Jason said. 'I've not worked on a film before. But I've published numerous articles in academic journals.'

'I see.' The man had no screenwriting experience and yet he presumed to tell me how to do my job? Struggling to hide my irritation, I said, 'Well, every scene in a movie needs to move the action forward. This is just two people talking about the scenery.'

Jason frowned. 'It establishes that the heroine is interested in the past.'

'No,' I said. 'At most it shows she's read a guide book.'

'I disagree.'

I took a deep breath. 'Listen, Jason, I don't mean to be rude, but *Swords and Sandals* is a story, not a documentary.' I held out the typescript. 'I appreciate the work you've put into this, but we can't use it. I'm sorry.'

Jason's blue eyes locked on mine. I tilted up my chin. After a moment, he took hold of the typescript and stowed it back in his desk. Relieved that we'd avoided further discussion of his turgid efforts at screenwriting, I opened my copy of the script.

'The first changes I've made are on page one,' I said, and read out my rewrite of the opening scene. It sounded good, I thought. In an effort to be conciliatory, I asked, 'Any comments, Jason?'

'What you've written is much livelier than the original.'

'Thanks,' I said. 'Marcus did say to add sparkle.'

'Yes, he did,' Jason said, 'but I think you need to tone it down.

The lines you've given to Chloe don't work. She comes across as unlikeable.'

'She does not! She's fun and feisty. A modern young woman.'

'If a woman said *that* to me –' He pointed to an inked line on my script, 'I'd think she was a slut. No offence.'

'None taken,' I said, through gritted teeth. I was proud of that line. It was humorous. It sparkled. 'We'll leave it in for now. I'll have a think about it.' I scribbled a note. This script meeting was not going the way I'd envisaged.

'It got worse,' I said to Conor. 'When we reached the part of the script set in the past, we argued over something on practically every page.'

'When you say argued,' Conor said, 'do you mean that you actually had a row?'

'No,' I said, 'but we came close to it. There's this one scene where Lysander – the ancient Greek hero – takes Chloe for a ride in his chariot and they end up making love in the grass under an olive tree. It's the most romantic sequence in the entire film, but Jason said it could never have happened.'

Conor grinned. 'The ancient Greeks never had sex in a field?'

'Please take this seriously,' I said, thinking that it wouldn't hurt him to be a bit more supportive. 'According to Jason, warriors like Lysander did not drive their girlfriends around the countryside in their chariots. We didn't have a full-scale shouting match, but our discussion did become a little heated. In the end, I told him there was no way I was cutting that scene, and he'd just have to put up with it.'

Conor raised his eyebrows. 'And you're still angry with him because . . .? Sounds like you had the final say.'

'Only after arguing with Jason for hours. And in all that time, the wretched man didn't even offer me a coffee.'

'Heinous crime to deprive you of caffeine,' Conor said. I picked up a scatter cushion and threw it at him. He laughed and threw it back. I reminded myself that it was Jason I was annoyed with, not my boyfriend.

'We got less than halfway through the script,' I said, 'and then Jason had to go off and give a lecture. Which means I'm going to have to spend more time with him over the weekend if we're going to complete the new draft by our Monday deadline.'

'Really?' Conor sat upright. 'You've not forgotten that we've got comps for my mate Andile's matinée tomorrow? And later we're going to that new bar in Covent Garden?'

'No, don't worry,' I said, quickly. 'I've asked Jason to come here on Sunday morning. At least that way I won't have to get up at stupid o'clock to drag myself over to the other side of London.' I sighed. 'Seeing as we're out all day tomorrow, I'm thinking I might go over *Swords and Sandals* one more time tonight.'

'Forget the script,' Conor said. 'I have plans for this evening.'

'You do?' I said. 'I thought we were staying in tonight?'

'We are.' Conor's mouth lifted in a wicked smile. Before I realised what was happening, he seized hold of my hand, pulled me down beside him on the bed, and kissed me hard. My stomach tightened as his hand slid under my top.

My phone rang.

'Don't answer it,' Conor said.

'I have to. It could be work.' Like most freelancers, who never know where their next job is coming from, I could never bring myself to ignore a ringing phone. I sprang off the bed, located my mobile on my writing desk, and snatched it up just as it stopped ringing. I checked the caller ID and sighed.

'Who was it?' Conor said.

'Jason,' I said. 'Well, I'm not phoning him back. There's nothing he can possibly want to say to me that can't wait until Sunday.' My phone announced the arrival of a text. 'Oh, for goodness' sake, now he's texting me! *"If you're certain you can't use the scene I wrote, will you consider moving one of the other modern-day scenes to some ruins? They could be the ruins of Lysander's palace, and Chloe realises this when she travels back to his time. JH."*'

I thought for a moment, running through a couple of scenes from the film in my head. 'Actually,' I said, 'that's not a bad idea.' I should have come up with it myself, I thought.

'Then don't reject it because it's his idea and not yours,' Conor said.

'As if I would,' I said, although I was tempted to do just that. Instead, I texted back: *Agreed. But we're definitely keeping the chariot scene.* Before Jason could respond, I switched off my phone. 'Cut! I'm not going to think any more about work tonight.'

'Good to know,' Conor said. 'So, where were we?'

I took off my top and threw it aside, and then I unzipped my skirt and let it fall to the floor.

'Scene One, Take Two,' I said.

Chapter Four

On Sunday morning I awoke with a start, to find Conor's hand shaking my shoulder.

'There's someone at the front door,' he said. Groggy from lack of sleep – we'd got home late and I'd been disturbed in the night by Amber, whom I hadn't seen all weekend, coming in even later and crashing about in the kitchen – I fumbled on the bedside table for my phone and checked the time, gasping when I saw that it was already gone ten o'clock.

'Oh, no!' I wailed. 'I must have forgotten to set my alarm. And now Jason Harding's here.' I sat up, shivering at the touch of the cold morning air on my bare skin. The mirror on my dressing table showed me a reflection of a girl with bed hair who'd done a hideously bad job of taking off her make-up the night before. 'Please, *please*, can you let him in? And keep him occupied while I sort myself out?'

Conor groaned and pulled a face, but pushed back the duvet and got out of bed. Locating his clothes, which like mine were lying in a heap on the floor, he stepped into his boxers and jeans and, struggling to do up his shirt, went off to open the front door, while I grabbed my dressing gown and made a dash for the bathroom. Having washed in record time, and flung on a jumper and a pair of jeggings, I picked up my copy of *Swords and Sandals* and hurried along the landing in search of Conor and Jason, discovering them standing in the kitchen, mugs of coffee in hand. Conor, who could always be relied upon to fill any gaps in conversation with an anecdote from his theatrical career, was telling Jason about the time he had gone on as an understudy and got better reviews than the lead he was covering. Jason's face was expressionless, but I suspected he was less enthralled by the story than I'd been the first time I'd heard it.

'I'm so sorry, Jason,' I said, interrupting Conor's monologue and narrowly avoiding tripping over Jason's rucksack, which he'd left by the doorway. 'I overslept.' As soon as the words were out of my mouth, I realised how unprofessional they sounded.

'Not a problem,' Jason said.

'It's OK, Laurel,' Conor said. 'I explained that we went out last night and didn't get in 'til the early hours.'

Thanks for that, Conor, I thought. I'd hoped this meeting with Jason would run more smoothly than the last one, but it was hardly getting off to a good start.

Jason drained his coffee. 'Would you prefer it if I went away and came back this afternoon?'

'No, not at all,' I said, quickly. 'We've got a lot to get through today. Come into the living room, and we'll make a start.' To Conor, I added, 'Would you mind making me a coffee?'

'Er, OK,' Conor said. I flashed him a smile.

Leaving Conor in the kitchen, and with Jason and his rucksack following obediently in my wake, I strode along the landing to the living room and opened the door, only to be confronted by the sight of Amber's friend Tom asleep under a duvet on the sofa. On the floor beside him were half a dozen empty beer bottles and an open pizza box containing a half-eaten pizza. The room stank of stale alcohol. Oh, for goodness' sake, I thought, he's not been here for weeks – it would have to be last night that he chooses to pass out on our sofa. I looked back at Jason, who raised one quizzical eyebrow. I felt the beginnings of a headache.

'I'm so sorry,' I said. 'I didn't know we had a guest staying. I'll turf him out.' And open the windows, I thought. Marching across the room, I said, loudly, 'Tom, you need to wake up.' I prodded his arm. 'Tom – it's morning.' No sign that he'd heard me. 'Tom! Wake up!'

He muttered something unintelligible and rolled over on to his stomach. For one brief moment, I considered rousing him by throwing a bucket of water over him, but decided that would be too cruel. And the flat did have another room we could use as a workspace, although I'd be mortified if Jason Harding saw it in the state it was in right now . . .

'Looks like we're going to have to work in my room.' I led Jason back along the landing, stopping outside my bedroom door. Conor looked out of the kitchen.

'Everything all right?' he said.

'Not entirely,' I said, jerking my head towards the living room. 'Tom's asleep in there.'

'Amber's Tom?' Conor said.

'Yes,' I said. 'Except he isn't Amber's Tom. He's Freya's Tom.'

'What?'

'They've just got engaged.'

'So why is he asleep on your sofa?'

'I've no idea,' I said, wearily. Conor vanished back inside the kitchen. To Jason, I said, 'Would you give me a minute?'

'But of course,' Jason said.

Thankful that he seemed in a more amiable mood than he'd been at our last meeting, I dived into my bedroom, shutting the door behind me. Gathering up yesterday's clothes from the floor, I shoved the bright red lacy underwear into the laundry basket and hung up the dress. I tossed a stray shoe under the bed, straightened the duvet, and swept various items of make-up from the surface of my dressing table into a drawer. And breathe, I thought, as I opened the bedroom door.

'Come in, Jason,' I said, picking up my *Swords and Sandals'* script and sitting down on the bed. Jason came into the room and looked around, his gaze passing over the collage of photos I'd framed and put on the wall, the dream catcher above my bed, the fairy lights I'd strung around the windows, and coming to rest on the shelves of DVDs.

'I thought most people streamed films these days,' he said.

I shrugged. 'I started buying DVDs when I was a teenager and never got out of the habit. If I can, I'll see a film for the first time in the cinema. If I like it, I'll buy it on DVD. Of course, not every film gets a cinema release any more, which I think is a shame. For me, nothing beats watching a story unfold on the big screen.'

Jason's gaze returned to the shelves 'I don't see any books.'

'I don't read much,' I said. 'I'd rather watch a movie.'

'Evidently,' Jason said. For the first time since I'd met him, his mouth lifted with the suggestion of a smile.

'Books, films, it's all storytelling,' I said.

'Which people have done for millennia,' Jason said, 'in one form or another. We can't be sure, but I can well believe that while they sat around their cooking-fires, the hunter-gatherers of the Palaeolithic era – stone age man – would tell each other tall tales about their prowess with a spear or such like.'

'Are you talking about cavemen?' I pictured a group of men, women, and children dressed in animal skins, huddled together around a fire, distracting themselves from the terrors of the darkness beyond the firelight by making up stories.

'Well, yes,' Jason said. 'Although the people I'm thinking of didn't necessarily live in caves.' He fished his copy of the script out of his rucksack. 'We should crack on, don't you think?'

To my surprise, he sat down next to me on the duvet – I'd assumed he'd take the chair – only inches away from me. Suddenly, ridiculously, I was acutely aware of his masculine presence filling the bedroom.

'Absolutely,' I said, shifting along the bed away from him and rifling through the pages of my own copy of *Swords and Sandals*.

'You'll find we were up to page fifty-three,' Jason said. 'Now, I've had a few thoughts about—' He fell silent as Conor materialised in the doorway holding two mugs of coffee.

'I'm going to head off now,' he said, passing one mug to me and the other to Jason. 'My parents are expecting me for lunch. I'll call you tomorrow, yeah? After my rehearsal.'

'Oh – OK,' I said. He hadn't mentioned he was visiting his parents this weekend, but then again, there was no reason why I needed to know his every move. I started to stand up with the intention of accompanying him as far as the front door and sending him off with a long, lingering kiss, but he motioned me to stay seated.

'You're working,' he said, backing out of the room. 'I'll see myself out.' I heard his heavy tread going down the stairs, and the slamming of the front door. I took a sip of the coffee he'd made me, and told myself I didn't mind that he'd never invited me to meet his family, and that he usually managed to have some reason to not to come with me when I visited mine. Not that my parents had been particularly keen to renew his acquaintance since he and I'd got back together – even though I'd been deliberately vague as to why we broke up.

I noticed that Jason was staring at me.

'Sorry,' I said. 'You were saying?'

My bedroom door, which Conor had left ajar, swung wide open. Amber, looking very glamorous in a brightly patterned silk dressing gown, came into the room, her eyes widening when she saw Jason sitting next to me on the bed.

'Oh – I didn't realise you were entertaining,' she said.

'I'm not entertaining, I'm working,' I said. Or trying to, I thought. 'Amber, this is Jason Harding. Jason – Amber Wallace, my flatmate.'

'Ah – you're Laurel's historical advisor,' Amber said. 'The archaeologist.'

'I am an archaeologist,' Jason said, 'but I've been brought in on *Swords and Sandals* as a writer as much as an advisor.'

Well that explains a lot, I thought irritably. Marcus should have made Jason's position clear to me from the start. As to why a guy with no experience of screenwriting had been hired to

26

rewrite the script of a major feature film, I couldn't begin to fathom.

Aloud, I said, 'Amber, I don't mean to be rude, but Jason and I have a deadline to meet.'

'On my way out the door,' Amber said. 'You need to get that script written. Just make sure you give all the best lines to any female character aged twenty to thirty. By the way, is Tom still here?'

'Out cold on the sofa,' I said.

'Aw – what is he like?' Amber smiled and left the room.

'It's as busy as Piccadilly Circus in here this morning,' I said to Jason. 'I am *so* sorry.'

'Please don't apologise,' Jason said. 'I know what it's like to live in shared accommodation from when I was a student.'

'It's not always like this,' I said, eager to dispel the impression that I lived the lifestyle of an eighteen year old. 'Amber and I can go days without setting eyes on each other. And Conor doesn't live here. He shares a house with two other guys.'

'Ah,' Jason said, evidently not much interested in my domestic arrangements. 'Anyway, going back to *Swords and Sandals*, I've come up with another reason why Chloe might be drawn back through time to ancient Greece.' My heart sank. Please don't tell me you've written another scene, I thought.

'We've already discussed that,' I said. 'We can't keep going over it again and again – not if we're going to whip *Swords and Sandals* into a fit state to present to Marcus tomorrow.' I looked directly into Jason's blue eyes. He held my gaze but, to my relief, made no further demur. Letting out my breath, I went on, 'So, we were on page fifty-three . . .'

For the next few hours we made good progress. When Jason pointed out that a twenty-first-century woman was unlikely to win a swordfight against a Greek warrior trained in the art of warfare since childhood, I was, on reflection, inclined to agree with his expert opinion and cut that particular scene. When I refused to cut a scene in which Chloe persuaded Lysander to get up off his throne and dance with her, Jason's eyes narrowed, but he didn't argue. We took a short break for lunch – Jason appeared surprised when I expressed a need to eat, but accepted a sandwich – but other than that we ploughed on until we came to the end of the film, the moment when Chloe had to decide whether to return to her own time or stay in the past for ever with the man she loved. The last page of the script was blank except for a scrawled note in Marcus's handwriting: *Does she go or stay?*

'She goes back to her own life,' I said, quickly, 'and he goes back to his.' In case Jason was in any doubt, I held out my copy of the screenplay, to which I'd attached my final scene for the film. 'Here, take a look at what I've written. I'm proud of this ending. It's bitter-sweet – and very commercial. I know Marcus is going to love it.'

Jason shook his head. 'She stays.'

Here we go again, I thought.

'Why would she go back?' Jason went on. 'What could possibly make her choose to return to the twenty-first century?'

'Honestly?' I said. 'How about music any time she wants it, without having to find a guy who can play a lyre? Supermarkets full of food that doesn't have to be hunted and killed with a spear? *Movies?* I could go on.'

'But in ancient Greece,' Jason said, 'she has the one thing she can never have in the present. She has Lysander.' He raked his hand through his hair. 'I don't believe we're having this conversation. It's not as though Chloe and Lysander are real people.'

'They're real to me . . .'

Chloe and Lysander walk hand in hand through an olive grove . . . She watches him as he spars with his warriors . . . He takes her in his arms . . .

'That is, I see them in my head,' I said. 'They seem real.'

Jason gave me a long look. 'Then let them have their happy ending. Rewrite the script and have them stay together.'

'I can't,' I said. 'I've given them the right – the inevitable – ending for their story. Read it, and you'll see what I mean.'

Again, I held out my typescript, and this time Jason took it and read it.

'Well?' I said. 'What do you think?'

Jason laid the script carefully down on the bed. I realised I was holding my breath.

'It's good,' he said. 'It's . . . real. Sad, but satisfying. I'm impressed.'

'Thank you,' I said, quietly. Not that I had any intention of letting Jason persuade me to alter the film's final scene – this was the ending I was going with for tomorrow's script meeting, whatever his opinion – but knowing that he rated my storytelling was a definite bonus. 'I think we've done a good job.'

'Overall, I have to agree with you,' Jason said. 'It took a while, but we got there.' I glanced towards the window and saw that it had grown dark outside without either of us noticing.

'Would you like a drink to celebrate?' I said. 'I've wine in the fridge – or beer, if you prefer.'

'A tempting offer,' Jason said, 'but I ought to head off home.'

I thought of the woman I'd seen storming out of his office. 'Someone expecting you?'

'No,' Jason said, getting to his feet and shouldering his rucksack. 'But I do have a pile of my students' essays waiting for me to grade them.'

'Ah – another deadline,' I said, standing up also. 'Well, I hope you find fewer historical mistakes in your students' papers than you found in the script.'

'So do I,' Jason said, a smile taking the sting out of his words. I found myself smiling back at him, noticing for the first time the laughter lines at the corners of his eyes, and his thick dark eyelashes. He should smile more often, I thought, as I stood looking up into his face. He was so much more attractive when he smiled . . .

I reach up, draw down Jason's head, and tangle my fingers in his hair . . .

And cut! Cut! Cut! Cut! My heart was beating very fast.

'I – I'll see you tomorrow,' I said, pivoting on my heel and heading out of the bedroom. I reminded myself that no one could see the movies in my mind, but it was only with difficulty that I prevented myself from breaking into a run.

Jason, oblivious of the effect of his smile on my over-active imagination, followed me along the landing and down the stairs. I flung open the front door, and he stepped past me into the small paved garden that separated the flat from the street.

'Goodnight, Laurel,' he said.

'N-night,' I stuttered. He went through the front gate, got into a car, and drove off.

I shut the door and stood at the bottom of the stairs, leaning against the wall until my heart had slowed to its normal beat and the unruly sensations I'd experienced as I'd gazed up at Jason Harding's handsome face had faded. Get a grip, Laurel, I told myself firmly. So what if I'd noticed that my writing partner – as I now had to think of him – was a good-looking guy? I knew a lot of good-looking men.

Amber's voice called, 'Was that your archaeologist leaving?' I looked up and saw her watching me from the landing.

'Yes, he's gone.' I walked slowly up the stairs. 'Is Tom still here?'

'Oh, no, he went home hours ago,' Amber said, following me as I went along the landing to the kitchen.

'Would you like some wine?' I said.

'Er – about that bottle of wine you had in the fridge,' Amber said. 'Tom and I may have drunk some of it last night . . .'

I opened the fridge and took out the now almost empty bottle of chenin blanc.

'Just as well Jason couldn't stay for a drink,' I said.

'You invited him to have a drink with you?' Amber said. 'Not that I blame you. That man is gorgeous. Why didn't you tell me?'

'I don't think Jason is particularly good looking,' I said. 'We worked well together today, much better than at our first meeting, but I'm not attracted to him.' Ridiculously, I felt my face grow warm.

'So I wasn't interrupting anything apart from screenwriting when I burst in and found you two cuddled up on your bed?' Amber said.

I rolled my eyes. 'You seem to have forgotten that I'm in a relationship. The only action that took place in my bedroom today after Conor left was on the pages of *Swords and Sandals*. I don't believe in gratuitous sex scenes. Not in a screenplay, and certainly not in my life.' I poured what was left of the wine into a glass. It was barely half full.

'Oh, lord,' Amber said. 'I didn't realise Tom and I'd drunk that much of your wine.' She clasped her hands together in front of her and in an angst-ridden voice that wouldn't have been out of place in a melodrama from the Golden Age of Hollywood, said, 'I know I've done wrong. I stole something precious from you. Can you ever forgive me?'

'It won't be easy after what you've put me through,' I said, holding the back of one hand against my forehead, and sighing dramatically. 'But I'll try.'

'Have you ever thought of becoming an actress?' Amber said.

'No,' I said. 'You'll never find me in front of the camera.'

'Just as well,' Amber said. We both laughed. I took a sip of the remaining chenin.

'What was Tom doing here, anyway?' I said. 'I thought his days of passing out on our sofa were over. His fiancée must be a very understanding woman if she doesn't mind him staying out all night.'

'Freya doesn't know,' Amber said. 'She was away the entire weekend. A hen party.'

'That was quick,' I said, 'considering she and Tom only got engaged last week.'

'Oh, it wasn't her hen party,' Amber said. 'Tom told me that he and Freya are invited to no fewer than five weddings in the next few months.'

'Five!' I exclaimed. Although, now I came to think about it, roughly the same number of my old school-friends had announced that they were getting hitched this year. 'I guess you and I are both getting to *that* age.'

'What age?'

'Oh, you know. The age when singletons start to think about the next stage in their lives. Maybe moving in with a partner, buying a house together, marrying, having children.' Fleetingly, I tried to picture me and Conor a few years from now as a couple living in marital bliss, but the images were insubstantial, flickering in and out of focus in my head before blinking out, like an old movie shown on a projector when the film reel breaks. I gave myself a mental shake. Conor had only been back in my life for three months. It was far too soon for either of us to be thinking of taking our relationship to the next level.

Amber's voice broke in on my thoughts. 'I can't help wondering if Tom felt pressurised to propose to Freya. What with so many of their friends tying the knot.'

'That seems extremely unlikely,' I said. 'Obviously I don't know Tom as well as you do, but he strikes me as a man who knows his own mind.'

Amber didn't appear to be listening. 'I hope he's not making a huge mistake,' she said. 'He was very eager for me and him to go out last night. I rather get the impression that Freya keeps him on a tight leash.'

'You really don't want him to marry her, do you?' I said.

'I want him to be happy,' Amber said. 'I can't see Freya making him happy. Not the way I could. If only he'd let me.' She hung her head. Her long dark curls fell forward over her face.

I stared at her, telling myself I was mistaken, and she hadn't just told me that she wanted to be more than a friend to Tom.

Choosing my words with care, I said, 'You've always insisted that you and Tom have never been anything other than best mates. Have your feelings towards him changed?'

She looked back up at me. 'Tom and me . . . Nothing's ever happened between us, but that doesn't mean I haven't sometimes wondered if one day it might.'

'Does Tom know?'

'That I'm in love with him?' Amber said.

'Oh, Amber—'

'Tom has no idea. I didn't know myself. Not until he told me he was marrying another woman.' Amber's eyes brimmed with tears. 'When I went into the living room this morning, he was still asleep. I stood there watching him, and all I could think was how much I wanted him, how wonderful it would be to share his bed and wake up next to him each day, to be with him. I love him. And I can never tell him.'

I was lost for words. Some screenwriter I am, I thought.

'Promise me that you won't repeat any of this to Conor,' Amber said.

'I won't if you don't want me to,' I said.

'I couldn't bear it if anyone else knew how I feel about Tom,' Amber said. 'I didn't mean to tell you, but I had to talk to somebody. I'm so unhappy.' A tear ran down her face. She wiped it away.

'Oh, don't cry,' I said. 'I can't imagine what you're feeling right now – I know it must be hard for you – but you'll get through it.'

Amber gave a barely perceptible nod of her head. 'I will get through this,' she repeated, as if to convince herself as much as me. 'I'll going on playing the role of Tom's best mate, and I'll watch him get married with a smile on my face. And if it all goes wrong, I'll be there for him.'

I put my hand on her arm. 'And I'm here for you whenever you need me.' It was strange to think that I'd only met Amber a year ago, when she'd rented the spare room in my flat. We'd become such good friends since then.

'Th-thank you, Laurel,' Amber said. 'And straight back at you.' For a moment, I thought she was going to cry again – my own throat felt a little tight – but instead she managed a brief smile. 'Are you seeing Conor tonight?'

'No, he's visiting his parents,' I said.

33

'So if I were to run out to the supermarket and get another bottle of that white wine you like,' Amber said, 'you'd be available to share it with me?'

'For sure,' I said. 'Tell you what, why don't we have a proper girls' night with a takeaway and one of my DVDs?'

'Sounds good to me,' Amber said. 'I'll go get the wine; you order us a pizza and pick out a film.'

We left the kitchen, and Amber headed off to the supermarket. I rang our local pizzeria and ordered the delivery of an extra-large pepperoni, and went back into my bedroom. My gaze slid along my shelves and the spines of the DVDs that made up my collection: thrillers, westerns, old black and white musicals, historical dramas, science fiction epics, and the rom-coms that were my favourite type of movie, although possibly not the best choice of viewing for Amber, who'd hoped to star in her own romantic comedy, but instead had been cast in a tearjerker.

With a sigh, I left my beloved rom-coms on the shelf and picked out a psychological thriller.

If only life was like a movie and we could rewrite the script.

Chapter Five

When I walked to the station on Monday morning, the day was fine, warm enough to make me think spring had finally sprung, but by the time I came up out of the underground, the sky had clouded over. As I turned into Wardour Street, once the centre of the British film industry and still the home of a few independent film makers like Farley Productions, I felt the first drops of rain. Stopping under an awning outside one of the street's many bars and coffee shops to rummage fruitlessly in my bag for an umbrella, I noticed Jason Harding sitting at a table in the window of a café on the other side of the road, and not unexpectedly found myself perfectly able to look at him, without feeling in the slightest bit attracted to him. I almost crossed over the road to join him, but then I saw he was not alone and that, to my surprise, the man sitting with him was *Swords and Sandals'* director, Drew Brightman, easily recognisable from his shock of white-blond hair, although rather more portly than I'd have expected from photos I'd seen of him in the media, with fleshy jowls that threatened to become a double chin in later life – I'd read somewhere that he was thirty-five, but I thought he looked older. I watched curiously as Drew leant towards Jason, thumping his hand on the table as if to emphasise what he was saying, before it occurred to me that being caught spying on a movie director through a plate-glass window might not be the best way to further my career as a screenwriter. I continued walking, quickening my pace as the rain began to fall in earnest. Presumably, Drew was also attending this morning's script meeting. It wasn't unknown for a director to do so.

Arriving at the tall red-brick building that housed Farley Productions, I hurried through the sliding doors leading into the reception area and, having announced my arrival to the receptionist, sat in one of several comfortable armchairs provided for visitors. A few minutes later, one of Farley Productions' staff – a beaming girl in her early twenties who introduced herself as 'Eadie, Marcus's new production assistant' – came to convey me through the company's airy, open-plan work space, where several dozen men and women sat at desks, talking on phones or tapping away at keyboards, leaving me in a meeting room with instructions to help myself to refreshments. I lost no time in pouring myself a coffee and selecting a blueberry muffin from the cakes, pastries, and fruit that had been left on a small table under the window. Hanging my coat and bag on the back of a chair, I took a seat at the larger table in the centre of the room, and placed my copy of *Swords and Sandals*, pens, and a supply of Post-it notes in front of me. A moment later, Marcus and Shannon, looking every inch the power couple in a suit and tailored dress respectively, came into the room, Eadie bounding in after them like an eager puppy. We exchanged the usual greetings, and they arranged themselves around the table, Marcus at one end, Shannon at the other, setting out scripts, notebooks, and iPads and, in Marcus's case, placing his mobile within easy reach. I noticed Shannon look pointedly at the clock on the whitewashed brick wall and then at her husband.

'We'll give them another five minutes,' he said, just as Jason and Drew came into the meeting room. 'Ah – here they are. Morning, Drew. Morning, Professor.'

'Hey, guys and gals,' Drew said, sitting down opposite me with the table between us.

'Good morning,' Jason said, sitting next to Drew.

The director's gaze fixed on my face. 'You must be Jason's co-writer?'

Well, that's telling me, I thought. Before I had a chance to reply, Drew turned his head towards Marcus.

'So what have you got for me?' he said.

'Over to you, Laurel,' Marcus said. Hastily I opened my copy of *Swords and Sandals*.

'The first change I – Jason and I – made is on page one . . .'

Three hours and many cups of coffee later – with Marcus, Shannon, and Drew asking questions and scribbling notes, and Jason observing the proceedings in silence – I read out the last scene.

'Fade to black,' I said. 'The End.' I closed the script and looked from Marcus to Shannon and back again. They were giving nothing away. I told myself very firmly that they couldn't fail to like what I'd done with the script. It contained some of the best lines I'd ever written.

'Good job,' Marcus said.

Yes! I had to make a conscious effort not to punch the air. I smiled across the table at Jason, but his attention was all on Marcus.

'That ending,' Marcus went on. 'I love it. Shannon?'

'It works for me,' Shannon said. 'Very moving. It would have made me cry, if I ever cried at films. Which I don't. I particularly like the very final scene where Chloe is sitting in a café overlooking the beach where Lysander once drove her in his chariot. She's desperately sad that the past is lost to her, but when the English guy she was talking to in the bar right at the beginning of the film asks if he can join her, you know her life will go on. She's where she's meant to be.'

'Well, it's been a long time coming,' Marcus said, 'but I'm ready to sign off on this screenplay.'

And the credits roll, I thought, with my name among them.

'So, Drew,' Marcus said, 'do you reckon we have a shooting script?'

'Not quite yet,' Drew said.

I drew in my breath. Was Drew Brightman about to criticise my carefully crafted, snappy, yet convincingly realistic dialogue?

'OK, Drew,' Marcus said, with a barely suppressed sigh. 'What are your thoughts?' Am I imagining it, I wondered, or is my producer friend not best pleased with his hotshot director right now?

Drew leant forward, resting his elbows on the table. 'Chloe should be an archaeologist, not a tourist.'

An *archaeologist*? I shot Jason a look.

'Interesting,' Marcus said.

'I can't claim the credit,' Drew said. 'It was Jason who came up with the idea.' He smiled benevolently at my co-writer. 'Tell them what you said to me this morning.'

Jason cleared his throat. 'If Chloe is an archaeologist working on a dig in Greece rather than a girl on a beach holiday, it gives her a connection to the past – a reason why she's ripped away from her own time. It would certainly explain how she's able to understand Lysander when he's speaking in ancient Greek which, I have to say, is something that's been bothering me since I first read the script.'

Unbelievable! After all the time Jason and I'd spent together – and with Chloe and Lysander – he'd gone running off to Drew with a whole new scenario for their story. Hidden from view under the table, my hands curled into fists.

'Great idea, yeah?' Drew said.

Marcus regarded Drew silently for a moment, and then his face broke into a smile. 'An archaeologist heroine. I like it. How about you, Shannon?'

'It could work,' Shannon said, 'but it would take *Swords and Sandals* in a whole new direction.' She doesn't want this, I thought.

'Exactly,' Drew said. 'Jason's idea is that we replace the opening scenes of Chloe in a beach bar with scenes of her digging up an ancient ruin. You do a lot of work in Greece, don't you, Jason? You can bring that first-hand experience to *Swords and Sandals*.'

'I have worked on excavations in Greece,' Jason said.

'I hear what you're saying,' Shannon said, 'but my issue is that we're looking at another rewrite for which we simply don't have the time. In case you've forgotten, Marcus, filming on *Swords and Sandals* starts in *five weeks*.' She *really* doesn't want this, I thought.

'I know, I know,' Marcus said. 'We need a shooting script and we need it fast.' His gaze travelled around the table and came to rest on me. 'What are your initial thoughts on Jason's new scenario, Laurel? If we were to go with an archaeologist heroine, how would you rewrite the scene immediately after the opening credits?'

Caught off my guard, my mind went blank. I couldn't think of a single line of dialogue, let alone a new opening scene for a major motion picture. I gawped at Marcus, resisting the temptation to tell him that in my opinion, the screenplay was fine left exactly the way I'd written it . . . And then I was looking at a close-up of Chloe digging in the ruins of Lysander's palace, discovering a small stone statue of the woman like the one in Jason's office . . . or a statue of a Greek warrior . . . or a sword . . .

'Laurel?' Marcus said.

'I see Chloe sitting on a fallen marble column in the ruins of Lysander's palace, which has recently been discovered by archaeologists,' I said. It's OK, I told myself, you've got this, pitching ideas to producers is what you do.

'I should point out,' Jason said, 'that if this is the first time the site has been excavated, she may not know whose palace it is.'

'She doesn't know.' I made myself smile, although it may have been a little tight. 'Not yet. She's holding a sword that she's found. It's Lysander's sword — although she obviously doesn't know that yet either.'

Jason leant forward across the table. 'It's an incredible moment when you find an object like that.'

'Is it?' I said. Personally, I couldn't see the attraction of scrabbling around in the mud for bits of rusty metal, but if Chloe were an archaeologist . . .

With infinite care, scarcely daring to breathe, Chloe lifts the sword from the earth that has hidden it for centuries and weighs it in her hands. It is broken and dull, but thousands of years ago, a warrior would have wielded it in battle, its deadly, shining blade carving arcs of light through the air . . .

Aloud, I said, 'Cut to the next scene. Chloe is cleaning the earth off the sword. I assume she'd do that?' I glanced at Jason, and he nodded. 'Another archaeologist, a guy, interrupts her, and invites her to go with him and some other people to . . .' Again, my imagination faltered.

'A team of archaeologists who've been working all day in the hot sun would most likely head for the nearest taverna,' Jason said.

'An authentic Greek taverna,' Drew said. 'I'm liking this.'

'They go to a taverna,' I said. Playing for time, I stood up, walked to the window and gazed out as though lost in thought. The street outside, what I could see of it through the raindrops running down the glass, might have once been the centre of the British film industry, but on a grey day like today, the view was not inspiring. I turned around to face the room, convinced that I was going to have to tell Marcus I was all out of ideas . . . and the film in my head began running again.

'The guy – the other archaeologist – comes on to Chloe,' I said, 'but she's not interested. She tells a female friend that she's fed up with casual one-night stands, and she wants to find her soulmate. While the others are joining in with some Greek dancing, she slips away to the ruins . . .'

Chloe's mind drifts back to the find she made earlier in the day. She thinks of the man who might have wielded the sword, the warrior who once lived, fought, and loved in this place where she spends her days digging in the earth. What was his name? What did he look like? What sort of man was he?'

'So, she's clambering around the excavation, alone in the dark, when she turns her ankle, falls, hits her head—' I paused for dramatic effect. 'And the rest is history.'

'Literally,' Jason said.

'*Yes*,' Drew said.

'Shannon?' Marcus said.

40

'It's your call, Marcus,' Shannon said.

'Archaeologist it is then,' Marcus said.

'Great,' Drew said. 'Well done, Jason.'

I thought, well done *Jason*? Well done for nothing other than dropping me right in it. Unwittingly, I scowled across the table at my so-called co-writer. He smiled. I looked away. The man was *insufferable*.

'We've got as far as we can for now, I think,' Marcus said. 'Eadie, would you have this typed up please? And email the new draft – draft twenty-eight – over to Jason and Laurel.' He held out his copy of draft twenty-seven, on which he'd noted the changes Jason and I had made. Clasping the script with both hands, Eadie galloped out of the room. Marcus and Shannon pushed back their chairs and stood up. Jason, Drew, and I followed suit.

'Thanks for coming in today,' Marcus said. 'As Shannon reminded me, we don't have much time, so I'm going to ask Jason and Laurel to bring in the new draft – I sincerely hope it's the final draft – on Thursday morning. Does that work for you, Drew?'

The director consulted his phone. 'Yeah. I'll have my people liaise with yours to confirm.'

Somewhat belatedly, Marcus said, 'Are you available on Thursday, Jason?'

'I can be,' Jason said.

'I'll be there,' I said, quickly.

Lingering only to chorus our goodbyes, Drew, Jason, and I filed out of the meeting room. The two men immediately fell into conversation, strolling side by side across Farley Productions' open-plan office towards the reception area. I followed after them, glaring at Jason's back, still trying to get my head around the fact that he hadn't run his *great new idea* past me before pitching it to our director, and making me look an incompetent idiot in front of Marcus and Shannon in the process. Traitor, I thought. What sort of co-writer does that?

In reception, Jason and Drew came to a halt, the director talking animatedly, with many wild gesticulations, my perfidious writing partner hanging on his every word. Even as I glowered at him, Jason beckoned to me to join them. Not trusting myself to speak to him without saying something entirely unprofessional, I kept walking.

Outside, it was raining heavily. Turning up my collar, I stomped along the slippery pavement, inadvertently stepping in a puddle, which did nothing to improve my mood. By the time I'd reached the junction of Wardour Street and Shaftesbury Avenue, I could feel the rain trickling down my neck inside my coat.

From behind me, I heard Jason say, 'Laurel, wait up.'

I whirled around to face him, and saw that he was holding a large black umbrella.

'You're getting drenched,' he said, stepping up close to me so that the umbrella kept the rain off both of us.

'What do you want, Jason?' I said, shifting away from him, even though it meant that I was once more standing in a downpour.

'You left before we arranged when we're going to meet up to work on the script,' he said. 'Is tomorrow any good for you? I'm lecturing until two o'clock, but after that I'm free for the rest of the day.'

'Whatever,' I said. 'Tomorrow or the day after, it makes no difference to me.'

'Shall we reconvene in my office?'

'Fine.'

'Alternatively, we could start work this afternoon?' Jason said. 'If you're free?'

'I'm not,' I said. An empty afternoon lay before me, but I needed some time out – time away from him. 'The screenplay of *Swords and Sandals* can stay as I wrote it for one more day.' Turning my back on him, I resumed walking through the rain towards Piccadilly Circus. To my intense irritation, he fell into step beside me, holding his umbrella overhead, matching his stride to mine when I quickened my pace. We walked the rest of the way along

42

Shaftesbury Avenue in a silence broken only when we were waiting for the traffic lights to change so we could get across the road, and Jason told me to watch out – too late – as the wheels of a passing taxi sent a spray of water on to the pavement, soaking my legs. This day just gets better and better, I thought.

The cars and buses came to a halt. With Jason still hovering at my side, I crossed the road, and headed in the direction of the station, almost colliding with a cluster of tourists taking photos of Eros despite the rain. I tried to dodge through them, but they were too interested in posing for the camera to get out of my way.

'Laurel—' Jason planted himself in front of me, forcing me to stand still.

'What?' I snapped, pushing wet hair back from my face. 'What is it you want?'

'I was wondering if I might buy you lunch?' Jason said. 'In return for your hospitality yesterday.'

'No, you may *not*,' I said. 'I have to go – I can't talk to you right now.'

He frowned. 'Is something wrong? You seem upset?'

'You think?' Fury reared up inside me. 'I go into a script meeting expecting *my* draft of *Swords and Sandals* – which I happen to think is one of the best things I've ever written – to be signed off as a shooting script for a major feature film. Instead I find that you've come up with a whole new storyline, and rather than having the common courtesy to discuss it with me, you decide to pitch it to the film's director on the sly, effectively stabbing me in the back.'

'That's not what happened,' Jason said. 'I had every intention of running my idea past you yesterday, but when I tried, you wouldn't listen. Whenever I make a suggestion, you shout me down—'

'That's simply not true—'

'And I did not speak to Drew *on the sly*, as you so charmingly put it,' Jason said. 'He asked me to bring him up to speed on where we were with the script before the meeting, and when I mentioned that I thought making Chloe an archaeologist would give her character a depth it lacked, he agreed.'

'Chloe was fine just the way I wrote her.' I was shouting at him now. 'And I don't appreciate being made to look a fool.'

'I didn't—'

'Goodbye, Jason,' I said. 'I'm going now.' Incandescent with rage, the blood pounding in my head, I strode away from him. I heard him call my name, but I did not look back.

Chapter Six

'I can't write with him,' I said. 'I just can't.'

Until then, while I stomped around the living room, Amber, still dressed in her barista's uniform – her go-to occupation when she was between acting jobs – had been sitting in an armchair, listening to my litany of complaints about Jason Harding without interruption. Now, she said, 'You kind of have to. What with him being your writing partner.'

'I didn't know he'd been hired as a writer when I agreed to work with him,' I said. 'I've half a mind to call Marcus and tell him that either Jason goes or I do.'

'Just a suggestion,' Amber said, 'but maybe wait until you've calmed down before you start making phone calls. Don't send Marcus any texts either.'

'I'm perfectly calm,' I snapped. 'I'll simply tell Marcus that Jason and I have irreconcilable creative difference, and I can't – I won't – work with him.'

'Why don't you just tell him you and Jason had a stand-up row?' Amber said.

'Because he'd think I was unprofessional—' I broke off in dismay. When I'd abandoned Jason by the statue of Eros, my one thought had been to get away from the infuriating man. A hideously unpleasant tube journey jammed into a steaming carriage, and a walk home from the station buffeted by wind and rain, had only increased my resentment at the way he'd manipulated the script meeting. Now, it came to me that yelling at him in the middle of Piccadilly Circus may not have been one of my finer moments.

'I've messed up,' I said. 'Working on *Swords and Sandals* was my chance to take my screenwriting career to another level, and I've blown it.'

Amber rolled her eyes. 'You creative types,' she said. 'Everything's a drama.'

'You don't understand,' I said. 'Jason was the star of that script meeting. I was way down the cast list. I was an extra.'

'Then you're going to have to play the scene with him or walk off the set,' Amber said. 'Of course, if you walk, you may never work for Farley Productions ever again.'

She's right about that, I thought. Marcus had given me the opportunity to prove I could deliver the script of a full–length feature film. If I let him down, if I refused to work with Jason, he wouldn't give me a second chance. Besides, I'd grown fond of the film's hero and heroine in the short time I'd known them. I wanted to tell their story.

'I can't walk away from *Sword and Sandals*,' I said. 'I can't abandon Chloe and Lysander.'

'Who?' Amber said.

'They're the main characters.'

'You creative types are *very* strange,' Amber said. I smiled at that. Then I remembered how I'd screamed at Jason before flouncing off, leaving him standing in the rain. I sank down on the sofa.

'I don't know how I'm going to face my writing partner tomorrow,' I said. 'I can't just rock up at his office and act as though nothing happened. I'm going to have to say something.'

'I think the word you're looking for is *apologise*,' Amber said.

I winced at the thought, but knew she was right.

'Keep the scene short,' Amber said, 'and the dialogue sincere.'

'I will,' I said.

'I'm sure Chloe and Lysander will appreciate it,' Amber said.

She hesitated, and then added, 'When you saw Marcus today, I don't suppose he happened to mention if he'd watched my showreel?'

'Er, no, he didn't,' I said.

'I guess if he'd wanted to call me in to audition, I'd have heard from his casting director by now,' Amber said. 'What do you think?'

'I've honestly no idea,' I said. 'Sorry.'

Amber sighed. Then she looked at her watch. 'Oh – I didn't realise the time. I need to go and get changed, and put on some make-up. I've said I'll go over to Tom's place tonight. Freya's back and she's very keen to show me her ring. According to Tom.'

'You're seeing him again so soon?' An alarm bell went off in my head. This wasn't going to help her get over her unrequited infatuation. 'Is that a good idea? I mean, after what you told me . . .'

'My best friend and his fiancée have invited me round to talk about their wedding plans,' Amber said. 'And I'm fine with that.'

If you say so, I thought. If I was writing Amber's story, I'd be cutting any scenes with Tom in them.

Amber got to her feet. 'Do you have any plans for tonight?' she said.

'Apart from going to my room and thinking about what I've done?' I said.

Amber smiled, but then her face grew serious. 'You know something, Laurel,' she said, 'instead of rewriting scripts for Marcus Farley, you should write your own original screenplay.'

'A rom-com?'

'Why not?'

'Perhaps I will one day,' I said.

Amber went off to get ready for her night out. I stayed sitting on the sofa, my mind drifting back over our conversation. *An original screenplay*. It had been years since I'd written anything that hadn't been commissioned by other people . . . A movie began playing in my head, a flashback, a memory . . .

★

As nineteen-year-old Laurel sits editing her screenplay outside the café, there's a sudden gust of wind, and the loose pages are blown off the table and scattered along the street. She leaps up from her chair and chases after them, frantically trying to catch them before they blow away, falling to her knees and scrabbling on the pavement. A passer-by, a man in his early thirties wearing a designer suit, stops and helps her gather them together. It's only when he hands the pages back to her that she recognises him as producer Marcus Farley. The third assistant director she's dating, who's worked in the film industry longer than she has, pointed him out when he treated her to lunch at the famous Silver Screen restaurant, only a few days ago.

'Thank you, Mr Farley,' Laurel says.

He looks at her curiously. 'Do I know you?'

'No,' she admits. 'My name is Laurel Martin. I'm a screenwriter. That is, I want to be . . .'

The sound of rain lashing against the windows brought me back to the present. It was still only early evening, but very dark outside. I got up and drew the curtains, and sat back down on the sofa.

That long-ago summer. I'd thought my third AD boyfriend and I were starring in an epic love story, but within months we'd broken up and were seeing other people. As for my blatantly autobiographical screenplay about a young woman working in her first job in London, I blushed as I recalled how I'd thrust it into Marcus Farley's hands . . .

Now, ten years later, I was not about to let a stupid argument with Jason Harding wreck my chance of becoming Farley Productions' go-to screenwriter for feature films.

Chapter Seven

The following morning, determined not to be late and give Jason any more reason to doubt my professionalism than I had already, I arrived at his locked office ten minutes early. To pass the time until he returned from wherever he was giving his lecture – and to distract myself from thinking about the excruciatingly embarrassing apology I was going to have to make – I started reading my print-out of *Swords and Sandals – Draft Twenty-eight*. Annoyingly, I was now unable to think of the heroine as anything other than an archaeologist.

Absorbed as I was in the script, it was a shock to glance at my watch and see that I'd been standing outside Jason's office for nearly half an hour. The thought came to me that he'd decided he couldn't work with a woman who behaved like a stroppy adolescent. I checked my phone. To my relief, there was no message from Jason telling me that our writing partnership was over. Reluctant though I was to call him – if our conversation was going to be as difficult as I expected, I'd rather we had it face to face – I tried his number, but his phone was switched off. I thought, so how long do I hang around waiting to see if he turns up.

The sound of footsteps made me look hopefully along the corridor. Unfortunately, it wasn't Jason who came around the corner, but the woman I'd seen storming out of his office the first time I'd gone there. As she drew level with me, she came to a halt and looked me up and down.

'Can I help you?' she said, in a tone that made it very clear that she was actually saying, *Who are you and why are you loitering here?*

'No, I'm fine, thanks,' I said. 'I'm waiting for Dr Harding.'

'Are you one of his students?' the woman said.

'No, I'm just visiting,' I said. When she continued to regard me suspiciously, I added, 'He's expecting me.'

'Well, if he isn't in his office, you'll most likely find him in one of the lecture theatres on the ground floor,' the woman said. She continued down the corridor until she reached the last door. Giving me one final quizzical look, she unlocked it and went inside.

I thought, now what do I do? Deciding I'd hung around outside Jason's office quite long enough, I retraced my footsteps along the corridor and took the lift down to the ground level. There was no one in the lobby to ask directions, but I spotted a small sign on the wall that pointed me through a pair of swing doors and along another corridor towards Lecture Theatres One, Two, and Three.

Arriving outside Lecture Theatre One, I put my ear to the closed double doors, and when I couldn't hear anything, opened one door just a crack. Inside, I saw rows of tiered seating filled with students diligently writing in notebooks, while in front of them a woman stood talking with great enthusiasm about 'sherds' – whatever they were. I closed the door quietly and moved on to Lecture Theatre Two, which was empty and in semi-darkness. As I reached Lecture Theatre Three, the doors opened and a jostling bunch of students burst out. Seeing me standing there, the last of them held the door open for me. I stood in the doorway and looked inside, down past the rows of seats to a screen on the far wall. On the screen there was a black and white photo of a striking dark-haired woman wearing an ornate bejewelled headdress and necklace. In front of the screen, I saw Jason standing by a lectern, chatting easily with a few more students and apparently taking much more pleasure in their conversation than he did in mine. Even as I stood there staring at him, he glanced up, starting when he saw me, but then raising a hand and beckoning me in. Taking a deep breath, I walked slowly down the stairs that ran down the side of the hall, and slid into a seat in the front row. Jason said something I couldn't hear to the students and they immediately began shouldering backpacks, collecting up coats, and drifting away from him, up the stairs to the door.

I looked at Jason, and he folded his arms and looked evenly back at me, his face expressionless. I heard the door at the top of the stairs slam shut and knew that he and I were alone. The silence between us lengthened. My mouth felt dry and I swallowed several times. Then, suddenly, we both spoke at once:

'Jason—'

'Laurel—'

We broke off.

My heart thumping, I said, 'Jason, I owe you an apology. Yesterday, I was completely out of order.'

'You were upset.'

'I was angry,' I said, 'and I took it out on you. Inexcusable, I know, and I understand if you'd rather not carry on working with me, but I hope you'll—'

'Laurel, stop.' Jason stepped away from the lectern and came and stood directly in front of me. 'Yesterday, I was angry too. In my opinion, I'd done nothing to justify your accusing me of perfidy in the middle of Piccadilly Circus. But now I've had time to think it over, I can see that you had every right to be annoyed with me. It simply never occurred to me that you'd see my talking to Drew Brightman as . . . How can I describe it?' He ran a hand through his hair. 'A breach of professional etiquette?'

'Something like that,' I said. My heartbeat slowed to a normal rate.

'In my defence,' Jason said, 'it was Drew who offered me the job in the first place, so I wouldn't have expected him to lead me astray.'

'*Drew* offered you the job? Not Marcus?'

'When Drew decided he needed an expert to bring authenticity to the script, one of his assistants got my name from the university. I thought working in a field so different to my own might prove interesting . . . and the rest is history.'

Now that, I thought, explains a lot.

'I didn't think you'd turn up this afternoon,' Jason went on, 'otherwise I wouldn't have stayed here after my lecture talking to my students.'

'I'd never miss a script meeting,' I said. 'However mad I was at my writing partner. It would be worse than standing up a guy on a date.'

'We're still partners then?'

A wave of relief washed over me. 'Yep, seems like we're stuck with each other until we deliver a shooting script.'

'And you're no longer mad at me?' His blue eyes met mine.

'Not right now,' I said. From nowhere, the thought came to me that I couldn't stay mad at a guy with such beautiful eyes. I pushed the thought aside. 'Not when we have a deadline to meet. Shall we go up to your office? We need to get writing.'

'Sure,' Jason said. 'I'll just get my lecture notes.' He went to the lectern. My gaze drifted to the screen behind him, and the photograph of the jewel-bedecked woman.

'Who's that?' I asked, gesturing at the photo.

Jason turned to the screen. 'Her name,' he said, 'is Sophia Schliemann. She was married to the nineteenth-century archaeologist Heinrich Schliemann.'

'Never heard of him,' I said. 'Nice bling she's wearing.'

'That bling, as you call it,' Jason said, 'is a three-thousand-year-old archaeological artefact.' Turning back to face me, he added, 'Have you, by any chance, read Homer's *Iliad*?'

I shook my head.

'But you've heard of it?' he said. 'It tells how Helen, a Greek queen, ran off with a Trojan prince, and how the Greeks besieged the city of Troy for ten long years to get her back.'

'Oh – you're talking about the story of *The Trojan War*,' I said.

'I loved that film. Not that I remember it very well – I must have been about ten when I saw it.'

'I suspect that watching a Hollywood movie is a somewhat different experience to reading Homer,' Jason said, dryly. 'Anyway, Sophia's husband *had* read the book and, unlike most archaeologists of his time, he believed it was more than a concoction of myths and legends, and that it was based on real historical events. He was proved right when he found Troy's ruins. Well, almost right – it's a long and controversial story. The jewels Sophia is wearing were found during his excavations.'

I stared up at the photo. 'So that headdress could have been worn by a Greek queen?

'Whoever owned it was undoubtedly a person of high status,' Jason said, 'but whoever she was, she definitely wasn't Helen – if she ever existed – if that's what you're thinking.'

'You can't know for sure,' I said.

'Oh, but I can,' Jason said, his eyes shining. 'It's all to do with the level at which it was found.'

'The level?' I said, bemused. 'Sorry, Jason, but I have no idea what you're talking about.'

'I can explain it to you,' he said, with a quick smile, 'or lend you a book about it, if you're interested.'

The thought of ploughing through an archaeology textbook made me shudder.

'I'll take your word for it,' I said. Jason's smile faded. For a moment I thought my lack of enthusiasm had offended him, but then I realised he was looking past me towards the back of the hall. I swung around in my seat and saw the woman who'd accosted me outside Jason's office descending the stairs.

'Jason?' she said. 'I'm sure I'm timetabled to give a lecture in here this afternoon.'

'We were just leaving,' Jason said. He reached behind the lectern, and the screen went blank.

The woman reached the bottom of the stairs. 'Aren't you going to introduce me to your visitor before you go?' she said.

'Laurel, meet my colleague, Emily Page,' Jason said. 'Emily, this is Laurel Martin.'

'You found him then,' Emily said to me, her gaze darting between us.

'Thanks to you,' I said. To Jason, I added, 'I met Emily outside your office. She told me where you'd be.'

'I see,' Jason said. 'Right. Well, you and I should get out of here. We've a lot of work to do.'

'Absolutely,' I said, standing up.

'You two are working together?' Emily said.

'Yes, we are,' I said.

'Oh. I thought perhaps this was a social visit. How stupid of me.' She gave an exaggerated sigh. 'As if Dr Harding would take time out of his crowded schedule to spend an afternoon with a friend.'

Jason said, 'Enough, Emily.'

'Only teasing,' Emily said, as the door to the lecture theatre swung open and a number of young men and women began clattering their way loudly down the stairs. 'Ah – here are my third years.'

'We'll leave you to it, then,' Jason said. Picking up his lecture notes, he strode off up the stairs two at a time.

Gabbling a hasty goodbye to Emily, I hurried after him, squeezing past the students now flooding into the lecture theatre. I caught up with him in the lobby.

'That woman never knows where to draw the line,' Jason muttered, stabbing at the button that would summon the lift. 'I can do without her telling me how to run my life.' The lift doors opened, and we stepped inside. I waited for Jason to resume talking, but he remained silent, staring straight ahead of him as though he'd forgotten I was there. While the lift creaked up to the fourth floor, I stood beside him, stealing glances at his profile – his mouth was set in a tight line – and speculating as to why Emily Page's innocuous comments had so riled him. He'd described her as a colleague, but I couldn't help wondering if she was more than that. She'd certainly behaved in a very familiar manner towards him. Not that Jason Harding's private life was any concern of mine.

The lift juddered to a halt and the doors slid open. We walked in silence along the corridor to Jason's office, he let us in, and we sat down on opposite sides of his desk.

He cleared his throat. 'What I said about Emily – I shouldn't have said it. She means well.'

Without thinking, I blurted, 'Are you and Emily a couple?'

Jason's eyes widened. 'No, we are not,' he said, apparently aghast. 'Why would you think that we were?'

I shrugged. 'You seemed close.'

'We're old friends. We've known each other since we were students at Oxford. She's actually married to another archaeologist friend of mine – I introduced them. You, Laurel Martin, have an overactive imagination.'

'Is that a bad thing for a screenwriter?' I said.

For the first time, I heard Jason Harding laugh. 'Probably not,' he said. 'Talking of screenwriting—' He opened a drawer, brought out a copy of *Swords and Sandals*, and placed it on the desk in front of him. 'My good friend Emily is forever telling me I work too hard, but we do need to make a start on this.'

'Too right we do.' I retrieved my laptop and my own copy of the script, which I'd printed out the previous evening, from my bag. 'Let's start with the scene where Chloe finds the sword.'

Chapter Eight

Lysander places his hand on his heart. 'I have been struck by Eros's arrow,' he says. 'I love you, Chloe . . .'

The scene where Lysander declared his love was *so* romantic. If only my life was more like a movie, I thought. If only twenty-first century men were more like my ancient Greek hero.

I let the page of typescript fall from my hand on to the untidy pile of loose pages on Jason's desk.

'It's a wrap,' I said.

On the other side of the desk, Jason raised one eyebrow. 'It's a what?'

I hadn't expected to get through the entire rewrite in just one afternoon and evening, but once I'd started writing the new opening scene for the film, the dialogue had come easily. Jason had raised no objections to anything I'd written, and he'd come up with some excellent suggestions as to how we might tweak the rest of the script to fit in with a plot that involved an archaeologist heroine. It was all going so well, with the pair of us bouncing ideas off each other, that even when the darkness outside Jason's office windows showed us that night had fallen without us being aware of it, neither of us wanted to call a halt and begin again in the morning. Instead, Jason had made a sortie to a student bar, returning with coffee for me, beer for him, numerous packets of crisps, and a large bar of chocolate, and we'd carried on writing.

Now, I smiled, and put down my pen.

'A wrap. It's a phrase used on a film set to tell the actors and the crew that filming is finished,' I said. 'We've nailed it, Jason. *Swords and Sandals* – our version – is a great script. Our work here is done.'

'Well, I may not know much about film-making,' Jason said, 'but I happen to agree with you.' He leant back in his chair, stretching out his arms, working the stiffness that came of spending the best part of a day hunched over a desk out of his shoulders. 'There are two beers left. Would you like one?'

'Sure, why not?' I said. He opened the last two cans and passed one to me.

'Cheers,' he said.

'To Chloe and Lysander,' I said, clinking my can with his.

We may have got off to a bad start, I thought, but it felt good working with him today, with me doing the actual writing and him acting as a sounding board and making suggestions. Marcus had been right when he said we'd make a terrific team. I smiled at Jason and he smiled back, before raising his beer can to his mouth and taking a long draught. I studied him as he drank, my gaze sliding from his stubbled face, to his broad chest, to his muscular arms – at some point, he'd rolled up the sleeves of his shirt to above the elbow. He must work out, I thought, he didn't get those muscles sitting at a desk or in a lecture theatre. Or maybe it's digging up archaeological artefacts that's given him the body of an athlete . . . long hours of shifting earth under a hot Mediterranean sun . . .

Jason standing in the middle of a ruined city, leaning on a spade, shirtless, tanned, jeans hanging low on his hips, his stomach taut . . .

'I should make a move,' I said, before my imagination went into overdrive.

'I'll walk you to the station,' Jason said. 'This area is as safe as any other part of central London, but some of the pubs get rowdy at night.'

I almost told him there was no need – I was, after all, perfectly used to negotiating the streets of London after dark – but it struck me that if I did, he might think I couldn't wait to get away from him.

'As long as I won't be taking you out of your way,' I said.

'Not at all,' Jason said.

As it turned out, I was glad of Jason's presence on the walk to the station, not because I needed an escort to protect me from the wild revellers of Aldgate, but because he knew a far less circuitous route than that recommended by my phone. When I arrived home, just after midnight, the flat was in darkness, but I could hear the sound of the TV coming from the living room, so I knew that Amber hadn't yet gone to bed. Still on too much of a high after such a successful writing session to think of going to bed myself, I paused only to toss my coat and bag into my room, then went along the landing and flung open the living room door – and shrieked when the flickering light from the TV showed me not my flatmate but the dark silhouette of a man lounging on the sofa. An instant later, I realised that rather than an intruder with a compulsion to watch late-night reality shows, the man was Conor. I switched on the main light.

'Jeez, Laurel,' Conor said, pointing the remote at the screen and turning off the television. 'What's with the screaming?'

'I didn't know it was you lurking on my sofa,' I said. 'Why were you watching TV in the dark?'

'I prefer it,' Conor said. 'You must know that.'

'I don't – I mean, I didn't,' I said. I was, I realised, woefully ignorant of Conor's small screen viewing habits, even after dating him for more than a year. On and off. 'We hardly ever watch TV together.'

'I can think of more interesting things to do with you of an evening than slump in front of a television.' Conor said, with a wolfish smile.

'Just as well not everyone feels like that,' I said, 'or I might never work again. What are you doing here, anyway?'

'Aren't you pleased to see me?'

'Of course I am.' I crossed the room and sat on his lap. He put his arms around me and kissed me briefly on the mouth.

'My rehearsal finished on time for once,' he said, 'and I found myself at a loose end. I decided to come here, and Amber let me in. She was in a very good mood, as she'd been called in last minute to a casting for *Swords and Sandals*, and when I arrived, her agent had just phoned to tell her she's got the part of Thais.'

I sat bold upright. 'Oh, that's such great news! Thais is a minor role, but she's got some cracking lines. Is Amber in her room? I wonder if she's still awake? I must go and congratulate her.' I made to get off Conor's lap, but he kept hold of me, his arms around my waist.

'I wouldn't,' he said. 'Amber is in her room, and I'm pretty sure she's awake, but she's not alone.'

I gaped at him. 'You mean she's got a man in there?'

'Yep,' Conor said. 'Why are you so surprised?'

'It's a bit unexpected, that's all,' I said. 'She hasn't had a . . . an overnight guest the entire time she's been living here.' It struck me that the reason for Amber's chaste lifestyle might well have something to do with Tom.

'Well, she's making up for it tonight,' Conor said, with a grin. 'I had to turn up the TV to drown out the cries of passion.'

'Conor!'

'Too much information?'

I rolled my eyes 'Did you get to meet the guy?'

'Only very briefly before Amber dragged him off to her lair.'

'Anyone we know?' I asked.

'I don't know him, but you do,' Conor said. 'Harry Vincent.'

I gasped. 'Jago – the actor who plays Jago – is in Amber's bedroom? But what on earth is he doing in there?'

Writing the 'Jago' storyline for long-running soap *Fields of Gold* for the last three years, I'd become fond of the character – as had many of the show's female viewers – and I was sorry when Harry Vincent, who played the brooding farmer, had decided to leave. Not that I could blame him for wanting to use Jago's popularity as a springboard to further his career, even if it meant that I was out of a job. Fortunately for me, only a few days after I'd written the episode in which Jago came to a gory demise – which was yet to be filmed – I'd been hired to work on *Swords and Sandals*.

Conor laughed. 'I'd have thought it was obvious what he was doing.'

'What I meant,' I said, 'as I'm sure you know, is how did Amber and Jago – Harry – get together? It's not like she's ever met him before. At least, not as far as I'm aware.' I'd got to know Harry well over the last few years at the end-of-season wrap parties held in the *Fields of Gold* studio bar and often ran into him at other industry events, and neither he nor Amber had ever mentioned that they knew each other.

'Strangely, neither of them volunteered that information,' Conor said. 'They had other things on their minds. As do I. Let's go to bed.'

Deciding that further speculation about Harry and Amber could most certainly wait for another time, and increasingly conscious of a delicious heat low in my stomach, I got off Conor's lap, and led the way to my bedroom. As soon as the door was closed, he seized hold of me and kissed me, grinding his hips against me, before pulling his shirt off over his head without bothering to unbutton it. Desire lanced through me, but I took a moment to let my gaze linger on the smooth planes of his waxed chest. Then I turned around so that my back was to him, and knowing he was watching, slowly stepped out of my dress and peeled off my underwear. I smiled at him once, over my shoulder, and then I walked across the room, deliberately swaying my hips, and climbed into bed. Conor quickly rid himself of the rest of his clothes and retrieved a condom from his wallet, before pulling back the duvet and lying down next to me, crushing me to him, kissing me hungrily, his tongue probing deep in my mouth. I felt the weight of him as he covered my body with his, and then he was inside me, his hips thrusting, pleasure coursing through me, my fingers digging into his back, waves of sensation, ever more intense . . . Lights, camera, action . . . and action . . . and . . . and . . .

Conor's body arched and shuddered. 'Jenny,' he groaned. 'Oh, Jenny.'

He grew still, and then he rolled off me and on to his back. Sighing contentedly, he shut his eyes. I lay rigid beside him, telling myself I'd misheard him, that his calling out another girl's name when he was having sex with me meant nothing. Shivering, although my body was bathed in sweat, I sat up, reached for the switch at the side of the bed, and flicked on the main overhead light.

'Who is Jenny?' I said. And please don't lie to me, I thought, because if you're cheating, I'd rather hear it from you than someone else. Conor's eyes opened, and he raised himself on one elbow.

'Jenny is a character in the play I'm rehearsing,' he said, yawning. 'Why do you ask?'

'Just now you said her name.'

'Did I?' He sounded genuinely surprised. 'I must still be in character from rehearsal. Dominic – my role – had a lot of scenes with Jenny today.'

'As long as it's only acting you're getting up to with her,' I said.

Conor frowned and sat up. 'Laurel, don't go there. You can trust me. You must know that.'

'I – I do trust you,' I said. Most of the time, I thought. He leant towards me and kissed me, before lying back down on the bed. I switched off the main light, and the fairy lights and sank down next to him. A minute or so later, his even breathing told me that he was asleep. No one with a guilty conscience, I thought, could fall asleep that easily. And yet . . .

Careful not to wake Conor, I slid out of bed. By the light of the street lamp outside my bedroom window shining through a gap in the curtains, I put on my dressing gown and, taking my phone with me, crept out of the bedroom and padded along the landing to the living room.

61

Sitting at the dining table, I googled Conor's play, *Sometime, Never*, and saw that there was indeed a character named Jenny. Feeling more than a little foolish, I was about to go back to bed when I saw that I had a text.

Hello, Laurel. Are you home yet? Jason. Half an hour had passed since it had been sent.

Bemused, I texted back. *Am home. L xx.* Almost immediately, my phone vibrated. I hit the answer icon.

'Hey, Jason,' I said. 'What's up? Have you thought of another anachronism in the script?'

'No, nothing like that,' he said. 'I just wanted to make sure you'd got home OK.'

'Oh, that's so kind of you,' I said, touched. 'But I got back with no trouble at all. Thanks for checking in with me though. I hope you didn't stay up waiting for me to reply to your text.'

'No, I was up anyway. Just going over a few notes for the paper I'm giving at a conference next week.'

'You're still working? After all the hours we put in today? Your friend Emily's right – you work too hard.'

'I don't think so,' Jason said. He paused, and then he added, 'I enjoyed today, Laurel.'

'Likewise,' I said.

'As for our script, if I was grading it, I'd give us an A.'

I laughed. 'We were on fire.'

'The ancient Greeks would have said that the Muses were with us.'

'The what?'

'The Nine Muses,' Jason said. 'The Greek goddesses of the arts. All poets – all storytellers – depended on them for inspiration. Erato was the goddess of song, Thalia the goddess of comedy . . . between them, they pretty much had the arts covered.'

'Useful women to know if you were an ancient Greek creative,' I said. 'Although I'm guessing there wasn't an ancient Greek goddess of screenplays.'

'No, sadly,' Jason said. 'But if you were of a mind to ask a

Muse for inspiration, I reckon Calliope would be your best bet. Her statues usually depict her in the act of writing.'

'I'll hold that thought,' I said. I was almost sure I heard Jason laugh.

'See you on Thursday, Laurel,' he said. 'Goodnight.'

'Night, Jason,' I said, and we ended the call. I sat for a while thinking over the conversation, and it struck me that once you got to know him, the ruggedly handsome Dr Jason Harding was a really nice guy.

Going out of the living room, I crept back along the landing and into my bedroom. The light from outside the window showed me that Conor was sleeping soundly. I let my dressing gown fall to the floor and slid into bed next to him.

I do trust him, I thought, as I relaxed into sleep. What happened – what he did – it's all in the past. It's not going to happen again.

Jason placed his phone on his desk, and leant back in his chair. The unease he'd felt since watching Laurel vanish into the dark maw of the tube station, the guilt that he hadn't thought to offer to drive her home, began to fade. He told himself it was ridiculous to be concerned about her making the journey across the city alone, but he was glad he'd called her.

Recalling that he still had hours of work to put in on his real job, he picked up the print-out of his half-written research paper, and started to read, occasionally making a note or referring to one of the hardback books stacked on the floor beside him. He imagined his co-writer's reaction to his academic prose – she'd probably tell him it needed more sparkle – and he smiled. Laurel might be woefully ignorant of ancient history, but she had a sharp mind, and she certainly knew how to tell a story.

More than once as he worked on through the night, Jason's mind wandered back to the talented Laurel Martin, in her flat on the other side of London. How she'd ended up with a boor like that actor fellow for a boyfriend, he couldn't imagine.

Chapter Nine

I'd just stepped out of my bedroom when Amber's overnight guest, his face shadowed with dark stubble, emerged from her room, closing the door behind him.

'Hey, Laurel,' he said.

'Morning, Jago,' I said.

'It's Harry,' he said, amiably.

'Of course it is,' I said. 'Sorry, Harry. It's going to take me a while to stop thinking of you as Jago. You are him, in my mind.'

'Which is exactly why I decided to leave *Fields of Gold*,' Harry said. 'I've enjoyed the experience of being part of a long-running soap, but I've become so identified with Jago, I was starting to worry that casting directors wouldn't see me for anything else.'

'So what's next for Harry Vincent?' I said. 'I suppose you're back to auditioning?'

'You don't know?' Harry's mouth lifted in the lazy smile that had sent the viewing figures for *Fields of Gold* sky-high and made a lot of TV executives very happy.

'Er, no,' I said. 'Why would I?'

'Amber said that you're one of the writers on *Swords and Sandals* . . .'

'I am indeed,' I said.

'Haven't you seen a cast list?'

'No, I haven't. Do you have a part in the film?'

'I signed a contract yesterday,' Harry said. 'I'm playing a guy called Lysander. Waves a sword around and rides horses.'

'Oh, *Harry*!' I squealed. 'You're the *star*.' Impulsively, I hugged him, and he lifted me up and swung me around in his arms, both of us laughing. 'Congratulations,' I said, when he put me back on my feet. 'I'm so pleased for you.'

'Thanks, Laurel,' Harry said. 'I've acted in feature films before, but this is the first time I've played the lead. And it's all happened so fast. I haven't got my head around it yet.'

'You'll be great as Lysander,' I said. 'He's the perfect role for you – he has a *lot* of action scenes.'

'Yeah, I'm hoping I'll be allowed to at least do some of my own stunts. When I met the film's producers, one of them seemed to think I could, but the other wasn't so keen.'

'Let me guess,' I said, 'Marcus Farley was all for letting the star of a major motion picture race a horse-drawn chariot along a beach, but Shannon Farley told him it wouldn't be covered by the film's insurance.'

'Ah – you know Marcus and Shannon,' Harry said.

I nodded. 'I've worked for them many times, but not on a project as massive as *Swords and Sandals*. It's a first for me as much as for you.'

'Exciting times,' Harry said. He hesitated, and then he added, 'I will miss Jago, you know. I don't suppose you'd tell me what happens in his final scenes?'

'You know I can't tell you that,' I said. 'All the writers on *Fields of Gold* sign a contract in blood never to give away the plot. You may be a big movie star now, but you'll have to wait until the day before filming to get the script like everyone else.'

'Fair enough,' Harry said. 'At least I won't have to wait as long as the audience. I shoot Jago's last episode next week, but I reckon it'll be another two months before it's shown on air.'

'Something like that,' I said. 'Plenty of time for the press and your fans to come up with all sorts of wild theories as to what's going to happen to him. I fully expect more than one showbiz reporter will claim to have discovered that he's abducted by aliens.' I put my hand over my mouth. 'Oh, you won't tell any-body I said that, will you? If it got out . . .'

Harry laughed. 'And on that note, I'm going home.'

Having seen Harry off the premises, and recalling that I'd left Conor dozing in my bed with the promise that I'd make us breakfast, I went to the kitchen, switched on the kettle, and located the necessary ingredients for scrambled eggs on toast. I rarely bothered with more than a coffee and a yoghurt in the morning when I was on my own, but Conor liked a cooked breakfast. A moment later, he appeared in the kitchen doorway.

'Breakfast is still a work in progress,' I said. 'Sorry for the delay. I was talking to Harry.' I put a couple of slices of bread in the toaster. 'Did he tell you he's been cast as Lysander in *Swords and Sandals*?'

'No, he didn't mention it,' Conor said. 'But last night, Amber didn't give him a chance. Is it a good part?'

'He's the lead,' I said. How could he not know that? I'd talked about Chloe and Lysander often enough.

'Right,' Conor said. 'Hey, I've just remembered that I never told you what the director of *Sometime, Never* said to me yesterday . . .'

Reminding myself that Conor had a lot on his mind with the new play, and I couldn't reasonably expect him to remember every detail of my script, I carried on making breakfast, while he brought me up to date on the excellent progress he and his fellow cast members had made in rehearsal, and his satisfaction with his own role in particular. We carried our plates and mugs into the living room and sat at the dining table to eat, which was another thing I rarely did when I was on my own.

Conor had only eaten a couple of mouthfuls when he put down his knife and fork and laid his hands flat on the table.

'Everything all right?' I said.

'Er, yeah,' he said. 'Listen, Laurel, last night I came here for a reason. I was planning to ask you something. Before we got sidetracked.' His brown eyes stared straight into mine. I thought, why is he looking so serious? A number of possible questions a guy could ask his girlfriend suggested themselves.

'So, what was it you wanted to ask me?' My voice sounded unusually high.

'How would you feel about my moving in with you?' he said.

'Y-you w-want to live – us to live – you want to move into my flat?' I stuttered. I thought, do I want Conor and me to live together? Am I – are we – ready to make that sort of commitment? I realised I didn't know the answer. My stomach twisted into a knot.

'It wouldn't be for long,' Conor said. 'My landlord wants the house I've been sharing for his daughter, so he's not renewing our tenancy agreement. Me and the other guys have found a three-bedroomed flat to rent, but it's being renovated, and we won't be able to move in for a couple of weeks.'

'Oh—' I said. 'I see. You need somewhere to stay temporarily.' I picked up my mug of coffee, but my hand was shaking so much, I had to replace it on the table before I spilt it. Fortunately, Conor didn't notice.

'I don't have rehearsals this weekend,' he said, 'so I could bring my stuff over on Saturday. Would that be OK?'

Pulling myself together, I said, 'It's fine by me, but I'll have to check with Amber.'

Conor raised his eyebrows. 'I don't see what it's got to do with her. It's your flat.'

'Yes, but it's been Amber's *home* for nearly a year now.' Mentally crossing my fingers, I added, 'I'm sure she won't mind if you crash here for a bit, but I'm still going to ask her. It's the right thing to do.'

Conor shrugged and resumed eating, while I pushed the food around my plate. Eventually, I decided it was as well he hadn't asked me to live with him. Our contemporaries might be ready to start playing happy families, but we were fine as we were for now.

'You don't have a lot of space here,' Conor said, 'so I'll just bring essentials like clothes, and store the rest of my stuff at my parents' house. Maybe you could clear a few drawers for me?'

'Er, yes, I could do that,' I said. How I was going to fit his belongings into my already chock-full chest of drawers and wardrobe, I had no idea. 'I'll move some things around.'

'Great,' Conor said. 'If you stay at mine on Friday night, you can help me with my packing, yeah?'

'That makes sense,' I said, although I doubted he'd need my assistance to pack a couple of suitcases.

Conor smiled at me, and then glanced at his phone. 'Time I went to rehearsal,' he said, pushing back his chair. I hastily gulped down the rest of my breakfast, and the two of us went out of the living room and down the stairs. He kissed me lightly on the mouth, before heading off in the direction of the station.

Now to tackle Amber, I thought.

I returned to the kitchen and made two mugs of coffee, before going to my flatmate's room, and knocking on her door.

'Come in, Laurel,' Amber called.

Juggling the two mugs, I opened the door and went inside. Amber, who was sitting at her dressing table in her dressing gown, brushing her hair, swung around to face me.

'Did Conor tell you my good news?' she said.

'He did,' I said, placing her coffee within easy reach – next to an empty champagne bottle – and sitting down on the bed. 'Many, many congratulations.'

'Thank you,' Amber said. 'I know Thais is a small part, but I'm over the moon!'

'You may only have a few lines,' I said, 'but you're in a lot of scenes.'

'That's what they told me at the casting,' Amber said. 'And what's even better is that the first three months of the shoot is on location on a Greek island. But I suppose you know that.'

'Marcus did mention that they're filming in Greece over the summer,' I said. 'I'm sure you'll be working most of the time rather than sunning yourself beside a swimming pool, but I may be just the tiniest bit envious of you right now.'

Amber laughed. 'It's all because of you, Laurel. If you hadn't recommended me to Marcus, I'd never have been called in to audition. We should go out and celebrate.'

'Now that's a plan.' My gaze slid to the champagne bottle. 'It looks like you've been celebrating already. You and Harry. Last night. How did that happen?'

'It was after my audition yesterday,' Amber said. 'I knew most of the actresses who were auditioning for Thais, and once we'd been in to see the casting director, a few of us went for a drink in a lovely old pub just around the corner from Farley Productions. Maybe you know it?'

'I've been there with Marcus and Shannon,' I said. 'Go on, Amber. Don't keep me in suspense.'

'After we'd been there an hour or so, Harry and this older guy walked in – Harry told me later that it was his agent. They had one drink at the bar, and the agent left, but Harry stayed on. I got up from our table to buy a round, and happened to stand next to him.'

'Quite by chance!' I said.

'I happened to stand next to Harry Vincent in a crowded pub,' Amber insisted 'He asked me if he was right in thinking he'd seen me earlier at Farley Productions, I told him I was there auditioning for *Swords and Sandals*, and he said he'd just signed a contract. We got talking, and he joined me and my friends at our table. After my friends had gone home, he and I had a few more drinks. And one thing led to another. You know how it is.'

'Scene one, boy meets girl,' I said. 'Scene two, they share a bottle of champagne. Scene three, they spend the night together. What happens in scene four? Are you going to see him again?'

'No, I won't be seeing him again,' Amber said. 'That is, I will *see* him again at some point, as we're going to be working on the same film, but I won't be . . . hanging out with him.'

'So last night wasn't the first episode in a long-running series?' I said. A thought struck me. 'Isn't it going to be a bit awkward being on set with him in Greece?'

Amber shook her head. 'I made it clear to him that last night was strictly no strings, and he was fine with that. We didn't even swap numbers.'

'But why not? Harry's a nice guy, he's easy on the eye, and he's single. Not to mention that he's a successful and talented actor on the verge of international stardom.'

'He's all of that,' Amber said, 'and I can confirm he certainly knows how to play a love scene. But he isn't Tom.'

'Oh, Amber,' I sighed.

'I'm not planning to spend the rest of my life carrying a torch for a man I can't have,' Amber said, 'but my head isn't in the right place at the moment for me to even think about getting into a relationship with Harry – or anyone else. Last night was great, but it isn't going to lead to anything more.'

'But you and Harry could be so good together . . .'

Harry and Amber, arm in arm, walking along the red carpet at a premiere, cameras flashing, crowds cheering . . .

'Laurel, listen to me,' Amber said. 'I've a really good feeling about my role in *Swords and Sandals*. This is *my* time. I don't want or need a man complicating my life right now.'

Swiftly rewinding the film in my head, I thought, why can't my friends keep to the scripts I write for them, rather than wildly improvising?

'I meant what I said about you and me going out to celebrate,' Amber went on. 'What about tonight? Or would you prefer the weekend?'

'Tonight works best for me,' I said. 'I've a lot on this weekend.'

'Of course, you'll be seeing Conor,' Amber said. Getting a part in *Swords and Sandals* must have put her in an exceptionally good mood, because she managed to say Conor's name without a grimace. I decided I'd best make the most of it.

'Actually,' I said, 'I wanted to ask you something about Conor. He has to move out of the house he's been sharing, and he can't get into his new place until it's decorated. I was hoping it'd be OK with you if he stayed here for a bit? It would only be for a few weeks.'

The silence that followed stretched on and on, until it became distinctly uncomfortable.

'I don't know, Laurel,' Amber said, eventually. 'Having a boy-friend stay over the odd occasion is one thing, but sharing a flat with him, having him around all the time . . . It could be difficult.'

'I don't see why,' I said.

'Bathroom,' Amber said. 'Remembering to lock the door every time I took a shower.'

'Seriously?' I said. 'When don't you lock the bathroom door?'

'What about the kitchen then?' Amber said. 'Does Conor know how to load a dishwasher? I've shared flats with guys before, and none of them did any household chores. I don't mean to be sexist, but men are much better at creating a mess than clearing it up.'

'That's simply not true,' I said. 'At Conor's place, where he's living now, they have a cleaning rota.'

'Hmm,' Amber said. 'How long did you say he would be staying?'

'Just a couple of weeks,' I said.

'OK,' Amber said. 'I guess I can put up with him for that long. Just make sure you show him where we keep the Hoover.'

'Thanks, Amber,' I said. 'I'll call Conor and let him know that he'll have a roof over his head.' I got to my feet.

'I must call my parents,' Amber said, 'and inform them that their eldest daughter is no longer an out-of-work actor.'

'They'll be so proud of you,' I said.

'They'll be relieved that for once I'm not phoning to ask if I can borrow some money,' Amber said.

I laughed, and went out of her room. Reaching for the handle to close the door, I saw that she was already holding her mobile to her ear. I pulled the door shut, but I could still hear her excited voice announcing her good news to the person who'd answered the call.

I went to my own room and sat down at my desk.

There was surely no reason for me to worry about Amber just because the first person she'd chosen to call about her role in *Swords and Sandals* was Tom.

Chapter Ten

'And the final shot is of Chloe and the other archaeologist sitting together on the beach,' I said. For dramatic effect, I waited for a count of ten, before adding, 'The End.'

Earlier this morning, I'd arrived in the meeting room at Farley Productions to find Marcus and Shannon already seated at opposite ends of the table, and Drew Brightman lounging on the chair nearest the door. After helping myself to coffee, I took a seat across from Drew, placing the new draft of the script on the table in front of me. A few moments later, Jason appeared in the doorway. Drew pointed to the chair next to him, but Jason either failed to see or chose to ignore the gesture and, having favoured me with one of his rare smiles, walked around the table to sit beside me. It surprised me how ridiculously pleased I was to have him there, how conscious I was of his presence, even while I talked Marcus, Shannon, and Drew through the rewritten script.

Now, the credits had rolled and the lights had come back on. I looked straight at Marcus, catching his gaze and holding it. He'd listened without interruption to me reading aloud the changes Jason and I'd made, other than laughing in all the right places, so it wasn't entirely unexpected when his face broke into a smile.

'I like it,' he said. 'I like it a lot. Shannon?'

'It's good,' Shannon said. 'Personally, I don't think we're going to get a better version of *Swords and Sandals* than this one. But it's your call, Marcus.' She too was smiling. I realised I'd been holding my breath. However much he might like the script, I knew Marcus had too much respect for his wife's commercial expertise to sign it off without her approval.

'Drew?' Marcus said. 'Have we got a shooting script?'

'Possibly,' Drew said. 'Although I do have one suggestion.'

My heart plummeted. Just when it was all going so well.

'I'm not saying Jason and Laurel haven't done a great job,' Drew said, 'but what *Swords and Sandals* still needs is something that will set it apart from other films of the same type.'

'What exactly do you have in mind?' Marcus said. Shannon sighed audibly.

'What I propose,' Drew said, 'is that in the scenes in the film that take place in the past, the dialogue is in ancient Greek. With English subtitles.'

There followed a stunned silence. Surely, I thought, he *cannot* be serious. *Swords and Sandals* is destined for a big-screen multiplex, not an art-house cinema showing foreign language films.

Marcus cleared his throat. 'A film with subtitles isn't going to get the audience it deserves,' he said. 'An interesting idea, though.'

'But simply not viable in today's market,' Shannon said, quickly.

'I disagree,' Drew said. 'Shooting scenes set in the past in an authentic language is exactly the sort of innovative film-making that wins awards.'

Shannon's mouth became a thin tight line.

Drew leant across the table towards Jason. 'Would you be able to translate the historical section of *Swords and Sandals* into ancient Greek?'

Jason raised one eyebrow. 'I could,' he said.

Nooo, I thought, don't encourage this madness. My dialogue needed to be spoken aloud, not reduced to a line of text while the actors spouted words that no one in the audience could understand. Briefly, I considered kicking my writing-partner under the table, but decided that I didn't know him well enough to be sure he'd understand the message I was trying to put across.

'Drew, we have less than five weeks until we start filming,' Shannon said. 'We can't afford any delays.'

'How long would a translation take you, Jason?' Drew said.

Jason shrugged. 'Hard to say. At least a year. But that's a conservative estimate.'

'That long?' Drew said. 'Oh, well it was just an idea.' For a moment, he looked crestfallen, but in the next instant, he brightened up. 'And I have so many ideas as to how I'm going to film *Swords and Sandals*.' Suddenly he was beaming across the table at me and Jason. 'I have my shooting script.'

I was certain I wasn't the only person seated at the table who felt weak with relief.

'Great,' Marcus said, hastily. 'If I could have that draft?' He held out his hand, and I passed him my copy of the script. 'Laurel and Jason, you've done an excellent job.' He stood up, bringing the meeting to an end.

The next few minutes were taken up with hand-shaking, air-kissing, thanks for hard work, and hopes that we would all work together again. Once we were outside the meeting room, Shannon went off to her office, while Marcus shepherded Drew to reception, where a driver was waiting for him, Jason and I following. There were more farewells, and then I and my writing partner, just the two of us, were standing in the street.

'Are you walking to Piccadilly Circus?' I asked Jason.

'No, not today,' Jason said. 'I'm heading over to Bloomsbury. I'm meeting a colleague – a fellow archaeologist – at the British Museum.'

'So this is where we part,' I said. I'd met him less than two weeks ago, and yet – after a false start – we'd worked so well together. Suddenly, I felt reluctant to simply say goodbye to him and walk away.

Jason shifted his weight from one foot to the other, but, like me, made no move to go. 'How crazy was that suggestion of Drew's that I should translate *Swords and Sandals* into ancient Greek?' he said.

I grimaced. 'I thought you were seriously considering it,' I said, 'telling Drew it would take you a year or more.'

'That was an exaggeration,' Jason said, 'but I had to say something to put him off. I may know very little about film-making, but I'm pretty sure that the twenty-first century cinema-going public wouldn't appreciate a movie in which the actors speak in a rough approximation of the language of Homer. And if I'd had any doubts, the look of sheer horror on your face when Drew brought the matter up would have convinced me it was a bad idea.'

'You may be my favourite co-writer right now,' I laughed.

A smile flickered across his face. 'We made a good team.'

'We did,' I said. We both fell silent. I reminded myself that our writing-partnership, good as it had been, was over. 'I guess the next time we see each other will be at the *Swords and Sandals'* premiere.'

Jason raised one eyebrow – a habit of his, I now realised. 'You think we'll get tickets for the premiere?'

'Of course we will,' I said. 'And for the after-party.'

He considered this for a moment. 'I don't know that I'll be going to either. I'm not much of a one for parties.'

'But you have to go,' I said. 'Sitting in the dark, watching a film on the big screen, seeing the story you've written brought to life, your name in the credits – you can't miss that! And afterwards, you get to drink champagne.'

'Premieres and after-parties are your world, not mine,' Jason said. 'I'm an archaeologist, not a screenwriter. Much as I've enjoyed my foray into the film industry, it's back to academia for me now. *Khaire*, Laurel.'

'Sorry?' I said. 'What did you say?'

'It means farewell in ancient Greek.'

'*Khaire,*' I said. 'Would Lysander have said that to Chloe when she returned to her own time?'

'I'm sure he did,' Jason said. With a smile, he turned away from me and headed off along Wardour Street in the direction of Tottenham Court Road. I started walking in the opposite direction towards Shaftesbury Avenue.

Knowing I might never see him again made me feel empty inside.

'You should invite Laurel Martin as your plus one to the opening of Philip's Etruscan exhibition,' Emily said.

'Why would I do that?' Jason said, leaning forward and resting his elbows on the dining table, toying with his empty wine glass.

'Because she's all you've talked about all evening,' Emily said.

Jason raised one eyebrow. 'It was you who asked me to tell you about my venture into the film industry. As Laurel is – was – my co-writer, naturally her name has cropped up once or twice.'

Emily turned to her husband, who was sitting on her right, opposite Jason, who was on her left. 'I think Jason should give Laurel a call, don't you agree?'

'I think we all need another drink,' Philip said. 'I'll fetch another bottle.' He got up from the dining table and headed to the kitchen. Jason concealed a smile. In all the years they'd known each other, Philip had always refused to get involved in Emily's attempts to act as a matchmaker.

'Listen, Emily,' Jason said. 'I very much enjoyed *working* with Laurel Martin, but that's all. I'm not interested in dating her.' It had been exhilarating working with Laurel, he thought, picturing her sitting at his desk in his office, her sheer enthusiasm for the screenplay. The way she talked about Chloe and Lysander as if they were real people . . .

'That girl really messed you up, didn't she?' Emily said, suddenly. 'She's the reason why you're thirty-three and still single.'

Jason stared at her in disbelief. Surely she wouldn't dredge this up? Not after all this time.

'I assume you don't mean Laurel,' he said.

'No, of course not, I'm talking about Tèa. Because of her – what she did – you've never let any woman get close to you since. You bury yourself in work—' Emily broke off, biting her lip. 'I'm sorry, Jason. I shouldn't have said any of that.'

No, you shouldn't, Jason thought. He reminded himself that if he found his old friend irritating at times, she probably felt the same about him.

'It's fine, Emily,' he said, and smiled to show he meant it. 'But can we talk about something other than my love life? It's not as interesting as you think.'

'That was rather my point,' Emily said, with a heartfelt sigh.

Philip came back into the room, carrying a bottle of red. 'More wine, Jason?' he said, sitting down at the table. Thankful for the interruption to his and Emily's conversation, Jason held out his glass.

The evening went on. The wine was drunk. Inevitably, the talk turned to archaeology: an exciting find on a site in Sicily, who had or had not got funding for their next dig. Laurel Martin's name did not crop up again.

Chapter Eleven

I wrapped the last of the glasses in newspaper, placed it carefully in the cardboard box with the others, and sealed the box with tape.

'Anything of yours left in here?' I asked Conor.

'I don't think so,' he said. He opened each kitchen cabinet in turn. 'No – all the shelves are bare.' He held up the rubbish sack containing the saucepan without a handle, the kettle that didn't work, and the burnt roasting tin we'd discovered lurking at the back of a cupboard. 'I'll take this out to the rubbish. You start clearing my stuff out of the bathroom.' Picking up an empty box, I went out of the kitchen and headed up the stairs.

The previous evening, I'd arrived at Conor's place to find his housemates, Greg and Lucas, already packed up and loading their belongings into Greg's van. Conor, as he'd told me proudly, had thought to buy a new suitcase and a number of storage boxes. Unfortunately, he'd yet to begin filling them with his worldly goods, and the famed cleaning rota had been forgotten in the upheaval of vacating the house. As his parents had agreed to pick up the majority of his possessions at lunchtime the following day – I'd finally get to meet them, a prospect that pleased and terrified me in equal measures – and the landlord was coming to inspect the house mid-afternoon, I'd suggested we make an inroad into his packing straight away, but this idea was brushed aside in favour of a farewell drink with Greg and Lucas in the pub. By the time the two of us had got back to the house, Conor had other things on his mind – not that I was complaining – and it had been after eight o'clock that morning when we'd dragged ourselves out of bed and begun frenziedly emptying drawers, folding clothes, wiping down kitchen counters, washing the hall floor, and binning the detritus of the three years he'd been sharing the house.

Going into Conor's bathroom, I deposited the box on the floor, wincing when my reflection in the mirror above the sink showed me cobwebs in my hair, a smudge of dirt on my face, and a streak of oven grease on my shirt. Glad that I'd thought to wear old clothes suitable for a house clearance – I was planning to change into a dress before Conor's parents arrived – I glanced round the bathroom and saw that it was as empty as the rest of the house, except for one shelf which was groaning under the weight of male grooming products. No wonder Conor smells so good, I thought, as I transferred his razor and shaving foam to the box, along with pre-shave cream, aftershave, several bottles of cologne, shampoo, conditioner, shower gel, facial scrub and moisturiser. And a lipstick. Which certainly wasn't Conor's. Or mine. I'd done my make-up in his bathroom often enough, and it was conceivable that I'd absent-mindedly left a lipstick behind, but I'd never worn that pale pink colour – I preferred more dramatic shades, red or brown. This lipstick belonged to some other girl.

Suddenly, my legs began to shake. Still clutching the lipstick, I sank down on to the edge of the bath. My reflection in the mirror over the sink showed that my dirt-smeared face had gone very pale . . .

Laurel rings Conor's doorbell. The door is opened by his housemate, Greg.

'Laurel . . .' he says. 'Conor's not here. I don't know what time he'll be back.'

'No worries,' Laurel says. 'I'll come in and wait for him.'

'He's filming today,' Greg says. 'He could be hours yet.'

'I don't mind,' Laurel says. 'I haven't anywhere else I have to be. I was supposed to be meeting a friend, but she had to cancel.' She puts a

foot on the doorstep, expecting Greg to move out of her way, but he stays where he is.

'Yesterday, they didn't wrap until midnight,' he says.

'Greg, can I come in?' Laurel says.

'Er . . . yeah, of course,' Greg says. He stands aside so Laurel can enter the house. 'Maybe you should give Conor a call. Let him know you're here.'

'I will – if he isn't back very soon,' Laurel says, walking past Greg and up the stairs to Conor's room.

An hour passes, and there is still no sign of Conor. Laurel calls him, but his phone is switched off, which presumably means he's still on set and won't be home for a while yet. Laurel stretches out on his bed and scrolls through her friends' posts on social media, smiling when she spots a photo of her and Conor taken a few days ago at a party. *We look good together,* she thinks.

The door to Conor's room swings open. Laurel looks up to see a girl standing in the doorway, blonde, mid-twenties, strikingly beautiful. Not Greg's girlfriend, whom Laurel has met, but a girl she's never seen before, although it's easy enough to guess who she is.

'Hello,' Laurel says, sitting up. 'You must be looking for Lucas. His room is next to this one.'

'Who are you?' the girl says.

'I'm Laurel. Conor's girlfriend.'

The girl frowns. 'Conor,' she says. 'Who is this woman and why is she in your bedroom?'

It is then that Laurel sees Conor, standing behind the girl, looking over her shoulder. The expression on his face, eyes wide, mouth hanging open, in other circumstances would have been comical.

'Laurel?' Conor barges past the girl and into the room. 'What—? Why are you here?'

Laurel tries to frame a response, but the words won't come. Sick to her stomach, she forces herself to stand up, return her phone to her bag, and hoist her bag on to her shoulder.

'Laurel,' Conor says. 'Please, I can explain—' He puts his hand on Laurel's arm. She stares at him, and he lets his hand fall. She stumbles

80

past him, past the blonde girl, and down the stairs, wrestles open the front door, and runs out into the street. She hears Conor calling her name, but she keeps on running . . .

I stared at the lipstick resting in the palm of my hand. Not again, I thought. Please don't let him have cheated again.

'Laurel, can you hear me?' Conor's voice came from downstairs. 'My parents are here.'

I gasped, and sprang to my feet. Conor's parents had arrived early – and I looked a state. Not knowing what to do with the lipstick, I shoved it in the pocket of my jeans and attempted to wipe the dirt off my face with my hands. To my dismay, I only made it worse. Intending to make a dash for Conor's room and my over-night bag, I ran out on to the landing, only to see him and a middle-aged couple standing in the hall at the foot of the stairs, looking up at me expectantly. The man bore a striking resemblance to Conor, except that his hair was grey. The woman, casually smart in roll-neck jumper and black trousers, was dark haired like her son, with no sign of grey at all.

'There you are,' Conor said. 'Come and meet my mum and dad.'

My face was covered in grime, my hair was unbrushed, and I was wearing my oldest clothes. And I'd just found possible evidence that my boyfriend had slept with another woman. Whose name, now I came to think of it, might very well be Jenny.

'Hello, Laurel,' Conor's mother said. 'It's lovely to meet you.'

Somehow, I managed to stutter, 'Y-you too.' Fixing a smile on my face, I walked slowly down the stairs.

This was *not* how I'd have written the scene where I met Conor's parents for the first time.

'That's nearly everything brought in from my car,' Conor said, placing his suitcases in the centre of my bedroom floor, next to the cardboard boxes containing sundry items that hadn't gone to his childhood home with his parents, and the clothes that hadn't fitted in the suitcases. His TV was standing on my writing desk, while his iPad, laptop, and gaming console were marooned on top of my chest of drawers.

'There's more?' I said.

'Just a couple of carrier bags and the lamp,' Conor said. 'One more trip will do it.' Whistling cheerfully, he headed back to his car. I waited a heartbeat, and then I retrieved the lipstick from the pocket of my jeans.

I wouldn't have described my first meeting with Conor's parents as an episode from one of TV's more lurid soaps – I didn't slap my boyfriend's face and accuse him of cheating on me – but it wasn't a scene from a heart-warming, uplifting rom–com either. As we'd carried boxes out to his parents' car, I'd done my best to join in with their lively conversation, but distracted as I was by the evidence of their son's infidelity, my ability to come up with witty dialogue deserted me, and they must have thought me a very dull girl. By the time they'd driven off, I couldn't think straight. I'd helped Conor load up his car, watched him deal with the landlord, sat next to him while he drove across London to my flat, listening to him singing along to the radio, and I simply couldn't bring myself to confront him with my suspicions. Now, surrounded by his belongings, the idea that he'd cheated on me felt increasingly unbelievable.

I weighed the lipstick in my hand, and reminded myself that Conor wasn't the only guy to have a woman stay overnight in his shared house. Greg's girlfriend, Hayley, was there every weekend, and I'd bumped into so many girls parading in and out of Lucas's bedroom that I couldn't remember their names. A stray lipstick could belong to any one of them. Just because I'd found it on Conor's bathroom shelf, it didn't mean its owner had spent the night in his bed.

If Conor and I are going to make a go of our relationship, I thought, I have to get a grip on my imagination. I have to trust him.

I tossed the lipstick into the bin.

Chapter Twelve

I read through the email one last time – just to make sure I hadn't done anything stupid like type 'xx' after my name – and pressed send. Now all I could do was wait for a response. Closing my laptop, I went out of my bedroom and into the living room.

Amber, curled up in a chair, her feet tucked under her, looked up from her book. 'Finished work for today?' she said.

'I have,' I said, sinking down on to the sofa. 'On Monday morning, the commissioning editor of a new TV series will find my email in her inbox telling her all the reasons why she has to hire me.' I sighed. 'This is the worst part of being a freelance writer – it's a wonderful moment when you hand over your final draft, but then you're basically unemployed until your next successful pitch.'

'Tell me about it,' Amber said. 'I was out of work so long, I was thinking I might never act again. But then I got *Swords and Sandals*.'

'And the rest is history,' I said. 'Literally. As Jason Harding might say.'

'Have you been in touch with him?' Amber said.

'Who, Jason?' I said. 'No. Why would I?'

Amber shrugged. 'You told me how much you liked working with him. I was thinking maybe you had plans to continue your partnership.'

Since Jason and I'd parted outside Farley Productions, and gone our separate ways, I'd hardly thought about him, but now I pictured him smiling one of his rare smiles. There was no reason for me to contact him. He was no longer a character in my story. I was surprised how much that thought saddened me.

'I'd happily work with Jason again,' I said, 'but *Swords and Sandals* was a one-off for him. He was adamant that he's an archaeologist, not a screenwriter. That's another downside of freelancing. You work closely for a short time with people you like, you almost become friends, then the job is over and you never see them again.'

'I know what you mean,' Amber said. 'I once did a film with this guy and . . . let's just say we went for another take every time we left the set, but I haven't seen him since the wrap party.'

'That,' I said, 'is not what I'd call a *working* relationship.' Suddenly becoming aware that I was hungry, and recalling that Conor had said he'd be back in time for us to eat together, I checked my watch. 'Conor's late. Rehearsals must have overrun again.'

'Any news about when he's moving into his new flat?' Amber said. 'Has he chased up the landlord?'

'No, not yet,' I said. 'With the hours he's rehearsing, he hasn't had a chance.'

'You did say he'd only be staying a couple of weeks, but it's been twice that long already.'

Here we go again, I thought. If Amber and I ever fell out, it would be because of Conor. 'It's only been three weeks, and he'll move out as soon as his new place is refurbished.'

'If you say so,' Amber said. 'It wouldn't surprise me if him and all those boxes he's left cluttering up the landing are still here when I get back from Greece.'

'That won't happen. He'll be long gone by then.' I made a mental note to ask Conor if he could possibly take a few more of his belongings to his parents' place. Not that I was going to admit it to Amber, but I was growing tired of having to squeeze past the boxes every time I walked from the living room to the kitchen. And I could have done without Conor's TV on my writing desk — sitting typing on my bed did not feel very professional. Deciding I needed to change the conversation to a less contentious topic than my boyfriend, I said, 'What are you up to this weekend?'

'I'm going with Tom, Freya, and her bridesmaids for a curry,' Amber said, without enthusiasm. 'Tom thinks it'll be a good opportunity for the wedding party to get to know each other. He's got it into his head that Freya and I are going to become great friends. As if that's ever going to happen.'

To me it seemed perfectly reasonable for Tom, oblivious as he was to Amber's feelings, to picture his fiancée and his groom's girl bonding over a biryani, but I didn't say this to Amber.

'I can't stop thinking about him,' Amber said. Her voice was calm, but I saw that her hands were clenched together so tightly that her knuckles were white. 'Even when Harry was sleeping next to me in my bed, I lay awake thinking about Tom.'

For the last week, she hadn't mentioned Tom's name. I'd dared to hope that her unreciprocated passion was fading. Evidently, I was wrong.

'I'll never get over him,' Amber said.

'You *will* get over him,' I said. 'Even if you don't believe it right now.'

'But I don't want to get over him,' Amber said. 'What I want is for him to cancel his wedding.'

I decided it was time for some tough love. Steeling myself, taking a deep breath, I said, 'Tom is marrying Freya. Deal with it and move on.'

'They're so wrong for each other,' Amber continued as if she hadn't heard me. 'That time I went round to Tom's flat so that Freya could show off her ring, all she did was moan at him: he was late home from work, he'd bought the wrong wine. I don't know how he stands her whining voice, I really don't. If there was something I could do to break them up . . . Make him realise it's me he should be with, not *her*.'

'Enough, Amber!' I said. This, I thought, has to stop right now.

'You try to come between Tom and the girl he loves, and you're the one who's going to get hurt.'

Amber stared at me wide eyed. I folded my arms and stared back at her, until she looked away.

'You're right,' she said, eventually. 'I can't make Tom love me.'

Finally, I thought, I'm getting through to her. 'No, you can't,' I said. 'You have to accept that he's never going to be your leading man. He can still be in your movie, but only in a supporting role.'

'Maybe he can. But I don't see myself ever becoming best friends with Freya.' She bit her bottom lip.

'It'll get easier—' At the sound of feet stomping up the stairs, we both turned our heads towards the door. An instant later, Conor put his head round the doorframe, and any further discussion of Amber's future relationship with Tom's fiancée was necessarily brought to a close.

'Evening all,' Conor said.

Amber mumbled something that could have been a greeting, and then ostentatiously returned her attention to her book.

'Hey, Conor,' I said, before he could register her aloofness. 'How was rehearsal?'

'Good,' Conor said. 'Laurel, could I talk to you a minute?'

'Sure,' I said, getting to my feet. 'See you later, Amber.' I followed Conor along the landing and into my bedroom, and sat down next to him on the bed.

'I've just had a call from Greg,' Conor said. 'He's decided he's had enough of London, and he's moving back to Cumbria.'

'Goodness,' I said. 'I never saw that coming.'

'Neither did I,' Conor said, 'but apparently, he's been thinking about going back up north for a while, and what with the delay on the flat, he's decided that now is the right time. He's planning to buy a place in the village where he was brought up.'

'Sounds like he's already got the cameras rolling,' I said. A thought struck me. 'I wonder how his girlfriend feels about him leaving the metropolis to go in search of his northern roots.'

'Oh, Hayley's going with him,' Conor said. 'She and Greg think a Cumbrian village would be a great place to raise kids. Apparently.'

'So they've scripted their happy ending,' I said.

'Yeah,' Conor said. He hesitated, and then went on, 'Obviously I'm pleased for Greg and Hayley, but their riding off into the sunset means that Lucas and I can no longer afford the new flat. We need to find a two-bedroomed place with a less exorbitant rent, which won't be easy in London.'

'Ah,' I said. I had a fairly good idea where this conversation was heading, and it wasn't in a direction that Amber was going to like.

'I was hoping it's be OK with you if I stayed on here a bit longer than we originally planned,' Conor said.

I thought, what do I say to him? I could hardly tell my boyfriend that my flatmate had taken against him. Besides, even if I wasn't ready to make a lifetime commitment to the guy, I wasn't in any desperate hurry for him to move out of my flat.

'I know you'll want to run it past Amber,' Conor said. 'Would you like me to ask her myself?'

'No — I'll speak to her.' I thought for a moment. 'Actually, there's no need for either of us to say anything to Amber unless she asks why you're still here.'

It was, I thought, fortunate on so many levels that Amber would be spending the next three months away on location in Greece.

Chapter Thirteen

'Have you ever thought of writing a play?' Sadie Wilson, the actress playing the part of Jenny, asked me.

'No, I've only ever been interested in writing for the cinema or TV,' I said. Recalling that Sadie had only worked in theatre, I added, 'I enjoy watching a play, though. Especially one as good as *Sometime, Never.*'

'And especially a play with someone you know in it?' Sadie said. We both looked towards the far side of the crowded theatre bar, where Conor was deep in conversation with the actors who were playing the male and female leads.

'Well, yes, that too,' I said, raising a hand and waving as Conor glanced around and saw me looking at him. He smiled, kissed the female lead on the cheek, and began edging his way through the crowd towards me and Sadie.

The opening night of *Sometime, Never* at the Walbrook – a two hundred and fifty-seat theatre in Finsbury Park – might not have been as glamorous an event as the film premieres I'd attended in Leicester Square, but the atmosphere in the auditorium as the audience waited for the house lights to dim and the play to begin had been every bit as exciting. The first thing I'd done, once I'd taken my seat, was to read my programme, feeling my face flush when I saw the name of Jenny in the list of characters – a forcible reminder of my unwarranted lack of trust in Conor. Not for the first time, I'd resolved never to let my imagination run away with me ever again.

The play itself had proved to be a dark comedy – while it didn't have the audience laughing hysterically, it certainly made them chuckle, and Conor had performed brilliantly, transforming into a character so unlike himself it was uncanny. I'd had a thoroughly enjoyable evening's entertainment, and I wasn't surprised when the cast took their bows to enthusiastic applause. There was no after-party as such but, like many small theatres, the Walbrook stayed open for an hour or so after the actors left the stage, and tonight was no different, with the cast, and members of the audience who were so inclined, gathering in the bar. After I'd given Conor my exuberant congratulations, he'd introduced me to his fellow actors, and I'd fallen into conversation with Sadie. That she was in her late forties and married with a teenage son made my lipstick-inspired suspicions seem even more foolish.

'Hey, you!' Conor appeared at my side, and slid an arm around my waist. To Sadie, he said, 'It went so well tonight. Even the quick change in Act One went right.'

Sadie laughed. 'For the first time.'

To me, Conor said, 'We'd never managed that quick change before. Until tonight, one of us was either late coming on stage, or only wearing half a costume.'

'Even with all those extra rehearsals?' I said.

Sadie arched her eyebrows. 'There weren't that many,' she said. 'I'd have liked more.'

'We were a little under-rehearsed,' Conor said, 'but we got away with it.' He drained his pint. 'Time we made a move, I think, Laurel. I'm exhausted.' I quickly swallowed my remaining wine. Sadie and I exchanged air-kisses, and Conor ushered me towards the door.

We spent the train journey home discussing Conor's outstanding performance, the audience's reaction to the play, and some delicious backstage gossip about several members of the cast.

'I'd love to see it again,' I said, as I unlocked the front door, and we trundled upstairs. 'What night are your parents going?

Maybe I could go with them.' And hopefully show them that their son's girlfriend wasn't entirely lacking in social skills.

'It'd be more interesting for you to come to the final perform-ance,' Conor said. 'Plays can change so much over the course of a run.'

'Well, I wouldn't mind seeing it a couple more times,' I said.

'Am I that good an actor?' Conor said, striking a pose and admiring himself in the mirror at the top of the stairs.

'You are,' I said. Noticing that Amber's door was open, but the room was in darkness, I added, 'Looks like Amber went out again. She told me she was having a night in with a glass of wine and a good book.'

'Do you think she'd like to see *Sometime, Never*?' Conor said.

No, I thought, Amber would not like to see the play. Not if you're in it.

'I doubt she'll have time,' I said. 'She's flying out to Greece in three days.'

We went into my bedroom. I kicked off my shoes and tossed my bag and coat on the chair. Conor took off his jacket and came and stood in front of me.

'It'll be good to have this flat to ourselves,' Conor said, lifting his hand and brushing his thumb over my mouth. A shiver ran along my spine as he reached behind me and unzipped my dress.

'I thought you were exhausted,' I said. He laughed softly, and kissed me.

'I reckon I can manage one more performance tonight,' he said.

The sound of voices dragged me out of a deep sleep, Amber's voice, high pitched, dissolving into giggles, and a slurred male voice. Then I heard a loud thud – as if someone had overturned a chair – that made me sit bold upright in bed.

'What the——?' Conor said, half-raising himself off the bed on his elbows.

'I think Amber may have brought home another overnight guest,' I said.

Conor groaned and rolled over on to his stomach. I lay down beside him. There was a burst of raucous male laughter, followed by a long silence. I shut my eyes and willed myself to fall sleep.

I heard Amber say, 'Come in here. No, *here*. My bedroom.'

The male voice, still slurred, but now horribly familiar, said, 'You're the best. Y'know that, Amber? My best girl.'

I heard Amber's bedroom door slam shut.

No, I thought. Surely not? I sat up again and switched on the light. 'Conor, wake up.'

'I'm not asleep,' Conor muttered. 'No chance of that.' He sat up also, blinking and rubbing his eyes.

'It's Tom,' I said. 'Amber has Tom in her bedroom.'

'Tom who's getting married?'

'Yes, *that* Tom.'

Conor grinned. 'Presumably no one told him that the duties of a groom's girl don't include shagging the groom.'

'Cheating isn't funny,' I snapped. 'It's just plain wrong.'

Conor rearranged his face into a suitably solemn expression. As well he might, I thought.

'You're shocked, and I get that,' he said, 'but who she has sex with is none of your concern. And I need to get some sleep or I'll be too exhausted to make that quick change tomorrow.' He lay down on his side, facing away from me. I switched off the light, and lay down next to him.

If Amber was a character in a film, I thought, I'd most definitely be rewriting her storyline.

Chapter Fourteen

When I woke up the following morning, my first thought was: Amber slept with Tom last night.

My phone told me it was only seven a.m., but I knew there was no way I was going back to sleep, not with the thoughts that were buzzing around my head. Careful not to disturb Conor, who was sleeping soundly, I slid out of bed, found my dressing gown and laptop, and crept out on to the landing. It was then that I heard the sound of crying coming from Amber's room.

I was still shocked that she and Tom had spent the night together, but she was my friend, and I couldn't listen to her weeping without worrying about her. It occurred to me to wonder if Tom was still in her bedroom – if he was, I should make myself scarce – or if he'd already left the flat, in which case, judging by what I could hear, Amber might welcome a proverbial shoulder to cry on. For a while, I hovered on the landing in an agony of indecision, but then, taking a deep breath, I knocked on her door.

'Is everything OK in there?' I said. There was a short silence, and then the door opened to reveal Amber dressed in pyjamas, her eyes red and her face wet.

'Did I wake you?' she said. 'I'm sorry.'

'I was awake anyway,' I said. 'What's wrong? What's happened?'

'I did something really stupid last night.' She turned away from me, stumbled across her room, collapsed on top of her duvet, and burst into tears, great heaving sobs that racked her entire body.

I sat down on the end of her bed and waited until she was all cried out. Spotting a box of tissues on the windowsill, I picked it up and placed it within her reach on her pillow. 'Can I get you a glass of water? A cup of tea?'

'N-no,' she said, raising her head. 'Thank you, though.' With a visible effort, she sat up. Reaching for a tissue, she blew her nose. 'Tom was here last night.'

'I know,' I said. 'I heard you talking and recognised his voice. He sounded drunk.'

'We were both drunk,' Amber said. 'Yesterday, he rang and suggested we meet for a drink, just me and him, before I went to Greece. I nearly turned him down, but I figured it was my last chance to see him for months.' Her voice caught in her throat, and I thought she was going to start crying again, but she got herself under control. 'He was so sweet and funny – the way he used to be – and I didn't want the evening to end. I persuaded him to come back here and open another bottle of wine. We were laughing and drinking, and then I kissed him. I got it into my head that if I slept with him, he'd leave Freya for me.'

I stared at her. 'I'm sorry, Amber, but that is *so* wrong – on so many levels.'

'I know,' Amber said. 'I wasn't thinking clearly. I wanted him so badly.'

'So did you . . .?'

'Did Tom and I have sex last night?' Amber said. 'No, we didn't. I took him into my bedroom and lay down with him on my bed but however much I told myself that he and I should be together, I knew deep down that he was only there because he was completely wasted. And that one night of drunken sex wasn't going to make him feel the same way about me as I felt about him.' She stared off into the distance, as if she was replaying the scene, the way I ran films in my head. 'Suddenly, I was stone cold sober. I pushed Tom away, and told him I couldn't have sex with a guy who was in love with another girl. He looked confused, but didn't argue. He said he'd better go, and called a cab, but there was an hour's wait. He texted Freya so she wouldn't worry, and she texted back that she'd come and get him.'

'Freya came here!'

Amber nodded. 'She drove across London in the middle of the night to pick up her drunk fiancé. Who, by the time she arrived, had fallen asleep on the sofa. It was awful.'

'Was she very angry?' I said.

'No, not at all,' Amber said. 'She was lovely. She kept apologising for Tom, saying he was lucky to have such a good friend as me. I felt so guilty, and her being so nice made it worse. She woke Tom up, and he gave her this look of *adoration*. And then, with her still thanking me and hoping I'd have a fab time in Greece, and him saying nothing at all, they went home.' A tear ran down Amber's face. 'I despise cheating – the lies, the hurt it causes – yet last night I deliberately set out to *seduce* Tom.'

'But you didn't sleep with him,' I said, wishing I hadn't been so quick to think she had.

'In the end I didn't,' Amber said. She wiped her face with her hand. 'I still feel dreadful though.' I looked at her tear-stained face and my heart went out to her.

'You're not the first girl to make a bad choice when you've had too much wine,' I said. 'And it sounds like Tom wasn't exactly unwilling.'

'He was blind drunk.'

'That's no excuse for cheating on a fiancée. Listen, Amber, you almost did something shameful last night, but you came to your senses and stopped before you went too far. Try not to beat yourself up about it.' I risked a smile. 'And don't do it again.'

Amber didn't appear to appreciate my feeble attempt at raising her spirits. 'It's all such a mess,' she said. 'Tom won't want to know me after this – not that I can face him. I can't possibly go to his wedding. And I've no idea how I'm going to explain that to my family. They're all so excited about it – my brother is invited to his stag night.' She started at the ringing of her phone, and retrieved it from the floor beside her bed. The colour drained from her face. 'Oh, no – it's Tom. I can't talk to him now.'

'You'll have to speak to him sometime,' I said. 'What with you being his groom's girl.'

'Not for much longer, I'm sure, after last night,' Amber said. The phone stopped ringing. And started again.

'Best hear what he has to say and get it over with,' I said. Amber sighed, but she hit the answer icon.

'Hey, Tom,' she said, her tone unnaturally bright. 'How are you?'

'I have the most god-awful hangover,' Tom said, his voice loud and clear over the phone's speaker.

'Well, you did drink more than your fair share of the wine last night,' Amber said.

'Guilty as charged,' Tom said. There was a long silence, and then he added, 'I have to ask you something. About last night.'

'W-what do you want to know?'

'Oh, lord, this is mortifying,' Tom said. 'Last night, I was completely pissed. I remember us going back to your place, but after that, most of it's a blur. I woke up this morning with no idea of how I got home.'

'Freya drove you,' Amber said.

'Yes, she told me this morning before she went to work,' Tom said. He cleared his throat. 'There's no easy way to say this, so I'll come straight out with it. Last night – me and you – did something happen?'

Feeling acutely uncomfortable, I caught Amber's eye and mouthed 'Shall I go?' She shook her head.

'Tom! What are you implying?' she said.

'I've been getting these flashbacks in my head – you and me – your bed – and then a blank.'

'Oh my days,' Amber said, with a peal of laughter. 'I'm very fond of you, Tom, you know I am, but you, me and a bed . . . *Ugh!*'

'I'm serious,' Tom said.

95

'Seriously, let's just not go there.'

'Amber, did we have sex last night?' Tom said.

'No, we did *not*,' Amber said.

'Are you sure?'

'I'm absolutely, positively sure,' Amber said. 'Nothing happened last night. Except for you giving me a disgusting slobbery kiss on my cheek and repeatedly assuring me that I was your best friend *ever*, before doing your usual trick of passing out on the sofa.'

'Oh, thank god,' Tom said. 'Sorry, if I've embarrassed you, Amber, but I had to ask. I had to know if I'd betrayed Freya's trust in me. If I hurt her, I couldn't live with myself.'

Amber's eyes were suddenly very bright. 'Tom, you're a lovely guy, and I'm sure you'd never do anything to hurt Freya, but maybe you should think about making some lifestyle changes, like cutting back on the alcohol.'

'That's what I'm thinking too,' Tom said. 'I've turned thirty. Soon, I'll have a wife. In a few years, I could have kids. It's time I started behaving like a responsible adult. Speaking of which, I need to get off the phone and go to work, before I make myself late. The leisure centre can't open without its Assistant Manager.' He paused. 'Bye, Amber. Safe flight. Have a great time in Greece.'

'Have a fab summer, Tom,' Amber said. 'Bye now.' She ended the call.

'Now that,' I said, 'was an Oscar-winning performance.'

'You think?' Amber said. 'Well, I'm not proud of it. In all the years I've known Tom, that's the first time I've lied to him.'

'It was only half a lie. And if you'd told him the whole truth, it would only have made him feel bad and you feel worse.'

'If I'd told him the truth, if he knew how I feel about him, I'd lose his friendship for sure,' Amber said. 'And I can't imagine not having him in my life.' She rubbed her temples. 'I ought to get up and get dressed – I planned to start my packing for Greece today – but I'm so tired. And I'm getting a headache.'

'It's still early,' I said. 'Why don't you go back to bed for a bit?' Amber nodded. I patted her arm, stood up, and went to the door.

'Laurel—' she said.

'Yes, what is it?'

'Freya's so right for Tom. And her voice isn't at all whiny.'

I smiled. Amber was going to be fine. All she needed was time. And now that she knew how it felt to regret in the morning something you'd done the night before, perhaps she'd be less judgemental towards Conor.

Chapter Fifteen

'That was delicious,' I said. Placing my knife and fork together on my empty plate, I glanced around the pub, which was just down the road from the Walbrook Theatre. Apart from three men clustered by the bar, Conor and I had the place to ourselves.

Conor, who rather than relaxing over his cod and chips, had been texting between every mouthful, raised his eyes from his phone. 'Sorry, Laurel, did you say something?'

'Only that I enjoyed my meal.' Knowing that I was incapable of leaving a ringing phone unanswered, I'd switched my mobile on silent while we ate. It wouldn't, I thought, have hurt Conor to have done the same. As the nearest thing to a date we'd had since he'd moved into my flat, this meal was far from the romantic tête-à-tête I'd envisaged when I suggested it. Pushing aside my irritation, I said, 'With food this good, I'm surprised there aren't more customers.'

'There never seem to be many people in here at lunchtime,' Conor said, 'but it does fill up in the evening. If we want a drink after the show comes down, the other actors and I prefer to stay in the theatre bar.'

'Naturally,' I said, biting back the observation that lately there weren't any evenings when Conor didn't stay for a drink with the other actors after the show. 'Your adoring public expect you to be available to sign autographs.'

'That has happened occasionally,' Conor said, seemingly oblivious to the fact I was teasing him, 'but we haven't had the crowds of fans that turn up at stage doors in the West End.' He beckoned to the waiter. 'Could we have the bill, please.' To me, he added, 'I'll get this.'

I didn't argue with him. Not that I expected him to pay every time we ate out – we usually split the bill – but he'd been living in my flat rent-free and eating his way through my fridge for almost three months now, so I didn't think it hurt him to wine and dine me once in a while. Almost immediately, I realised how churlish this would seem to anyone else. Except, possibly to Amber, who rather than thaw towards Conor in the days before she left for Greece, had avoided him completely. The last thing she'd said to me, before she got into the cab that was taking her to the airport, was to say that she supposed Conor would be gone by the time she got back. Since then, the only communication I'd received from her were photos on WhatsApp of deserted beaches and calm blue seas, with captions like: *Not all work and no play here on Kyros lol! Fab day out at this beach :) xx* – which reassured me that she wasn't spending her every spare moment pining for Tom – but I dreaded receiving a message asking me how Conor's flat hunting was going.

'Ready to go?' Conor said, placing a couple of notes and a handful of coins in the small tray the waitress had left on the table for that purpose.

'Absolutely,' I said, standing up and shrugging on my jacket. 'I've less than an hour before I have to be at Farley Productions. I do wish I'd some idea of what it is Shannon wants to discuss with me.' When Shannon's assistant had called me to arrange the meeting, I'd naturally asked him what it was about, but all he would say was that Shannon needed to speak to me urgently.

'Presumably she has another script she wants you to beat into submission,' Conor said.

'I like to think what I do has a bit more artistry than that,' I said, 'but I hope you're right—' I realised that Conor was once again studying his phone.

'Sorry, this is important.' He finished reading whatever was on the screen. 'I need to get myself backstage. The company manager will have a hissy fit if I miss the half.'

'Oh, don't let me make you late,' I said, hastily.

Outside the pub, looking along the road, I saw that the Walbrook's doors were open and the matinée audience were already streaming inside.

'Break a leg and all that,' I said, my actor friends having drummed into me never to utter the words *good luck* to a performer – but Conor was already hurtling towards the theatre, and didn't hear me. I stood and watched him until he vanished into the alley that led to the stage door. He did not look back.

As I headed towards the nearest underground station, I reminded myself that an actor about to go on stage needs to focus on his forthcoming performance, not his girlfriend. If Conor was inattentive, it was because his mind was on his work. I had no reason to feel neglected.

Arriving at Farley Productions, I'd barely taken a seat in reception, before Shannon's assistant, Devon, a lanky young man reputed to share her enthusiasm for spreadsheets, appeared to collect me.

'Is the meeting today just me and Shannon?' I asked him, as we walked through the open-plan main office, and up the stairs to the first floor. 'Or will Marcus be there too?'

'Oh, no,' Devon said. 'Marcus won't be there. He's off on location with *Swords and Sandals*. He flew out to Kyros last week.'

'Marcus is in *Greece*?' I said.

'Yep,' Devon said. 'Eadie – his PA – is out there too. I volunteered to go in her place if she didn't fancy it, but strangely, she was very keen to jet off to a Greek island.'

I laughed. 'Who'd have thought it?' I wondered if Marcus was actually needed on Kyros, or if, with his boundless enthusiasm for every aspect of film-making, he'd simply been unable to keep away.

By now, we'd arrived at the suite of offices that were Marcus and Shannon's domain. I followed Devon into the outer office, where he and Eadie shared the task of guarding the doors that led into their bosses' presence.

'I'll check if Shannon's ready for you,' Devon said, reaching for his desk-phone just as the door to the inner office opened – and Jason Harding walked out.

'Hey, Jason,' I said, startled at how pleased I was to see him. 'We meet again.'

'Indubitably,' he said. 'Sorry, I can't stop. I have to get back to Aldgate.'

'Oh. Right. See you, then.'

'I do hope so, Laurel. I hope we'll see each other very soon.' With that he headed off, leaving me gratified, if more than a little bemused, by his unexpected desire for my company in the near future.

Shannon, wearing a pale blue structured dress that emphasised her enviably slender figure, stepped out of her office. I'd only known her as a producer, but seeing her standing there, framed by the doorway, her braided bun and vertiginous heels adding inches to her five foot ten height, it was easy for me to picture her sashaying along a catwalk in Paris or Milan – which, according to Marcus, was how she'd paid her way through business school.

'Laurel,' she said. 'Do come in.' I joined her inside the room. Instead of sitting behind her desk, she settled gracefully in one of the leather chairs grouped around a coffee table in front of the floor to ceiling windows, and gestured to me to do the same.

'As I've just explained to Jason Harding,' she said, once I was seated, '*Swords and Sandals* has run into some problems. Marcus has flown out to Kyros to get a clearer idea of what's going on, but it seems that Drew's pursuit of his vision has resulted in an unfortunate amount of friction between him and some of the actors.'

I was right, I thought, Shannon is not a fan of Drew, and with good reason, it seems. Not that it was unheard of for directors and actors to clash over the interpretation of a character or the script, but it was hardly professional.

'There have been other issues,' Shannon went on. 'The film is falling way behind schedule.'

Again, not a unique situation, but regrettable.

'And then there's the script,' Shannon said. 'Drew wants to make some more changes.'

Oh, surely not, I thought. That script is *good*. Aloud, I said, 'So that's why you asked me and Jason here today. You want us to do another rewrite.' Not a new project, then, but I was far from averse to spending more time with Chloe and Lysander. Or with Jason, for that matter. We made such a good writing team.

'It's a bit more complicated than that,' Shannon said. 'Drew, as you may have gathered, is not the easiest of directors to work with, but he seems to have taken a shine to you and Jason. He's requested that the pair of you join the film unit on location – they've another month of filming in Greece before they're due to return to London for the rest of the shoot.'

'He wants us to go to Kyros?' Excitement soared up inside me.

'It's a big ask, I know,' Shannon said, 'but we'd like you to fly out – with Jason, who's already said he'll go – on Thursday.'

'The day after tomorrow!'

'Is that too soon for you?' Shannon said.

'No, that works fine for me,' I said, hurriedly.

'I take it you want the job?' Shannon said.

'Yes, please,' I said. 'I most certainly do.' I couldn't stop smiling.

'Good,' Shannon said. 'I've had a contract prepared for you.' She stood up, went to her desk, and returned with several sheets of paper neatly stapled together, which she handed to me, and a fountain pen which she placed on the table.

'Where do I sign?' I said.

'I appreciate your enthusiasm,' Shannon said, 'but perhaps you'd like to read the contract before you sign it?'

'Ah – yes, I should do that,' I said.

'Take all the time you need,' Shannon said, sitting down opposite me and leaning back in her chair. 'There are two copies – one for you and one for us. I'll need your signature on both.'

I made myself read slowly and carefully through the contract, which was standard for the industry, and similar to other contracts I'd signed with Farley Productions. Apart from my fee. Which was so much higher than the amount anyone had paid me before that I almost asked Shannon if there'd been a mistake. Fortunately, I came to my senses before I made a fool of myself. What to me was an extraordinary amount of money, was only what a screenwriter working on a feature film, away for a month on location, would expect to be paid. All the small, low-budget productions I'd worked on, learning my craft, had led me to this moment. I was ready for this.

'Is the contract acceptable to you?' Shannon said.

'Yes, it is,' I said, signing my name with a flourish, and passing the contract back to Shannon.

'I won't bore you with the details,' Shannon said, 'but there's a lot riding on *Swords and Sandals*.'

'That's what Marcus told me,' I said.

'When you're in Greece, if you have any issues – especially with Drew's vision for the film – take them straight to Marcus. Remember it's Farley Productions you're working for, not Drew Brightman.'

'I'll hold that thought,' I said.

Shannon smiled. 'In that case, I'd say we're all good.' She rose to her feet. Realising, the meeting was over, I hastened to do the same. 'Devon will email you the travel arrangements and so forth.'

'Thanks, Shannon,' I said. Thank you so much, I thought. You can rely on me to do a good job. I won't let you down. Fortunately, I managed not to blurt my fulsome thanks out loud.

I left Shannon's office and, having assured Devon that I could find my own way out of Farley Productions, skipped down the stairs and through the main office, resisting the urge to punch the air until I was out in the street.

Fishing my phone out of my bag, I texted Jason: *Can't wait to fly to Greece! Looking forward to working with you again! Laurel xx*. He replied almost immediately: *Likewise. See you at the airport. JH.*

Then I texted Amber: *Me and Jason flying out to Kyros day after tomorrow. Save me a sun lounger, lol! xx.* She texted back: *Yay! The writers are coming! Whoop! Whoop! :) xx*

It was only then that it occurred to me to wonder how Conor might react when I told him I was swanning off to a Greek island, leaving him alone in London.

Jason walked the short distance along the corridor from his office to Emily's. Her door was half open, and he could see her sitting at her desk, absorbed in reading her laptop screen. He rapped lightly on the doorframe to get her attention, and she looked up, smiled, and beckoned him in.

'Hi, Jason,' she said. 'Have a seat.'

Jason removed a stack of books from a chair, placed them on Emily's desk between the pot plant and the framed photo of Philip, and sat.

'I'm afraid I won't be coming with you to the Humanities department dinner next week,' he said. 'The day after tomorrow, I fly to Kyros. I'll be gone a month.'

'*Kyros!*' Emily closed her laptop. 'I haven't heard anything about a dig there this summer. Are you heading up a team? Why didn't you tell me this before?'

'If I was planning an exploratory excavation on a Greek island, you'd be the first to know,' Jason said, 'but much as I'd like to look for the lost Mycenaean settlement of Kyros, I'm going there to do more work on *Swords and Sandals*.' Even as he spoke, he felt his spirits rise – exactly as if he was indeed about to embark on a new dig.

'I thought your screenwriting days were over,' Emily said.

You're not the only one, Jason thought. When Shannon had told him more rewrites were needed, he'd been surprised at how proprietorial he'd felt towards *Swords and Sandals*. Even so, he'd only accepted the job with the proviso that Laurel would also be flying out to Kyros. He knew by now that there was no way he could write a screenplay without her.

'Turning down the offer would have felt like leaving a job h
done,' Jason said. 'And I'll get to work with Laurel again.'

Emily's eyes widened. 'She's also going to Kyros? You'll b
spending a month with her on a sunlit island in the Aegean?'

Jason sighed. He'd walked right into that one. 'Even if I was
attracted to Laurel, which I'm not,' he said, wearily, 'she's unavail-
able. She has a boyfriend.' At least, she did when I last saw her, he
thought.

Emily pouted. 'How annoying of her,' she said.

Chapter Sixteen

ried to call Conor between his matinée and evening show, but when he failed to answer his phone, I decided to wait for his return from the theatre and give him my news face to face. It was nearly three a.m. – I was attempting to watch a DVD, but was having trouble keeping my eyes open – when I heard his footsteps on the stairs.

'In here, Conor,' I called, switching off the movie. He came into the living room, standing just inside the door.

'I thought you'd be asleep,' he said. 'You didn't need to wait up for me.'

'I wouldn't normally,' I said. 'How did the play go tonight?'

'As always, the audience loved it.'

'That's great,' I said. 'Listen, before we go to bed—'

'I'm not going straight to bed,' Conor said. 'I'm going to take a shower.'

'Before you do,' I said. 'I've some good news to tell you. At least, I hope you'll think it's good news.'

Conor frowned. 'That sounds ominous.'

'No, it really is good news,' I said. 'This afternoon I signed a new contract with Farley Productions. More rewrites needed on *Swords and Sandals*.'

For a moment, Conor stared at me blankly, and then he said. 'Oh, yeah, right, you had a meeting. That's great news, babe. I wouldn't have stayed out so late if I'd known we had something to celebrate.' Crossing the room, he sat down beside me on the sofa, and planted a kiss on my mouth. I tasted stale beer and inhaled the scent of cigarettes that his cologne wasn't strong enough to mask.

'There's more,' I said, watching his face carefully, trying to gauge his reaction. 'Drew Brightman – the director – wants me and Jason Harding to go out to *Swords and Sandals'* Greek location. The day after tomorrow, I'll be flying to the island of Kyros.'

'Awesome,' Conor said. 'I'm chuffed for you.'

I'd just told my boyfriend that I was leaving the country. Did he have to sound quite so enthusiastic?

'The downside,' I said, 'is that my going to Greece will mean that we'll be apart for a month.'

Conor shrugged. 'That's not long in the grand scheme of things.'

'Well, no, when you think about it, it's hardly any time at all.' I was tempted to ask Conor if he'd miss me while I was away, but it came to me that what I wanted was for him to say he'd miss me without my prompting, while at the same time, remaining totally supportive of my taking the job. Almost immediately, I realised most people would consider this incredibly needy – not an attractive trait in a girlfriend.

'There is one thing though,' Conor said. 'Are you OK with my staying on in the flat while you're away?'

'Oh – I hadn't thought about that,' I said, taken aback.

'I may as well stay on here, don't you think? It's pointless my moving out and leaving the place empty.'

'I guess,' I said. There was no reason why he shouldn't stay on, but the idea of him living in *my* flat while I was away seemed a little strange, although I didn't quite know why. 'What about Lucas? If you stay on here, you'd be leaving him without a housemate?'

'Oh, I meant to tell you,' Conor said, 'he's now thinking of renting a studio apartment. I may do the same. Unless . . . How would you feel about my staying on here once you're back?'

'After I'm *back* from Greece?' I said.

'It's going well, us living together, isn't it?' Conor said.

My mouth literally fell open. 'Are we living together?'

'It seems like we are,' Conor said. 'I think we should make it official, don't you?'

'Oh – I—' When had Conor started thinking of himself as my live-in boyfriend? Surely, I thought, this significant change in my life to one half of a co-habiting couple shouldn't have escaped my notice?

'Laurel?' Conor said.

'Oh – Conor—' I felt a sudden rush of guilt. My boyfriend had asked me to *share his life* and all I'd done was gawp at him. 'I love you, Conor,' I said. I *do* love him, I thought. I really do. 'But as for us living together – I don't know if I'm ready.'

Conor put his hand over mine. 'Don't say any more,' he said. 'We don't need to make any decisions tonight. How about I stay on here while you're away, and then, when you get back, we'll see how it goes, yeah?'

'Are you OK with that?' I said, hoping I didn't sound as relieved as I felt.

He nodded. 'My timing was bad. I shouldn't have sprung all this on you when you're about to fly off to Greece. We'll talk about it when you're back.' With a wolfish smile, a flash of white teeth, he added, 'I'll join you in bed as soon as I've had that shower.'

While Conor took himself off to the bathroom, I headed to my bedroom, pausing to close Amber's door, which had swung open, on my way. *Amber.* If Conor and I set up home together, I'd presumably lose her as a flatmate. Given how she felt about Conor, I might even lose her as friend. I reminded myself that neither of us had expected her to be living in my spare bedroom for ever.

I went into my room and switched on the fairy lights. Going to draw the curtains, I stood by the window for a moment, looking up at the clouds scudding across the sky.

I thought, is Conor really able to commit to living with me?

'It didn't mean anything. I've deleted her number . . .'

No, I thought, do not go there, Laurel. That was all over months ago.

Hurriedly, I shut the curtains, and started taking off my clothes. I was naked and about to get into bed when Conor, also naked, came into the bedroom, holding a towel in front of him. His gaze travelled over my breasts and down my body to my legs. Smiling wickedly, he let the towel fall from his grasp so I could see the effect I was having on him.

And then he proceeded to show me that if I did decide to live with him when I was back from Greece, it might not be the worst decision I ever made.

Chapter Seventeen

'Laurel – wait up.' That was Jason's voice. I looked back over my shoulder and saw him striding towards me, taller than most of the travellers trundling wheeled suitcases through Departures. With some difficulty, weighed down as I was with the tote bag on my shoulder, I manoeuvred my two large cases around to face him. For travelling, he'd chosen to wear a long-sleeved T-shirt and jeans. A rather better sartorial choice than mine, I felt, as the sleeveless top and short denim skirt I was wearing in anticipation of Greece's hot climate was proving inadequate in the milder temperatures of Heathrow's Terminal Five.

'Good to see you, Jason,' I said. 'Do you know where we need to go to drop off the cases?' Having dragged my suitcases around the airport for fifteen minutes without finding the drop-off point, I was extremely pleased to see my fellow traveller. Not that I'd have had any qualms about flying out to Greece on my own – even though my only experience of foreign travel was a package holiday with my family when I was eleven – but I certainly wasn't averse to having his company on what I was beginning to suspect would be a long and tiring journey, with a change of planes at Athens before we flew on to Kyros.

'Yes, it's this way,' Jason said. His gaze went to my luggage. 'Would you like a hand?' He, I noticed, had only one holdall and his ubiquitous rucksack.

'Please,' I said, gratefully passing him my larger case.

Jason strode off through the airport, slowing his pace when he noticed me lagging behind – that morning when I'd put on my high-heeled ankle boots, all I'd thought about was how stylish they were, now I wished I'd worn flats – and we joined the long snaking queue for the drop-off desk.

'I wondered why we had to be here two hours before the flight,' I said, after half an hour of standing in line, shuffling forward, pushing my suitcase before me. 'Now I know.'

'Haven't you flown before?' Jason said.

'Not since I was a child,' I said.

He raised one eyebrow. 'Are you nervous about flying?'

'No, not at all,' I said. 'It's just that every time I've thought about jetting off somewhere exotic, it's never worked out. Conor – the guy you met at my place – and I were planning to go on holiday, but then we split up—' I bit my lip. Why had I said that? I'd no desire to regale Jason with the messy history of my relationship with Conor. 'Anyway, this trip will be only the second time I've been abroad. What about you, Jason? Are you an inveterate traveller?'

'I've worked on digs all over the Mediterranean—' Jason began, breaking off as we finally arrived in front of the drop-off desk, and had to present our passports and boarding passes for inspection

Having dropped off our luggage and passed through security, we meandered through duty free, Jason waiting patiently while I pounced on the perfume testers and gleefully sprayed myself with expensive scent that I'd no intention of buying – which, I felt, earned him the role of my perfect travelling companion before we'd even boarded the plane. The departure lounge was crowded, but we found a couple of seats with a view of a large screen showing the time and destination of each flight leaving that day, and sat.

'Looks like some flights are delayed, ours included,' Jason said.

'That's annoying,' I said, eager to begin the first leg of my foreign adventure.

'The joys of air travel,' Jason said. 'I'll stay here and keep our seats, if you want to go for a wander round the shops to pass the time.'

111

'Now that,' I said, 'is a great idea.'

Leaving Jason guarding our seats – which turned out to be a wise move as the number of delayed flights mounted up and the departure lounge became ever more crowded with increasingly disgruntled passengers searching for somewhere to sit down – I went and explored the shops and food outlets that were on every side, returning to Jason with sandwiches and coffee. After we'd eaten, he went off for a wander, returning with more coffee and a newspaper, which he quickly became absorbed in reading. I flicked idly through the colour supplement, my mind drifting back to the moment earlier in the day when I'd said goodbye to Conor.

Standing on the pavement outside my flat, I'd told him that I'd miss him and promised that I'd phone him as soon as I arrived on Kyros. His only words to me had been, 'Safe journey and all that,' and then he'd put his hands in his pockets and stood watching in silence as I clambered into the back of the cab that was to take me to the airport, before giving me a brief wave and going back inside. As goodbye scenes went, it was sadly lacking in drama and emotion, I felt. Unlike the farewell I'd written for Chloe and Lysander . . .

On shaking legs, Chloe walks across the clearing towards the cave that is the portal to her own time.

'Chloe—' Lysander's voice, the voice she will never hear again, brings her to a halt.

Chloe turns around to face him. He raises a hand in farewell, and then places it on his heart. Chloe's eyes brim with tears, but she forces herself to walk away . . .

I reminded myself that unlike Chloe and Lysander, Conor and I would see each other again in just one short month. Passionate farewells, with declarations of love and attendant weeping and wailing, were all very well for lovers parting for ever in ancient Greece. Such scenes did not belong in a twenty-first-century London street. I asked myself what I would have done if Conor had gone down on his knees and begged me not to go to Kyros,

112

and knew that whatever he'd said, I still would have got into the cab.

Suddenly, Jason said, 'The gate number for our flight's just come up.'

'At last!' I said, leaping to my feet and hefting my bag on to my shoulder. A thought struck me. 'Have you been to Kyros before?'

'No,' Jason said. 'When I worked in Greece, it was on another island and in Athens – Laurel, we need to get to the plane.'

We set off across the lounge in the direction indicated by a sign pointing to the departure gates.

'So how long were you in Athens?' I asked.

'I lived there for three years,' Jason said, 'but I left seven years ago, and I've not been back to Greece since.'

'How come?' I said.

'I had no reason to go back.'

'I don't understand,' I said. 'With ancient Greece being your area of expertise, I'd have thought you couldn't keep away.'

Jason came to an abrupt halt and turned to face me. 'When I lived in Athens,' he said, quietly, 'I was engaged to an Athenian girl. It didn't work out.'

'Ah,' I said, as heat flooded my face. 'I'm so sorry, Jason. I didn't mean to cross-question you. If I'd known, I wouldn't have said anything, obviously—'

'No apology necessary,' Jason said, 'but, as I'm sure you can understand, I'd rather not discuss this in the middle of an airport. Or at all.' He resumed walking. Excruciatingly aware that I'd inadvertently discovered a side of Jason Harding that he'd rather have kept hidden, I hurried after him.

We joined a stream of travellers heading towards the departure gate, arriving just as it opened. After the hours of waiting, there was now a flurry of activity as we and our fellow passengers marched along the covered walkway that led on to the aircraft, and found our allocated seats.

'Would you like to be by the window?' Jason asked, breaking the silence that had fallen between us.

'Most definitely,' I said, sliding into the window seat, stowing my bag under the seat in front of me, and fumbling to fasten my seat belt. Jason favoured me with a smile warm enough to convince me that he'd forgiven my earlier lack of tact.

'May I?' he said, and showed me how the seat belt fastened.

I looked out of the window, but as yet there wasn't much to see other than airport buildings and another plane taxiing towards a runway. Glancing towards Jason, I saw that his attention was all on a paperback open on his lap. I thought over the little he'd said about his time in Athens – and what had brought his living there to an end. It must have been a hideously bad break-up if it still pained him to talk about it, I thought. I told myself that Jason Harding's private life was nothing to do with me, but I longed to hear more of his story.

I felt the aircraft begin to move. In just a few hours, I thought, I'll be in Greece. Excitement bubbled up inside me.

Jason raised his head from his book and glanced at this watch. 'We're cutting it fine if we're going to touch down in Athens in time to transfer to our connecting flight before it leaves for Kyros,' he said.

I also checked the time and did some calculations in my head. 'We'll still have half an hour after we're due to land before the Kyros plane takes off,' I said. 'Surely that's plenty of time?'

'Let's hope you're right,' Jason said.

Chapter Eighteen

I sat on a bench in Athens International Airport, surrounded by
our luggage. A short distance away, Jason was deep in conversation with the woman at the information desk. I couldn't hear
what they were saying, but he didn't look happy. Ten minutes, I
thought. If we'd arrived ten minutes earlier we'd have made it.

For most of our flight, Jason had occupied himself with his
book. I'd gazed out of the window as we flew over the clouds,
fascinated by the occasional glimpse of the tops of snow-capped
mountains or winding river valleys, before my eyelids had grown
heavy and I'd drifted off to sleep – who knew that sitting in an
airport and then on a plane could be so exhausting? Jason had
woken me up when the fasten-seat belts sign came on, but by
then the light was going, and all I could see from the window as
the plane began its descent was sea, a jagged coastline, and the
dots of light that were the houses and roads of Athens.

We'd landed smoothly, but there was no time for me to savour
the experience of finally arriving in Greece, as we leapt up so as
to be first off the aircraft, collected our cases from the baggage
area, and literally ran to Departures – to discover that half an
hour was not enough time to make the connection and our
onward flight was already in the sky.

My immediate reaction had been to call the *Swords and Sandals'*
production office – it was their job to sort out travel for cast and
crew, after all – but, unsurprisingly given that it was now gone
eight o'clock at night, there was no answer. If I'd been on my

own, I'm sure I'd have panicked, but thankfully Jason was there to point out that our obvious course of action was to retrace our steps to arrivals, go through customs, and book ourselves on the next flight to Kyros. It was only when we inquired at the information desk, that we'd discovered the next direct flight to Kyros was in three days' time.

While I'd stared at the woman behind the desk in shock and disbelief, Jason had calmly asked about alternative routes to the island. It soon became clear to me that I had little to contribute to the ensuing discussion of complicated journeys involving changing planes and ferries in places I'd never heard of, so I'd left him to it.

Now, he came and sat beside me.

'It turns out there's no way of getting to Kyros tonight,' he said.

'So we're stuck in Athens,' I said.

'For one night at least,' Jason said. 'Before we do anything else, I suggest we try to find ourselves a hotel – I did once spend a night sleeping on a bench in an airport, but it's not an experience I'm keen to repeat.'

'I'm with you there,' I said, my enthusiasm for travelling growing less by the minute. 'Let me try the production office one more time.' I scrolled through my address book, and suddenly spotted Marcus Farley's personal mobile number. Rescuing stranded screenwriters wasn't in a producer's job spec, but I hit the call icon, and heard the phone ringing. Come on, Marcus, I thought, answer your phone.

A male voice said, 'Marcus Farley.'

'Marcus!' I said, putting my phone on speaker. 'Am I glad to have got hold of you.'

'Laurel?' Marcus said. 'Have you landed already?'

'Yes and no,' I said. 'Jason and I are stranded in Athens. Our flight from London was delayed and we missed our connection to Kyros. The next flight isn't until Sunday—'

'Not to worry,' Marcus said, immediately. 'It's unfortunate that you won't be here for another couple of days, but I'll have

Eadie sort you out seats on the next Kyros flight. Are you both happy to stay in Athens until then?'

'I guess,' I said. 'Jason?'

'That does seem to be the best course of action,' Jason said.

'In that case,' Marcus said, 'Eadie will book you hotel rooms for the next three nights.'

'Oh, thank you so much,' I said. A wave of relief washed over me.

'Leave it with me – Eadie will get back to you,' Marcus said, and ended the call.

'Two days in Athens,' Jason said. 'I thought I'd never come back. It seems I was wrong.'

A couple of hours later, and we were in the back of a taxi edging through the traffic in central Athens bound for the hotel where Eadie had booked us rooms. I sat next to Jason, feeling very glad he was there with me, rather than my having to make this unexpected detour on my own. Stealing a look at him now, I saw that he was gazing fixedly ahead, apparently deep in thought. I couldn't help wondering if he was remembering the girl he'd loved and lost all those years ago. Was he still carrying a torch for her after all this time? I pictured him walking hand in hand with a stunning dark-haired Greek girl along these very streets.

Leaving the busy traffic on the main thoroughfares behind, the taxi turned down one narrow side street and then another. It was too dark to see much, other than the buildings lining the street were tall, narrow and had shuttered windows. The main roads we'd driven along earlier had been brightly lit and their pavements thronged with people, but this area appeared to be deserted.

We drew up outside a building with a sign in English as well as Greek proclaiming it to be the Aphrodite Hotel – the light spilling out of its plate-glass entrance was a welcome sight in the dark, empty street. Jason and I got out of the taxi, and the driver fetched our cases from the boot. By now, I was too tired to protest when Jason paid the fare – he'd get the money back on expenses, anyway. Neither did I object to his help with carrying

117

my luggage into the hotel's marble-tiled reception area or his doing most of the talking to the smiling young man behind the reception desk – he told us his name was Andreas – who checked us in.

'Here are your keys,' he said, handing two key cards to Jason. 'Your room is on the fourth floor. Our rooftop restaurant is closed, but the bar stays open until midnight.

'And the other room?' Jason said. 'Is it on the same floor?'

Andreas looked puzzled. 'You have a reservation for one room only,' he said.

'No,' Jason said, 'we have two.'

Andreas studied his computer screen. 'I assure you there is only one room booked for Martin and Harding on our system.'

'That can't be right,' I said.

'Obviously a mistake has been made,' Jason said, 'but it's easily remedied. We'll book another room.'

Andreas' face fell. 'I am sorry, but that will not be possible. There are no more rooms available. The hotel is full.'

'Seriously?' I said. 'You're completely booked up?'

'It is the tourist season,' Andreas said, 'and the Aphrodite is a very popular hotel. We are within easy walking distance of all the major sites and museums.'

Jason drummed his fingers on the reception desk. 'It seems we have a problem. I would like to speak to your manager.'

'She will only tell you the same,' Andreas said.

'Even so,' Jason said. At that moment, a door behind the reception desk, which had been ajar, swung wide open. A woman, older than Andreas, appeared in the doorway.

'Good evening,' she said. 'I am the manager. Can I help you?'

'I certainly hope so,' Jason said. 'Earlier this evening, a reservation was made for us for two rooms. Now, your colleague tells us there's only one room available.'

The manager looked questioningly at Andreas. He spoke to her rapidly in Greek, and she replied in the same language, while peering at the computer screen. Then she turned back to Jason and me.

'Unfortunately, there has been some confusion over your booking,' she said, 'and there is only one vacant room in the Aphrodite. All I can do is offer my apologies. If you wish, I will try to find you a second room at another hotel.'

Jason frowned. 'Laurel, we need to discuss what we're going to do. In private.' Pivoting on his heel, he marched across the reception and out of the hotel. I joined him on the pavement. My first night in Greece, I thought, was *not* going well.

'So what's happened is that the Aphrodite messed up our booking,' Jason said. 'Although the manager has instructed Andreas not to admit that to us.'

'You understood what they were saying?' I said.

'I didn't live in Greece for three years without picking up the language,' Jason said. 'Now, what do you want to do? I'm happy for you to have the room while I go elsewhere.'

'No, I wouldn't want you to do that,' I said, alarmed at the thought of him vanishing off into the night. Honesty compelled me to add, 'I'd rather not stay here alone. Which you probably think is ridiculous.' I hoped that the light from the hotel wasn't enough for him to see the flush of embarrassment I could feel spreading across my face.

'I'd never think that,' Jason said. 'Most people would feel the same if they arrived in a strange city where they didn't speak the language in the middle of the night. We'll both go to another hotel.'

I gave him a grateful smile. Then a blindingly obvious solution occurred to me. 'Jason, don't take this the wrong way, but we could share the room. That is, if you didn't mind.'

Jason gave me a long look. '*You* don't mind?' he said.

'No, I . . . I'm not coming on to you or anything.' Now my face was on fire. 'It's just that I'm practically asleep on my feet.'

'I've no problem sharing a room with you,' Jason said. 'I've slept four to a tent before now.'

'Then we'll share,' I said. 'We'd best go in and tell Andreas we want the room before he gives it away to someone else.'

We went back inside the hotel, collected our keys from an

inordinately polite Andreas — I had a strong suspicion that the mix-up over our reservation was down to him — and with Jason man-handling our luggage into the lift, went up to our room on the fourth floor. Walking ahead of Jason, I unlocked the door, and went inside, trundling the smaller of my cases in after me. My gaze travelled over a large wardrobe and an easy chair, and came to rest on a double bed. It'll be fine, I told myself, we can keep our clothes on. It's no different to falling asleep next to him on the plane. I moved out of Jason's way so that he could bring in the rest of our luggage.

'It's not quite midnight,' he said. 'I'm going to head up to that rooftop bar Andreas mentioned, and buy us some bottled water.'

'Good idea,' I said, realising I was thirsty. He went out, which gave me the chance to take first turn in the en suite bathroom and swap the clothes I'd travelled in for a loose-fitting T-shirt and shorts — I wouldn't have felt comfortable parading in front of Jason in my thin strappy pyjamas when we were sharing a bedroom. Examining the bed, I discovered it had only one sheet and one thin blanket, but I found others in the wardrobe and hastily arranged them on either side of the mattress. This, I felt, made sharing a sleeping place a little less intimate than if I'd had to join Jason actually *in* the bed under the covers. Too tired to think about unpacking, I sat down on the end of the bed to await Jason's return. Which was when I remembered I'd promised to phone Conor as soon as I'd landed on Kyros. Hurriedly, I called him, but when his phone went through to voicemail, I was forced to acknowledge that he wasn't going to answer. I left a message telling him that I was fine, that I was in Athens and why, but I was hurt by his apparent lack of interest as to whether I'd arrived safely at my destination. The arrival of a text from Amber: *Eadie says the writers are stuck in Athens! See you Sunday! xx,* only added to my annoyance with my errant boyfriend.

Restless and on edge, I went to the window and opened the curtains, and found myself looking out over the rooftops of Athens, at night a patchwork of darkness and light, stretching as far

120

as I could see. My attention was drawn to a plateau that rose high above the city, glowing against the night sky, its illuminated slopes steep and rocky, its summit crowned by what appeared to be a massive structure formed from huge stone columns, brightly lit from within.

Jason came into the bedroom. 'The bar was just closing, but I got us water,' he said.

'Thanks,' I said. 'Jason, what's that building on the hill that's lit up so brightly?' He came and stood beside me.

'The hill is the Acropolis,' he said, 'the highest point in the city. The building is the Parthenon. It's an ancient temple that once housed a golden statue of Athena, the Greek goddess of wisdom. It suffered a lot of damage over the centuries from earthquakes, wars, and looting, but now it's being restored . . .' He stared intently at the glowing hilltop. 'The Acropolis is one of the most important archaeological and architectural sites in the world. I'll give you a guided tour tomorrow, if you like.'

I wasn't especially eager to see the ruins of an ancient Greek temple, but it would have seemed ungrateful to refuse his offer. And it wasn't as it I had anything else planned.

'Sounds good to me,' I said.

'We should aim to get there as close to eight a.m. when it opens as we can,' Jason said. 'Certainly by mid-morning. Later in the day, it's overrun with tour parties.'

'That'll mean an early start,' I said, hoping I sounded more enthusiastic than I felt.

'Yes, we should call it a night,' Jason said.

'Er, yes, we should,' I said. Feeling stupidly self-conscious, I moved away from the window, lay down on the bed, and pulled up the covers. Jason stayed gazing at the Parthenon a while longer, and then, having set the alarm on his phone, picked up his holdall and vanished into the bathroom. When he reappeared, he was wearing a short-sleeved T-shirt and cut-off trackies. He switched off the overhead light. Then he switched it on again. He cleared his throat.

'Are you cool with us sharing this bed?' he said. 'I don't mind sleeping on the floor.'

I would so have preferred to have the bed to myself, but I couldn't bring myself to ask him to sleep on a hard floor. If I'd felt any sort of physical attraction to him — or if he'd given any indication that he was interested in me in that way — I might have felt differently, but as it was, we were simply two co-workers, making the best of an awkward situation.

'It's fine, Jason,' I said. He switched off the light for the second time. The room was just light enough for me to see him walk around the bed, and then I felt the mattress tilt as he lay down next to me. I rolled on to my side, with my back to him, and shut my eyes. Conor, I thought, wouldn't have been too pleased to know I was sharing a bed, however innocently, with another guy, but he need never know — and I was too tired to care what he thought.

I'd almost drifted off to sleep, when Jason said, 'It's strange for me being back in Athens. I feel as if I've stepped back into the past. Being here, looking out of the window, seeing the Acropolis, it's bringing it all back. Téa and I . . . Her name was Téa . . . What we had . . .'

I opened my eyes and turned over to face him. He was lying on his back, staring up at the ceiling.

'I thought my future was here in Athens with Téa,' Jason said, 'and then she met someone else . . . And I have no idea why I'm telling you any of this . . .' Wide awake now, I waited for him to go on, but he remained silent.

'I don't mind listening,' I said.

'It's been a long day,' Jason said. 'I'll stop reminiscing and let you get to sleep.' He shifted on to his side. After a moment, I did the same.

'Night, Jason,' I said, resisting the temptation to beg him to tell me more.

Seven years, I thought, and he's still not over her.

Chapter Nineteen

The lift doors slid open and Jason and I stepped inside, joining a young man and a young woman holding the handles of a buggy in which sat a small, blonde-haired toddler.

The man said, '*Guten Morgen.*'

'*Guten Morgen,*' Jason replied, and proceeded to chat to the man in what appeared to me to be fluent German, until the lift stopped at the next floor and the young German family got out.

'How many languages do you speak?' I said, as the lift continued to descend.

'Five modern foreign languages,' Jason said. 'English, Greek, German, French, and Italian. And I speak various forms of what most people refer to as ancient Greek. And Latin. I say *speak*, but, of course, we can't know exactly how ancient languages sounded when spoken aloud.'

I gaped at him. 'You have got to be the cleverest man I've ever met.'

Jason shrugged. 'It's no big deal. Learning languages has always come easily to me.'

That morning, woken not by an alarm, but by sunlight streaming through the window, I'd raised my head off the pillow to find Jason already up, dressed, and loading his rucksack with water and sunscreen. It had been an effort to drag myself out of bed, but once I'd showered, dressed in clothes suitable for sightseeing – a T-shirt, shorts, and flat sandals – I was wide awake, and more than ready for the continental breakfast of cold meat, cheese, olives, tomatoes, and strong Greek coffee, served in the open-air rooftop restaurant, along with a view of the Acropolis and its monumental buildings, now a pale honey colour in the sunlight. While we ate, Jason had made suggestions as to places we might go later in the day, after we'd climbed the Acropolis hill, and as I'd never heard of any of the sites he mentioned, I'd simply agreed with him. My memories of mind-numbingly boring school trips to museums notwithstanding, there was, I thought, no reason why we shouldn't have a good day out. Especially if I could persuade my tour guide to show me not only the archaeological sites, but other tourist attractions like the shops.

I'd had no reply from Conor to my voice mail. Jason had made no further mention of his ex.

Now, the lift arrived at the ground floor, and deposited us in reception, where Andreas was once again smiling behind his desk, wishing us a cheerful good morning, his eyes widening in surprise when Jason replied to him in Greek. Leaving the hotel, we walked through quiet residential streets, until we turned into a lively, tree-lined thoroughfare – Jason told me it was called Athinas Street – bustling with both tourists and Athenians, and with the Acropolis visible in the distance. We strolled past shops selling inexpensive everyday clothes, household goods, and live chickens and ducks – nothing that tempted me to ask Jason to stop so I could browse – pavement kiosks doing a brisk trade in newspapers and canned drinks, and a large covered food market, where Jason said he'd bought meat and fish when he'd lived in Athens.

Athinas Street ended at a square – Monastiraki Square, Jason said – which we cut across, before entering a maze of narrow, winding cobbled lanes lined with pastel-coloured houses, traditional tavernas with wooden chairs and tables outside on the pavement, and souvenir shops that I thought might be well worth investigating after we'd had our fill of sightseeing. Everywhere I looked, I saw brightly coloured flowers tumbling from earthenware pots and trees in stone planters, their branches providing a welcome shade.

'It's so pretty here,' I said to Jason, getting out my phone and taking a photo of a small stairway with a pot of scarlet flowers on every step.

He nodded. 'This is the heart of Athens, the Plaka district. One of my favourite parts of the city.' He glanced at his watch. 'I don't want to rush you, but it's already going to be getting hot up on the rock.'

Taking the hint, I put my phone back in my bag, and we continued walking, emerging out of Plaka's dappled shade into bright sunlight. Jason put his hand on my arm, drawing me to a halt.

'What?' I said. 'Ooh . . .' In front of us was the Acropolis hill, crowned by the Parthenon. The sheer size of it took my breath away.

Jason smiled. 'You've seen nothing yet,' he said.

A short walk along the broad promenade encircling the hill brought us to the entrance to the site where we purchased tickets. Once inside, we followed a rough, winding path up the hillside, passing the ruins of two Greek theatres – with their tiered seating, very much like modern open-air theatres – and rounding a bend to arrive at a flight of marble steps leading up to an imposing archway.

'This is the Propylaia,' Jason proclaimed, spreading his arms wide, 'the grand entrance through which all visitors to the sacred rock must pass – now and in the past.' In a less stentorian tone, he added, 'Watch yourself, it's easy to slip on the steps.'

We walked through the archway and out on to the summit of the Acropolis. When I looked up at the ruins of the Parthenon, its rows of towering marble columns gleaming against the clear blue sky, I actually gasped.

'Impressive, huh?' Jason said.

'It's *awesome*,' I said. 'I know people use that word all the time when they only mean that something's cool or OK, but I am in awe.'

'You and me both,' Jason said. 'Even though I've seen it many times.'

'I have to take a photo,' I said.

'Would you like me to take a picturesque shot of you sitting on a fallen column?'

'Please,' I said, eagerly handing him my phone and sitting on one of the many blocks of marble scattered across the site so he could take my picture with the Parthenon in the background, before persuading him to sit next to me and take a photo of the pair of us. After our photography session, we wandered over the summit, Jason's description of what the various ruined temples would have looked like thousands of years ago, and his tales of the ancient Greeks, the citizens of Athens, climbing the sacred rock in a winding procession, bringing gifts to the golden statue of Athena – 'she was partial to a new dress' – making the past come alive for me in a way schoolbooks never had.

'Maybe we should write a scene for *Swords and Sandals* set on the Acropolis,' I said. 'Lysander could bring Chloe to Athens in his chariot. She'd be fascinated to see the Parthenon as it once was.'

'I hate to disappoint you,' Jason said, 'but it's impossible for Lysander and Chloe to come here. He was a king, and therefore has to have lived between three to four thousand years ago in what archaeologists call the Mycenaean age. By the classical era, when the buildings you see here were constructed, ancient Greece no longer had kings.'

'So it wouldn't be *authentic* for Chloe and Lysander to come here,' I said, which made Jason smile.

'If you've seen enough,' he said, 'I think we should start back down the hill. I've just spotted the first coach party. It'll be unbearably crowded up here soon.'

Until then, we'd had the site practically to ourselves, but now I saw a sizeable group of people streaming through the Propylaia. Pausing only to drink some water – the sun was now high in the sky and fierce – the two of us headed back down the winding path to the foot of the hill. From there, a short walk along the promenade brought us to the Acropolis Museum, which, Jason informed me, housed artefacts discovered on the hill.

We wandered for an hour or so among the statues in the museum – I became so absorbed in what Jason was saying, about traces of paint revealing that a white marble girl had once been brightly coloured, that it was a shock to turn around and see that his impromptu lecture had attracted a small crowd of eavesdroppers – and then, at his suggestion, we went to the museum's restaurant, an open-air terrace, for lunch.

'What made you become an archaeologist?' I asked as we ate our Greek salads. 'It must take years of study. Were you a very studious child?'

'No, not especially,' Jason said. 'Like most small boys, I preferred kicking a football to reading, much to the dismay of my librarian mother and bookseller father. Then – I must have been about nine – my parents gave me a book of Greek myths, and one of the stories in particular caught my imagination. It was the tale of a hero who sailed from Greece to the distant land of Colchis and stole a golden fleece from its king. The hero's name was Jason.'

'I can see why that might have appealed to you.'

'Yes, it was my namesake who got me into Greek myths and legends,' Jason said. 'As I got older, I became fascinated by the people who first told those stories, and when it came to deciding what I wanted to study at university, archaeology was an obvious choice. After I graduated, I managed to get myself a job as a field archaeologist in Greece, and I spent the next three years dividing my time between Athens and a dig on an uninhabited island where we were excavating an eighth-century sanctuary to the goddess Artemis . . .' He stared off into the distance, as if he were watching a movie in his mind, the way I did. 'We'd been uncovering floors and the remains of walls for weeks without finding any artefacts, but then I found a potsherd – a piece of broken pottery. I can still remember how amazing it felt to hold it in my hands, and know I was the first person to set eyes on it in nearly three thousand years.'

'I don't think I'd be thrilled to have dug for hours under a hot sun only to come up with a smashed pot,' I said. 'Now if you'd found a sword like Chloe . . .'

'I did once find a dagger,' Jason said, 'but that was after I'd returned to England and taken the job at Aldgate. I was leading a team of archaeologists excavating a Roman site, many of them my students. They were most impressed. I felt quite the hero that day.'

I smiled. 'So you don't spend all your time giving lectures and marking essays?' I said.

'No, I still get to dig for hours,' Jason said, dryly. 'Fortunately for me, as uncovering the past – literally – is why I became an archaeologist. Why I do what I do.' One side of his mouth rose in a shy half-smile. 'For all that, I'm glad to be in a position to pass my skills and knowledge on to the next generation.'

'I kind of gathered that,' I said, recalling the eager students clustered around him in the lecture theatre at Aldgate. 'Maybe if I'd had a teacher as enthusiastic about history as you are when I was at school, I'd have been interested in the past too.'

'Didn't you like history lessons?' Jason said.

'I didn't like any lessons,' I said. 'No, that's not true. I liked English – when we had to read a book, I watched the film version – but I spent most of my schooldays staring out of the classroom window, daydreaming. Needless to say, I didn't pass many exams, but I was an enthusiastic member of my school's Film Society. We used to make our own short films, which was when I discovered that I loved writing scripts and that I was good at it—' I broke off. 'I shouldn't have said that. You must think I'm totally up myself.'

'Not at all,' Jason said. 'You are a good writer, Laurel. You're very talented.'

'Flatterer,' I said, flushing with pleasure. 'But thank you.'

'I wouldn't say it if it wasn't true,' Jason said.

If this were a date, I thought, I'd say it was going really well. I reminded myself that the undeniably attractive man smiling at me across the table was my co-writer, not a potential lead in my very own rom-com. We were eating a meal together at a table for two, talking and laughing, but this was most certainly *not* a date.

'What about after school?' Jason said. 'Did you do some sort of Film Studies course?'

I shook my head. 'I spent the summer after I left school googling *How to become a screenwriter*. I discovered that the best way was to get a job – *any* job – in the film industry, and persuade the commissioning editor you just happen to stand next to in the lunch queue to take a look at your brilliantly written screenplay. I was working as a very junior PA in a post-production company when, quite by chance, I met Marcus Farley . . .' I smiled at the memory. Unsurprisingly, Marcus hadn't optioned the script I'd thrust into his hands that day, but he must have seen something in my writing that he liked, because a few weeks later, I'd had a call from Farley Productions offering me a job as one of a team of writers developing a pilot for a TV show. 'Marcus gave me my first screenwriting credit,' I said. 'After that, when I pitched for work, commissioning editors took me a lot more seriously. Then they began to call me.'

Jason leant back in his chair and looked at me thoughtfully. 'I have to say that screenwriting seems a rather precarious way to make a living.'

'It is,' I said. 'I never know where my next job is coming from – or when. That's why I rent out my spare bedroom – just in case the screenwriting dries up. But I can't imagine ever wanting to do anything else but write.'

'Given how important your writing is to you,' Jason said, 'I'm surprised you agreed to have me foisted on you as a co-writer on *Swords and Sandals*.'

'If I'm honest, I wasn't best pleased to start with,' I said, 'but I am now.'

'So am I,' Jason said. We exchanged smiles. When, I thought, had Dr Jason Harding started smiling so often?

'So where is my tour guide taking me this afternoon?' I said.

'The National Archaeological Museum,' Jason said. 'They have an impressive collection of finds from the palace of Mycenae.'

'Mycenae?' I said. 'Oh – Lysander lived in Mycenaean Greece.'

'He did,' Jason said. 'You'll see artefacts similar to those he would have owned. That is, he could have owned them, if he wasn't a character in a movie.' He stroked his bearded chin. 'Why am I talking about Lysander as if he actually lived and breathed?'

'Welcome to my world,' I said.

'You remember when we talked about the Trojan War?' Jason said, suddenly, as we approached the steps leading up to the entrance of the National Archaeological Museum – an imposing building with rows of columns along its façade that reminded me of the Parthenon.

'Helen, a Greek queen, ran off with a Trojan prince,' I said, 'and the Greeks sent an army to fetch her back.'

Jason nodded. 'According to legend, Helen was an exceptionally beautiful woman – allegedly, the most beautiful woman in the world. Many kings and princes sought her for their wife, but she married Menelaus, King of Sparta. When she ran off with Paris, a prince of Troy, Menelaus called upon his fellow Greek kings, his sworn allies, to help him get her back.'

'So they all upped and sailed off to Troy?' I said.

'It took a while to round them up,' Jason said, 'and some of them tried to get out of going, but eventually they did set sail, led by Menelaus' brother Agamemnon, King of – cue drum roll – Mycenae.'

'I see where you're going with this,' I said.

'I thought you might,' Jason said. 'In the early days of archaeology, back in the nineteenth century, the site of the fortified citadel of Mycenae was well known, but it was Schliemann – the guy who was so keen to prove that the Trojan War was a real historical event – who excavated it with the aim of confirming it was the legendary Agamemnon's palace. He made some spectacular finds. Let's go inside, and you'll see what I'm talking about.'

We climbed the steps of the museum, and entered a central atrium, with doors to the left, right, and straight ahead, and joined the short queue at the ticket desk. When we reached the front of the queue, before I had a chance to find my purse, Jason had taken out his wallet and purchased our entrance tickets.

'Let me give you the money for mine,' I said.

'No, it was my idea that we came here,' Jason said. He hesitated and then added, 'There is something I'd like you to do for me, though, if you're willing?'

'Depends what it is,' I said.

'You just need to shut your eyes and let me guide you into that room,' Jason said, indicating the doorway straight ahead of us.

'OK,' I said, bemused.

'Here, give me your hand,' Jason said. 'Don't open your eyes until I tell you.'

I put my hand in his and closed my eyes. Feeling a little foolish – there were a fair number of people milling around the entrance hall, and anyone who noticed us would think us very odd – I let him lead me a short distance.

'You can open your eyes now.' He let go of my hand.

I did as he said, and gasped. I was standing in front of a display cabinet, looking at a mask, a face of shining gold, the bearded face of a man, his eyes closed as if he were asleep. I stared at the mask, mesmerised by the bright metal, unable to look away.

In a voice scarcely above a whisper, Jason said, 'I have seen the face of Agamemnon.' A shiver ran down my spine.

'Is it really his image?' I said.

'Sadly, no,' Jason said. 'That was what Schliemann said when he first saw it, but it's centuries older than the time when warriors from Mycenae went to fight beneath the wall of Troy. It's a death mask found in the grave of a man of high status, most likely a king.'

'It's stunning,' I said. 'It must be priceless.'

'It is,' Jason said. 'Now, look around you,'

Tearing my gaze away from the mask, I saw that it was situated in the centre of the room, surrounded by more display cabinets containing a resplendent array of gold artefacts.

'All this was found at Mycenae,' Jason said.

'I think I'm beginning to understand what makes you want to dig up ancient ruins,' I said.

With Jason at my side, I walked slowly from display to display, marvelling at golden masks, necklaces and diadems, breastplates, cups and signet rings, and bronze weapons, coming to a halt in front of a bronze sword, with a hunting scene – as Jason pointed out to me – etched into the blade and inlaid with gold.

'Could Lysander's sword have looked like that? I said, peering closely at the outlined figures of spearmen and lions.

'Most of the swords in this room were made to be art, not weapons used in battle,' Jason said, 'but it's possible Lysander had a bronze sword similar to that one.'

I smiled and got out my phone. 'Put your hand in front of that sword,' I said.

Jason raised one eyebrow, but did as I asked, placing his hand on the glass of the display cabinet.

'Now curl your fingers,' I said. 'A bit more. That's it. Now it looks as though you're holding Lysander's sword.' I took a photo.

Jason rolled his eyes. 'I'm so glad that none of my archaeologist colleagues were here to witness that,' he said, but I saw a smile flicker across his face.

Chapter Twenty

I unlocked the door to our hotel room and went in, dumping my bag on the floor and sitting down on the bed to take off my sandals.

'Have I worn you out?' Jason said.

'No, not at all,' I said. 'I've had a brilliant day. Thank you.'

'You're welcome,' Jason said. 'Not that it's ever a hardship for me to visit an archaeological site or museum, but I had a good time today too.' Sliding his rucksack off his shoulder, he added, 'I wouldn't mind taking a shower, unless you want to?'

'You go first,' I said.

While Jason went off into the bathroom, I retrieved my phone from my bag, and scrolled through my photos, smiling at the picture of him and me in front of the Parthenon and the shot of him apparently grasping the hilt of the sword that I couldn't help thinking of as Lysander's. After we'd seen the Mycenaean gold, we'd strolled through the other galleries of the museum, and I'd listened entranced as Jason talked about bronze sculptures – a life-sized galloping horse and its boy rider, a bearded muscular god whose sculptor had made him appear to be balancing on his toes as he cast a spear – and the scenes of everyday life in ancient Greece depicted on numerous red and black vases. I'd returned to the hotel with my head full of bronze swords and monumental ruins, and an unexpected desire to do more sightseeing.

I was about to return my phone to my bag, when it occurred to me to check my messages. Which was when I discovered a text from Conor: *Sorry I missed your call. Talk soon xx*. To my dismay, I realised that I hadn't given him a thought all day. Feeling like the worst girlfriend ever, I called his phone.

'I got your text,' I said, when he answered. 'Sorry I didn't get back to you sooner. I've been out most of the day.'

'No worries,' Conor said. 'How's the location?'

'I'm not at the location,' I said. 'I'm still in Athens. I texted you. There are no flights to Kyros until Sunday.'

'Ah, yes,' Conor said. 'I remember. Listen, Laurel, I can't talk to you right now. I shouldn't have left my phone switched on. I'm at the theatre.'

'Of course you are,' I said. 'Sorry. I didn't think to check the time before I rang you. I'll call you tomorrow.'

'I have to go into the theatre early tomorrow,' Conor said. 'We've an extra rehearsal. Give me a call when you get to – what is it?'

'Kyros,' I said. 'The name of the island is Kyros.'

'Yeah, that,' Conor said. 'Laurel, I've just heard the call for Act One beginners. I have to go.'

'Conor—' I stared at my mobile. He'd rung off without saying goodbye. And without any apparent regret that we hadn't had a chance to talk. That, I thought, was *not* the conversation I was hoping to have with my boyfriend. I reminded myself that we'd only been apart for two days, and that before he'd moved into my flat, we'd gone a lot longer without the need to talk on the phone. And that I should have known better than to call him when he was backstage.

'The shower's all yours.'

Jason's voice made me jump. I looked up from my phone and saw him standing by the door to the bathroom. It took me a few seconds to register that all he was wearing was a towel wrapped around his waist. And that his naked torso, with its dusting of dark gold hair on his chest, was every bit as sculpted as that of the nude male statues of gods and heroes I'd been staring at all afternoon. Fairly sure that admiring my co-writer's muscular physique

134

was not only inappropriate but unprofessional, I dragged my gaze up to his face.

'Great,' I said, a little breathlessly. 'I won't be long.'

Jason peered intently at me. 'I hope you don't mind my mentioning it,' he said, 'but you're slightly flushed. I hope you've not had too much sun today.'

'No, I'm good,' I said. 'Never felt better.' Shoving my phone in my bag, I went to the larger of my unpacked suitcases, pulled out a change of clothes — a sleeveless shirt dress — and sauntered into the bathroom. Shutting the door behind me, I leant against it, my face hot, my pulse racing . . .

The towel falling from Jason's waist . . . Me slowly unbuttoning my dress . . . His arms around me, my head resting against his hard, unyielding chest, his hands stroking my back . . .

And cut, I told myself, determinedly pushing the erotic image of a naked Dr Jason Harding to the back of my mind.

I'd never written a gratuitous sex scene, and I wasn't about to start now.

Jason and Laurel had eaten a meal of moussaka in the hotel's rooftop restaurant — sitting at a table for two under the stars, the Acropolis shining brightly in the distance — and were lingering over their second carafe of wine, when Laurel asked him if he'd ever dug up any priceless objects like those discovered at Mycenae.

Jason shook his head. 'Archaeology is as much about everyday objects as hoards of gold and silver. Seemingly unimportant finds like cooking pots or loom weights can tell us so much about the people who owned them — what they ate or the clothes they wore.' I need to stop lecturing her, he thought. She's not one of my students.

'What about how they partied on a Saturday night?' Laurel said, draining her wine. 'How they loved?'

'That too,' Jason said. 'Even the most unenthusiastic archaeology undergraduate would be able to show you evidence that the ancient Greeks enjoyed a lively and varied sex life.'

'When they weren't hacking each other to pieces on the battle field,' Laurel said. 'I saw Lysander's sword this afternoon, remember.' She laughed, and Jason laughed too. Her remark wasn't particularly amusing, but her laugh was infectious. Then her face grew thoughtful. She leant forward, resting her chin on her steepled fingers, and Jason caught the scent of her perfume. 'What happened to the people who lived at Mycenae?' she said. 'How did it become a ruin?'

'We don't know exactly what happened,' Jason said. 'The archaeological record shows that around three thousand years ago, the Mycenaeans abandoned the palace after a series of fires, but we don't know why – they may have been driven out by invaders – and their entire civilisation vanished.'

'Apart from the stories,' Laurel said, dreamily. 'Tales told and re-told. History becoming legend. The most beautiful woman in the world. Your namesake, who stole a golden fleece.' She turned her head to look at the brightly lit Parthenon.

Jason sat silently, studying her face in profile. His gaze drifted to her bare shoulders and to the curve of her breasts just visible above the neckline of her dress. She is beautiful, he thought. How did I not notice until now how beautiful she is?

'So, Dr Harding,' Laurel said, turning back to face him, 'which important archaeological site are you taking me to tomorrow?'

At that precise moment, Jason couldn't remember the name of a single site in the whole of Greece. With an effort, he gathered his thoughts. It occurred to him that Laurel's new-found enthusiasm for archaeology might not extend to another full day of sightseeing.

'Perhaps you'd like to do something different tomorrow?' he said. 'Whenever my family visited me in Athens, my sister's favourite excursion was to the shops and chain stores on Ermou Street. It is, apparently, an extremely good place to buy women's footwear.'

Laurel thought for a moment, and then she said, 'We're only

in Athens for one more day, and I'd much rather spend it exploring ancient ruins than trying on shoes. If we happen to pass a souvenir shop, I'd like to buy myself a memento of our time here, but it's not vital.' Almost shyly, she added, 'After all we did and saw today, I know how Chloe felt when she found Lysander's sword. It was as though she'd made a real connection to the warrior who'd wielded it all those centuries ago.'

'You understand why I do what I do,' Jason said. He picked up his wine glass and was surprised to find it empty. As was the carafe.

'I think I do understand,' Laurel said. 'Would you like another drink?'

'No, let's call it a night,' Jason said. An itinerary for the following day began to take shape in his mind. 'We'll need to make another early start tomorrow if we're going to fit in everything I'd like to show you.'

They left the terrace and travelled down in the lift in a companionable silence. Laurel unlocked the door to their room, and as soon as they were inside, pulled an article of clothing out of one of her overflowing suitcases and went into the bathroom, emerging wearing a loose, knee-length shirt. Jason took his turn in the bathroom, stripping down to his boxers, before recalling that Laurel might consider his sleeping beside her in just his underwear inappropriate, and putting his T-shirt back on.

In the bedroom, Laurel was already lying on one side of the bed, wrapped in a sheet and blanket. Jason switched off the light and lay down next to her, careful to leave as much space between them as he could without falling off the mattress, and pulled his own sheet and blanket up to his waist.

'Goodnight, Laurel,' he said.

'Night,' she muttered sleepily.

Jason lay on his back, acutely conscious of the woman lying next to him, her gentle breathing, the now-familiar scent of her, and felt himself growing aroused. It's just a physical reaction, he told himself, turning his head to look at her. There was enough light in the room for him to see that she was sleeping soundly, her lips slightly parted, a strand of hair fallen across her forehead.

Resisting the urge to reach out and brush the hair off her face, Jason rolled on to his side, facing away from Laurel, and shut his eyes, but sleep evaded him for a long time.

Chapter Twenty-one

'This is the Agora,' Jason said.

After an early breakfast, we'd left the hotel and once again walked to Monastiraki Square. From there, a short walk took us past several ancient monuments, the library of Hadrian, the Tower of Winds – Jason remarking that it was hard to walk through Athens and *not* come across an archaeological site – and brought us to the Agora, which, Jason informed me, was Athens' ancient market place, although now all that was left of it was trees, grass, overgrown low stone walls, and three massive statues. Next to the Acropolis, like the rest of the city, it was overlooked by the Parthenon. On one side it was bounded by a sloping hillside with a Greek temple on top – the temple of Hephaestus, according to Jason – and on the other by a modern structure, a long, low building with a colonnade running along its length. I looked quizzically at my tour guide.

'That's a reconstruction of a *stoa*,' Jason said. 'A covered walkway where merchants set up their stalls.'

'An ancient Greek shopping mall?' I said.

'Exactly,' Jason said, 'although this one houses a museum. Imagine the Agora with more buildings like that, and crowds of people doing their marketing, discussing business or politics, and listening to the speeches of philosophers.'

For a while, we wandered among the ruins, Jason's expert eyes picking out details I'd never have noticed, and in my mind the rambling expanse of grass and stones became a lively, bustling market, the tourists I saw carefully picking their way over the uneven ground becoming stallholders and their ancient Greek customers. I took a photo of Jason on my phone, and he took one of me on his, and then we paid a short visit to the museum, Jason's commentary on the exhibits – 'It's a *krater*. A vessel used to mix wine and water at all-male drinking parties that ended with gangs of rowdy young men staggering home through the streets, much like central London on a Saturday night' – once again attracting the attention of other visitors to the museum who stood near enough to overhear. I felt very fortunate to have him there to bring the past alive for me.

When we went back out into the Agora, the noon heat hit us like a blast from a furnace.

'Let's take a break from ancient monuments for a bit,' Jason said. 'Monastiraki flea market is only a short walk from here. It's the best place to go if you're after a souvenir.'

The flea market turned out to be an area of narrow, crowded pedestrian streets with tiny open-fronted shops selling everything from T-shirts emblazoned with 'I Heart Greece' to exquisite leather handbags and gold jewellery, hand-carved olive-wood bowls, brightly painted china, and old vinyl records. Hoping to find myself a souvenir that was specifically Greek, I marched resolutely past gorgeous sundresses and sarongs, but halted outside a shop selling red and black vases of all shapes and sizes, similar to those I'd seen at the National Archaeological Museum.

'I'm guessing these aren't the genuine article?' I said.

'You're right there,' Jason said. 'They're mass-produced for the tourist market. Like the figurine of the goddess Athena I have in my office.'

'Is that a souvenir of your time in Athens?' I said. In the next instant, I remembered that amongst Jason's memories of Athens were some he'd most likely prefer to forget.

'No, my sister, Nicola, gave it to me when I got my first degree,' Jason said, with an indulgent smile, which I took to indicate that he was fond of his sister, and that he hadn't registered my lack of tact. 'She found it on the internet. Athena being the goddess of wisdom, it seemed to her an appropriate gift for her scholarly brother.'

I looked at Jason, his dark blond hair falling in his eyes, the darker stubble on his chin, his muscular body which his T-shirt did nothing to conceal, and all I could think was that he was hardly my idea of a scholar.

'See anything you like?' Jason said.

I gaped at him. 'W-what?'

'The vases?'

'Oh – yes – the vases.' I pictured my flat. Now that Conor had scattered his possessions throughout, there were few free surfaces on which to put a Greek vase, whatever memories of Athens its presence might bring back to me. 'I don't know that any of them would look right at my place.'

We continued edging our way through the crowds, until we'd almost reached the end of the street.

'Nothing that catches your eye?' Jason said.

There was, I reminded myself, no way he could know that his body had caught my eye more than once. Get a grip, Laurel, I thought. You have a boyfriend. You can't keep fantasising about the muscles under another guy's T-shirt.

'Not yet,' I said. Spotting a shop selling inexpensive trinkets and jewellery on the far side of the street, I edged through the oncoming tide of tourists, and went inside, Jason following with commendable patience at my heels. While I browsed trays of silver rings, beads, and bangles, he squeezed his large frame past racks of sunglasses and counters piled high with baseball caps, and occupied himself by leafing through a rail of men's shirts. I'd given up on the jewellery, and was trying on straw sunhats in front of a mirror – not that a sunhat would make much of a souvenir, but the sun outside was extremely strong – when he came and stood behind me, something glittering gold in his hand.

'How about this for a souvenir?' he said. 'I found it in the back of the shop.'

'What is it?' I said, turning to face him.

A smile playing about his mouth, he held out a headband – a circlet of gold leaves. 'It's a crown of laurel leaves,' he said. 'Archaeologists have discovered countless pieces of jewellery with a laurel leaf design like this. They were apparently extremely popular with the women of ancient Greece.'

'*Laurel* leaves?' I said, looking at the circlet more closely. It was made of wire, but in the dim light of the small shop it glinted like real gold.

His smile became broader. 'Turn back to the mirror.' I did as he asked, and he placed the circlet gently on my head.

'It's not quite as magnificent as the gold headdress found at Troy,' he said, 'but it suits you.' I studied my reflection, liking the effect of the gold against my dark brown hair.

'It's lovely,' I said. 'A perfect souvenir. I'm going to buy it.'

In the mirror, Jason's eyes met mine. 'The face that launched a thousand ships,' he said.

I thought, is he talking about me?

'That's what was said of Helen of Troy.'

'Ah,' I said. For an instant, as he'd looked into my eyes, I could almost have believed he was flirting with me. I obviously needed that sunhat. 'One day, you'll have to tell me the whole story of the Trojan War.'

'It would be my pleasure,' Jason said.

I went to the till and made my purchases, and then the pair of us went out into the street, where it was even hotter than before. I stowed the headband in my bag, put my new hat on my head, and gratefully accepted a drink of the bottled water that Jason had been lugging around all morning in his rucksack.

'Shall we get some lunch?' I said.

'Yes, let's get out of the midday sun for a while,' Jason said. 'There's a café a couple of streets away that I used to go to when—' He stopped speaking as a woman, dark haired, early thirties, trying to negotiate her way through the swarming tourists while holding a bag of shopping and the hand of a small girl, jostled against him.

'I am so sorry,' she said in slightly accented English. Then, taking off her sunglasses, she peered up into Jason's face. 'Jason?'

He stared at her.

'Don't you recognise me, Jason?' the woman said. 'Have I changed so much?'

Jason's eyes widened. 'Téa,' he said softly.

I only just stopped myself from gasping aloud. *Téa.* The woman who, seven years ago, had broken Jason's heart. In a city as large as Athens, what were the chances of their bumping into each other – literally – on a crowded street? I couldn't make up a scene like that.

'Téa,' Jason repeated. 'You've hardly changed at all. It's just that . . . I never expected to see you.'

Téa gave him a tentative smile. Her long dark hair caught up in a pony-tail, wearing a T-shirt dress that clung to her curvaceous figure in all the right places, she was, I had to admit, quite pretty, if nothing like I'd imagined her. If she was an actress, I thought, she'd be cast as the mother in a TV advert.

'I never thought to see you again either,' she said. Her gaze went from Jason to me. 'Are you going to introduce me to your girlfriend?'

'This is Laurel,' Jason said, 'but she isn't my girlfriend. We're colleagues, in Athens for a couple of days on our way to a job in the Cyclades.' He paused, and then said, 'Laurel, meet Téa.' I waited for him to add something to his introduction of his ex, other than her name, but he didn't.

'Hello, Laurel,' Téa said. Her smile was rather desperate now, I thought. 'Jason and I . . . we also worked together once. Before I was married.'

I wasn't quite sure why she felt it necessary to inform me of her marital status, but made myself smile back at her. 'Hi,' I said, common courtesy making me add, 'good to meet you.

Turning her attention back to Jason, Téa said, 'Stefanos and I got married. A couple of years after you left Athens.'

There followed a long silence, during which Jason and his ex stared at each other, apparently having lost the power of speech and I wished myself anywhere but in that hot, crowded street. Oh, my goodness, I thought, is this awkward or what? If I was on a film set right now, I would so be calling out 'Cut!' Then, to my surprise, I saw the ghost of a smile appear on Jason's face. He turned to the little girl, who all this time had been quietly holding Téa's hand.

'And who is this?' he said.

'This is my daughter, Mikaela,' Téa said. She spoke to her child in Greek, and the little girl said something in the same language. She was an enchanting, elfin creature, with dark hair like her mother's and huge dark eyes . . .

Jason says, 'Téa, I have to ask you . . . Is she . . .?'

'Yes, she's yours,' Téa says.

'Why didn't you tell me?'

'I didn't know.' A tear runs down her face. 'I only realised when Stefanos told me he couldn't father children . . .'

'Does she speak English?' Jason said.

Téa laughed. 'She's only four, Jason.'

And cut once again, Laurel, I thought. Jason and his ex are *not* characters in a soap opera. Apart from which, he hasn't seen the woman for seven years — he can't possibly be her daughter's father.

Jason crouched down in front of the child and spoke to her in Greek. At first Mikaela hid her face in her mother's skirt, but then, as Jason continued to talk to her, she looked at him, and finally, she smiled shyly at him, and even spoke a few words. Slowly, he straightened up to his full height.

'She looks a lot like you, Téa,' he said, 'but she has Stefanos' eyes.'

'Yes, she does,' Téa said. There was another silence, and then she said, 'I have to go. *Adío*, Jason. Stefanos will be so surprised when I tell him I saw you after all this time. Goodbye, Laurel, I am pleased to have met one of Jason's colleagues.'

'Likewise,' I said, not sure if I meant it, but saying it anyway.

'*Adío,*' Jason said.

Holding her daughter's hand, Téa started walk away.

'Téa – wait,' Jason said. She came to a halt. Jason spoke to her in Greek. She replied in the same language, and briefly touched his arm. Then she turned away, and vanished into the crowd.

'That was an unexpected reunion,' Jason said. He shook his head as though to clear it. 'What were we talking about before Téa tripped over me? Oh, yeah. Lunch.' Outwardly, he appeared calm and relaxed, but I couldn't believe that the encounter with his ex hadn't affected him.

'Are you OK?' I said.

'Why wouldn't I be?'

'Because you've just been accosted in the street by your ex,' I said. 'Anyone would find that difficult.' Especially if you're still carrying a torch for her.

He regarded me silently for a moment, and then he said, 'I'm fine, Laurel. I'll admit it was strange seeing Téa again after all these years, but it hasn't taken away my appetite. Let's get some lunch.'

We went to the café Jason had spoken of earlier, a small family-run place which had as many locals as tourists amongst its lunchtime clientele. While we ate our stuffed vine leaves, Jason talked animatedly about a dig he'd be working on once he was back in London, and I talked about film-making, surprising Jason when I explained that scenes in a movie are shot out of order, the schedule determined by the availability of studios and locations rather than the story. By the time we were drinking our Greek coffee – I was developing quite a taste for it – I'd decided that whether or not he'd found the encounter with Téa painful, he had no intention of discussing her with me.

'Where are going this afternoon?' I asked, as he set his empty coffee cup down on the table.

'As long as you don't object to a longish walk,' he said, 'I thought I'd show you the Filopappos Hill. Ancient Greek poets and musicians believed it was inhabited by the Muses and would go there to seek inspiration.'

'Then we should definitely walk up that hill,' I said. 'From what Shannon told me, I've a feeling that when we get to Kyros, we're going to need all the inspiration from the Muses we can get.'

Chapter Twenty-two

'This view is incredible,' I said.

'Agreed,' Jason said. 'I reckon it's the best view in Athens. Look this way – you can see the Aegean.'

There'd been a coach parked right by the entrance to the Filopappos Hill, but its passengers had apparently gone elsewhere, for as we'd walked up a sloping, pine-shaded path to the summit, Jason and I'd had the place entirely to ourselves, except for a pair of tortoises we'd spotted ambling through the long grass, and the chirping cicadas. Now, we stood on the hilltop, beside the ruins of the marble monument that gave the hill its name, looking out over the city of Athens as far as the Aegean Sea.

I sat down on a rock. 'It's so peaceful up here,' I said. Jason sat next to me.

'It's one of my favourite places in the whole city,' he said. 'When I lived in Athens, I'd often come here with a group of friends at weekends. Sometimes, I'd come up here on my own and read a book.' He fell silent, shading his eyes against the sun with his hand, gazing into the distance. I thought, did he come up here with Téa? Is he thinking about her now?

He said, 'These last two days in Athens, showing it to you, have made me realise I shouldn't have stayed away so long.'

'I'm so glad, Jason,' I said. 'Now, maybe you'll be able to move on.'

His blue eyes met mine. 'Move on from what?'

'Well, the past,' I said.

'It's kind of hard to move on from the past when you're an archaeologist,' Jason said.

'I mean *your* past,' I said. 'Listen, forget I said anything. It doesn't matter.'

'*My* past?' Jason gave me a long look. 'Are you, by any chance, talking about the past I share with Téa?'

I nodded. 'The way you were with her this morning,' I blurted, 'I could see that you still have feelings for her.'

'You think I'm still in love with her?' He sounded incredulous.

'Aren't you?' I said.

'No, Laurel,' Jason said, his voice quiet now. 'I'm not in love with Téa. I did love her once, and she hurt me very badly – so badly that I left Greece and cut myself off from everyone I knew here – but I was over her years ago.'

'But—You told me you don't like to talk about her,' I said.

'Yes, strangely, I don't enjoy talking about a failed relationship, and a bad time in my life that I'd rather not remember.'

'This morning—'

'I didn't recognise her,' Jason said. 'Not at first. Then, when I did recognise her, I felt nothing. No, that's not true.' His forehead creased in thought. 'Téa and I had a bad break-up, and I was hurt and angry with her for a long time, but if I've thought about her at all in the last few years, it's been with indifference. Seeing her this morning with her child, hearing she was married to Stefanos – not the man she left me for, incidentally – I found, admittedly to my astonishment, I could only be glad that things had worked out for her.' He paused, before adding, 'Which is more or less what I told her.'

'I guess I'll have to rewrite the scene where you're pining for your ex-girlfriend,' I said.

Jason raised one eyebrow. 'Have you been running a film in your head with me and Téa as the romantic leads?'

For a horrible moment, I thought I'd offended him, but then I saw he was smiling.

'What can I say?' I shrugged. 'It's what I do.'

148

He took the bottle of water out of his rucksack and drank. 'You really do have an over-active imagination,' he said.

'Which, as I've told you before, can only be a good thing for a screenwriter. Anyway, it wasn't a rom-com, it was a soap opera.'

He laughed at that, and I laughed too, and when we fell silent, all I could think was how good it felt to be sitting there on a hill-top in Athens with him. I held out my hand for the water bottle and he passed it to me. His gaze wandered back to the view over the Aegean.

'Can you hear music?' he said, suddenly.

Even as he spoke, I heard a trill of musical notes. I scanned the hillside, but the scrub that grew around the summit concealed the musician from view.

'It's coming from lower down, I think,' Jason said. He sprang up, holding out a hand to haul me to my feet, and I followed him down the hill towards the music.

A short distance below the crest of the hill, we came across a girl wearing a tie-dyed dress, a bandana tied around her long dark hair, sitting cross legged on the stony ground and playing a flute. She took no notice of us – I suspected she was so caught up in her art that she wasn't even aware she had an audience – but we lingered a while, spellbound by the haunting tune in that des-erted place among the rocks and thorny bushes, before Jason's touch on my shoulder drew me back to the path.

'The place we've just come from,' he said, 'the area cut into the rock, is the ruins of the shrine of the Muses.'

'Maybe that girl was seeking their inspiration,' I said.

'I'm sure she was,' Jason said. 'We live in a rational age and no longer expect to find gods and nymphs inhabiting every moun-tain and stream, but musicians and poets still climb this hill and leave offerings for the appropriate muse.' He pointed to a small, pyramid-shaped pile of pebbles at the edge of the path. 'That cairn was probably built by different people walking past, who each added a stone.'

'Ooh . . .' I said. 'Could I . . .?'

'I don't see why not.'

Feeling a little self-conscious, I found a smooth round pebble and placed it on the cairn. An instant later, to my surprise, Jason did the same. I shot him a look.

'What?' he said. 'I'm simply asking Calliope, the Muse of Screenwriting, to help us with *Swords and Sandals*.'

'Goodness, Dr Harding,' I said. 'You need to rein in your imagination. You're mistaking legend for historical fact.'

'I'm merely allowing myself a little dramatic licence,' Jason said with a grin. 'Is this moment worthy of a photo, do you think?'

'Definitely,' I said.

Jason took his phone out of his pocket. 'We need to stand closer together,' he said, putting his arm around my shoulders. For an instant, as he took the picture, I felt the heat of his body pressed against mine, and a tightening in my stomach. Then he let his arm drop and stepped away.

'Will you send it to me?' I said, my voice sounding unusually high. Ridiculous, I thought, to react like that when a guy casually drapes an arm around you. I must have had too much sun.

'Of course,' Jason said. 'Shall we carry on down the hill? I'm thinking it's time we headed back to the hotel.'

We resumed walking.

Just once, as we made our way down the sloping paths, I thought I heard music drifting down from higher up the hill, but it was too faint for me to be sure.

Lying under the thin blanket, Jason could see Laurel silhouetted against the window. She'd been standing there for a while, gazing out at the Parthenon, but now she turned back to the room and crept slowly around the bed. There was a sudden thump as something fell to the floor.

'Laurel?' Jason said. 'Are you OK?'

'I'm fine,' Laurel said. 'Although the suitcase I just knocked over may not be.' Jason felt the mattress shift slightly as she lay

150

down next to him. 'Did I wake you up? Sorry. I was taking one last look at the Acropolis by night.'

'I wasn't asleep,' Jason said.

After a moment, Laurel said, 'I've had such a good time these last two days.'

'So have I,' Jason said. It occurred to him to wonder what her reaction would be if he told her that he couldn't sleep for thinking about her, that he longed to take her in his arms and kiss her. Reluctantly, he decided this was not a conversation to have while he and Laurel were sharing a bed due to circumstance rather than choice.

'Night,' Laurel said

'*Kalinikta*,' he said. 'That's Greek for goodnight.'

'*Kalinikta*,' Laurel repeated.

Jason was overwhelmed by a sudden rush of fondness for her. He was mildly astonished to realise that it was the first time in seven years – the first time since Téa had betrayed his trust and left him – that he'd felt anything more for a woman than a purely physical attraction.

It came to him then, that while he rarely thought about her, he'd allowed what had happened between him and Téa to cast a long shadow over his life – and it had taken seeing her again for him to acknowledge that. But now . . .

These last few days with Laurel in Athens, he'd felt more alive than he had in a very long time.

Chapter Twenty-three

From Kyros's small airport, the main road headed north along the coast. Looking out of the car windows, in one direction I had a view of a range of mountains, green on their lower slopes, bare rock higher up, and in the other direction, beyond the hotels and apartments of the tourist resorts that sprawled along the shore, tantalising glimpses of an impossibly blue sea. Spiros, our driver from the airport to our accommodation in the promisingly named Paradise Holiday Village, remarked that this part of the island had beaches as fine as any in the Mediterranean.

Once we'd driven past Lanissi the island's capital, the hotels and villas became far fewer. Soon, we were driving through groves of silver-leaved olive trees and terraced fields of vines. The road began to climb, circling around a steep mountainside, following the winding coastline in a series of frankly terrifying hairpin bends. The vista on the seaward side changed to one of sheer cliffs plunging down into the Aegean, and small deserted coves – Jason remarked that they could surely only be reached by boat. I saw cacti and thorn bushes and the occasional dark cypress tree, and once, to my delight, Spiros had to stop the car to allow a herd of goats to cross from one side of the road to the other. I watched, fascinated, as they made their sure-footed way up the mountainside among the rocks.

It was well past midday when we left the mountains and began to descend once more towards the sea. Spiros turned off the main highway on to a side road that brought us to a village of white houses with blue-painted shutters at their windows, and a pretty square shaded by trees, where locals and a few tourists were sitting outside a taverna. Spotting a small hotel, I assumed this was where Jason and I would be staying, but Spiros drove straight through the village and on to a dirt road, little more than a rough track, that followed the meandering, rocky shoreline for about half a mile before rounding a headline and petering out altogether.

In front of us were two white villas, facing each other across a turquoise swimming pool. There was a paved terrace by the pool, where there were a number of sun loungers, terracotta pots containing red and purple flowers, and a picnic table, and then a stretch of grass from which steps cut into a gently sloping rock face led down to a crescent-shaped beach of pristine white sand. But what really caught my eye, as I got out of the car, was a wooden gazebo-like structure, four wooden posts and a roof of woven palm leaves, under which someone had placed a small wooden table and a couple of chairs, overlooking the sea. There, I thought, is the perfect place for me to sit and write.

Tearing my gaze away from my new writing space, I saw a dark-haired woman about my age, wearing a smart skirt and blouse, come out of one of the villas.

'*Kalimera*,' she called, as she walked towards us. 'Dr Jason Harding and Ms Laurel Martin?'

'That's us,' Jason said. '*Kalimera*.'

'Hi,' I said.

'I am Katerina,' the woman went on, 'Deputy Manager of Paradise Holiday Village. I welcome you to Villa Penelope and Villa Daphne.' She pointed to each villa in turn and handed both me and Jason a set of keys. 'The villas are self-catering, but it is arranged for Ms Martin and Dr Harding to take meals at any of the restaurants in the Paradise Holiday Village, where we are delighted to welcome so many of the *Swords and Sandals'* film unit as our guests.'

I glanced along the coast, but couldn't see beyond the rocks that encircled our beach. It seemed we had no near neighbours.

'Where is the rest of the Holiday Village exactly?' I asked.

'It is that way,' Katerina said, pointing along the coast. 'It is a very short walk.'

'Good to know,' I said, having no desire to take a long walk every time I fancied a sandwich.

'I go now,' Katerina said. 'Please come to Reception or telephone if you find more questions. The telephone number and a map are in the welcome pack in the villas. I hope very much that you enjoy your stay here with us on our beautiful Kyros.'

'Thank you,' I said, my gaze drifting back to my writing space, with its panoramic view of the beach, the sea and the sky. 'I'm sure we will.'

While Katerina had been welcoming us to her island, Spiros had unloaded our cases from the boot of his taxi. After a brief discussion in Greek, the two of them got inside the car and drove off.

I examined the label attached to my keys.

'I'm in Villa Daphne,' I said.

'That's appropriate,' Jason said. 'The name Daphne, in Greek, means Laurel. In mythology, she was a nymph who escaped the amorous advances of the sun god Apollo by turning into a laurel tree.' He smiled self-deprecatingly. 'Sorry – I'm trying not to lecture you every time I open my mouth, but I can't seem to stop myself.'

'That's OK,' I laughed. 'I like hearing about the ancient Greeks – and that I have an ancient Greek namesake.' I inclined my head towards the other villa. 'Who was Penelope?'

'She was the wife of Odysseus,' Jason said. 'One of the Greek kings who fought at Troy. She waited faithfully for twenty years for him to return to her from the war.'

'The Trojan War lasted *twenty years*?'

Jason shook his head. 'No, Troy was besieged for ten years before it fell, but it took Odysseus another ten years to sail home again.'

'It doesn't sound like he was in much of a hurry.'

'It wasn't entirely his fault,' Jason said. 'An enchantress, Circe, seduced him and kept him on her island for a year. Then he was shipwrecked and – well, it's a long story, but he was detained by the sea nymph Calypso.'

'That old excuse,' I said. 'Sorry I'm late home, darling, I was seduced by a witch and then I hooked up with a nymph. But it didn't mean anything. Now make me a moussaka.'

'Your take on antiquity is refreshingly original,' Jason said.

I laughed. 'Rewrites are what I do.' My attention strayed to the swimming pool. Sparkling in the sunlight, it looked very inviting. I smiled at Jason. 'What do you reckon we should do first? Unpack or try out the pool?'

'See you in the water,' Jason said, heading off around the pool to Villa Penelope. Hoisting my bag on to my shoulder, I wheeled my cases over the grass to Villa Daphne, unlocked the door, and went inside.

I found myself in a large, airy room with whitewashed walls, a tiled floor, and a small kitchen area. The room was sparsely furnished with a low, rough-hewn wooden table and four chairs – they had wooden frames and canvas seats, which reminded me of the sort of chair provided for directors on film sets, and proved to be unexpectedly comfortable when I sat in one. Two dark wooden doors opened on to bedrooms with double beds, wooden shelves, and hooks for clothes. A wrought-iron spiral staircase took me up to a mezzanine floor, where another door opened out on to a roof terrace. Here, I found a sun lounger large enough for two, shaded by thin cotton curtains hanging from a wooden frame, like a four-poster bed. I thought, I'm going to be spending a whole month in this delightfully rustic villa by the sea, and I smiled.

Back downstairs, I dragged a suitcase into a bedroom and rifled through its contents, throwing clothes on to the bed, until I found a bikini and got changed. I took a minute to check my phone – I'd emailed Eadie that we'd arrived on Kyros, and she'd replied, informing me that a script meeting was scheduled for the following day – grabbed my sun hat, sunglasses, and a towel, and went outside.

As I was spreading out my towel on a sun lounger, Jason came out of the other villa, a pair of swim shorts hanging low on his hips. Carelessly tossing a towel on to the ground, he walked around the pool to the far end, and stood poised on the poolside – giving me a delicious view of the ridges of muscle on his toned stomach. I had to remind myself very firmly that if I expected to have a good working relationship with my co-writer while we were in Greece, I needed to resist the temptation to ogle his body every time he appeared without a shirt.

Smiling at me, Jason lifted his arms above his head, raised himself on the balls of his feet, and dived into the pool.

Surfacing, shaking water out of his hair, he said, 'Aren't you going to join me?'

'For sure,' I said. Thankful that so many Saturday mornings in my childhood had been spent with my father teaching me and my brother to swim and to execute a proficient dive, I walked to the side of the pool and launched myself smoothly into the pleasantly cool water. Having swum a few widths, I floated on my back for a while, before climbing the steps and stretching out on a lounger, watching Jason from behind my sunglasses as he swam lengths, cleaving through the water with a powerful crawl.

The sun grew stronger. My attention wandered to the gazebo, and the view of the sea, sky and rocky headland shimmering in the heat. It was very quiet, the only sound the occasional splash of water. This place is idyllic, I thought. Paradise indeed, and me and Jason have it all to ourselves. Just me and him. The two of us. Suddenly it came to me that after Jason went off to sleep in his villa, I would be alone in mine. I would be spending the night completely alone in an isolated villa. I couldn't help thinking of a number of movies that featured a heroine alone in a house, with no one around for miles. None of them had ended well.

I sat upright on the sun-lounger. At some level, I recognised I was being totally irrational but I also knew I didn't want to spend my nights alone in Villa Daphne with Jason too far away in Villa Penelope to hear me scream.

From the pool, Jason called, 'Are you coming in again?'

'Not right now,' I said. Swimming to the steps, he climbed out of the pool, and lay down on the sun lounger next to mine.

'I could get used to having a swimming pool right outside my door,' he said.

'You and me both,' I said. 'It's lovely here . . . but it's very remote. I can't help feeling a little nervous about staying in the villa on my own at night.'

Jason raised himself up on his elbows. 'Would you prefer it if we shared one of the villas?'

A wave of relief swept over me. 'I'd so much rather we shared. If you wouldn't mind.'

'It's fine with me,' Jason said. 'No problem at all. I should have thought of it myself – I know you're not used to travelling on your own.' He lay back on the sun lounger. 'I'll dry off and then I'll fetch my stuff over to Villa Daphne.'

I thought, he is such a nice guy. I, too, lay back in the sun, and shut my eyes. A short while later, I heard the scrape of a sun lounger on the tiles around the pool as Jason stood up, and then I heard him moving his things into Villa Daphne. I should go inside and unpack, I thought. I will, in a few minutes. And then we should go in search of the Holiday Village. I wouldn't mind a glass of cold white wine . . .

I was half asleep when the sound of an approaching car jerked me awake. I sat up to see it come to a halt at the end of the track. A rear passenger door opened and, to my delight, Amber, looking very fetching in a floral sundress, jumped out. I waved and stood up, and it was then that I saw Harry Vincent emerging from the other side of the car. Amber bounded towards me across the grass, while Harry, who was holding two carrier bags, followed rather more slowly. The car drove off in a cloud of dust.

'You're here on Kyros at last!' Amber said, giving me a hug. 'Eadie told me you'd arrived, but I wanted to see for myself!' She gestured at the villas and the pool. 'This place is fabulous. Harry and I were worried that you and Jason would be sleeping in tents on the beach.'

'Why?' I said. *Harry and I?*

'Oh – you wouldn't know,' Amber said, 'but there aren't any

large resorts in this part of the island, and the film unit has taken over practically every villa and studio apartment to be had. Most of us are in the Paradise Holiday Village, or in Eloussa, the pretty little town just up the road, but the producers and the stars –' She smiled at Harry, who gave an exaggerated bow '– are in a luxury hotel further along the coast.'

'We come bearing gifts,' Harry said. 'Food and wine. And our company, if you'll have us.'

'This way you and Jason can relax and settle in after your long journey,' Amber said, 'and you won't have to trek across miles of barren rock before you can eat.'

'Miles of rock?' I said.

'It's a five-minute walk,' Harry said. 'Amber is being over-dramatic.'

'Well, I am an actress,' Amber said. 'Ah – there's Jason.'

I turned my head to see Jason come out of Villa Daphne.

'We have visitors,' I said to him. 'You've met my friend Amber. And of course, Harry needs no introduction.' Harry rolled his eyes.

'Hello again, Amber,' Jason said. 'Harry.' The two men shook hands. 'Are you an actor too?'

Harry's eyes widened. 'Er, yes, I'm playing Lysander.'

'Oh, my days,' Amber said, 'you have no idea who Harry is, do you, Jason?'

'I'm afraid I don't,' Jason said. 'Sorry.'

'He's Harry *Vincent*,' I said. When Jason gave no sign of recognising the name, I added, 'He used to play Jago in *Fields of Gold*.'

'Right,' Jason said.

'Have you ever watched *Fields of Gold*?' I said.

'Much as it pains me to admit it,' Jason said, 'I can't say that I have.'

'I did try to tell you, Harry,' Amber said. 'You're not as famous as you think you are.' To me, in a stage whisper, she added, 'He's had so many British guests at his luxury hotel asking him to pose for photos, that he's getting completely up himself.'

'He's always been up himself,' I said. 'Now he's a *movie star*, he'll only get worse.'

Harry laughed.

To Jason, I said, 'You'll be glad to hear we won't have to mount an expedition in search of Sunday dinner – Amber and Harry have brought it to us.'

'And just to prove that I'm so not up myself,' Harry said, 'I'll do the cooking. If you'll point me in the direction of the kitchen.' He looked from one villa to the other.

'In there – Villa Daphne,' Jason said. 'I'll give you a hand, if you like.'

The two of them went inside the villa.

'So,' I said to Amber. 'How do you like acting with Harry Vincent? Have you been sticking to the script or have you been improvising?'

Amber raised a finger to her lips and nodded towards the open door of the villa. 'Let's go and take a look at the sea,' she said.

We walked across the grass to the gazebo and sat in the chairs.

'I can see you sitting here to write,' Amber said.

'That's what I thought,' I said. 'Actually, I have a great idea for an original screenplay. A rom-com set in Greece. With you and Harry playing the leads.'

'About me and Harry,' Amber said, 'I wouldn't want you to get the wrong idea. We're not a couple. Not officially.'

'But you are . . . seeing each other?' I said.

'Yes, Laurel, I'm sleeping with him,' Amber said. 'But no one knows about us – apart from Harry's driver, and Harry's assistant – so please, *please*, keep it to yourself.'

'Are you sure no one else knows?' I said. 'A film unit on location is usually quick to notice if the leading man acquires a new squeeze.'

'We've been careful.'

'You've not been spotted sneaking into Harry's trailer?'

Amber shook her head. 'I've snuck into his hotel room a few times, but I've kept well away from his trailer. It hasn't been easy – you know what it's like when you have a bunch of actors waiting to be called to set with nothing to do but gossip – but so far, we seem to have got away with it. The women I'm sharing a villa with – Christina, who works in the production office, and Nisha, who's a make-up artist – know I'm seeing someone, but I'm sure they haven't realised it's Harry.'

It seemed to me much more likely that the entire production team and everyone in the make-up department were fully aware that Harry had a love interest off as well as on screen, but I kept my opinion to myself.

'Would it be so terrible if people knew?' I said. 'It's hardly the first time two young, single actors have found romance on a film set.'

'But Harry is *famous*,' Amber said. 'He hasn't been able to go for a drink in Eloussa without some English holiday maker asking for his autograph. The last time he went swimming in the sea – and this was at his posh hotel's private beach – a guy swam up to him with a waterproof camera and took a close-up. What he and I want is a bit of privacy.'

'I get it,' I said. 'You want to be able to gaze into your boyfriend's eyes without having to worry that your romantic moment is being studied as a masterclass in acting for rom-coms by the rest of the cast, or being uploaded on to the internet from a fan's mobile.'

'Exactly,' Amber said. 'But Harry isn't my *boyfriend*. Him and me . . . it's just a summer fling. Uncomplicated and fun. After the whole debacle with Tom, it's just what I need.' Her dark eyes met mine. 'When I first came out to Greece, I was a wreck – although I hope I'm a good enough actress that I didn't let it show – but Harry's changed all that.' With a smile, she added, 'It was something you wrote that brought us together again.'

'Really?' I said. 'Well, I'm happy to have been of service.'

'Up until about a month ago,' Amber said, 'I hadn't seen much of Harry – although he always said "Hi" when we were on set together. We happened to be standing next to each other between takes, when he mentioned he was having trouble learning his lines for Lysander and Chloe's big love scene, and wondered if I'd mind going over them with him. And I thought, why not?'

I smothered a grin. I knew for a fact that when he was in *Fields of Gold*, Harry had often demonstrated his ability to work a twelve-hour day, go home with a new script, and turn up the following morning word-perfect. That he was having difficulty learning Lysander's lines seemed to me extremely unlikely.

'The next day was Sunday, our day off,' Amber went on. 'Harry borrowed one of the unit cars, and we drove along the coast until we found an empty beach with no gawping holidaymakers. We worked on his lines, and swam and sunbathed, and . . . Well, an experienced screenwriter like you can probably tell where this plot is heading.'

'Scene One. Morning. On a beach in Greece,' I said. 'Scene Two. Evening. In a movie star's luxury hotel bedroom. There really isn't much suspense in this story.'

Amber laughed. 'And what about you and your writing partner?' she said. 'How's that going?'

'Oh, me and Jason are great,' I said. 'I don't know what I'd have done without him in Athens. He used to live there, so he knows the city well, and was able to show me around. We had such a good time.'

Amber shot me a look.

'What?' I said. 'Jason and I didn't get off to a great start, but it turns out he's a really lovely, thoughtful guy.'

'Good to know, but how is your and Jason's *writing* going?' Amber said. 'Christina-in-the-production-office told me that the writers were coming out to fix the script. Can you fix it?'

'We don't know yet which bits want fixing,' I said. 'We have a script meeting tomorrow, so we'll find out which scenes need rewriting then.'

'I may be able to give you a heads up,' Amber said. 'Last week they were filming the scene where Chloe and Lysander are about to part for ever, when Drew Brightman suddenly announced he wasn't feeling it, and flounced off back to his hotel.'

'How unprofessional,' I said. No wonder the film is behind schedule, I thought.

'You have no idea,' Amber said. 'Drew may be a genius, but someone needs to tell him that shouting and screaming at an actress until she's reduced to tears because she didn't play a scene exactly the way you wanted it on the first take isn't going to help her give her best performance. And informing an award-winning cameraman he doesn't know how to line up a shot doesn't win you friends among the crew.'

'Sounds like tomorrow's script meeting could be interesting,' I said. 'I'll have to warn Jason.'

The sound of male voices came to us from the direction of the villa. I turned my head to see Jason and Harry, who was carrying a beach umbrella, standing by the picnic table. After some discussion, they set up the umbrella so the table was in shade, and went back inside.

'You have to admit that guy is hot,' Amber said.

I laughed. 'I couldn't possibly say, but I'm sure his fans would agree with you.'

'Not Harry,' Amber said. 'Well, Harry *is* hot, but I'm talking about Jason.'

'Jason is—' Images of Jason wandering around the hotel room in Athens in a towel and Jason poised to dive into the pool flashed into my head in quick succession. Cut, I thought. *Cut!* 'He's an attractive man,' I said, 'but it's perfectly possible to notice a guy's got the body of a Greek god without wanting to sleep with him.'

Amber arched her eyebrows. 'I wasn't suggesting you did. I do know that you have a boyfriend.'

Conor. I'd said I'd call him when I got to Kyros, but I hadn't given him a thought. A wave of guilt washed over me.

'Any news about when he's moving out of the flat, by the way?' Amber said.

I have to tell her that Conor may *not* be moving out, I thought, and I have to tell her now. It's only fair.

'Not yet,' I said. 'He – we – thought he might as well stay on for a bit. So that the flat isn't empty while I'm in Greece. When I get back to London . . . we've talked about us living together.'

162

For what seemed an age, Amber regarded me in silence. 'Do you want to live with Conor?' she asked, eventually.

Doubts about living with Conor slithered nefariously back into my mind. Was I ready for this? Was he?

'Laurel?' Amber prompted.

'I . . . I'm not sure,' I said.

'Well, let me know when you decide,' Amber said, 'because if Conor's going to be a permanent fixture in your flat, I'll need to move out.'

I sighed. 'I'm so sorry, Amber, but I think you're right.'

'No need to apologise,' Amber said. 'If you and Conor are going to make a success of a serious, committed relationship, you'll need your own space. And I'm not about to cast myself in the role of the annoying flatmate.'

Not to mention that you can't stand Conor, I thought.

'It's like you said,' Amber went on, 'we've reached *that* age. The credits are rolling on our singleton, flat-sharing years. We're about to start shooting a whole new script.'

It struck me that Amber was making this particular scene of our new film a lot easier for me to write than she might have. Whatever happens, I thought, whether or not Conor and I live together, whenever she moves out of the flat, Amber and I are going to stay friends.

'I'm not making any decisions 'til I get back to London,' I said. 'I've come to Greece to fix *Swords and Sandals*' screenplay, and that's all I want to think about right now. When I'm not lying in the sun, that is. I'd like to see something of Kyros, as well. I'm on a beautiful Aegean island – I'm literally living in paradise – and I want to make the most of it.'

'Sounds like a plan to me,' Amber said. 'Ah – lunch is ready.' I looked towards the villa to see Jason, carrying a tray of plates, and Harry, carrying a bottle of wine and four glasses, come out on to the terrace.

'Let's go eat,' I said.

★

'So the first night I'm in the hotel dining room,' Harry said, 'a woman comes over to my table and tells me that she's delighted I've recovered, and it'll do me good to have a holiday and regain my strength before I have to start bringing in the harvest.'

I rolled my eyes. 'How on earth is she going to feel once she's watched your last episode of *Fields of Gold*?'

Jason's face took on a quizzical expression. To Harry, he said, 'The woman believed you were the character you portray in the series?'

Harry shrugged. 'It happens. Since then, I've had my evening meal sent up to my suite.'

'I don't blame you,' Jason said.

'Don't get me wrong,' Harry said. 'Most of the time I'm happy to talk to fans – I'm flattered that they want to talk to me – but it's hard to be sociable with complete strangers when you've just got back from a long, demanding day at work and all you want to do is chill. It's been great coming here this afternoon and not having to think about any of that.' He smiled at Amber. 'Or worry that someone's going to see us holding hands.' He took hold of Amber's hand, which was resting on the table, and kissed it.

It really had been a lovely afternoon, I thought. The four of us had eaten Harry's delicious seafood pasta, and drunk wine, and the conversation had flowed as easily as if we'd all known each other forever. Harry, who as well as being an actor was a qualified stuntman, plied Jason with questions about ancient warriors' fighting techniques. Jason and Amber talked about ancient Greek theatre, which Amber had studied at drama school. I talked about seeing the Parthenon and the face of Agamemnon, and climbing the Filopappos Hill. I didn't say anything about adding stones to the cairn – that was just between me and Jason. Neither of us mentioned that while we were in Athens, we'd shared a bed.

Having finished our lunch, we'd gone to the beach and whiled away the remainder of the afternoon swimming in the Aegean – Amber and Harry in borrowed swim gear – and soaking up the sun. Now, with the sun low on the horizon and the sky streaked with red and gold, the four of us were once again seated at the picnic table. I looked at Harry and Amber, and I thought, she's right, every couple needs their own space – even if they're only having a summer fling. My gaze slid to Villa Penelope, unoccupied now that Jason had moved his belongings into Villa Daphne. Catching Jason's eye, I tilted my head towards the empty villa, and then towards Amber and Harry. A smile of understanding appeared on Jason's face, and he gave a barely detectable nod of his head.

'Jason and I are staying in Villa Daphne,' I said to Harry, 'but we have the keys to Villa Penelope, so if you ever need a hideaway . . .'

Harry's gaze flicked from me to Jason and back to me again. 'I didn't realise you were sharing one villa.'

Without thinking, I said, 'There are two bedrooms.' My face flushed.

Whether or not Harry noticed my confusion, all he said was, 'It would be good to get away from the incessant surveillance of the camera phone.' He thought for a moment, and then went on, 'If you guys wouldn't mind giving us a minute—' He stood up, and held out his hand to Amber. She looked bemused, but allowed him to help her to her feet and lead her across the grass, so that they were too far away for Jason and me to hear what they were saying.

After a short while, during which Jason and I didn't even pretend we weren't watching them – quickly looking away when Harry put his arms around Amber and kissed her – they returned to the table.

'We've a favour to ask you,' Amber said.

'How would you feel about us both moving into Villa Penelope for the rest of the shoot?' Harry said.

'Hmmm, let me think about that,' I said, putting my head on one side. 'Are you planning on throwing glitzy showbiz pool parties every night?'

'Not when I have a five a.m. call time,' Harry said.

'What do you reckon, Jason?' I said. 'Do we want a famous movie star as a neighbour if he refuses to include us in his glamorous celebrity lifestyle?'

'I can live with that,' Jason said.

By midnight, having acted out a convoluted script that involved creeping in and out of a luxury hotel, persuading Harry not to throw his suitcases out of the window and climb down after them – 'Jason and I will take them down in the lift, Harry. If you want to avoid anyone seeing you leave the hotel, go out the fire exit' – with the help of Harry's assistant, Will, a gangly young man who wrote down every instruction Harry gave him on an iPad, and Harry's driver, the four of us had successfully transferred Harry and Amber's belongings to their new location. Whether or not Christina-in-the-production-office and make-up-artist Nisha, who had walked in just as Amber and I were wheeling her suitcases out of their shared digs, believed my assertion that I was in need of her company in my lonely dwelling on the shore, I was unable to tell – but Amber had later complimented me on my talent for improvisation.

'Is your life always like this?' Jason said to me, after Harry and Amber had walked off hand in hand to Villa Penelope, leaving me and my writing partner together by the pool.

'Rom-com meets adventure with a touch of cloak and dagger?' I said. 'Usually only in my head.'

Jason laughed 'It's been a long day,' he said. 'I'm for my bed.'

'You and me both,' I said. 'Writing Harry and Amber's script has tired me out.'

We went into Villa Daphne. Yawning, I retrieved the keys from a hook by the door.

'I'll lock up, if you like,' Jason said.

'Thanks,' I said, placing the keys in his outstretched hand.

'*Kalinikta,*' he said, softly. We were standing very close together, so close that I could feel the heat radiating from his body. I became aware of a fluttering in my stomach . . .

Jason bends his head and kisses me. I taste wine on his lips, and sunlight and salt water on his skin . . .

'See you tomorrow, Laurel.'

'Night,' I said, and sprinted into my bedroom.

Once inside, the door firmly closed, my heart thumping, I sank down on the bed. I told myself there was no reason for me to feel guilty. I'd done nothing wrong. Yes, I found Jason Harding attractive – he was an attractive guy – but it wasn't as if I was going to do anything about it. I wasn't the sort of girl who has a few glasses of wine in the sun and kisses the nearest available male – other than in my head – just because he has an incredible body. I had a boyfriend at home in London. Whom I really needed to call.

I checked the time on my mobile. Just gone midnight on Kyros, so it would only be ten o'clock in London. Not too late to phone. I found Conor's number and hit the call icon. The phone rang and rang, but just when I thought it would go through to voicemail, he answered.

'Laurel?' he said. 'Laurel, is that you?' It was hard to hear him over a cacophony of shouted conversation, shrieks of laughter, and the thud of rock music.

'Yes, it's me,' I said. 'Conor, I can hardly hear what you're saying.'

'Hold on,' he said. The shouting and music gradually faded. 'Can you hear me now?'

'Yes, that's fine,' I said. 'Where are you? It sounds like you're in a club?'

'Was in the flat,' Conor said. 'In street now. Too much noise inside. Couldn't hear you.' As he spoke, his voice became increasingly slurred. I realised he was drunk.

'What's going on?' I said. 'Who's in my flat?'

'Having a house party,' Conor said. 'Or do I mean flat party?' He roared with laughter. 'Jus' my mate Andile and some other people.'

'Who?' I demanded.

'My ver' good friends,' Conor said. 'Not anyone you know.'

Unbelievable. I'd been away less than a week and he'd filled *my* flat with *his friends,* whom I'd never met, and who were no doubt as wasted as he was, and spilling beer all over the living-room carpet even as we spoke. I remembered the state of his, Greg, and Lucas's place after they'd had one of their house parties – the cigarette burns, the broken glass – and shuddered.

'You might have asked me before you threw a party in my flat,' I said.

'You don' mind, do you, Laurel?' Conor said. 'You don' mind. Ver' good friends of mine.'

I did mind, but there seemed little point in saying this – or anything else for that matter – to Conor at this precise moment.

'I only phoned to let you know I've arrived on Kyros,' I said. 'I'll say goodnight, and let you get back to your *very good friends.* I'll call you tomorrow.' When you're sober.

Conor made no reply.

'Did you hear me?' I said. 'Conor? Are you there?' There was still no answer. He'd hung up on me.

I slammed the phone down on the bed. When Conor had suggested staying in the flat while I was in Greece, he hadn't mentioned his intention to turn it into party central. What was he *thinking?* And yet . . . Was I being unreasonable? Did I really expect him to ask my permission to invite a few friends over? After all, if we did ever make the commitment to live together, it wouldn't be *my* flat we were living in, but *our* home. *If* we made that commitment.

Reminding myself that I didn't have to think about any of this until I was back in London, I got myself ready for the night, my temper soothed by the touch of my silk pyjamas against my skin, and the cool cotton sheets, as I slid into bed. I shut my eyes, scenes from earlier in the day replaying in my mind . . . hot sand beneath my feet, deliciously cold wine, laughter, Jason's blue eyes, sunlight on water . . .

As I drifted off to sleep, London seemed very far away.

Chapter Twenty-four

When I woke up, the first thing I did was go to the window, open the shutters, and look out, resting my arms on the sill. Another day in paradise, I thought, as I gazed at the view of the rocky coastline and the calm sea, its surface as smooth as a mirror, and the clear blue sky overhead.

'Good morning, Laurel.'

Jason's voice made me jump. Turning my head, I saw him seated on a sun lounger beside the pool, paperback in one hand, cup of coffee in the other, wearing just a pair of swim shorts.

'You're up early,' I said. And looking good on it, I thought, taking in his newly acquired suntan.

'I wanted to get a swim in before we have to leave for – what is it? – the unit base?' Jason said.

I nodded.

'You've just missed Will,' Jason went on. 'He turned up with provisions – not only for Harry and Amber but for us as well. As instructed by Harry, apparently.'

'That was kind of him,' I said. 'So we won't need to trek to the restaurant for breakfast?' Our sortie the previous night had shown me that the main part of the Paradise Holiday Village – studio apartments and villas very like ours, reception, a shop, restaurants and swimming pools – might be five minutes away by car, but would take considerably longer to reach on foot.

'Not for a week at least,' Jason said. 'I fear that young Will has emptied every shelf in the Paradise supermarket.'

I laughed, and withdrew into my bedroom. Having showered and dressed in a pink sleeveless top and white shorts – suitable work gear for a Greek island location, I felt – I raided our supplies for bread, fruit, and cheese, and joined Jason, also now fully dressed, outside by the pool for breakfast. While we ate, I relayed to him what Amber had told me about Drew's stomping off set, but he'd already been brought up to speed by Harry the previous afternoon – some serious male bonding had apparently taken place while the two of them were fixing lunch and the sun umbrella – and was far more interested in how he might arrange to borrow one of the unit cars.

'Kyros is mentioned in several ancient sources,' he said, 'but no one has ever done an archaeological survey of the island. I'd like to take a look around and see if I can spot any signs of early settlement.'

'Am I invited?' I said.

'But of course. I hoped you'd want to accompany me.'

'I'd love to. As long as you're willing to tell me what I'm looking at.'

'It would be my pleasure as always,' Jason said. 'But you have to promise to tell me to shut up if you get bored.'

'I could never get bored listening to you talk about archaeology, Professor,' I said, my voice sounding much more coquettish than I'd intended.

'I'm glad to hear it,' Jason said, 'because I'll never tire of talking to you about it.' His mouth lifted in a lazy smile.

I thought, are we flirting? A flush crept over my face. To cover my confusion, I picked up my coffee cup, only to find it empty. I put it back down on the ground beside my sun lounger.

'Laurel—' Jason got to his feet. I looked up at him, shading my eyes with my hand. The thought came to me that I'd never tire of looking at him.

'W-what is it, Jason?' I said. He held out his hand. I took it, acutely conscious of the feel of his strong fingers closing around mine, as he helped me to stand.

'Our driver is here,' he said.

★

170

Spiros turned the car off the winding coast road and on to a wide track leading to an area of bare, flattened earth behind a wire fence. This, he informed Jason and me, as he brought the car to a halt by the barrier that marked the entrance, was usually an empty coach park — a little-used stop-off point for the few sight-seeing tourists who ventured north of Lanissi. Now the unit base for *Swords and Sandals*, the space was packed with trailers, vans, and cars, and several vehicles whose function eluded me until I realised they were horse boxes. Beyond the parked trailers, I caught a glimpse of azure sea.

A middle-aged man, wearing a badge that proclaimed him to be 'Security', approached the car. He and Spiros exchanged a few words in Greek, and the security guard spoke briefly into a two-way radio, before raising the barrier to let us through.

'I drop you here,' Spiros said, stopping at a point where the main track through the base branched into two. 'The production office is sending a runner to meet you. They will call me when you wish to return to your villa.'

Jason and I got out of the car, and Spiros drove off along the smaller track — presumably to spend the day in the company of the other unit drivers.

'You have me at a disadvantage,' Jason said. 'I assume you know who or what a *runner* is — other than an athlete — while I do not.'

'Yes, I do know,' I said. It struck me that who did what on a film set was one of the few things that I knew far more about than Jason did. 'A film unit is made up of various departments, like the camera crew, sound, or make-up. In the assistant direc-tors' department you have the first assistant director, who runs the set, the second AD, who is based in the production office and organises the shooting schedule, the third AD, who directs the extras, and then the runners, who basically run errands for every-one else. They travel the actors — that is, they fetch them when they're needed on set — get the star's lunch orders, and all that sort of thing, often literally at a run.'

'So it's an entry level job?' Jason said.

'Exactly,' I said. 'It's hard work and long hours, but it's the way a lot of people get their start in the film industry.'

Right on cue, a young man – he couldn't have been more than about twenty – tanned and with a shock of dark hair, clutching a radio and a clipboard, appeared from amongst the assorted parked vehicles and jogged over to us, introducing himself as, 'Yannis, here to take you to the production office,' where Marcus Farley was expecting us.

Yannis led us through the unit base, pointing out the make-up and costume trucks, informing us which trailer belonged to Harry Vincent, Ella Anderson, who was playing Chloe, and the other key actors, and – most importantly – where we would find the catering van. Passing a large tent, which was the holding area for the extras – four men dressed in voluminous white robes, all wearing sunglasses and baseball caps that detracted somewhat from their ancient Greek costumes, were seated outside playing cards – we arrived at a long silver trailer. Yannis sprang up the steps and knocked on the door, just as his radio suddenly crackled into life. He put it to his ear.

'Copy,' he said. To me and Jason, he added, 'I'm wanted on set. I have to go.' Jumping down the steps of the trailer, dodging among the vans and trucks, he sprinted away.

'That young man's job title is certainly very apt,' Jason said, as the door of the trailer was opened by Marcus's production assistant, Eadie.

'So good to see you guys!' she said, beaming at us. 'It must have been awful for you, missing your connecting flight. I hope the hotel I found for you was OK?'

'It was a lovely hotel, thank you, Eadie,' I said. 'And missing the flight wasn't so bad.' I glanced sideways at Jason. 'I enjoyed every moment of my time in Athens.'

'As did I,' Jason said. 'If we'd had to stay longer, I wouldn't have minded in the least.'

'Oh, that's fab,' Eadie said, moving to the side of the doorway so that we could enter.

Inside the trailer, which was furnished as an office, with desks and filing cabinets, we found Marcus Farley, pacing up and down while talking on a mobile, Christina, the Greek girl I'd met the previous night, an older woman, and a man of about thirty-five, all sitting at laptops. When they saw me and Jason, they stopped tapping at their keyboards, and smiled at us expectantly.

Marcus ended his call, and proceeded to introduce us to the assistant producer, Nigel, and second AD, Tilda. 'Eadie you've met, of course,' he said, 'and this is Christina, who's also assisting me while we're in Greece.'

'Hello again,' I said to Christina.

'You know each other?' Marcus said.

'We're staying in the same accommodation,' I said, vaguely, trusting that Marcus had more important things on his mind than to inquire as to the exact circumstances that had led to my meeting his Greek production assistant.

'Take a seat,' Marcus continued, gesturing to four low chairs and a coffee table positioned in the middle of the trailer, on which were four copies of *Swords and Sandals*. 'Drew's filming down on the beach right now, but he'll be along any minute to talk over the changes he wants for the script. We'll have a working lunch – and then I'm thinking you'd like to visit the set?'

'Absolutely,' I said, eager as always to watch the filming of a script I'd written. 'You've not been on a film set before, have you, Jason? You'll find it fascinating.'

'I'll look forward to it,' Jason said. He and I sat down next to each other. The production team returned their attention to their laptops. Eadie went to the far end of the trailer, which was set up as a kitchen, and made everyone coffee. Marcus made another call. I picked up one of the scripts and flicked through it, failing to spot any dialogue that I'd want to rewrite. Jason drummed his fingers on his knee.

After half an hour, Eadie fetched a lunch of calamari and chips for Marcus, Jason, and me from the catering van, before going off to eat her own meal. Nigel announced he was taking a break and left the trailer. There was no sign of Drew.

'Can you find out when we might expect our director, please, Tilda?' Marcus said. The second AD spoke into a radio, which sprang into crackling life.

'OK, Yannis,' she muttered. 'Yeah . . . No . . . No, you stay where you are . . . Copy and out.' To Marcus, she said, 'Drew's decided not to break for lunch. He's pressing on until he gets the perfect shot.'

Marcus barely concealed his irritation. To me and Jason, he said, 'Sorry, guys. You may have to hang around for some time.'

I put my now-empty plate down on the coffee table. 'If Drew's going to be a while, why don't Jason and I go and watch the filming now rather than later?'

'Yeah, why not?' Marcus said, wolfing down the last of his fried squid. 'I'll come with you.'

Once we were outside the air-conditioned trailer, the fierce heat of the midday sun made me very glad that I'd thought to wear the sunhat I'd bought in Athens – Jason had donned a baseball cap, while Marcus's head was occupied by his designer sunglasses. The three of us set off between the rows of parked vehicles, in the direction of the sea, coming to a halt at the edge of the coach park.

Before us, a stony path led down to a curving beach of pale golden sand. Directly in front of us, a woman in her late twenties, draped in a bright blue, sleeveless tunic-style dress, gold glinting at her throat and her wrists and in her blond hair, which was elaborately styled with plaits wound around her head, stood ankle-deep in the sea, holding her skirts up out of the water. A group of young women, similarly dressed, stood nearby. Further along the beach, a man wearing a purple tunic sat astride a white horse.

With a rising excitement, I said, 'It's Chloe and Lysander.' For the first time, I was actually seeing them – other than in my head.

A smile appeared on Jason's face. 'And Thais,' he said.

'So it is,' I said, shading my eyes against the light so I could see the women more clearly, and recognising Thais – Amber – among

174

them. Looking at them in their brightly coloured flowing tunics, it would have been easy to imagine that somehow, like Chloe, I'd fallen back into the past – if it wasn't for the camera operator with the hand-held camera and the boom operator standing next to the women, the larger camera mounted on a dolly near the horseman, the other cameras on tripods, and members of the film unit and their assorted equipment milling about the beach. A short distance away from the actors, in the shade of an easy-up, a free-standing awning on a metal frame, Drew Brightman sat in his director's chair, deep in conversation with an older grey-haired guy. Three other crew members, two men and a woman, had also crowded under the easy-up and were standing behind a monitor. As we watched, Drew finished whatever it was he was saying, stood up, and walked over to Chloe – actress Ella Anderson – and started talking to her with much wild gesticulation. She stood listening to him with her hands on her hips, a rather aggressive stance, it seemed to me, but when Drew stopped talking, she merely shrugged and turned to face the sea. Drew stomped back to the easy-up.

'Now what's wrong?' Marcus muttered under his breath, and started down the path to the beach. I went after him, turning around when I realised Jason wasn't following to see him take his phone out of the pocket of his shorts, and hold it up in front of him.

'Jason!' I said. 'You can't take photos of the set!'

He lowered the phone. 'Whyever not?'

'Think about it. A production company uses photos of the making of a film for publicity. They hire an official stills photographer. They don't want anyone else selling photos to the gossip columns or plastering them all over the internet.'

'Ah, yes,' Jason said. 'I see that could be an issue.'

'I'm not saying you'd do that,' I said, 'but in any case, you need to switch off your phone.'

'Pity,' Jason said. 'I was hoping I could take a photo of the two of us on the set.'

175

The thought that he'd want a photo of me and him together made me feel warm inside.

'Oh, come on, then,' I said. 'Do it now. Quickly. Before someone sees us.' I went and stood next to him, and he took our photo with the set in the background. 'Send it to me later?'

'I will,' he said. 'And I swear I won't post it on social media.' With a boyish grin, he returned his phone to his pocket. 'Anything else I need to know about on-set etiquette?'

I thought for a moment. 'Well, it's best not to talk to any of the actors unless they talk to you first,' I said. 'Even if they're apparently just standing around doing nothing, they could be going over their lines in their head, or getting into character. And don't ask them for their autographs, obviously.'

'I shall try to restrain myself,' Jason said, with another grin.

By now, Marcus had reached the awning, and was talking intently to Drew. Jason and I hurried down the path to the beach and across the sand to join them.

'Drew – our writers are here,' Marcus said. Drew nodded his head in our direction, but for all that he'd requested our presence, he didn't appear particularly pleased to see us. Marcus's mouth tightened, but he covered any awkwardness by introducing the man I'd seen Drew talking to earlier as first AD, Ollie Byrne – despite his grey hair, I reckoned he was only about forty – and the other men standing in the shade of the easy-up as the director of photography and Drew's personal assistant. The woman he introduced as the script supervisor. I made a mental note to explain to Jason that she wasn't a writer like us, but ensured the script's continuity when filming.

'So let's do this, Ollie,' Drew said, sitting down in his chair. Miraculously, Yannis and another runner appeared with folding chairs for me, Jason, and Marcus. They also offered us bottles of water, which all of us accepted. Even in the shade of the easy-up, it was oppressively hot. My sleeveless top was sticking wetly to my back.

The first AD and the DoP walked out from under the awning

into the bright sunlight. I became aware of a cessation of movement around the set, as the various members of the crew saw them. A girl of about Yannis' age ran on to the set brandishing a clapperboard.

'She'll be the clapper loader,' I whispered to Jason. 'The camera department's tech assistant.'

'Nice and quiet all round, please, guys,' Ollie said. 'Stand by for a take.' He repeated the words into a radio – which I guessed was for the benefit of the crew at the other end of the beach. Excitement stabbed through me – no matter how many times I visited a film set, I found these moments just before the camera rolled electrifying. I glanced at Jason, his gaze riveted on the set, his hands gripping the arms of his chair, and I thought: he feels it too.

The clapper loader held the clapperboard in front of the camera.

'Turn over, please,' Ollie said.

The camera operator said, 'Rolling.'

The sound guy said, 'Sound speed.'

The camera operator said, 'Mark it.'

The clapper loader said, 'Scene twenty-nine, take seventeen,' and shut the clapperboard. Such a satisfying sound, I thought.

'And action . . .'

Chloe wades into the shallows holding her ankle-length skirts up above her knees. The water is deliciously cool. She wonders if the serving girls who have accompanied her on this expedition to the beach ever swim in this sea as she did only a few weeks ago – or will do three thousand years in the future, depending on how you looked at it.

'Do you know how to swim?' she asks them. They shake their heads. Thais says, 'The king is here.'

Chloe looks towards the palace, shading her eyes with her hand. Lysander, mounted on his favourite stallion, is riding towards her along the beach. She wades out of the sea and stands on the sand, waiting for him to come to her, aware that her heart is beginning to beat a little faster. He urges his horse into a canter, halting just a few feet away from her, and springs from the horse's back.

'Leave us,' he says to the servants. The girls hasten to obey, heading up the beach in the direction of the palace. To Chloe, he says, 'I returned from the hunt to find you had left the women's quarters. I feared—'

'What?' Chloe says.

'When I found you were gone,' Lysander says, 'I feared you had returned to your own time.'

'I've told you often enough that I have no way to do that,' Chloe says.

Lysander's sensuous mouth lifts in a smile. He places his strong hands on Chloe's waist, bends his head towards hers, and kisses her . . .

'Cut!' Drew shouted.

The actors froze. Harry lifted his head from Ella's, and let go of her waist. Drew stood up and marched over to them.

'I need more from you, Ella,' he snapped, his voice carrying to us clearly on the still air. 'And you, Harry. This is a scene of intense emotion, but I'm getting nothing from you. You're supposed to be an *actor*. Try and do some *acting*, why don't you?' Without waiting for an answer, leaving Harry and Ella staring after him, he stomped back to the easy-up and flung himself into his chair.

Outrageous! I gaped at Drew, aghast. Harry and Ella's acting had been so charged with emotion that when Chloe and Lysander had kissed, my eyes had filled with happy tears. As for the way Drew had spoken to Harry – that was *not* giving an actor direction; that was downright rude.

I glanced at Marcus but his face was unreadable. Drew's assistant was standing behind me, so I'd no way of judging how he regarded Drew's outburst, but I noticed the script supervisor giving the director a look of pure disdain.

Putting his mouth close to my ear, Jason whispered, 'What Drew just said to Harry. Is that how directors normally talk to their cast?'

'No, it isn't,' I whispered back. 'Disrespecting an actor like that is completely out of order.'

A flurry of movement drew my attention back to the set. Two women, both wearing broad-brimmed sunhats, who'd been standing out of shot, now hurried over to Ella and Harry who were talking quietly together by the sea. One held an umbrella over Ella's head as a sunshade, the other – who I now saw was the make-up artist Nisha – dabbed at her face with a make-up brush and reapplied her lipstick. Having peered closely at Harry's face, she contented herself with mopping his brow. The actors must be unbearably hot out there on the beach, I thought, with the sun blazing down and the heat reflecting up from the sand.

'We'll try again,' Drew said.

Ollie called out, 'OK, guys. Going again.'

Nisha and the other woman scurried off the set. The horse, which, once its rider had dismounted, had obligingly trotted over to its handler, was now led back to Harry. It had, I noticed, neither saddle not stirrups, but with a display of enviable athleticism, Harry swung himself up on to the blanket covering its back and rode to the other end of the beach. Cameras were re-positioned. A guy from the Art department raked smooth the sand where the horse's hooves had churned it up. The actresses playing Chloe's serving women, who'd settled themselves among the rocks at the top of the beach where there was some shade, were shepherded back to the set by the third AD.

Ollie said 'Quiet please, everyone . . . Stand by . . . Turn over.'

'Sound speed.'

'Scene twenty-nine, take eighteen.' The clapperboard slammed shut.

'Set.'

'And action . . .'

Ella waded into the sea. Harry began riding along the beach towards her.

Turning to Amber and the servant girls, Ella said, 'Do you know how to swim?'

Amber took a step forward away from the other girls. There was a long silence.

'No, no, no,' Drew yelled, leaping to his feet. 'Cut!'

There was a cry from one of the other actresses as Amber's

knees buckled and she crumpled to the sand. Ella ran out of the sea and knelt down next to her. The other girls gathered around them, along with several members of the crew.

Ella shouted, 'We need medical assistance here.'

Ollie spoke rapidly into his radio, as did the third AD. At some level, I knew I wasn't actually helping Amber by running on to the set to join the cast and crew standing over her prone body and offering well-meant, if contrary advice – 'Put her head between her knees.' 'No, don't move her.' 'Wait for the medic.' – but I ran over to her all the same, with Jason following close behind and Marcus coming after him.

'Out of my way!' Harry, his arrival on the scene unnoticed until then, leapt from his horse's back without drawing rein. Actresses and crew sprang aside to let him through. He dropped to his knees and clasped Amber's hand.

'Amber, sweetheart, can you hear me?' he said.

Amber's eyes flickered open. Sliding his arm under her shoulders, Harry helped her to sit up.

'Can we give her some air, please,' he said. Actresses and crew shuffled back. Jason stepped past the other onlookers and handed Harry an open bottle of water. With a quick smile of thanks, Harry held it to Amber's mouth, and helped her to drink. Tendrils of dark hair were clinging to her forehead, and he gently brushed them out of her eyes. Even although she was wearing make-up, her face looked very pale.

'What the hell is going on?' Drew elbowed his way through the on-lookers.

'Amber fainted,' Ella said.

'This is what happens, Drew,' Harry said, 'if you keep people working eight hours without a break in this heat.'

'Well, she's all right now, isn't she?' Drew said 'Get her on her feet. We need to do another take.'

'Not now we don't,' Marcus said. He crouched down beside Harry. 'Amber, the unit medic is on her way, but you'll feel a lot better if we get you out of the sun. Can you stand up?'

Amber moaned and slumped against Harry's chest. 'I feel dizzy,' she said, 'I'm sorry.'

'Stand up, you stupid girl,' Drew said. 'We need to do another take since you ruined the last one.'

There was a collective intake of breath from the onlookers. Ella's hands flew to her face. Marcus shook his head as though to clear it. I thought, Drew *cannot* be serious.

Harry's eyes narrowed and his jaw clenched. 'Enough,' he said, the menacing tone of his voice sending a cold shiver along my spine. 'This time, Drew, you've gone too far.' In one smooth, sinuous movement, he stood up, Amber in his arms, her head resting on his shoulder. His gaze fastened on Marcus. 'Have the medic meet us at my trailer,' he said, and walked off the set.

Drew's eyes bulged and his face turned bright red. 'Don't you walk away from me, Harry Vincent,' he yelled. 'Come back.'

Harry ignored him and kept walking. Under the startled gaze of everyone on the beach, he began to climb the path up to the unit base.

'Harry Vincent,' Drew bellowed. 'It's you I'm talking to.'

'Leave it, Drew,' Marcus said.

'No one walks off my set,' Drew spluttered. 'Who does he think he is? Someone get him back here now.'

'Better to let him take some time out,' Marcus said, as Harry reached the end of the path and was lost to sight amongst the vehicles in the coach park. 'Ollie, please radio Eadie and ask her to check in with Harry and Amber, make sure the medic knows where to find her, and let me know how she is. Have everyone else take a half-hour break.' To Drew, he said, 'You and I'll take a look at the footage we've already got on the monitor.' Seizing the director unceremoniously by the arm, he steered him across the sand and into the easy-up's shade.

'OK, stand down, everyone,' Ollie said, raising his voice so that it carried across the beach. 'Crew back on set in thirty, please.'

'I'll be in my trailer,' Ella said and headed off up the beach, the other actresses following in her wake. The third AD, grips, horse and trainer, and make-up artists drifted away from the set, past me and Jason, and up the path to the unit base. Their conversation was muted, but I overheard several people mention the names 'Harry' and 'Amber' in the same breath.

Well, I thought, if the cast and crew of *Swords and Sandals* didn't already know that Harry and Amber are together, they certainly do now.

Chapter Twenty-five

Concerned about Amber – I recalled an episode of *Fields of Gold* in which a character got heatstroke and ended up in intensive care – Jason and I went straight from the beach to Harry's trailer. We arrived to find Will and Eadie chatting together at the foot of the steps leading up to the door. Their smiles when they saw us reassured me somewhat that my fears for my friend's health were exaggerated.

'How's Amber doing?' I said.

'She's all good,' Eadie said. 'That is, she will be, as long as she keeps out of the sun for a bit and drinks plenty of fluids. According to the medic.'

'Were you down on the beach when it all kicked off?' Will asked. 'Did you see what happened?'

'Is it true that Harry took a swing at Drew?' Eadie said, with what seemed to me undue relish.

'Yes, we were on the beach,' I said. 'No, Harry didn't hit Drew.' However much he may have wanted to. 'Who told you that?'

'One of the guys in craft services,' Eadie said, vaguely.

'He said he'd heard it from an extra, who'd heard it from a runner,' Will said.

'But he doesn't speak much English so he may have misunderstood,' Eadie said. 'Will, I need to get back to the production office. Shall we have a drink later, at the hotel?'

Will nodded. 'Yeah, see you later.' To me and Jason, he said, 'I'll let Harry know you're here.' Bounding up the steps, he rapped on the trailer door, and when it opened, spoke in an undertone to whoever was on the other side. Harry appeared on the top step.

'Come on in,' he said.

I'd visited film sets many times, but I'd never had the opportunity to see inside a star's trailer before, and at the sight of Harry's luxurious on-location living quarters, my mouth literally fell open. At one end there was a kitchen, complete with microwave, large fridge, and breakfast bar. In front of me was a living area, furnished with squashy sofas, throws and cushions, deep pile rugs, and a large-screen TV, and at the other end of the trailer, a bedroom which could be separated from the rest of the interior by a curtain. Now, the curtain was drawn back to reveal Amber, still in costume, sitting on a double bed, her back propped up against the headboard by snowy white pillows. To my relief, she looked much recovered, if still a little pale.

'Hey, Amber,' I said. 'How are you?'

'I'm fine now,' Amber said. 'Really I am. Apart from being mortified that I passed out like that.'

'You could've had heatstroke,' Harry said, sitting down on the side of the bed and waving Jason and me to a sofa. 'Remember the episode of *Fields of Gold* when Jago's sister got heatstroke, Laurel? She was dangerously ill.'

'I do remember,' I said.

'But I haven't got heatstroke,' Amber said. 'I just had a little too much sun and not enough water.'

'It could have been a lot worse,' Harry said. 'And it's entirely Drew's fault, demanding take after take in that merciless heat. I've been on some tough shoots – I've played a love scene standing up to my waist in icy water and spent an entire night running up and down a hill in chain mail – but I've never worked with a director who has such little consideration for his actors.' He put his hand over Amber's. 'Sorry, I know I'm ranting, but I've had just about all I can take of Drew Brightman and his flippin' vision—' A knock on the door interrupted him. 'See who that is please, Will.'

Will opened the door. 'It's Yannis.'

The young runner hovered in the doorway. '*Yia sou,* Harry,' he said. 'I've come to let you know you're needed on set.'

'What about me?' Amber said.

'You're not needed again today, Amber,' Yannis said. 'Drew's decided there's enough footage of the wide shot with you and the extras, so we're going to move on to Ella and Harry's close-ups.'

'No, we're not,' Harry said. 'Because I'm not coming back to the set. And you can tell Drew Brightman that, Yannis.'

The young runner swallowed uneasily. 'I don't understand.'

'Go to the set and tell Drew Brightman that he's going to have to find himself another actor to yell at,' Harry said. 'I quit.'

Amber gasped. 'But you can't, Harry. You can't just walk off a motion picture.'

'Watch me,' Harry said.

Oh, for goodness' sake, I thought, he can't be serious. 'You don't mean that, Harry,' I said.

'I do, though,' Harry said. His liquid gaze, the warm brown eyes that had melted the insides of Jago's female admirers, became as hard as flint. 'Yannis, please do as I ask.'

'Wait, Yannis,' I said. 'Harry, you can't ask a runner to deliver a message like that – Drew will go ballistic.'

Yannis ran his hand through his thick dark hair, muttered something in Greek, and backed out of the trailer. He clattered down the steps and I heard the crackle of his radio, followed by his voice speaking rapidly, again in Greek, followed by silence. I glanced at Jason.

'What did he say?' I asked.

'Sounded like he's sending for reinforcements,' Jason said.

Harry reached for his phone, which was on a table by the bed. 'I need to call my agent. I should let him know what's happened before the proverbial hits the fan.'

Oh, my days, I thought, he *is* serious. He's going to walk out on *Swords and Sandals*. And the movie can't get made without its leading man. Fighting a rising panic, I said, 'Harry, if you quit this film, if you break your contract, it could wreck your reputation as an actor. It could ruin your career.'

'I'll take that chance,' Harry said.

'It's not just about you,' I said, struggling to keep my voice calm. '*Swords and Sandals* is a long way from a wrap. Without you to play Lysander, I can't see it reaching the big screen.'

'Not my problem,' Harry said. Leaping to his feet, he strode out of the trailer, slamming the door behind him, effectively preventing those of us inside from eavesdropping. I went to a window and looked out, to see him already talking on his phone, an incongruous sight in Lysander's costume of tunic and leather boots. Yannis stood a short distance away, clutching his radio in both hands.

Jason and Amber came and joined me by the window.

'I think Harry really is going to quit,' Amber said.

'It's very unlike him to behave like a *star*,' I said, my gaze following Harry as he paced up and down outside the trailer, 'but I think you could be right.'

Amber's hands fluttered about her face. 'This is all my fault,' she said. 'Harry's going to throw away his career – everything he worked so hard for – because of me. If I hadn't fainted—'

'No, Amber,' I said. 'It's Drew Brightman who's to blame and no one else.'

Outside, Harry appeared to have concluded his call. He stood staring at his phone for what seemed like a long time, although in reality it was probably less than half a minute. Then he returned to the trailer, flinging open the door and kicking it shut.

'My agent is handling things from now on,' he said. 'I'm out of here. Please send for my car, Will.'

'Are you going back to the villa?' Amber said.

Harry frowned. 'I guess so. For now. Until I can get a flight to Athens.'

'Shall I come with you?' Amber said. 'To the villa, I mean.'

Before Harry could reply, a loud rap on the door made all of us start. Without waiting to be asked, Will went to open it.

'It's Marcus Farley—' he began, as *Swords and Sandals*' producer stepped past him and into the trailer. I felt weak with relief. If anyone could get the cameras rolling again, it would be Marcus.

'Afternoon, Marcus,' Harry said, folding his arms and jutting out his chin.

'Hey, Harry,' Marcus said. Spotting me and Jason, he nodded at us, and looked at Amber. 'How are you, Amber? Eadie tells me you're feeling a lot better.'

'Oh, yes, I'm fine now, Mr Farley,' Amber said. 'Totally recovered. Thank you for asking.'

'Good to hear,' Marcus said. Lowering his lean frame on to a sofa and crossing one linen-clad leg over the other, he turned his attention to Harry. 'Have a seat, Harry. We need to talk.'

Harry remained standing, his body rigid. 'It's my agent you need to talk to, not me,' he said.

'I will,' Marcus said, 'but I'd prefer to speak to you first, if I may.' To the rest of us, he said, 'Could you guys give me and Harry the room, please.' He smiled, but his tone made it clear this was not a request. As one, the four of us started moving towards the door.

Harry drew in his breath, but he sat down on the other sofa, facing Marcus.

'Whatever,' he said. 'I'll hear what you have to say, but my mind is made up – there's no way I'm going back on that set.'

'Sing, O Muse, of the rage of Achilles,' Jason murmured, half an hour later, as he and I sat next to each other on the steps of Harry's trailer, which were, by now, fortunately in the shade. Amber had taken herself off to wardrobe to change out of her costume. Will and Yannis had wandered over to Ella's trailer, which was parked across from Harry's, and were chatting with Ella's dresser.

'What did you say?' I asked Jason.

'It's the first line of the *Iliad*,' Jason said.

'I see,' I said. 'Actually, I don't see. Why are we talking about the Trojan War right now?'

'Achilles was the greatest of the Greek warriors who fought at

Troy,' Jason said. 'He quarrelled with Agamemnon, the leader of the Greek army, withdrew from the battlefield, and sulked in his tent, refusing to fight.'

'Are you suggesting a quarrel between an ancient warrior and a king is in any way similar to a row between an actor and a director?'

'Harry is sulking in his trailer and refusing to return to the set, is he not?'

'Well, yes,' I said. Curiosity prompted me to ask, 'Did Achilles return to the battlefield.'

'Eventually,' Jason said. 'After Hector, the Trojan champion, killed Achilles' boyfriend, Achilles killed Hector in revenge. Then Achilles was killed by an arrow.'

'The ancient Greeks weren't much into the happy-ever-after, were they?' I said. 'The final scenes of the Trojan War definitely need a rewrite.'

Jason laughed, and then fell silent as the door of the trailer opened and Marcus came out.

'Whyever did I become a film producer?' he said.

'I'm guessing Harry's still saying he's going home?' I said.

'He's adamant,' Marcus said. 'I'm going to talk to his agent – in the vain hope that he can make him see sense – but the future for *Swords and Sandals* is not looking good.' His eyes fixed on mine. 'You do realise that without Harry, filming can't continue?'

'Yes, Jason and I get that,' I said. Despite the heat of the late afternoon, I felt cold all over.

Jason cleared his throat. 'Marcus, before you call his agent, would you object to my having a word with Harry?'

'You think you can talk him round?' Marcus said.

'I can try.'

'Then go ahead by all means,' Marcus said.

Jason got to his feet, squeezed past Marcus, and went into the trailer. My head jerked up in surprise as Marcus let out a string of expletives. In all the time I'd known him, I'd never heard him swear.

'Sorry, Laurel,' he said.

I shrugged. 'No apology necessary. I've heard those words before. Just not from you.'

'Yes, well, I've never had to deal with an actor as stubborn as Harry Vincent before,' Marcus said. 'Mind you, I do see where Harry's coming from. If Drew Brightman had spoken to Shannon the way he spoke to Amber down on the beach, I wouldn't have been responsible for my actions.'

'Drew Brightman,' I said, 'is out of control.'

Marcus sighed. 'I'd heard rumours that he could be difficult, but I chose to ignore them. And – my bad – I persuaded Shannon to do the same.'

'But why?' I said.

'Have you seen his first feature film?' Marcus said, sitting down next to me on the steps.

I nodded. 'It's a good movie – I'll give him that.'

'It's brilliant,' Marcus said, 'and it made a fortune. Having him direct *Swords and Sandals* brought in the investors we needed to green light the film.'

'Well, forgive me if I'm speaking out of turn,' I said, 'but it seems to me that Drew has reached his sell-by date.' A thought struck me. 'Fire him – and Harry will stay.'

'Not an option,' Marcus said. 'The legal and financial repercussions are such that I can't fire Drew.'

'But if Harry walks, the film won't get made at all,' I said. 'I'd imagine the fallout from that would be dire too.'

'You have no idea,' Marcus said. 'Strictly between you and me, all that Shannon and I own, even our house, is tied up in the financing of *Swords and Sandals*. If the film doesn't get made – or if it does get made and it bombs – Farley Productions goes under, and Shannon and I lose everything.'

I gaped at him. 'You've gambled your home on a movie?' My stomach churned at the thought.

Before he could reply, Amber, now dressed in shorts and a T-shirt, appeared around the end of the trailer. Catching sight of me and Marcus, she came to a halt. As if on cue, the door of the trailer opened, and Harry came out.

'OK, let's do this,' he said, 'before we lose the light.'

As one, Marcus and I sprang to our feet and ran down the steps. Harry followed at a more sedate pace. When he reached the bottom, Marcus stood in front of him, and held out his hand.

'Thank you, Harry,' he said, his voice uncharacteristically solemn.

'Don't thank me, thank Jason,' Harry said, but he took Marcus's hand and shook it.

'Where's Yannis?' Marcus said.

'Here,' Yannis said, materialising between the producer and Harry.

'Please travel Harry to set,' Marcus said.

'One moment,' Harry said. He went to Amber, and putting an arm around her shoulders, spoke to her in a voice too quiet for anyone else to hear. Then he started walking in the direction of the beach.

'Travelling,' Yannis said into his radio, and hurried after Harry.

Jason walked slowly down the trailer steps. 'So this is how a film gets made,' he said. 'I'd never have expected so much of the drama would take place away from the set.'

Marcus laughed. 'Thanks to you, Professor, today's drama didn't become a crisis. I owe you a pint.'

It seemed to me that he owed Jason much more than a beer.

'You don't owe me anything, Marcus,' Jason said. 'I want *Swords and Sandals* to get made just as much as anyone else.'

'May I ask how you persuaded Harry to return to the set?' Marcus said.

Jason shook his head. 'Sorry,' he said. 'What happens in the trailer, stays in the trailer.'

I shot him a look. When had Jason Harding started talking like a character in a movie?

'Fair enough,' Marcus said. 'Right. Crisis averted. Script meeting necessarily postponed. I'm heading back to the production office. If you three come with me, I'll have Eadie arrange cars to take you back to wherever you're staying.'

'Thank you, but I won't need a car,' Amber said, her face going pink. 'I'm going to wait for Harry.'

'Of course,' Marcus said, giving her a benevolent smile that made her blush all the more.

'I'll see you back at the villas,' she said to me and Jason, 'but I'm not sure when. Harry and I are going to eat out tonight.' Her face aflame, she ran up the steps and into the trailer.

'Damn,' Jason said, 'I've left my baseball cap down at the beach. You go on ahead. I'll catch you up.' He strode off in the direction of the shore.

'So,' Marcus said. 'Harry Vincent and your actress friend. I did wonder what Harry was getting up to on the days he wasn't filming. I hope it works out for them.'

'That's so sweet of you,' I said. 'I didn't know you were a romantic.'

'I'm not,' Marcus said, 'but a broken-hearted actor can wreak havoc with filming schedules, and I've already had more than enough crises to deal with on this production.'

We began strolling towards the production office, and the conversation we'd had earlier came back into my head.

'Marcus,' I said, 'I know you love film-making, and how much you want to make this one, but to risk losing Farley Productions, to risk leaving your family without a roof over their heads . . . Is any film worth that?'

'Sometimes you have to take a risk to get what you want,' Marcus said. 'But I'm very glad that when I phone Shannon tonight, I won't have to tell that we're about to become bankrupt and homeless.'

He continued walking, his mouth curving in a smile, as though he hadn't a care in the world.

For the first time that day, I remembered that I also needed to make a phone call. To Conor. After our last phone call, the prospect did not make me smile.

Chapter Twenty-six

'I was so impressed seeing Harry ride that horse today without a saddle or stirrups,' Jason said, as we drank our after-dinner coffee. 'The Mycenaeans had neither, so it's historically accurate, but not, I imagine, easy for a modern rider.'

'Yes, most actors would need a stunt double for something like that,' I said.

Arriving back at Villa Daphne, Jason and I'd taken only the time needed to change into swimming gear before diving into the pool. We'd followed our swim with a meal we threw together out of the supplies so thoughtfully provided by Harry, me whisking eggs and Jason chopping onions and tomatoes for omelettes – we made as good a team in the kitchen as we did as writers – which we'd eaten by the pool, accompanied by a bottle of white wine, also provided by Harry. Inevitably, our conversation kept returning to the scene we'd witnessed on the beach, but despite my unabashed interrogation, Jason had steadfastly refused to divulge what he'd said to persuade Harry to return to the battlefield. Of Harry himself, and Amber, there was as yet no sign.

'Of course, Ella Anderson's costume is entirely wrong for the era,' Jason said.

'Are you telling me that Ella's costume is *inauthentic*?' I said.

'Don't worry, I won't tell Drew,' Jason said. 'Shall we open another bottle of wine?'

I glanced at my watch. Conor should be back from the theatre by now.

'Not for me,' I said, standing up from the table. 'I have to make a phone call, and then I'm going to call it a night.'

'I'll wish you *kalinikta,* then,' Jason said. 'I won't be far behind you.'

'*Kalinikta,* Jason.'

'Your pronunciation is improving.'

'Why, thank you, Professor,' I said, delighted that he'd noticed. Leaving him sitting by the pool, I went inside the villa and into my bedroom. Fishing my phone out of my bag, I sat on the bed and called Conor's number. It rang and rang – long enough for me to think he wasn't going to answer – before I heard his voice.

'I didn't think you were going to call tonight,' he said. 'I was asleep.'

'Oh, sorry,' I said. 'You don't usually go to bed so soon after you've got in from the theatre.'

'I didn't go to work today,' Conor said. 'I was too hungover. I rang in sick.'

'You missed a show because you were *hungover*?' I said. How could he be so unprofessional?

'Yeah, I threw quite a party last night,' Conor said. 'Shame you couldn't be there.'

'Yes, isn't it?' I said. 'Conor, I called you last night when the party was in full swing. Don't you remember?'

'Huh?'

'You don't remember cutting me off while I was talking to you?'

'No – I was wasted.' He laughed. 'It was a *very* good night.' Apparently, I wasn't going to get an apology.

Through clenched teeth, I said, 'Is my flat OK?'

'Oh, yeah, I've no complaints,' Conor said.

'That wasn't what I meant—' Let it go, I told myself.

'I've moved some of my stuff into Amber's room,' Conor went on, 'which has given me a lot more space.'

'You did what?' I said. 'You must know that even I don't go into Amber's room without asking her first.'

'Amber doesn't have to know.'

'That's not the point.'

'If it's such an issue for you, I'll move my stuff out again,' Conor said.

I hadn't seen my boyfriend for a week. The first time I called him, he was too drunk to talk to me. Now, we were squabbling over the location of a few boxes.

'You don't have to do that,' I said.

'OK, I'll leave my stuff where it is,' Conor said. I thought I heard him sigh, but I couldn't be sure.

I cast about for a less contentious topic of conversation, but my mind went blank. No doubt every other member of the film unit had already rung their significant other to tell them what had happened on the beach that afternoon, but knowing Amber's opinion of Conor, I wasn't comfortable discussing her love life with him.

'Laurel, why did you phone?' Conor said. 'Was there something in particular you wanted to say to me?'

'No, I just called for a chat,' I said.

'Well, now isn't a great time for me to talk to you,' Conor said. 'I have to get up in time for the matinée.'

'I'd better let you get some sleep then,' I said. 'We can talk tomorrow.'

'I'm going out after the evening show,' Conor said. 'I'm out after the show every night this week. Why don't you leave calling me 'til Sunday when I'm not working?'

'Maybe it's better if you called me?' I said. 'As I always seem to pick the wrong time.' I sounded petulant, I knew, but I couldn't help myself.

'If you want,' Conor said. 'Night, Laurel.'

'*Kalinikta,*' I said. 'That's goodnight in Greek.' To my annoyance, he'd already ended the call.

I sat very still and replayed our conversation in my mind, wondering how it was that after a week apart, Conor and I had so little to say to each other. I'd woken him up, so he was hardly

194

likely to be in the best of moods, but he could at least have *acted* like he was pleased to hear from me.

Placing my phone on a shelf, I washed, changed into my pyjamas, and slid into bed. By now, I was extremely tired – it had been a long and trying day, after all – but I found myself restlessly twisting and turning, unable to settle to sleep. It was a hot night, and my bedroom was stifling, even though I'd left the windows open to allow air in through the shutters. Kicking off the one sheet covering me, I lay on top of the bed in my skimpy nightwear, staring into the darkness. I told myself that Conor's reluctance to hold a late-night conversation meant nothing. There was no reason for my disquiet other than my over-active imagination.

The sound of an engine distracted me from the vague, uneasy thoughts slowly forming in my head. I heard the slam of a car door. Then there were footsteps going around the pool, Amber and Harry's voices, and Jason's voice – I couldn't make out what they were saying – followed by silence.

I rolled over and shut my eyes, but still sleep eluded me. I heard Harry's voice again, and then the sound of splashing. Sitting up, I swung my legs over the side of the bed, and going to the windows, opened a shutter just wide enough for me to peer out. Jason and Harry were in the illuminated pool, both of them swimming lengths, and from where I was standing in my hot, stuffy bedroom, the turquoise water looked cool and inviting. Suddenly wide awake, I closed the shutter, quickly swapped my pyjamas for a bikini, grabbed a towel, and went to join the guys.

Outside, the air was hot and still, the moon was full, and the night sky was sprinkled with stars. Jason was still gliding smoothly through the water, but Harry was now sitting on the edge of the pool. Dropping my towel on a lounger, I went and sat next to him, dangling my feet in the water.

'It's so hot tonight,' I said. 'I couldn't sleep.'

'Me neither,' Harry said. 'Amber went out like a light as soon as she got into bed, but I couldn't relax.' He sighed. 'I completely lost it this afternoon. That so isn't me.'

'I've worked with you long enough to know that,' I said.

'I don't care what Drew says to me,' Harry said. 'I can take it. But when he started on Amber – when I saw her lying on the sand – I was so angry with Drew, there was no way I was going back on that set. Not until Jason made me realise that it wasn't only my career I'd be damaging if I broke my contract, but Amber's too. Playing Thais means so much to her.'

'Her first featured role in a movie,' I said. 'Complete with a premiere in Leicester Square. Hopefully.'

Harry nodded. 'I couldn't deprive her of that.'

'It's for Amber's sake that you agreed to go on working with a dickhead like Drew,' I said, as with a sudden clarity, I understood how Jason got him back on set.

'I'd do anything for Amber,' Harry said. His gaze went to Villa Penelope, where Amber lay sleeping. 'I'm in love with her.'

'Oh, Harry.' Even as I smiled, I remembered what Amber had said to me the previous day: *It's just a summer fling.*

Harry was staring at me wide eyed. 'I shouldn't have told you that.' He ran his hand through his hair. 'I haven't told her. Why did I tell you?'

'Hold on a minute,' I said. 'Can we rewind a bit? You're in love with Amber, but you haven't told her?'

Harry shook his head. 'I made it very clear when we first hooked up that we were strictly no strings attached. Now, I can't seem to find the words to tell her that my feelings have changed and I want us to be a couple.' Unexpectedly, he grinned, 'I don't suppose you'd write me a script?'

'Absolutely not,' I said. 'Telling a girl you love her is a scene you need to write for yourself.'

'You think?' Harry said. 'I always found that Jago's lines went down far better with women than anything I ever came up with.'

I laughed at that, but I couldn't get the echo of Amber's words out of my mind: *Uncomplicated and fun . . . After the whole debacle with Tom, it's exactly what I need . . .*

'I know you and Amber are mates,' Harry went on, 'but you

won't say anything to her about what I've told you tonight, will you?'

'As if,' I said.

'I'm going to tell her how I feel,' Harry said, 'but I want to find the right moment.'

'The perfect shot in one take,' I said.

'Exactly,' Harry said. After a moment, he added, 'I know it wasn't just Amber's career I might have derailed if I'd walked off *Swords and Sandals*. Jason made me see how important this movie is to you too. It could be your big break, as we actors say.'

'That's what I'm hoping,' I said.

'I'm sorry if my threatening to quit freaked you out this afternoon. It won't happen again. Just so you know.' With a smile, Harry pushed himself into the pool, swam to the far end, climbed out, and went inside Villa Penelope.

Poor Harry, I thought. He and Amber aren't only not on the same page, but reading from a different script.

Jason swam over to the side of the pool where I was sitting and hauled himself out to sit beside me.

'I was trying to be discreet and keep my distance,' he said, 'given the nature of the conversation, but I couldn't help overhearing what you and Harry were saying.'

'I'm thinking you'd already guessed that Harry is a man in love,' I said, 'and by appealing to his feelings for Amber, you succeeded in getting him back on set when Marcus Farley failed.'

'I'll admit I suspected that Harry had been struck by one of Eros's arrows, as the ancient Greeks would have put it,' Jason said, 'but to be honest, once he'd finished ranting about Drew's over-inflated ego, his vanity, and his borderline personality disorder, he needed very little persuading.'

Eros, I thought, needs to get his act together and aim some of those arrows at Amber.

We lapsed into silence. I heard the chirrup of insects, and the lapping of the water against the side of the pool. The night air was heavy with the scent of flowers

'Laurel,' Jason said.

'Mmm?' I became aware that his thigh was brushing against mine.

'I understand how important telling Lysander and Chloe's story is to you,' he said. 'It's important to me as well. I want you to know that.'

'I do know that, Jason,' I said. 'And I wouldn't want to write this script without you.'

Jason's eyes met mine . . .

Then he bends his head and kisses me on the mouth . . .

Then he looked away and slid noiselessly into the pool.

Feeling distinctly light headed, I, too, lowered myself into the pool, relishing the caress of the cool water. Floating on my back, I stared up at the canopy of stars, and let the tensions of the day drift away. When Jason swam to the steps and climbed out, I did the same.

He picked up my towel. I held out my hand for him to give it to me but instead he placed it around me, his hands lingering on my shoulders . . .

His hands slide around my waist. I reach up and put my arms around his neck, desire lancing through me as he bends his head and kisses me, a deep, demanding kiss, his tongue in my mouth, both of us half naked, our bodies entwined, his arousal hard against my stomach through his swim shorts. I am breathless when he finally lifts his head from mine . . .

'I think it's time we called it a night,' he said, stepping away from me.

'Yes, you're right,' I said. We went into Villa Daphne and Jason stood watching me as I locked the front door.

'*Kalinikta,* Laurel,' he said.

'*Kalinikta,* Jason.'

We went to our separate bedrooms. I peeled off my bikini, quickly towelled myself dry, and stretched out naked on the bed, my body tingling as I replayed the scene by the pool in my head. Jason hadn't kissed me, but the way he'd looked at me, the way he'd leant towards me, I was sure he'd wanted to. And I'd very much wanted to kiss him, to feel the touch of his hand on my body, for him to pick me up in his arms, and carry me to his bed . . .

Jason's hands part my legs so he can kneel between my thighs. My gaze roams from his stubbled chin to the dark blond hairs on his sculptured torso and the line of darker hairs on his stomach, so different to the smooth, waxed planes of Conor's body . . .

Conor. My boyfriend. Who right now was asleep in my flat in London, blissfully unaware that I was writing scripts for movies featuring me having sex with another guy.

My heart was beating so hard I felt sure that Jason must be able to hear it on the other side of the wall. I reminded myself that he had *not* kissed me. And I'd made no attempt to kiss him. The footage of me and him naked in his bed was destined only for the cutting room floor. I had *not* cheated on Conor.

I stood up, put on my pyjamas, and lay back down on bed, thoughts tumbling around my head . . . I'd never cheat on a boyfriend . . . I'd never hurt Conor the way he'd hurt me . . . I wanted Jason . . . my body ached for him . . . I wanted him inside me . . . I'd never cheat . . .

Dawn was breaking before I finally fell asleep.

Chapter Twenty-seven

Woken by the sound of knocking, I sat up, rubbing my eyes.

'Just a sec,' I called. Groggily, I got out of bed, stumbled across the room and opened my bedroom door, to be confronted by my co-writer, wearing only a pair of jeans.

'I've just had a call from Eadie,' he said. 'Our script meeting is now scheduled for this morning, at today's unit base. A car's picking us up in half an hour.'

'Oh, my goodness,' I said. Suddenly, I was wide awake. 'I'll need to get a shift on.'

'This might help,' Jason said, handing me mug of coffee. 'Milk, no sugar, right?'

'You're getting to know me very well.'

A smile spread slowly across Jason's face. 'I hope so,' he said. No one, I thought, has any right to look as good as Jason Harding does first thing in the morning. With a conscious effort, I ignored the pleasurable fluttering in my stomach.

'I'll go and get myself sorted,' I said.

Backing into my bedroom, I shut my bedroom door, gulped down my coffee, and jumped in the shower.

Lysander stands behind her, reaching around her to hold the reins of the matching pair of black stallions that pull his chariot. He keeps the horses to a walk, heading inland away from the sea, following the course of an old, dried-up river bed. Reaching a grove of gnarled, silver-leafed olive trees, he brings the horses to a halt and leaps down on to the sun-baked earth. Chloe is about to jump down after him, but he puts his hands on her waist and lifts her down, setting her on her feet so close to him that their bodies are almost touching. For a long moment, he gazes searchingly at her face, then he takes her hand and leads her into the grove . . .

'We were so right to keep that scene in the script,' I said to Jason, as we stood watching Harry and Ella emerge from among the trees. 'It's so romantic. Harry's fans will love it.'

'As I remember,' Jason said to me, with a wry smile, 'it was you who, despite my misgivings at the time, insisted on keeping that scene. And you were right to do so. It is romantic.' He paused. 'I must admit, I'm envious of Harry.'

'Because he gets to play a romantic love scene with a beautiful actress like Ella?' I said.

Jason laughed. 'No – because he's had the opportunity to drive a replica of a Mycenaean chariot!'

Jason and I had arrived at the expanse of grass, thorn bushes, and trees with a vista of distant mountains that was today's location to find it in lockdown, with Yannis barring our way on to the set and informing us gravely that if we went any further we'd be in shot – Jason had looked somewhat alarmed at this, until I'd explained it simply meant we'd be on camera if we went any nearer to the action – and we had to wait for a break in filming, when Drew would join us in the production office for our script meeting. Despite the lure of the air-con in the production office trailer, which was parked a short distance away, both Jason and I had elected to linger outside and watch the filming.

Now, a loud crackle from Yannis' radio caused him to raise it to his ear. 'Drew is happy with the playback,' he said, 'and they're moving on to the next set up.'

'Translation, please, Laurel,' Jason said.

'Drew liked what he saw on the monitor and the crew are positioning the cameras for the next shot,' I said.

'Copy that,' Yannis said in response to a further crackle. To me and Jason, he said, 'I have to go. Drew will be with you in a few minutes.'

'OK, thanks, Yannis,' I said.

'*Kalí týchi*,' Yannis said, and darted off through the grass.

'Now I need a translator,' I said. 'What did he say?'

'He wished us good luck,' Jason said, with a grin.

For a while, we stood watching the activity in the field, but then, increasingly aware of the strength of the sun, we retreated into the production office trailer. I wouldn't have been surprised if we'd had another long wait before Drew finally deigned to meet with us – or if the meeting was again cancelled – but Eadie barely had time to provide us with ice-cold lemonade, before the door to the trailer was flung open and the director swaggered in, followed by Marcus.

'Sorry to have kept you waiting,' Marcus said, pulling up two chairs and sitting on one of them. 'Eadie, if you'd take notes for us.' To the assistant producer, the second AD, and Christina, he added, 'Would you take an early lunch, please, guys?' Apart from Eadie, the production team got up from their desks and trooped out of the trailer. I wondered if Marcus, in anticipation of *artistic differences* between his director and his writers, was getting rid of potential witnesses. Glancing surreptitiously at Drew, who had remained standing, rocking from foot to foot, I noticed that his face was more florid than usual. I was unable to decide if he was angry or excited – or merely sunburnt.

As soon as the trailer door had closed, Drew said, 'You know why you're here?' Without waiting for an answer, he went on, 'It's the script. It's not working. You need to fix it.'

I took a deep breath. 'Could you be a little more specific about what you'd like us to change?' Please don't ask me to rewrite my heart-rending, yet uplifting ending for Lysander and Chloe's story.

'I thought we'd found the right ending for this picture,' Drew said, 'but it only took one take of the scene where Chloe tells Lysander she is leaving him, for me to see that it's all wrong. You need to rewrite the script so that Chloe stays in the past.'

Do not argue with him, I told myself. You came here to do a job – now do it.

202

My heart plummeting, I said, 'I can do that.'

'I should hope so,' Drew said. 'You claim to be a screenwriter. That's why I brought you to Kyros.'

I *claim* to be a screenwriter? Did he actually say that? My hands clenched, my nails digging into my palm.

'I'm sure our writers are more than capable of rewriting the ending of *Swords and Sandals*,' Marcus said, 'but the question is whether we should change the picture quite so radically. Don't you agree, Laurel?'

I thought, Marcus doesn't want to change my ending any more than I do. And it's him I'm working for.

'Yes, Marcus,' I said. 'I do agree with you.'

Drew's face creased into a frown. 'I can't film the ending as it is now. It lacks authenticity. It's unfilmable.'

Unfilmable? I didn't trust myself to speak.

Jason leant forward. 'Drew, I appreciate that giving Chloe and Lysander a happy-ever-after ending may make *Swords and Sandals* more commercial, but have you considered the possibility that her staying in the past could lessen the authenticity of the film as a whole?'

Drew swivelled round to face Jason. 'What are you talking about?' he said.

'Don't you see that the very fact of Chloe returning to the twenty-first century affirms the ambiguity of whether she did actually travel back in time,' Jason said, 'and paradoxically, this causes the scenes set in the past to become more real in the audience's mind?'

I thought, it does? I gave Jason a long look. His face remained impassive.

'I hear you, Professor,' Marcus said. 'Drew, I wouldn't want you to compromise your artistic integrity for commercial reasons.'

I thought, you wouldn't?

Drew frowned. 'Are you suggesting I'd do that?'

'No, of course not,' Marcus said. 'All I'm saying is that I understand where you're coming from.'

Which is more than I do, I thought. Aloud, I said, 'I do think Jason has a point.' Although I've no idea what it is . . .

'So, Drew, what you want is for us to rewrite the ending so that Chloe's return to the present is more authentic?' Jason said.

'That's exactly what I want,' Drew said.

'In that case, we're all in agreement,' Marcus said, with a beaming smile. 'Splendid.'

'Yes, yes,' Drew said. 'And now you've come around to my way of thinking, I'll leave you to get on with it. I have a movie to make.' With a toss of his head, he spun on his heel, and strutted out of the trailer.

'Result!' Marcus leapt to his feet and punched the air. In a less exuberant tone, he said, 'Now it's over to you guys. Do you think you'll be able to tweak *Swords and Sandals'* ending in a way that doesn't require half the picture to be re-shot and won't cost a fortune – and will keep Drew in his happy place?'

'When do you need it?' I said.

'I can give you a week,' Marcus said. 'That way, we'll still have three weeks to fit new scenes into the schedule before we're due back in England.'

'I'd say a week's plenty of time?' I said. 'Jason?'

'You're the expert,' Jason said. I flashed him a smile.

'Then we're all good,' Marcus said. 'Email me any rewritten scenes as soon as you can, and I'll take it from there. Right now, I'd better go and see what Drew's getting up to before he has another stroke of genius.' He sighed, 'I haven't had to run around after anybody like this since my girls were toddlers.'

Marcus headed off to the set. Eadie summoned a car for me and Jason, and the two of us went outside to await its arrival.

'Thanks, Jason,' I said. 'Whatever you said to Drew was far too clever for me to follow, but it worked.'

'What I said to him was far from clever. It was pretentious nonsense.'

'Really?'

'Yep,' Jason said. 'I don't even know where it came from.'

'Maybe you were inspired by Calliope,' I said.

Jason laughed. 'Perhaps I was,' he said. 'And what about you, Laurel?' His gaze met mine and held it. 'Are you feeling inspired for this *final* final rewrite of *Swords and Sandals*? What are your initial thoughts?'

At that precise moment, gazing into Jason's blue eyes, I couldn't think at all . . .

Jason cups my face in his hands and runs his thumb over my mouth . . .

'I – I'll come up with something,' I said . . .

He bends his head and kisses me . . .

'Maybe you could write Chloe and Lysander another love scene?' Jason said.

'Mmm,' I said . . .

That night, I lie awake, knowing that Jason is only a few feet away from me, on the other side of the wall . . . I get out of bed, take off my pyjamas, walk naked to his bedroom, and enter without knocking. Jason is also naked, stretched out on his bed . . . reading the Iliad. *When he sees me, he throws the book aside. I lie down on the bed next to him . . .*

'There's our ride,' Jason said, as a large saloon pulled into a space between two trailers. Spiros got out and opened the passenger door . . .

In the morning when I return to my own room, I find a missed call from my boyfriend . . .

On shaking legs, I followed Jason to the car and climbed in.

Chapter Twenty-eight

'Shall we make a start on our love scene?' Jason said, as we sat on the terrace, after a late lunch of stuffed vine-leaves.

Our love scene? I stared at him.

'The rewrites?' Jason said.

'Ah, yes,' I said, hoping my face hadn't gone red. 'We should definitely make a start on the rewrites. I'll fetch a copy of the script.'

'See you in our Kyros office,' Jason said. Getting up from his chair, he set off around the pool to the rustic gazebo overlooking the sea.

Amber, who wasn't in any of the scenes being filmed that day, and had spent most of it sunbathing by the pool, suddenly sat up and took off her sunglasses.

'Harry's back,' she said, pointing to an open-top jeep approaching the villas – as it drew nearer, I saw Harry at the wheel. Springing off her sun lounger, Amber ran lightly across the grass to meet him. He brought the jeep to a screeching halt, jumped out and ran to her, taking her in his arms and kissing her very thoroughly – as if they'd been parted for rather longer than the few hours since he'd left for the location that morning.

Come on, Eros, I thought, it can't be that hard for you to make her fall in love with him.

I went into Villa Daphne and located my copy of *Swords and Sandals* in my bedroom. I also changed out of the T-shirt and shorts I'd worn to the script meeting into a bikini, with a sarong tied around my hips. By the time I emerged back into the sun-light, Amber and Harry had disappeared inside Villa Penelope. I headed towards the shore and Jason, who was leaning against one of the gazebo's posts, looking out to sea. He turned around as I reached him, his gaze travelling from my face, down my bikini-clad body, and up to my face again. My stomach tightened. Unless I was very much mistaken, the way my co-writer was looking at me was totally unprofessional . . .

He covers my body with his . . .

Get a grip, Laurel, I told myself, you have work to do. I smiled briefly at Jason, placed my script on the table and sat facing the sea. He dragged the other chair next to mine.

'So what have you come up with?' he said.

He slides his hand between us and guides himself inside me . . .

'I – I haven't, as yet,' I said. 'As Drew's taken against the scene where Chloe tells Lysander she's leaving him and going back to her own time, let's start with the scenes leading up to that see if there's anything we can tweak.' I picked up the script and started flicking through it. 'There's the scene where they declare their love for one another – I'm not changing that.'

'*I have been struck with Eros's arrow*,' Jason said, putting his hand over his heart just as Lysander did. 'Drew can't object to a refer-ence to Greek mythology.'

'Then it cuts to the tastefully low-lit love scene,' I said. 'That has to stay. Then, it's the next morning, and the priestess of Arte-mis arrives at Lysander's palace and informs Chloe there is a way she can return to her own time, but only if she leaves before the new moon rises in the sky . . .'

The priestess and her retinue leave the throne room. Chloe goes to the window and stands with her hands on the sill looking out over the parched grassland and olive groves that lie between Lysander's palace and the mountains. One day – in her time – here there will be white cube-shaped houses with blue shutters at their windows, hotels and swimming pools, shops selling flip-flops, beach towels, and mobile phone cases. There will be cars speeding along the coast road, tourist buses, and planes flying overhead. One day, more than three thousand years from now, a young archaeologist will fly to the island of Kyros, and in the ruins of a Mycenaean palace, she will discover a sword. Chloe has her work in that distant time, the studies that are so important to her. She has family and friends, people she loves and who love her. She has – had – the life of a woman whose world is not bound by palace walls. She could have it again.

Lysander stands up from his throne, steps off the dais, and walks across the tiled floor to join her at the window.

'Tell me that you will not go,' he says.

Chloe turns to face him, this warrior-king, so different from anyone she has ever met, a man whom she has come to love, a man who makes love to her with a passion unlike any she has ever known.

'I love you,' he says.

'I love you, Lysander,' Chloe whispers, 'but I cannot stay with you . . .'

'They argue,' I said. 'Eventually, Lysander tells her he won't have her stay with him against her will, but he won't watch her leave. He rides out from the palace in a rage, while Chloe goes to Artemis' sacred cave to ask the goddess to return her to her own time. At the last moment, Lysander rides up on his white stallion. He and Chloe exchange a look of love. He raises his hand in farewell and watches her walk away from him into the cave . . .' I frowned. When I'd delivered this version of the script to Marcus and Shannon, I'd been convinced that I'd found the perfect ending for Chloe and Lysander's story; now, my confidence deserted me.

'Is something wrong?' Jason said.

'I'm not sure.' I re-read the scene and my heart sank. The dialogue I'd been so proud of now seemed flat and unconvincing. 'I hate to admit it, but Chloe and Lysander's farewell scene isn't working for me any more – and I don't know why.'

Jason raised one eyebrow. 'I take it you're not having second thoughts about Chloe returning to her own time?'

'No, it's not that,' I said. 'Absolutely not. But something about this scene doesn't ring true. And I'm at a loss as to how to rewrite it.'

'May I?' Jason said I slid the script towards him and he read through the scene.

'Any ideas?' I said.

He closed the script. 'When you wrote that scene, I didn't know Lysander that well,' he said, slowly. 'Now I know him better, I feel certain he wouldn't just sit there on his horse and watch the only woman he's ever loved walk out of his live for ever. He'd fight for her, metaphorically speaking. Unless – and this is only a suggestion – something happens that forces him to let Chloe go.'

'Like what?'

'The Trojan War,' Jason said. 'What if Lysander is among the Greek kings summoned to fight at Troy? It's just an idea . . .'

Troy. I pictured Lysander armed for battle, a plumed helmet on his head, his sword in his hand. He was a king, but he was also a warrior, and he lived in violent times.

'Go on, Jason,' I said.

'So, Chloe sets out for the sacred cave,' Jason said, 'but Lysander comes after her. At the last moment, she cannot bring herself to leave him. They return to the palace –'

'They have another passionate love scene,' I said, making a note on the script.

'Yeah, why not?' Jason said. 'Lysander tells Chloe that he will make her his queen.'

'Yes!' I said. 'Oh, yes!'

A smile flickered across Jason's face. 'Chloe has decided to stay. Then a messenger arrives from Agamemnon, the commander of the Greek army, calling on Lysander to lead the warriors of Kyros to Troy. He can't take Chloe with him—'

'She wants to go with him,' I interjected.

Jason's eyes widened. 'Yes, she does. As an archaeologist, if I thought I had a chance to see the fabled city of Troy before it was a ruin, to speak with the Greek kings, Odysseus, Achilles, the heroes of the *Iliad* . . .' He shook his head. 'An army camp in Lysander's time is no place for a woman. The only women in the Greek encampment at Troy are spoils of war, captured, enslaved, and shared out among the men . . .'

'I would go with you,' Chloe says.

'Do not ask that of me,' Lysander says.

'Take me with you, Lysander.'

'I cannot.'

'Give me one good reason why.'

Lysander's dark eyes bore into hers. 'If I fall,' he says, 'if it is my fate to die beneath the walls of Troy, you will be left alone and defenceless. If Agamemnon doesn't take you as his bed slave, he'll give you to any king or warrior who wants you . . .'

'Lysander could refuse to go to Troy,' I said. 'Problem solved.'

'Not an option,' Jason said. 'Lysander has sworn to aid his fellow kings when they call on him. He won't break his sacred oath, not even for Chloe. He is a man of his time.'

'Chloe has read the *Iliad*,' I said. 'She knows the Trojan War lasted ten years. She is a woman of *her* time. She can't – won't – sit in Lysander's palace for ten years waiting for him to come back to her.'

'*If* he comes back,' Jason said. Hesitated, then he added, 'Archaeologists have found the graves of Mycenaean warriors at Troy.'

'He comes back,' I said. 'Chloe finds his sword.'

'She finds a three-thousand-year-old bronze blade,' Jason said. 'It's pure speculation that it could be Lysander's. It doesn't have his name on it.'

I thought, Helen's headdress, Agamemnon's mask, Lysander's sword . . .

'Whatever Lysander's fate,' I said, 'Chloe has no choice but to return to her own time.'

Jason nodded, solemnly. 'And for her sake, Lysander has to let her go.'

With images of Chloe and Lysander and snatches of dialogue swirling around in my head, I got to my feet, walked to the edge of the rocks, and stood gazing out over the sea. The sun was low in the sky, turning the Aegean's mirror-like surface to molten gold. After a moment, Jason came and stood beside me . . .

They leave the palace an hour before moonrise, Chloe sitting in front of Lysander on his white stallion, and ride through the woods. When they reach the clearing, Lysander dismounts and, placing his strong hands on Chloe's waist, lifts her down from the horse's back.

'I can go with you no further,' he says. 'Only women may enter Artemis' sacred place.'

His hands are still resting lightly on Chloe's hips. He kisses her, and then he folds her in his arms, holding her close. She rests her head against his chest.

'You must leave me now,' he says.

Chloe looks up into Lysander's dark eyes, and nods her head. He kisses her one last time, and then his arms fall to his sides. Chloe's throat is very tight, but she takes one step away from him and then another, before turning on her heel. In front of her, on the far side of the clearing, is the black fissure in the hillside that is the entrance to the cave.

'Chloe—' Lysander's voice makes Chloe turn and face him. He places a hand over his heart. Chloe's eyes brim with tears . . .

'So what do you think of my idea?' Jason said, dragging me back from a wooded hillside in ancient Greece to the present. 'Does it get your green light?'

'Absolutely,' I said. 'The final reel is already playing in my head.'

Jason's smile was dazzling. 'This seems a good time to mention that I have another idea that I'd like to – er – pitch to you.'

'Go ahead,' I said.

He stepped closer to me. A lock of his tousled hair fell forward over his forehead, a pulse was throbbing in his neck. Suddenly, all I could see was a close-up of his handsome, tanned face and the blue sky above his head . . .

Jason kisses me . . .

'It's a script I've been working on for a while now,' Jason said. 'The hero and heroine are an archaeologist and a screenwriter. I see the opening scenes being shot on location in Greece.'

My heart started beating very fast.

'I – I think that sounds like a screenplay we could work on together,' I said.

'That was my thought, too,' Jason said. 'I've written the first draft.' He reached up and cupped my face in his hands. My lips parted with a gasp as he ran his thumb over my mouth. Low in my stomach, I felt the sinuous unfurling of desire.

And then Jason kissing me was no longer only a scene in a movie playing in my head.

It was a gentle kiss at first, his cool lips brushing mine, but soon it deepened, his tongue exploring my mouth, His arms slid around my waist; I raised my hands to his broad shoulders and then around his neck, and as I'd so often longed to do, tangled my fingers in his hair, heat coursing through my body, a delicious ache between my thighs, as he crushed me to him, my bikini-clad breasts pressing against his bare chest, his erection hard against my stomach, even through his denim shorts. We were breathless when we broke apart.

'Laurel,' he said. 'Oh, Laurel . . .' He trailed a finger down my arm, and my skin tingled at his touch. 'Are we . . . do we have a shooting script?'

I smiled up at him. 'The cameras are already rolling.' I couldn't seem to stop smiling. Neither, it seemed, could Jason.

'Will you come out with me tonight?' he said. 'There's a place not far from here that's supposed to have a spectacular view of the Kyros sunset, and I'd very much like to take you to see it. I'll ask Harry if I can borrow the jeep.'

It took me a moment to realise he was asking me out on a date. I felt distinctly light headed – and it was most certainly not because I'd had too much sun.

'I'd love to go out with you tonight,' I said.

He kissed me again and it felt *so* good.

Chapter Twenty-nine

I surveyed myself in the full-length mirror. The calf-length, pale yellow sundress I was wearing showed off my suntan, I thought, and it went well with my flat sandals – given that I'd no idea how much walking I was going to be doing, I'd decided against heels. On impulse, I placed the laurel leaf headband I'd bought in Athens on my head, where it shone softly against my dark hair. Was it too much? It was a while since I'd gone on a first date . . .

Conor! Uninvited, unwanted, he forced himself into my mind.

I sank down on the bed. What was I *thinking* going out on a date with Jason Harding? I wasn't free. I had a boyfriend. I was in a relationship with a guy who wanted us to live together. And yet . . .

I thought of the way I'd felt when Jason had leaned in for a kiss, the taste of him, the scent of his skin. I thought of the time we'd spent together since we'd come to Greece. How lately, just seeing him was enough to make my heart flutter in my chest. Had Conor ever made me feel that way? He must have done, I supposed, but not in a long time. Now, his presence was more likely to cause me irritation.

My head reeled as it came to me in a rush that I was never going to live with Conor. The idea of living with him was unthinkable. I'd loved him once, but now, as I thought back over the weeks he'd spent in my flat, I realised that I'd fallen out of love with him months ago. And I certainly didn't trust him. We're finished, I thought. Our final credits have already rolled – even if I'm the only one who knows it.

I looked at my reflection in the mirror and said, 'Conor and I are over.' Saying it aloud made it real.

I felt as though a weight had been lifted from my shoulders, a weight I hadn't known was there until it was gone. I should call him, I thought. It's only right that I call Conor and tell him we're done. And that he needs to move out of my flat.

From outside the window, I heard voices: Amber and Harry talking to Jason while he waited for me on the terrace.

Jason.

I did need to speak to Conor, and soon, but now was not the time. Not when my and Jason's story was about to begin.

Determining to put Conor out of my mind, at least for tonight, I got to my feet. I checked my reflection in the mirror one more time – the headband was staying – shouldered my bag, and headed out of the villa.

On the terrace, Harry and Amber were sitting next to each other on a sun lounger. Jason, now clad in jeans and T-shirt, was leaning casually against the table, his thumbs hooked in his belt, his long legs crossed at the ankles, his rucksack by his feet. For a moment, I stood in the shade of the doorway, drinking in the sight of him. Then I stepped into the sunlight.

'Hey, guys,' I said. They all turned their heads. The look on Jason's face when he saw me, the appreciative glint in his eyes, melted my insides.

'Wow,' Amber said. 'Looking good, girl.'

'You look great,' Harry said. 'I'm saying that as your friend, by the way. I am *not* objectifying you. I just think you look nice.'

I laughed. 'Thanks,' I said. 'Good to know.'

'You're really rocking the summer festival vibe with those gold leaves in your hair,' Amber said. 'Not your usual look, but it suits you.'

I touched my hand to the headband. 'I bought it in Athens. I couldn't resist wearing it out tonight.'

Amber looked from me to Jason. 'Am I missing something here?' she said. 'Are you two going somewhere special?'

'Yes,' Jason said. He picked up his rucksack. 'Ready, Laurel?'

'Er, Jason, you might want this,' Harry said, producing a car key from the pocket of his shorts. He tossed it to Jason, who caught it in his free hand, without taking his gaze off me.

'Have a good evening,' Amber said.

With Harry and Amber watching us with undisguised interest, we walked around the pool and across the grass to the jeep. Jason opened the passenger door for me – I couldn't remember a guy ever doing that before – then went around to the driver's side, and we both climbed in.

'You look beautiful, Laurel,' Jason said softly, before starting the car and focusing his attention on the road.

My heart soared.

We drove along the rugged shoreline, with me exclaiming at the view revealed every time we went around a hairpin bend. Our route took us to the north-western side of the island, eventually bringing us to a small village, which Jason told me was our destination.

Leaving the jeep in a car park packed with tour buses, cars, and camper vans, we made our way through narrow, winding cobbled streets lined with white houses, cafés and tavernas, and shops selling pottery, paintings, shells, and natural sponges. Turning a corner, we came to a sunlit square, bounded by a low white wall, where a small crowd of people stood taking photos.

'That's where we need to be,' Jason said, setting off across the square. I followed him through the crowd until we found a space by the wall and a view of the rocky coastline, sea, and sky that made me gasp aloud.

In front of us was a wide, circular bay, surrounded by sheer black cliffs that plunged down into the blue Aegean hundreds of feet below. We were standing at the highest point of the village, which I now saw was carved out of the cliff-face, the white houses below us clinging to the black rock, the narrow streets snaking between them. A stone stairway led down to a beach, where a number of small, brightly painted boats were moored by a stone jetty.

'It's breathtaking,' I said. 'My breath is completely taken away. How did you know about this place?'

'I did some research before we left for Greece,' Jason said.

'I'm most impressed by your research skills,' I said.

'When I say research, I mean that I googled *Things to do on Kyros*,' Jason said.

I laughed and turned back to the view. Fishing my phone out of my bag I took several photos. Jason produced his phone, and did the same.

'Can I take one of both of us?' I said.

'Sure,' he said. 'Let's have the view in the background.' We stood with the incredible view behind us, and I took our photo. Then Jason draped his arm lightly around my shoulder, his fingers warm on my bare skin, and took a few more. I noticed there were now even more people in the square than when Jason and I'd arrived, and others were entering all the time.

'This seems to be a very popular spot to watch the sun go down,' I said.

'Yes, but it doesn't set for another hour and it's going to become oppressively crowded here long before then,' Jason said. 'We'll move to a vantage point less likely to come up in an internet search.'

He still had his arm around me and, for an instant, I thought he was going to draw me to him and kiss me. My stomach tightened and my heart began to race, but he simply smiled and, putting his hand on the small of my back, steered me through the ever-growing swarm of tourists, and into a street that took us from the square to the far side of the village.

We emerged from the village on to a path that ran parallel to the clifftop, circling around the base of a boulder-strewn hillside, with a handful of people – a few couples, a small group of teenagers – scattered about its slopes. Jason and I walked a short distance along the path – it was only a couple of metres away from the edge of the cliff, and I was extremely glad that Jason

216

positioned himself between me and the drop – until we came to a beaten track which led up the hill.

'Shall we climb up?' Jason said.

'Sure,' I said, thankful I'd not worn heels.

We followed the track upwards, our shadows long on the stony ground before us, until we were higher than any of the other people gathered on the hillside, with an unrivalled view of the village and the bay below. Jason sat on what appeared to be the remains of a low stone wall.

'Is this hill an archaeological site?' I said. 'Could a warrior-king have come here to watch the sunset thousands of years ago?'

'Much as I'd like to be able to tell you that we're sitting in the ruins of a Mycenaean palace,' Jason said, 'my professional opinion as an archaeologist is that this wall is no more than a hundred years old.'

'I can still imagine Lysander bringing Chloe here,' I said. 'I can see them sitting where we are now.'

'So can I,' Jason said, with a wry smile. 'Although, I wouldn't have done before I met you.' He opened his rucksack and brought out a bottle of white wine. 'Would you like a drink?'

'That's another of your good ideas,' I said.

I sat next to him on the sun-warmed stone. He unscrewed the wine and passed it to me. I raised it to my mouth, drank, and passed the bottle back to him. For a while, we passed the wine back and forth between us, looking out over the sea, while the sun sank towards the horizon, streaking the sky orange and scarlet, bathing the whitewashed houses in honey-coloured light. I thought how good it felt to sit with Jason on a Greek hillside, watching the sun slide into the Aegean. I willed Jason to kiss me. The sun became a fiery red orb, reflected in a sea of liquid metal, a path of dazzling light from the horizon to the dark cliffs. Jason set the wine bottle down on the ground and slid an arm around my waist. The sun began to dip beneath the surface of the sea; the sky turned crimson and purple as the light began to fade. Jason brushed a stray strand of hair from my face.

'I'm so very glad I met you, Laurel,' he said. And then he did lean in and kiss me, tasting of wine and sunlight, and a taste that was just him. I closed my eyes and kissed him back, desire lancing through me like a warrior-king's spear, knowing he wanted me as much as I wanted him.

When we came up for air and I opened my eyes, the sun had vanished beneath the horizon and the light was almost gone from the sky. Peering through the dusk, I saw no sign of anyone else on the hillside.

'It's almost dark!' I exclaimed.

'Time we started back down,' Jason said, returning the wine bottle to his rucksack.

I put my hand on his arm. 'Jason, thank you for bringing me here tonight. It was stunning.'

'It was,' Jason said, giving me a look that sent delectable shivers up and down my spine, 'and I'm not talking about the sunset.' He stood up and helped me to my feet. 'Are you hungry? I thought we'd eat at one of the restaurants in the village.'

'Lovely,' I said, suddenly realising that I was indeed ready to eat.

'Apparently, it's impossible to get a table to sit and watch the sunset unless you book days in advance, but once the sun's gone down, most of the tourists leave straight away.'

We retraced our path down the hillside – Jason lighting the way with his phone – and along the main thoroughfare through the village, and found a restaurant we both liked the look of. Jason spoke to the waiter in Greek, and we were shown to a table for two, where we ate a delicious lamb meal called *kleftiko* – I had more wine, but Jason drank water as he was driving – talking about everything and nothing, telling each other about our lives. Every time our eyes met it felt as if sparks of electricity were jumping between us, and as the lights came on in the white houses, the moon rose higher, and the cliffs became a dark silhouette against the night sky, I couldn't help thinking that if we were on a cinema screen, the whole audience would have been willing us to kiss.

When we were outside the restaurant, Jason took my hand, lacing his fingers through mine. Walking at his side as we returned to the jeep, I felt as though I was floating on air.

I wasn't sure exactly what was going to happen when we arrived back at the Paradise Villas, but I was ready to pitch my ideas.

Jason brought the jeep slowly to a halt. We got out — careful not to slam the doors, as there was no sign of Amber and Harry, and no lights on in Villa Penelope — walked around the pool to Villa Daphne, and went inside. Jason locked the front door. Then he put his hands on my hips, bent his head, and kissed me long and slow. When he raised his head, I placed my hands on his chest. His heart was beating hard.

'Will you share a bed with me again tonight, Laurel?' he said, looking down at me with hooded eyes.

'Like we did in Athens?' I said.

'Not entirely like we did in Athens,' he said.

My body flooded with heat. I was scarcely capable of coherent thought. 'Yes, Jason,' I whispered, 'I'll share your bed tonight.'

'Come with me,' he said.

Instead of drawing me into one of the bedrooms as I'd expected, he went to the spiral staircase. On quivering legs, I followed him up to the mezzanine. He opened the door to the roof-terrace, and we stepped out into the moonlight.

Jason held out his hand. My heart pounding, I put my hand in his, and he led me to stand beside the sun lounger. I watched him as he peeled off his T-shirt and his jeans, wanting him very badly, and then I took off my dress, and my gold headband. We lay down on the mattress, and kissed each other for a long time, our bodies moulded together, our legs entwined, his touch searing my skin.

He lifted his head and looked deep into my eyes, and then he reached around behind me to unhook my bra, groaning when his fingers fumbled with the clasp, smiling when I shifted my body to help him. Tossing the offending garment away, he kissed me again, and cupped my breast, his thumb circling my nipple until I moaned with pleasure, his hand moving smoothly down my body to caress the curve of my hip, slipping a finger into the waistband of my knickers and sliding them off, raising his hips from the bed to rid himself of his boxers so that both of us were naked. My gaze drifted down his body to his erection and my stomach clenched almost painfully with the need to make our bodies one.

I rolled on to my back, and he lent over me, kissing my forehead, the hollow of my throat, my shoulders, my breasts, stroking me between my legs, setting my blood on fire.

'Laurel, I need to—' He sat up and reached over the side of the sun lounger. I heard the sound of tearing foil.

Then he was covering my body with his, I was parting my thighs, and at last he entered me, and I was gasping and writhing beneath him as he thrust his hips against me, in slow motion at first and then faster, my legs wrapped around him, ecstasy surging through me, Jason groaning, my arms above my head, his hands grasping mine, our bodies moving rhythmically, the two of us in perfect sync . . .

When Jason woke up, it was still dark. Careful not to disturb Laurel, he fetched a blanket from his bedroom to cover them both, and lay down again on the sun lounger, his hands behind his head, watching as the sky above the horizon grew steadily lighter. Beside him, Laurel stirred and opened her eyes.

'*Kalimera,* Jason,' she said.

He slid an arm around her, drawing her close, and she rested her head on his chest. With her body soft and warm against him, it was hard to gather his thoughts, but he knew that he wanted more from her than one night of sex, however passionate.

'Laurel, I—'

'What is it?'

'I—what I'm trying to say is—' If I was an ancient Greek, he thought, I would so be asking the Muses for inspiration right now. 'I'm out of practice at doing this—'

Laurel raised her eyebrows. 'I wouldn't have guessed.'

'I don't mean I haven't had sex—' Way to go, Jason, he thought. Why don't you tell the woman you've just made love to that you've spent the last seven years having meaningless casual one-stands? Because women really like to hear things like that. 'What I meant,' he said, 'was that I've been single for a long time. I'm out of practice with dating – going on dates. Seeing someone. But what I'm trying to say is, can I see you again? Can we go on seeing each other?'

Laurel's smile told him everything he needed to know.

Chapter Thirty

I lay on a sun lounger on the terrace. The swimming pool, in the midday sunlight, was almost too bright to look at, the flowers in the terracotta pots splashes of vibrant colour against the white walls of the villa. With the cloudless blue sky overhead, it was a perfect location for a rom-com. I thought about Jason, and what he'd said to me up on the roof, and my heart brimmed over.

Amber, dressed like me in a bikini, came out of Villa Penelope, walked around the pool, and sat on the sun lounger next to mine. It occurred to me to wonder if she had the slightest inkling of how Harry felt about her. Get a move on, Eros, I thought.

'Hey, Laurel,' Amber said. 'Jason not around?'

'He went to the supermarket with Harry,' I said.

The second time Jason and I'd woken up, it was almost noon. For a while, we'd stayed lying on the sun lounger, our naked bodies spooned together, but eventually hunger had made us get up and go to our own rooms. Having showered and dressed, we'd eaten brunch out on the terrace, where Harry had joined us, announcing his intention of making a supermarket-run to replenish our stores – 'I could call Will and tell him to do it, but it seems harsh to make him work on a Sunday when the rest of the unit have a day off' – and Jason had elected to go with him. I'd since received a text from Jason informing me that they'd been inveigled into having a drink with Ollie and a couple of guys from the sound department. That Jason had thought to let me know he'd be away longer than expected made me feel warm inside.

'So,' Amber said, smiling broadly. 'You and Jason?'

'Me and Jason?' I sat up, took off my sunglasses and widened my eyes.

Amber laughed. 'You really are a hopeless actor, Laurel,' she said. Despite having established that we were alone, she lowered her voice conspiratorially. 'It's obvious you and Jason have a thing going on.'

'Depends what you mean by a *thing*,' I said. 'Jason and I are seeing each other. As of last night.'

'I knew it.' Amber clapped her hands. 'You and Jason are in a relationship!'

'Not yet,' I said. 'It's early days. But we may be at the start of one.' Jason and I aren't writing a pilot that never gets optioned, I thought, but a brand-new original screenplay. And we're the stars . . .

Except we weren't the only characters in this movie. Our names might be above the title, but Conor was still listed in the cast, unaware that the woman playing the role of his love interest had found herself a new leading man. I shivered, as though a cloud had passed in front of the blazing sun.

'Laurel, are you OK?' Amber's voice was full of concern. 'You looked at though you were out of it for a moment there. Have you been over-doing the sun-bathing? Shall I fetch you some water?'

'No, I'm fine,' I said. 'I remembered I need to make a phone call, that's all.'

I picked up my phone, which was lying next to me on the sun lounger, weighing it in my hand. What to say to Conor? If I confessed that I'd met someone else, would that make it worse for him? My stomach churned.

'Is it still cheating if you want to break up with a guy, but neglect to tell him before you sleep with another guy?' I said.

Amber regarded me silently for a moment, and then she said, 'Only if you still have feelings for the first guy and think you might go back to him.'

'I don't and I won't,' I said. 'Not this time. Conor and I are over.'

Amber let out a long breath, but made no comment. Not that I'd expected her to pretend she was sorry.

'I have to phone him,' I said, 'and tell him that we're finished, but I'm dreading making that call. Whatever I say to him, I'm going to hurt him, and I feel terrible about that.'

'You think Conor cares about you?' Amber said. 'Now you listen to me, Laurel Martin, don't you go off on a guilt trip. The only person that man cares about is himself.' She'd never had any time for Conor, but I was shocked by the vehemence with which she spoke.

'You *really* don't like him, do you?' I said.

'No, I frigging don't,' Amber said. 'For goodness' sake, Laurel, he cheated on you on a regular basis. He's a serial cheater.' She tossed her hair behind her shoulders. 'Have you any idea how many women he's slept with since he got with you?'

'Two — that I know of,' I said, as the various suspicions I'd harboured about Conor over the last year flickered on fast forward through my mind. 'Maybe more.'

'One of them was me,' Amber said.

What? I gaped at her, speechless.

'I slept with Conor,' she said.

'You and Conor? No. *No!*' Suddenly, I was on my feet.

'Laurel, hear me out,' Amber said. 'Please—'

'I thought you were my friend.' The blood was pounding in my head.

'Please, Laurel,' Amber said. 'Let me tell you what happened. It was before I knew you. Before I moved into your flat.'

I took a moment to process this. 'I suppose you think that makes it all right.'

'No, I—'

'You lied to me,' I said. 'Well, no, you didn't *lie*. But you let me think you'd never set eyes on Conor before I introduced him to you as my boyfriend.' It came to me in a sickening rush that whatever lies Amber had or had not told me, Conor had told me more.

'I didn't know he had a girlfriend when I slept with him,' Amber said, her voice small and quavering. Her eyes filled with tears, and she brushed them away with the back of her hand. I told myself that I didn't feel in the slightest bit sorry for her, and it was only because my legs were shaking so much that I sat back down on the sun lounger.

'Go on,' I said. 'When was it exactly that you shagged my boyfriend?'

She looked down at her hands. 'It was over a year ago,' she said. 'I was in a club – there were a whole crowd of us celebrating someone's birthday, but I didn't know many of the others. Conor was there. He asked me to dance, chatted me up, bought me a drink – several drinks – and when the bar closed, we went back to my place . . .' She raised stricken eyes to my face.

I felt sick to my stomach. I knew the exact night she was talking about. Conor had gone out to celebrate his housemate Lucas's birthday. I couldn't go – I was at a screening of an indie film I'd worked on – but a friend of mine was there, and she'd told me she'd seen Conor leave the club with a girl. When I'd confronted him, he'd denied it at first, but then he'd admitted it, said he was drunk, and it didn't mean anything. We'd had a god-awful row. It had ended with me telling him we were finished.

'I'm still listening, Amber,' I said.

'He stayed the night, and he took my phone number,' Amber said. 'I hoped he'd call me, but he never did. I was nothing to him. Just a girl he'd picked up in a bar and screwed.'

I thought, that's what he said to me – in so many words. My anger began to fade. Amber wasn't to blame. It was all down to Conor.

'I told myself I was an idiot to take a guy home from a club and think it was going to lead to anything more than a night of casual sex,' Amber said. 'About a month after that, I took the room in your flat.'

'After Conor and I'd broken up,' I said.

Amber nodded. 'I'd been living there a few weeks – long enough to feel that we were becoming friends – when you happened to mention the name of your lying, cheating ex. I decided it couldn't be the same guy. I mean, what were the chances? Besides, even if it was him, there seemed no point in telling you, not when it was all in the past, and best forgotten.'

'And then Conor and I got back together,' I said. I'd persuaded myself that Conor was bad news, but when he'd phoned out of the blue and asked me to meet him for a drink, all my feelings for him had come flooding back . . .

'Yes,' Amber said. 'I was so shocked when you walked into the flat with him. I panicked – I had no idea what to do or say – but Conor gave no sign that he knew me, so I went along with it. The next morning – before you were up – he cornered me in the kitchen, and begged me not to tell you what had happened between us. He made this long speech about how you were everything to him, how you'd barely forgiven him for what he described as his "one mistake", and if it was all raked up again, he could lose you for ever.'

'Do you think he meant it?' I said, not sure that I wanted to know the answer to this question, but compelled to ask it all the same.

'I don't know,' Amber said, slowly. 'He was very convincing – but then he does have some talent as an actor. At the time, it seemed to me that it was up to you if you wanted to give your cheating boyfriend a second chance. So I kept quiet.'

'But – wasn't sharing the flat just a tiny bit awkward for you?' I said. 'Seeing Conor over the breakfast table. Listening to me going on and on about him.'

'Not at first,' Amber said. 'It wasn't as though the three of us hung out together – he wasn't there that often.' She bit her lip. 'I felt so awful that I hadn't said anything when he cheated on you again – I could hear you crying at night – but I couldn't help being relieved you'd split up with him. I couldn't believe it when you took him back a second time. I found it hard to be in the same room with him after that.'

'Yes, you made your opinion very clear,' I said. 'I always wondered why you were so off with him.'

'I should have told you,' Amber said, 'but the longer I left it, the harder it became. I knew that if I did, you'd want me out of the flat that I'd come to think of as my home.'

'You're right about that.' It might have been irrational, but I couldn't have shared a flat with her knowing she'd slept with my boyfriend.

'Are you mad at me?' Amber said.

'No,' I said, and meant it. 'We're friends, aren't we?'

'We are,' Amber said. Again, her eyes welled up. I was feeling a little teary myself.

'I get why you didn't tell me about you and Conor when he asked you not to,' I said. 'What I don't understand is why you've told me now.'

'It's because I can't stand seeing you feeling guilty about falling for a lovely guy like Jason, when Conor is such a dick,' Amber said. 'You have nothing to feel guilty about, Laurel. Don't let Conor spoil what you have – what you could have – with Jason. Call Conor, get him out of your life, and please, *please,* don't let him back in.'

I sat silently, Amber's words reverberating around my head. Was she right when she said Conor only cared about himself? Did he have no feelings for me at all? I didn't want to think that was true. Whatever he felt for me, it wasn't enough to stop him playing around.

'I don't feel guilty about breaking up with Conor,' I said, getting to my feet. 'I've already written him out of my story. And this time there won't be any rewrites. I'll call him now.' Briefly, I considered running a script for the call past Amber, but then remembered that Conor wouldn't have a copy. I'd have to make it up as I went along.

'I'll be here when you're done,' Amber said.

Clutching my phone, I went into Villa Daphne. I'd left the shutters closed that morning and after the bright sunlight outside, the interior of the villa was dim and cool. I took a moment for my eyes to adjust to the light and helped myself to a bottle of water from the fridge, before going into my bedroom and shutting the door. I sat down on the end of the bed and drank some water. Then I squared my shoulders and called Conor's number.

The phone rang and rang, and went through to voice mail. I hit the end call icon.

I thought, now what? I wanted Conor gone from my life, but I wasn't about to break up with him by voicemail – no one deserved that. However hard it was for me, I had to talk to him. It was only right. I called Conor's number again, and got the same result. With a sigh, I got up from my bed and went back outside.

Amber, still sitting on the sun lounger, paused in the act of rubbing sunblock on to her long legs. 'That was quick,' she said. 'How did he take it?'

'I didn't speak to him,' I said. 'I got his voicemail. I didn't leave a message. I always seem to pick a time to phone him when he's not able to take my call.' I could imagine all too easily several scenarios in which Conor might not answer his mobile. It was a shock to realise I didn't care. 'I'll try him again later,' I said.

'Text him,' Amber said.

I arched my eyebrows. '*Hi Conor. We're finished. Soz. When you get this, move out of my flat and post the keys through the door. L. xx*? I don't think so, Amber.'

'I meant text him and ask him to call you.'

'Oh. I guess I could do that,' I said. 'But what if he calls when I'm with Jason? I can't talk to him in front of Jason. How would it look to Jason, if he found out Conor is living in my flat?'

Amber said, 'The guys are back. If you're going to text Conor, do it now.'

I heard the sound of the jeep's engine. A moment later, it came into sight and drew up at the end of the dirt track.

228

I thought, I'll phone Conor at a time that suits me not him. And there's no reason for Jason to know anything about it.

'I know I have to sort things out with Conor,' I said to Amber, 'and I will. In the meantime, can I ask you not to mention anything about him to Jason? Or Harry?'

Amber sighed. 'What a tangled web we weave,' she said. 'No. I won't tell Jason or Harry that you have a shite of an ex-boyfriend squatting in your flat. Just promise me you'll get him out of there as soon as you can.'

I nodded, and put my phone on silent.

Chapter Thirty-one

'We ought to get up,' I said to Jason, as we lay next to each other in a tangle of sheet and early morning sunlight.

'We should,' Jason said. 'The trouble is, I'd rather stay here in bed and make love.'

The previous day, we'd postponed rewriting Chloe and Lysander's story in favour of a lazy afternoon on the beach and an evening meal on the terrace with Amber and Harry, the four of us sitting around the candlelit table until nearly midnight. As soon as Jason and I were inside Villa Daphne, he'd taken me in his arms and kissed me, and he'd kept on kissing me as we'd stumbled into his bedroom, torn off each other's clothes and toppled into his bed. Now, remembering, I smiled. The love scene we'd played last night had most definitely demanded a closed set.

'I guess we could stay in bed a little longer,' I said.

Sometime later, I said, 'Now, I really am going to get up and make a start on those rewrites.'

'That's why we're here on Kyros,' Jason said, raising himself up on one elbow and watching me as I pushed aside the sheet. His gaze followed me as I walked around the bedroom, gathering up the clothes he'd rid me of the previous night. I trusted he liked what he saw.

'Meet me on the terrace for breakfast?' I said.

Jason nodded. 'Before you go, I had another idea about the script. I meant to tell you last night. Before I got distracted.'

'I'll certainly hear your idea,' I said. 'You have some extremely good ideas, as I discovered last night and again this morning. But please don't tell me you want to change the ending of *Swords and Sandals* yet again.'

Jason laughed. 'No, not the ending,' he said. 'It's the scene where Chloe is cleaning the sword and wonders who it once belonged to that I'd like to change. In my rewrite, she's not alone but with one of her fellow archaeologists. He produces a copy of the *Iliad*, and reads out some of the names of the kings who fought at Troy – there's a section in the book that lists their names – including Lysander's, and suggests that the palace they are excavating might have been his.'

'So Chloe already knows Lysander's name before she falls and hits her head,' I said.

'Exactly,' Jason said. 'It goes some way to explain why she's drawn back to *his* time. If indeed she is.'

'But is it likely that anyone – even an archaeologist – would just happen to have a handy copy of the *Iliad* lying around?' I said.

'Now you come to mention it,' Jason said, with a grin. He stood up – giving me a delectable view of his rear – took a battered paperback from a shelf, and flicked through the pages. 'My copy is in Greek, but I'll translate it for you.'

I thought, how am I supposed to concentrate on an ancient text when a man with the body of a Greek hero is standing in front of me naked? I dragged my gaze from Jason's taut stomach to his face and kept it there. I noticed that his stubble was now definitely long enough to be described as a beard, and that his hair had pale blond streaks in it from the sun. I thought, he is beautiful. He is passionate. And he is kind. He is the kindest man I've ever known.

Jason said, 'From Sparta came Menelaus of the loud war-cry with sixty black ships . . . Next came Odysseus, king of Ithaca . . .' He looked up from the book. 'Then came the men of Kyros, led by Lysander, no warrior could match his skill with a sword.'

'I like it,' I said. 'Although that may be because the guy pitching it to me doesn't have any clothes on.'

Jason laughed. 'In future, I'll only pitch to you when I'm naked.'

'I can live with that.' I stepped towards him and kissed him lightly. 'See you on the terrace, Jason.'

I went to my room, showered, and put on a bikini and a sarong. Looking around for my sunhat, my gaze fell on my mobile – a stark reminder that I still needed to speak to Conor. I sighed. I might be able to forget his existence for hours at a time, but until I *officially* ended our relationship, he would always be lurking in the back of my mind. I so need to call him, I thought. But not now, not just having got out of Jason's bed. Leaving my phone in my bedroom, I went out of the villa.

On the sunlit terrace, I found Jason already there before me, Amber, who was holding a large, brightly coloured beach bag, and Harry. They were all staring at a paper map spread out on the table.

'It's an easy route to follow,' Jason was saying. 'Keep to the main road until you reach Lanissi, and then follow the signs. They'll be in English as well as Greek.' He looked up and smiled at me.

'There you are, Laurel,' Amber said. 'Harry and I aren't needed on set today, so we're going to check out Lanissi beach. Oh! I've just had a thought. Why don't you and Jason come with us? You'd be very welcome, wouldn't they, Harry?'

Harry, who was standing behind Amber, was visibly startled. 'Yes, of course,' he said, violently shaking his head, and making cutting motions with his hands.' Jason shot him a quizzical look.

'Jason and I have to work today,' I said, quickly. Harry mimed mopping his forehead.

'Some other time then,' Amber said.

'Absolutely,' I said. 'Have a fab day on the beach, you two, while Jason and I are slaving over a hot keyboard.'

Harry laughed, a little too heartily it seemed to me, although Amber didn't appear to notice, and the two of them headed over to the jeep and drove off.

'What's up with Harry?' Jason said.

I smiled. 'It may be my imagination, but I'm guessing his plans for the day include declaring his feelings to Amber, and he didn't want an audience.'

Jason stared thoughtfully after the jeep. 'When you've something that important to say, you need to find the right time.'

You certainly do, I thought, as Conor once again intruded into the forefront of my mind. 'Shall we have breakfast?' I said brightly to Jason. Go away, Conor, I thought, I can't deal with you now.

'How about a swim and then breakfast?' Jason said. 'We don't want to work too hard. Not in this heat.'

'You're a bad influence on me,' I said. 'OK. Swim. Breakfast. And then we write.'

Jason peeled off his T-shirt and dived into the pool. I untied my sarong and dived in after him.

Now was most definitely not the right time for me to be thinking about Conor.

Chapter Thirty-two

'We did it,' I said. 'We've rewritten the ending exactly as Drew wanted, even if he didn't know it was what he wanted until you told him.'

'And all in just one day,' Jason said.

I'd never known a rewrite to go so smoothly and quickly. As soon as Jason and I'd sat down at the table under the gazebo overlooking the sea and started working on *Swords and Sandals*, the script had practically rewritten itself, dialogue coming into my head faster than I could scribble it down. At one point, unable to sit still, I'd leapt to my feet and, pacing back and forth, recited the lines aloud while Jason wrote, covering the script with his enviably neat handwriting.

'The Greeks would have said that your Muse was upon you today,' Jason said, leaning back in his chair.

'Yes, Calliope really came through for us,' I said.

'For you, Laurel,' Jason said. 'You're the writer here. All I did today was transcribe your words.'

'I might have come up with the lines,' I said, 'but you had the best ideas. Lysander going to Troy. The *Iliad*-reading archaeologist. I couldn't have written those scenes without you.'

'I'm sure you could,' Jason said.

'No – we're a team.' I picked up the script. 'I'm going back to the villa to type this up and email it to Marcus. Or do you want to do that?'

'Unless you're planning to sneak in a glaring anachronism,' Jason said, with a grin, 'it's totally fine with me if you do it.'

'I'm all out of anachronisms,' I said.

'In that case, I'm going for a swim in the sea. Come and find me once you've sent the email. Bring a towel, a bottle of wine and a corkscrew.'

After a brief but delightful hiatus while we kissed, Jason went down to the beach, while I returned to Villa Daphne. Locating my laptop in my bedroom, I was about to seek out a spot on the terrace shaded enough for me to see the screen, when my gaze fell on my phone, still lying on my bed where I'd left it that morning. It came to me that now, while I was alone in the villa with Jason well out of earshot, was as good a time as any I was likely to get for me to call Conor. Even so, it was with reluctance that I picked up my phone.

As I might have expected, I had a ton of emails in my inbox, as well as numerous messages and notifications on social media. And one text from Conor: *Got a missed call from you. In rehearsal all day so can't answer my phone. Nothing to tell you any way! Lol! See you in three weeks. Con xx*

I re-read the text several times before I fully understood that he was telling me not to bother to call him – and not to expect him to call me. With a sigh, I let my phone slip from my hand on to the bed. I'd forgotten that Conor was already rehearsing his next play, but I knew the sort of hours he worked when he was in rehearsal, virtually coming home only to sleep. It would be difficult, if not impossible, for me to talk to him other than late at night. Which, given that I was no longer sleeping alone, was definitely not a good time for me.

I read the text again. *See you in three weeks.* I couldn't get hold of Conor right now, but in three short weeks I'd be back in London, and I could tell him we were over to his face. Surely that was better than learning you were dumped in a late-night phone call from Greece? It couldn't be any worse.

There's never a right or easy way to end a relationship, I thought, and I can't spend the next three weeks trying to contact Conor.

Leaving my phone in my bedroom, I went out on to the terrace and set up my laptop with the script of *Swords and Sandals* beside it.

Determinedly, I banished my ex from my head and started to type.

'So Chloe never finds out what happens to Lysander after she returns to her own time?' Amber said.

'She might not know the end of his story,' I said, 'but she never forgets him.'

In the hours since Harry and Amber's return from what they described as a fabulous day on Lanissi beach – the only downside was that Harry had to wear his sunglasses the whole time to avoid being recognised – neither of them had said anything to indicate that their status had changed to 'in a relationship'. Now, as the four of us sat over our after-dinner Greek coffees on the terrace, discussing the changes that Jason and I'd made to the script, I was forced to conclude that Harry had failed to find the right moment to declare himself.

'What do you think happened to him, Laurel?' Harry said.

'I'm not sure . . .'

Lysander wakes in the royal bedchamber in his palace on Kyros, the clash of sword against shield, the thunder of his chariot's wheels, and the screams of dying men echoing in his head. Five years since I returned home, he thinks, and I have fought many times since then, but still I dream of Troy. He gets out of bed and goes to a window. The new moon has risen, a pale silver crescent; the stars are very bright. A man's voice floats up from the courtyard below the window: a palace guard making his rounds. Another guard replies that all is well.

Lysander rests his hands on the window ledge, and stands gazing up at the moon until he realises that the sky is growing lighter, and it will soon be dawn. He returns to his bed. Beside him, his queen stirs in her sleep. Lysander waits until she is still again — he knows nothing of such matters, but he has heard her women telling her that she needs rest before the coming of the child — and then curves himself protectively around her swollen body. Before the moon is full, he thinks, I will have a son . . .

I said, 'I think Lysander survives the Trojan War, sails back to Kyros, marries a convenient princess, has kids, and leads a long and happy life. He never forgets Chloe, but he knows they were never meant to be.'

'What do you think, Jason?' Amber said.

'I'm sure Laurel's right,' Jason said.

'Sounds like you two are planning a sequel,' Harry said. '*Swords and Sandals II: The Voyage to Kyros.*'

'It works for me,' I said. 'Would you star in it, Harry?'

'As long as Drew isn't the director,' Harry said.

'On that note, I'm going to call it a night,' Amber said. 'I'm back on set first thing tomorrow, and Nisha won't appreciate having to conceal black circles under my eyes.'

'I'll finish my coffee, and I'll join you,' Harry said.

Amber went off to Villa Penelope.

'Who is Tom?' Harry said.

'Sorry?' I said.

'This afternoon, when Amber and I were on Lanissi beach, she got a phone call from some guy called Tom.'

'Oh *that* Tom,' I said. 'He's Amber's best friend. They've known each other since they were at school.'

'He's just a friend?' Harry said. 'Are you sure? Because when Amber was talking to him, she walked right down to the edge of the sea, so I couldn't hear what she was saying. As though she didn't want me to hear. They talked for over twenty minutes. And the rest of the afternoon, she seemed distracted.' He raked his hand through his hair. 'Am I being paranoid?'

'Yes, you are,' I said, trying to ignore the clanging of the alarm bell in my head. 'Tom's engaged to a girl named Freya.'

'He's getting married?' Harry said.

'Yes, he is. Amber's going to be his groom's girl.'

'I see.' Harry sat silently for a moment, and then he said, 'Have I just made a fool of myself?'

'No, of course not,' I said. 'Unreasonable jealousy is perfectly normal when a man is in love. Remember when Jago punched his brother because someone told him the brother had slept with the girl Jago was crazy about?'

A smile appeared briefly on Harry's face. 'I do remember. But I never thought there was anything unreasonable in Jago's behaviour.' He glanced towards Villa Penelope. 'Would you guys do me a favour? Tomorrow night, would you mind going out so that Amber and I can have this place to ourselves?'

Jason looked at me. 'I think we can do that,' he said.

'For sure,' I said, hoping desperately that Harry and Amber's rom-com wasn't about to turn into a disaster movie.

'Thanks,' Harry said. 'Much appreciated. I have a plan . . .' Without elaborating, he headed off around the pool.

Come on, Eros, I thought, you're running out of time to sort this out.

'Shall we call it a night, too?' Jason sad. 'Shall we go up on the roof?'

My skin tingled as he slid his hand up under my skirt. I decided that I really couldn't think any more about Amber and Harry or phone calls from Tom that night. Not while Jason Harding was stroking my thigh.

'Now that,' I said, as my stomach clenched with desire, 'is most definitely one of your best ideas yet.'

Chapter Thirty-three

I lay face down on the beach towel, while Jason smoothed sun-cream on to my back.

'There,' he said. 'You're done.'

With some regret, for I'd been enjoying the sensations aroused in me by the touch of his hand on my skin, I fastened my bikini top and sat up.

'I could get used to living like this,' I said. Picking up the tube of sun cream, I started rubbing it into my legs.

Jason glanced towards my beach bag. 'I think your phone is buzzing.'

'So it is.' I reached into my bag. Please don't let it be Conor, I thought, as a cold shiver ran along my spine. When I saw the caller ID, I felt giddy with relief.

'Hey, Marcus,' I said.

'Afternoon, Laurel,' Marcus said. 'Is Jason around by any chance? I may as well talk to both of you at the same time.'

'He's sitting right beside me,' I said, putting my phone on speaker.

'Good afternoon,' Jason said.

'So I'm calling to let you guys know that I've signed off on your latest batch of rewrites – and with Drew's full approval,' Marcus said. 'I was bracing myself for another *interesting* discussion with our director, but it wasn't necessary.'

'That's so good to hear,' I said, punching the air.

'As always, you two have done an excellent job,' Marcus went on. 'I'd like you both on set when we film the new ending in case there are any last-minute dramas, but that won't be for another two weeks – it's scheduled for our last week of filming. I also have a message for you from Drew. He particularly wants you to know that he's very excited you've included a quote about Lysander from the *Iliad* in the script.'

'That's great,' I said, mouthing '*your idea*' at Jason.

'Yeah, Drew was jumping up and down like a child with a new toy when he read those lines,' Marcus said. 'Anyway, I'll see you guys in a couple of weeks. Until then, your time is your own. Relax. Enjoy Kyros. Anything you need, please get in touch with Eadie. Bye for now.' He rang off.

'I suppose Drew does realise that Lysander's fighting at Troy is pure fabrication?' Jason said.

'I doubt it,' I said, 'but I won't tell him, if you won't.'

Jason laughed. 'Do you think it's too early for a beer?'

'Not at all. You heard what Marcus said. For the next two weeks, we're on vacation. For now, all we have to do is lie in the sun, swim, eat, drink, and . . . I'm sure there must be something else we can do, but I can't think what.'

'I'll check my list of *Things to do on Kyros*,' Jason said, his face deadpan. 'Although it may need updating. Can I fetch you some wine?'

'You so can,' I said.

He headed off, up the steps that led from the beach to the villas. I finished slathering myself in sun cream, and looked out over the sea to the horizon, which vanished in a haze of heat. A boat, a small cruiser, sailed slowly past our cove and around the headland. It was too far away for me to see them clearly, but its deck was crowded with people – holidaymakers enjoying a boat trip, I supposed. I wouldn't mind taking a boat trip around the island, I thought.

Amber's voice said, 'Hey, Laurel.' I turned my head to see her coming down the steps and on to the sand.

'You've wrapped early today,' I said.

'First time this entire shoot,' Amber said. 'Harry actually

240

would have liked to do another take of the last scene we shot today, but he decided not to risk antagonising Drew by suggesting it.' She sat down next to me. 'I've just been talking to Jason – great news about the script being signed off.'

'It certainly is,' I said.

'Harry and Jason are doing an emergency supermarket run, but the way. We're out of wine.'

'I can't imagine how that happened,' I said.

'Me neither,' Amber said. 'Jason asked me to tell you he won't be long.'

'He's so thoughtful,' I said. I smiled. 'And hot.'

Amber laughed. Then she said, 'While the guys aren't around – I have to ask – have you spoken to Conor?'

'No,' I said. 'I can't get hold of him. I'll talk to him when I'm back in London.'

Amber stared at me. 'But he's *living in your flat*. Surely you need to get him out before you get back. Before *we* get back. You can't just rock up, tell him it's over between you, and expect him to skip happily out the door. You haven't thought this through.'

An image of me throwing Conor's boxes out of the window while he banged on the front door flickered in and out of my head. No, I thought, it'll never come to that. We're not characters in a soap.

'Please don't worry, Amber,' I said. 'I'll sort things out with Conor as soon as I'm home. It'll be easier that way for both of us. For now, let's talk about something – anything – other than my ex-boyfriend.'

Amber opened her mouth as though to protest, but evidently thought better of it, and turned her head to gaze out over the sea. Dismissing Conor from my mind, I did the same. The cruiser I'd seen before sailed back into view and vanished again. I shut my eyes and tilted my face up towards the sun.

'I had a call from Tom yesterday,' Amber said.

The peace of our small beach was shattered by a deafening klaxon in my head.

'He was full of his wedding plans,' Amber said. 'I – I couldn't help feeling—Well, if I'm honest, listening to him going on and on, I couldn't help myself feeling just the tiniest bit jealous of—'

'Don't go there,' I said, as my heart sank. 'Tom is with Freya now, and nothing you do or say will change that. He's never going to be yours.'

'You think I'm still carrying a torch for Tom?' Amber said, her eyes wide.

'Aren't you?' I said.

'No, I am not. I was over him months ago. I believe I told you this.'

'So you did,' I said. 'Sorry. But you did say you were jealous . . .'

'I'm happy for Tom and Freya,' Amber said. 'What I was going to say, before you interrupted, was that I couldn't help feeling a little envious of their relationship. They're so in love they want to spend their whole lives together. I think that's wonderful.'

'Just so I'm clear,' I said. 'What you want is to star in your very own rom-com?'

'I want my own happy-ever-after ending. Or at least a chance of one.' Amber smiled, dreamily, twirling a strand of her hair around her finger.

'Do you have any man in particular in mind for your co-star?' I said, choosing my words with the same amount of care I'd give to a pitch.

'I know exactly who I want for that role,' Amber said. 'Unfortunately, he hasn't read the script.'

My spirits rose considerably. 'Are we talking about Harry?' I said.

'Who else?' Amber said. 'I don't know how it happened, but I – I have feelings for him.'

'You mean you're in love with him?' I said.

'I am,' Amber said, a blush stealing over her face.

I clapped my hands. 'Oh, my days,' I said. 'That's brilliant.'

'You think?' Amber said. 'Harry told me when we first hooked

242

up that he had too much going on in his life right now – what with his career taking off into the stratosphere – to get into a serious relationship. At the time, I wasn't ready for anything more than a fling myself. But that's no longer enough for me.'

'You want your name next to his, above the title in the credits?' I said.

'Exactly,' Amber sighed. 'But I've no idea how to make that happen.'

'You could tell him?' I said, repressing the urge to inform Amber that Harry was crazy about her. After all, when he'd told me how he felt, he'd practically made me sign a confidentiality agreement.

'Oh, I can't do that,' Amber said. 'I don't want to scare him off. And don't you go saying anything to him either. Or Jason.'

A movie, every shot in soft focus, began playing in my head.

'Listen,' I said, 'Jason and I are going out tonight, so you and Harry will have this place to yourselves. Why don't you set the scene for romance? Put on a nice dress and spray yourself with perfume. Maybe suggest to Harry you go up on the roof to take a look at the stars.' Whatever plans Harry might have for the evening, it wouldn't hurt to give him a bit of encouragement, I thought.

Amber rolled her eyes. 'Because a kiss under the stars is all it'll take for Harry to decide he wants a steady girlfriend?'

'It works every time in the movies,' I said. 'And I've got a really good feeling about you and Harry . . .'

Chapter Thirty-four

'I hope we've given them enough time alone,' I said to Jason, as he turned the jeep on to the dirt track that led to the villas. 'I'd hate to arrive back just at the wrong moment.'

'It's gone midnight,' Jason said, 'and Harry told me they both have early calls tomorrow. They're most likely asleep by now.'

Earlier that evening, Jason and I'd left Harry and Amber sitting on the terrace — Amber looking stunning in a red dress and immaculate make-up — and Jason had driven us into Eloussa. We'd had a fabulous meal in a restaurant in the pretty main square, but our delicious *souvlaki* — lamb kebabs that melted in the mouth — hadn't distracted us from speculating on the movie that may or may not have been playing back at the Paradise Villas.

Jason brought the jeep to a halt. I saw that the villas were in darkness, with only the turquoise glow of the pool illuminating the night, and no sign of Amber and Harry. We got out of the jeep careful not to slam the doors and wake them, as it appeared they had indeed gone to bed. While Jason commandeered a sun lounger, I went into Villa Daphne and made us a coffee, before joining him.

'This is so frustrating,' I said. 'I feel like I've spent the entire night looking forward to watching the last episode of a TV series, and then the season ends on a cliffhanger.' I sighed. 'I guess it'd be wrong for us to wake up the hero and heroine and demand to know if they're now officially a couple?'

'I doubt they'd welcome our presence in Villa Penelope right now,' Jason said, 'but I'm sure that if they're in a relationship, we'll be the first to hear. I've never known a guy share so much about his personal life as Harry.'

'Don't you talk to your mates about your love life?' I said.

Jason cleared his throat. 'Me and my mates did talk about girls when we were young,' he said, 'but we're no longer horny teenagers.'

'So what do you talk about now?'

Jason thought for a moment 'Work, mostly. Who's speaking at which conference. Who's published an article in an academic paper, and what's wrong with it.' He smiled ruefully. 'Much as I love my work, I have to admit that I spend far too much time on it – as my friend Emily is forever telling me.' He drained his coffee.

'Shall we go to bed? I said. 'I'll set my alarm so that we can catch Amber and Harry in the morning before they go off to the location.'

'Actually, Laurel,' Jason said, gesturing towards the sea, 'you may not have to.'

'Oh?' I turned my head and made out the shadowy figures of Amber and Harry approaching the pool, hand in hand, their way lit by the blue rectangle of Amber's phone. When they stepped into the light of the terrace, I saw they were both smiling, and that Harry was carrying an empty champagne bottle. I also noticed that Amber's lipstick was no longer immaculate, and her dress appeared to be covered in sand, as did Harry's jeans. I told myself that the only reason he was carrying rather than wearing his shirt was because it was a very hot night.

'Hey, guys,' Harry said. 'Did you have a good evening?'

'We did, thanks,' Jason said.

'What about you?' I said. 'How was your evening?'

'Not too shabby,' Harry said. 'I asked Amber to marry me.'

'And I said *yes*,' Amber said.

For a moment, all Jason and I did was gawp at them. Then, with a shriek of delight, I was on my feet hugging Amber, and

Jason was shaking Harry's hand, and punching him on the shoulder, and then Harry was folding Amber into his arms for a kiss. Somehow, in the midst of it all, I ended up with Jason's arms around me, and with him planting a quick kiss on my lips – not that I was complaining.

'I'm so pleased for you,' I said, breathlessly, once we'd all stopped hugging and kissing.

'Many, many congratulations to both of you,' Jason said.

'Thanks, guys,' Harry said. 'We've already drunk one bottle of fizz in celebration tonight, but there's another bottle in the fridge if you'd like to share it with us.'

'Lovely,' I said.

'I'd be delighted,' Jason said.

'I'll fetch it,' Amber said. 'Come with me, Laurel. You can carry the glasses.'

Leaving Jason telling Harry once again how pleased he was, and Harry grinning from ear to ear, Amber and I went to Villa Penelope.

'This is such wonderful news,' I said, when we were inside. 'If a little unexpected.'

Amber laughed. 'It came as a surprise to me too,' she said. 'I was willing Harry to see me as more than a casual fling, but I never imagined he'd ask me to marry him. Then when he did, it seemed so right, I knew without any doubt he was the man I'm meant to spend my life with.'

'That's so romantic,' I sighed. 'When he proposed you must have felt as though you were starring in a Hollywood movie.'

'No, it wasn't like a movie,' Amber said. 'There was no soaring background music, no atmospheric lighting, and no beautifully crafted dialogue.'

'But surely Harry made a passionate speech declaring his undying love?' I said.

'Not exactly,' Amber said, 'but his proposal was very romantic. We'd eaten dinner on the terrace, and he suggested we go for a walk on the beach. Once we were on the sand, he took hold of my hands, and after stuttering a few times – most unlike him – he told me he loved me and asked me to be his wife. I said yes, obviously. Actually, I said, "Yes, please, Harry." And told him I loved him too, although he'd probably worked that out for himself. Then he produced a bottle of champagne that he'd hidden earlier behind a rock.'

'I have to admit that does sound romantic,' I said. 'Even without a soundtrack and lighting.'

'The way I feel about Harry, I don't need any special effects,' Amber said. 'I'm so happy, Laurel, I couldn't be happier.'

'I'm happy for you, my friend,' I said. 'And for Harry.' My eyes brimmed with tears. 'Oh, my goodness, I'm welling up.'

'And me,' Amber said, dabbing at her face with a tissue.

'So when's the wedding?' I said.

'Oh, we haven't got that far yet,' Amber said. 'We're going to live together first, but not until we've found a house that could become a family home. A place that's *ours*. I hope you won't mind if I keep my room in your flat until we do, and Harry stays over sometimes?'

'He can have his own key,' I said. 'Now, about that fizz . . .'

We exchanged smiles. Amber found the champagne, I picked up four glasses, and we re-joined the men.

'To Amber and Harry,' Jason said, once the champagne was poured. 'May you always be as happy as you are tonight.' We clinked glasses and drank.

'So now we know what happened to Lysander,' I said.

'We do?' Jason said.

'He survived the Trojan War, returned to Kyros, and married Thais,' I said.

Chapter Thirty-five

Lysander puts his arms around Chloe and she leans against him, relishing the warmth of his hard muscular body next to hers. She tilts up her chin and he bends his head and kisses her one last time. Her body is trembling by the time they break apart. She thinks, I can't do this.

'I love you,' Lysander says, placing his hand over his heart. 'I will always love you. Wherever you are, however far away. Now go.'

'I-I can't,' Chloe says. 'I love you. I can't leave you.' Her eyes fill with tears.

'You have to,' Lysander said. He puts his hands on her shoulders, and gently turns her around so that she is facing the cave that is the gateway to her own time. On shaking legs, Chloe takes a step towards it and then another. When she reaches the cave's dark entrance, she looks back at Lysander. She knows she will never see him again.

'On summer nights,' Lysander says, 'when you look up at the sky and see the stars, think of me, and know that long ago, I looked on those same bright stars and thought of you . . .'

'And cut!'

Drew got heavily to his feet and stomped over to the monitor, with Marcus right behind him. Ella reappeared in the entrance to the cave, and stood with her hands on her hips, waiting for the director's verdict on the scene. Harry shook his hair out of his eyes, and adjusted the position of the sword on his hip. His gaze travelled over the camera crew, the make-up artists, and the props guy standing on the edge of the set, and came to rest on Amber, who although she'd completed all her scenes the previous week, had chosen to watch the filming on this last day of the shoot. He smiled, and Amber smiled back. As yet, they hadn't told anyone of their engagement, other than me and Jason and their families back in England – Harry wanted to keep it out of the media for as long as possible – but I suspected that when the news did get out, no one who'd seen them together on Kyros would be inordinately surprised. It occurred to me to wonder if anyone – apart from Amber and Harry – suspected that my and Jason's relationship was no longer strictly professional. Probably not, I thought, as we'd seen so little of the cast and crew other than on set.

Jason, who was sitting in a folding chair next to mine, leant towards me. 'Drew has to be happy with that take,' he said, keeping his voice low so that only I could hear.

I nodded. 'Harry and Ella really nailed it.'

There had been times, during the past three weeks, when I could almost believe that the sunlit days by the pool, the nights in Jason's arms, making love under the stars, would go on for ever. We'd spent one day on the famed Lanissi beach, and taken a boat trip around the island – much to my delight, the boat had anchored in a deserted cove and we'd dived and swum from the deck. Jason had driven us to various places on the island that he thought might be likely sites for an ancient settlement – not that we'd discovered any long-lost palaces, but I was fascinated by his explanations of how odd features in the landscape could alert archaeologists to the presence of buried ruins. There had been wine in tavernas, walks on the beach in the moonlight, laughter-filled evenings with Harry and Amber, the four of us talking into the early hours . . .

Then, suddenly, it was the last week of the shoot. Each morning, Spiros drove us to that day's location, and we'd watched as Chloe and Lysander's story came to its poignant end. There had been one hairy moment when Ella had failed to hit her mark, and Drew's face had turned an interesting shade of purple, but other than that, filming had gone smoothly, without any requests from our director for even the most minute tweaks to the script.

Now, only one scene, Lysander and Chloe's final farewell, awaited Drew's approval, before *Swords and Sandals* would, as they used to say in the Golden Age of Hollywood, be in the can. First thing tomorrow, Jason and I, together with those actors who hadn't already flown home, would be returning to London, to be followed by the crew and the production team a couple of days later.

Jason nudged my arm. 'Drew's smiling.'

I watched as the director walked into the middle of the set.

'It's a wrap,' he said. 'Good work, guys.'

There was a burst of clapping and cheering from the crew. Drew held out his hand to Harry, who shook it, smiling at Drew with every appearance of sincerity – he was, I reflected, an extremely good actor – before hurrying over to Amber, swinging her up in the air, planting a kiss on her lips, and keeping his arm around her waist as they vanished among a throng of ADs, gaffers, sparks, runners, and make-up artists all congratulating them and each other on a job well done. That they would still have another six months of filming *Swords and Sandals* in a studio back in England, was, for the moment, forgotten.

I smiled at Jason, and then, unable to help myself, put my arms around him and hugged him. When we let go of each together, I saw that the crew had already begun to strike the set.

'Our work here is done,' I said. 'And now we get to party.'

Except for the outfit I was wearing that evening to the wrap party at the Paradise Holiday Village, and the jeans and T-shirt I was planning to travel in the next day, my clothes were packed, and my suitcases lined up by my bedroom door. I took one last look at my reflection in the mirror – my short flame-coloured dress, worn for the first time on this trip, looked good, I thought, and the gold headband I'd bought in Athens was the finishing touch – shouldered my bag, and reached for the handle of my bedroom door.

Inside my bag, my phone pinged. Automatically, I took it out and checked my messages – and found myself looking at a text from Conor: *What time do you land tomorrow? I need to know how long I have to tidy up the flat! Lol! Con xx*

I breathed in sharply. For the last few weeks, I'd not thought about Conor once and I didn't want to start thinking about him now.

I was tempted not to message back, but then it occurred to me that my nebulous plan of telling Conor that he and I were over as soon as I walked in my front door, did rather depend on his being there when I arrived. Amber was right – I hadn't thought this through.

I checked the email Eadie had sent me an hour earlier, detailing the travel arrangements for the following day – flights to Athens and London, a car to drive me home from the airport – and worked out the time I'd reach my flat, allowing for the two-hour time difference between England and Greece. I texted Conor back: *Landing Heathrow 5.15. Home an hour or so after that.* Unable to add the affectionate '*xx*' with which I habitually ended texts, I pressed 'send', I waited a full minute, but he did not reply.

Telling myself very firmly that I wasn't going to let my cheating ex spoil my last night in Greece, I switched off my phone and left the villa.

There was no one on the terrace, but I spotted Jason standing by the gazebo, looking out to sea, back-lit by the sinking sun. I walked across the grass and touched him lightly on his arm. He turned around.

'Laurel—' His voice seemed to catch in his throat. Putting his hands on my waist, he drew me to him, and kissed me on the mouth, a gentle, tender kiss that left me feeling light headed.

'Hey, Jason,' I said, gazing up at him.

'Harry and Amber have already left for the party,' he said. 'They were going to wait for us, but I took it upon myself to say we'd see them there.'

With an effort, I gathered my thoughts. 'We might as well leave straight away, then. I'll call Eadie and have her send us a car.'

'Don't call her yet,' Jason said. 'I've something I want to say to you. Now we're done with the filming of *Swords and Sandals* I've been asking myself what happens next. To us. You and me. When we're back in England . . .'

Suddenly, my heart was beating very fast.

'I'd like it if we could go on seeing each other,' Jason said. His eyes, as blue as the Aegean, locked on mine. 'I don't have your way with words, but what I'm trying to say is, when we're back in London, could we be a couple?'

'Oh – Jason—' And in that instant I knew that what I felt for him was more than desire, so much more than an attraction to a good-looking guy. It was love. I was in love with him. My head reeled. How had I not known this before?

'Laurel?' Jason's gaze searched my face. 'I'm asking if you'll be my girlfriend?'

I love you, Jason Harding, I thought. Not that I was going to tell him. Not yet. It was far too soon in our fledgling relationship for that.

'I'd say that was your best idea yet,' I said.

Jason's smile was broader than I'd ever seen it. 'I'll take that as a *yes*,' he said, putting his hands on either side of my face and kissing me long and hard.

'*The Archaeologist and the Screenwriter*,' I said, breathlessly, when he lifted his head from mine. 'A good working title, I think.'

'Shot on location in Greece – and in London.' He kissed me again. 'Tomorrow we fly home, and I imagine you'll have as much to catch up on as I do.'

An image of Conor sprawled on my sofa intruded into my head.

'Er, yes,' I said. 'I have a few things I need to sort out.'

'On Monday, I have to go into the university,' Jason said. 'Will you meet me after work? We could go see a film – and spend the night together. You could stay at my place or I could come to yours, whatever you'd prefer.'

It came to me then, that if I was ever going to inform Jason that I had an ex-boyfriend ensconced in my flat, I should do it now. There again, given that as soon as I arrived home, I'd be evicting Conor, I couldn't see any reason why Jason needed to know.

'I'll come to yours,' I said, banishing all thoughts of my lying, cheating ex from my mind. 'I'd like to see where you live.'

'It's a date,' Jason said. He lifted his hand to trail a finger around the neckline of my dress. 'Do you think this wrap party will go on late?'

'Probably – but we don't have to stay late,' I said. 'Not when we have an early flight in the morning.'

'Good,' Jason said, 'because I have plans for our last night on Kyros.'

'You want to start working on our screenplay?' I said.

'I do have a scene in mind,' Jason said. 'Its location is Villa Daphne, up on the roof.'

Chapter Thirty-six

'They're going to fall in,' Harry said.

I looked towards the far side of the pool where the younger members of the film unit, Yannis, Will and Eadie among them, had congregated to do shots, perilously close to the edge. Even as we watched, there was a shriek from Eadie as Will toppled backwards into the water. He surfaced unharmed, swam to the side, and heaved himself out, only for Yannis to push him back in and the others to jump in after him.

'This must one of those wild showbiz parties I've heard so much about,' I said.

Jason and I'd arrived at the Paradise Holiday Village to find the wrap party already in full swing, a crowd of actors and crew at the poolside bar, other groups scattered among the palm trees and cacti of the well-manicured gardens. Caught up in the chatter and laughter, I didn't remain glued to Jason's side, but more than once, as I talked to a stuntwoman or he clinked a bottle of beer with Ollie, our eyes had met across the heaving throng, and I'd felt deliciously warm inside. An hour or so after arrival, seeing him sitting with Amber and Harry by the pool, I'd felt such an overwhelming longing to be near the man I loved that it couldn't be denied, and I went and joined them.

Now, Amber said, 'Looks like Drew's had enough of the party.'

The four of us watched as the director, who had spent the evening taking to Marcus and ignoring everyone else — not that they minded, I'm sure — exited the bar, actors and crew parting before him. There was a lull in conversation as he swept past, and a chorus of polite 'goodnights', but no one attempted to delay his departure, and the talk started up again as soon as he'd gone.

'It's as well he's left,' Harry said. 'I might not have been able to resist chucking him into the pool if he'd stayed much longer.'

Underneath the table, Jason's thigh pressed against mine. His mouth close to my ear, he whispered, 'Have we been at this party long enough for us to leave as well?' I became aware of an intense heat between my legs, a wildfire spreading through my body.

'I'd say this was the ideal time for us to leave,' I whispered back. To Harry and Amber, I said, 'Jason and I are heading back to the villas. See you in the morning.'

'You're going already?' Harry said.

'Oh, don't go yet,' Amber said. 'It's our last night on Kyros. We should make the most of it.'

'Stay for another drink at least,' Harry said.

Before I could think of a tactful way to tell Amber and Harry that I didn't want another drink, Marcus emerged from the crowd and sat down at our table.

'Well, we did it,' he said. 'It hasn't been the easiest of shoots, but we got through it, and having seen the raw footage, I think we can be proud of the way *Swords and Sandals* is turning out. That said, I'm very glad that I'm flying home in a couple of days. And that there's a week off before filming starts again.'

'You must be so looking forward to seeing Shannon and your girls,' I said.

'I can't wait,' Marcus said. 'I expect you're eager to get back to that actor boyfriend of yours – what's his name again? Oh, yeah, Conor.'

I heard an intake of breath from Amber. Looking at Jason, I saw his brows draw together in a frown.

'I've just had a thought,' Marcus went on, before I could say anything to head him off. 'You should have your boyfriend send me his showreel. I've one or two projects in the pipeline that he might be suitable for.'

'Ah—' Suddenly I was unable to frame a single coherent sentence. Next to me, Jason's body went rigid. He took his hand off my leg.

'Anyway, my thanks to all of you for your hard work,' Marcus said, rising to his feet. 'Safe journey tomorrow. Don't forget about Conor's showreel, Laurel.' He beamed at each of us in turn before plunging back into the milling crowd.

There was a long, heavy silence. Jason drummed his fingers on the table. Amber shifted uneasily in her seat. My face grew hot.

Harry said, 'I'm going to get another drink. Coming, Amber?' The two of them stood up and walked purposefully over to the bar.

Sick to my stomach, I turned to Jason. 'What Marcus said about Conor—'

'You said you'd split up with Conor.'

'What?' I said. 'When did I say that?'

'We were at the airport,' Jason said. 'I distinctly remember you telling me that you'd planned a foreign holiday with Conor, but you broke up.'

'That was the first time we broke up,' I said, trying unsuccessfully to remember exactly what I'd told him. 'We got back together after that. But now it's over between us.'

'Is it?' Jason said. 'What are you not telling me?'

I thought, what do I say to him? I was tempted, fleetingly, to say that Marcus had got it all wrong, that Conor was out of my life, but even as the thought entered my head, I knew I couldn't lie to him.

'I'm no longer with Conor,' I said, 'but he is currently living in my flat in Hammersmith.' My throat and chest clenched painfully.

'You live with your ex-boyfriend?' Jason said. 'Forgive me if I'm having trouble getting my head around that.'

'He wanted us to live together – we drifted into it—'

'So he's your live-in boyfriend, and you're cheating on him with me.' His mouth became a tight line.

'No,' I said. '*No.* I wanted to break up with him before I slept with you—'

Jason stood up, knocking over his chair. 'I'm going back to the villa,' he said. Turning on his heel, he strode off along the side of the pool.

I leapt to my feet. 'Jason, wait – I'll come with you.'

He came to a halt, glanced back over his shoulder, and resumed walking. I ran after him, dodging a mildly inebriated PA who tottered into my path, vaguely aware of people turning startled faces towards us as I pursued him through the hotel's reception area, finally catching up with him as he reached the car park.

A number of the unit's drivers, still on duty, were chatting by their cars, Spiros among them. Catching sight of me and Jason, he got into his vehicle and drove up to us. Jason opened a passenger door, gestured wordlessly for me to get inside, and climbed in next to me.

The car journey from Villa Daphne to the party had taken only five minutes, but the return journey seemed to take far longer. Having said a few words in Greek to Spiros, Jason lapsed into silence. I did my best to reply to our driver's cheerful remarks about the business *Swords and Sandals* had brought to his island in general and his taxi firm in particular, but I was very relieved when he dropped us at the villas and, having wished us a smooth flight home, drove off.

Still in silence, Jason stalked across the grass and unlocked the door of Villa Daphne, with me stumbling after him. Once we were inside, he flung himself down in a chair. I shut the door, and perched opposite him.

In a voice devoid of any warmth, he said. 'I can't do this, Laurel – I've been here before. I can't be with a woman who's involved with another man.'

'I'm not,' I said. 'I know how it looks, but Conor and I are over.'

'I want to believe you,' Jason said. 'I'm trying to understand.' He raked his hand through his sun-bleached hair. 'I don't think we should have this conversation tonight. We should go to bed.'

'Do you want to sleep on the roof?' I said.

'You sleep up there if you want,' Jason said. 'I'll sleep in my room. Alone.'

'Oh—' A leaden weight settled in my chest. 'Jason, I'm not lying to you – I can explain—'

'Not now, Laurel,' Jason said. 'I need you to give me some space.'

'Jason, please—'

His eyes met mine, hard and unflinching.

Then he turned away, went into his bedroom, and closed the door.

Chapter Thirty-seven

When I woke up the following morning, I reached for Jason, only to find his side of the bed empty. For a moment, I couldn't think why he wasn't there. Then the events of the previous night came flooding back. Marcus's ill-timed remarks at the party. The cold anger in Jason's eyes.

I have to talk to him, I thought. I have to put things right between us.

My temples were throbbing with the beginnings of a headache, but I made myself get out of bed – not that I had any choice, with a plane to catch. Shuffling into the bathroom, the mirror showed me the reflection of a girl with a pale face and dark circles under her eyes. With a grimace, I stripped off my pyjamas, climbed into the shower, and turned it on full.

Once I'd dressed and put on a dash of mascara, I felt a little more like myself. I stashed last night's clothes and my headband in my suitcase, had one final look around the room to check I hadn't left anything, and wheeled my suitcase into the living area. Jason's door was still firmly shut, but I could hear him moving around inside his room. I thought, should I go to him now and ask – beg – him to let me explain about Conor? While I was still standing there in an agony of indecision, the door opened and Jason came out, carrying his rucksack and holdall. The expression on his face was unreadable.

'Shall we wait for our car outside?' he said. Without waiting for my answer, he went to the front door and unlocked it, holding it open for me to wheel my suitcases on to the terrace, following me out, and locking the door behind us.

Outside, the early morning air was cool and clear, a faint breeze stirring the surface of the swimming pool. Jason dumped his rucksack and holdall on the ground and sat on a sun lounger. I took the lounger next to his. Neither of us spoke. I tried to find the words to tell him that I knew I'd messed up and that I was sorry, but Calliope had deserted me.

'I'm going to take a last look at the view,' I said, when the silence became intolerable. Getting to my feet, I walked slowly across the grass to the gazebo that had been my writing room, and stood looking out over the sea, as I had done so many times before. The blue Aegean and the rugged coastline in the pale early morning sunlight was unbearably beautiful.

Someone tapped my shoulder, I swung around, hoping it was Jason, but it was Amber who met my gaze.

'The car's here,' she said.

'Already?' Turning away from the sea, I saw Jason and Harry carrying suitcases from the terrace to the dirt track where a people carrier and a car were parked next to each other. As I watched, Eadie emerged from the back of the smaller vehicle.

I said, 'Last night, Jason and I had a blazing row – just so you know.'

'Oh, Laurel –. Are you two still together?'

'I don't know.' Tears stung my eyes. I dashed them away. 'Anyway, we have to go.'

Amber's face creased with concern, but she nodded, and started off across the grass. My throat was tight, and my limbs felt heavy, but I made myself put one foot in front of the other and follow her over to the others, who were standing by the cars, luggage at their feet.

'Morning, Laurel,' Eadie said, sounding far chirpier than anyone who'd jumped fully dressed into a swimming pool only a few hours before had a right to sound. 'Can I have your keys?'

'Keys?' I stared at her blankly.

'The keys to your villa. I have to return them.'

'Oh – yes, of course,' I said, looking round for my bag. Focus, Laurel, I told myself.

'Here,' Amber said, handing my bag to me. Hastily, I found my set of keys to Villa Daphne and passed them to Eadie. My sojourn in Paradise was over.

There followed a few minutes of mild chaos while Eadie, in full production assistant mode, checked everyone had their passports and boarding passes and wished us a smooth flight, before getting into the smaller car, which drove off. Our driver loaded our cases into the people carrier. Amber and Harry climbed in and I followed them, taking the seat behind them, while Jason was the last to climb on board. He hesitated by the open door, and my stomach knotted as I thought he was going to take the seat next to the driver, but instead he sat down next to me. I twisted around in my seat to face him, willing him to look at me, but his gaze remained fixed on the seat in front of him and the back of Harry's head.

A pall of misery settled around me, and as the people carrier lurched along the track and on to the coastal road, I turned my face to the window. Sea and mountains, white houses and olive groves, passed by me in a blur.

We arrived at Kyros Airport without Jason and me having exchanged one word, and in the hustle of dropping off our cases and going through security, there was no opportunity for the sort of conversation I needed to have with him. In the departure lounge – where we met up with Will, and Ella Anderson and her assistant, who were all on the same flight to Athens – I somehow made myself sit on a hard plastic chair, replying more or less intelligibly when any of the others spoke to me, buffeted by a cacophony of airport announcements, until my face began to ache with the effort of not screaming aloud. Jason looked at me just once, unsmiling, and instantly looked away.

On the plane, I found myself sitting next to two strangers, a middle-aged couple, while Jason was seated across the aisle and a row ahead – too far away to speak, even if he hadn't immediately buried his head in a book. Fortunately, for I'd exhausted my reserves of small talk at the airport, the couple next to me had also armed themselves with paperbacks for the journey. The wife did ask me in an undertone if I'd recognised the extraordinarily handsome man sitting towards the rear of the aircraft, and when I shook my head, excitedly informed me that he was soap star Harry Vincent, but then returned her attention to her novel.

The plane taxied down the runway, gathered speed, and rose steeply into the air. I had one last glimpse of jagged mountains and blue sea, before we flew up through a bank of white cloud, and Kyros, the Greek island paradise where I'd fallen in love with Jason Harding, was lost to my sight.

Chapter Thirty-eight

'I believe we have adjacent seats on this flight,' Jason said. It was the first time he'd spoken to me since we'd left Kyros. 'Would you prefer the seat by the window? I don't care where I sit.'

I remembered him offering me the window seat on our outward journey from England to Greece, and how he'd smiled at my excitement that day, and misery surged up inside me. Fighting back tears, I slid across the row of seats. Jason took the seat next to me and fastened his seat belt. I took several deep breaths and, having got myself more or less under control, fastened mine. All around us, passengers were settling into their seats, but the plane wasn't full, and the seat next to Jason remained empty.

Not long afterwards, I became aware that the plane was moving, almost imperceptibly at first, accelerating along the runway, and climbing into the air. In three and a half hours, I would be back in London.

At Athens airport, we'd had a stopover of an hour before our connecting flight, but what with getting from Arrivals to Departures, saying goodbye to Ella and her assistant who were on a different flight to London, and queuing with Amber, Harry, and Will in a café for a belated first meal of the day, Jason and I'd not had a moment alone. I'd not felt like eating, but I'd forced down a few bites of a burger, and sipped a coffee, while Jason read a Greek newspaper, and Amber cast anxious glances at both of us. I was very glad when our flight was called, and we'd had to join the scramble for places in the queue to board the place, Amber and Harry being ushered past us into First Class, and Will sitting on his own several rows away ahead of us. It hadn't occurred to me to ask where Jason was sitting on this last leg of our journey to London. I'd had other things on my mind. Like trying to write the dialogue that would put right the mess I'd made of my life.

Now, glancing surreptitiously at Jason, I saw that he had his paperback open on his lap. I thought, I can't sit next to him for three and a half hours, not knowing what's going on with us – if there is still an us – while he reads a book.

'Jason,' I said, 'we have to talk.'

'I'm not sure that we do,' Jason said, 'but in any case, an aircraft is not the place.'

'Please, Jason,' I said, my voice catching in my throat. 'If you'd just give me a chance to explain.'

With a sigh, Jason closed his book. 'You lied to me, Laurel, if only by omission. You let me think you were single, but you're in a relationship with another man.'

'I no longer have any feelings for Conor,' I said. 'We're over.'

'In your head maybe,' Jason said.

'I tried to tell him,' I said. 'I tried to phone him, but I couldn't get hold of him. I decided to wait until I got back to London and tell him to his face—' At the time this had made perfect sense to me, but now it sounded a very lame an excuse. 'If I could rewrite the story of my time in Greece, I'd do things differently.'

Whatever reply Jason might have made to me was lost as a disembodied voice filled the cabin: 'This is the captain speaking. We are now entering a zone of turbulence. Please will all passengers return to their seas and fasten their seat belts. Thank you for your cooperation.' As the announcement was repeated in Greek, two flight attendants moved rapidly along the aisle, checking that the instructions were obeyed. Above our heads, the fasten-seat-belts sign glowed red. Suddenly, my mouth felt dry and my heart began thumping in my chest. I hadn't undone my seat belt since getting on the plane, but now I tightened it.

'What do you think's happening?' I said to Jason.

'Didn't you hear?' Jason said. 'We're going through some turbulence.' As he spoke, the plane seemed to lurch and bump – like a car going over a rough road surface – and then it dropped through the air. In the seats behind me, a woman screamed. Ahead, towards the front of the plane, a baby let out a high-pitched wail. Then there was another series of jolts. I gripped my seat's armrests and shut my eyes. Then I felt Jason take hold of my hand.

'Look at me, Laurel,' he said.

I opened my eyes. His face was only inches from mine. The plane bucked and juddered.

'This is nothing to worry about,' Jason said. 'It happens on a lot of flights. It's an inconvenience, nothing more.' He fell silent, but continued looking directly into my eyes, holding my hand in his. I sat trembling, feeling the warmth of his breath on my cheek, bracing myself for the next jolt from the plane, not entirely convinced that we weren't about to plummet from the sky, willing Jason to still want me, for me to have a future that included him. I wanted to tell him that I loved him before it was too late.

'We're through it,' Jason said.

I realised it had been some minutes since I'd felt any movement from the plane – and that the fasten-seat-belts sign had gone out. I began to breathe more easily. Muted conversation drifted through the cabin. There was a sudden burst of laughter from the woman in the seat behind me. A disembodied voice announced that passengers were now free to move about the cabin.

I said, 'I don't want to lose you, Jason.'

'You're not free to be with me,' Jason said. He let go of my hand.

'I am – I will be—' My eyes brimmed and a tear ran down my face. What could I say to make him believe me?

'You need to sort your life out, Laurel,' Jason said. Opening his book, he resumed reading.

I wiped my face with my hands, and stared out of the window at the clouds.

Chapter Thirty-nine

With just the slightest of judders, the plane landed, decelerating along the runway, crawling over an expanse of tarmac, and coming to a halt within sight of the arrivals building. The passengers began lining up in the aisle, ready to disembark.

I was back in England. Soon, I'd be walking through the door of my flat where Conor would be waiting. Much as I dreaded seeing him again, knowing I was going to cause him pain, I longed to get it over with.

Jason, who, after our one brief conversation hadn't spoken to me for the rest of the flight, stood up and retrieved his rucksack from the overhead locker.

'Jason,' I said. 'Please – listen – hear me out. We need to talk—'

He gave a long, drawn-out sigh. In a toneless voice,' he said, 'I meant what I said, Laurel. You need to sort your life out. Do that – and then we'll talk.'

The tightness in my throat began to ease.

'I – I'll call you – after—' I said. The words I hadn't spoken, that I'd call him after I'd written Conor out of my life, hung in the air between us. For an instant, Jason's eyes met mine, and he gave a brief nod of his head before stepping into the aisle, just as the queue began to move towards the exit at the front of the plane.

Feeling considerably less wretched than I had all day, I edged into the queue behind Jason and followed him out of the aircraft, and along the passenger bridge connecting the plane to the arrivals gate. Here, we met up with Amber, Harry, and Will – Harry greeting us with a heartiness that made me strongly suspect that my and Jason's relationship status had been the subject of some discussion between him and Amber during the flight. As a group we made our way through passport control and into the baggage collection hall, where the men gallantly joined the crush of passengers jostling to snatch their suitcases from the conveyor belt, while Amber and I stood a short distance away.

'You and Jason . . .?' she said to me in an undertone.

'I think there's still a chance for us,' I said, desperately hoping I was right.

Amber hesitated, and then she said, 'If you don't mind me asking, what did you tell him about Conor?'

'The truth,' I said.

'He knows Conor's living in your flat? And he's OK with that?'

'Not exactly,' I admitted. 'But as I'm going straight home to inform Conor that he needs to move out sharpish, it won't be a problem for much longer.'

Amber bit her bottom lip. 'I was going with Harry to his place,' she said, 'but I could come back with you – I could lurk in my bedroom while you talk to Conor – if you'd like some moral support.'

'Thanks, but I've got this.' Before I could remind her that this wasn't the first time I'd broken up with Conor, the guys appeared, Jason and Will dragging their luggage, followed by Harry pushing a trolley loaded with more.

'That's all of them,' Harry said. 'Let's get out of here.' He put on a pair of sunglasses and a baseball hat, and he and Amber, and Will started towards customs and the exit.

Jason passed me one of my cases, I went to take the other, but he held on to it. 'I'll help you with this,' he said, his voice brusque. 'It's heavy.'

I ventured a smile, but he was already heading after the others. Seizing my smaller suitcase, I hastened to join them.

The five of us walked through customs, and out into the brightly lit arrivals hall, where a small crowd – many of them cab drivers holding up signs inscribed with the names of the people they were meeting – waited to welcome newly disembarked travellers. Will spotted his driver immediately, and after a quick round of goodbyes and assurances that he'd see Harry and Amber at the studios, vanished into the crowd.

'There's our guy, Amber,' Harry said, gesturing towards a man in a suit and tie, bearing a card with the words 'Vincent and Wallace' scrawled on it in large black capitals.

'And there's mine,' Jason said.

I scanned the crowd for a sign saying 'Martin', my gaze passing over the cab drivers, what appeared to be three generations of a family excitedly greeting grey-haired elders, and a middle-aged couple hugging a twenty-something backpacker. Then I saw a dark-haired man, a shockingly familiar figure, push to the front of the crowd. In the same instant, he saw me, smiled in recognition, and headed straight towards me.

Conor.

The blood began pounding in my head.

'Hey, babe,' he said.

My stomach twisted painfully. I wasn't ready for this. I couldn't deal with him now. Not here in the airport, with Jason standing right by me.

'Why – What are you doing here?' I said.

'I thought I'd surprise you.' To my horror, he seized hold of me, clasping me so tightly that I could hardly breathe, and plastered his mouth on mine. My body went rigid, my mouth clamped shut against his wet, probing tongue. When he let me go, I jerked away from him. It was all I could do not to wipe my mouth with my hand.

I spun around towards Jason. His face was an unreadable mask. I heard Conor greet Amber and Harry, and their stilted replies. Then he was beside me, draping the dead weight of his arm around my shoulders before I could move out of his reach.

'Hi there,' he said to Jason. 'I'm Conor, Laurel's boyfriend.'

'I know,' Jason said. 'We've met.'

'Oh, yeah,' Conor said. 'I remember you now. You came over to our place to work on the *Swords and Sandals*' script.'

'I did,' Jason said. His eyes locked on mine. 'And now it's finished. Goodbye, Laurel.'

What? I stared at him. No, I thought. *No*. He can't be telling me we're over. That isn't what he's saying.

Stunned, I watched as Jason hugged Amber, shook hands with Harry, and in a scene shot in slow motion, walked away from me. Wanting to go after him, knowing that I had to deal with Conor, wracked by shock, I saw Jason go up to his driver, and the two of them head off in the direction of the car park.

'A man of few words,' Conor said. 'I seem to remember that about him.' He removed his arm from my shoulder. 'Let's head on home. I came by tube, but I assume you get a chauffeur now that you've hit the big time?' His laughter at his own joke made me wince.

'Yes, I have a car,' I said, wearily. 'Somewhere.' I looked in vain for my driver, but Conor spotted him before I did.

'You coming with us, Amber?' he said.

'No, I'm going to Harry's,' Amber said.

Conor grinned. 'Ah-ha. I get it.'

Ignoring him, Amber hugged me, murmuring in my ear, 'Good luck. Call me if you need me.'

Conor was already striding towards the driver, raising a hand to catch his attention. Taking hold of my suitcases, I stumbled after him.

Chapter Forty

The first thing I saw when I opened the door of the living room was a vase containing a bunch of pink roses.

'Those are for you,' Conor said. 'To welcome you home.'

Driving home from the airport, with Conor talking incessantly about his new play, assuring me I was going to love it, I'd shrunk into the corner of the car, horribly aware of what lay ahead when we reached my flat. Now, I breathed in the heavy cloying scent of the roses, and it turned my stomach. He'd never bought me flowers before. Of all the times for him to make a romantic gesture, why, oh why, did he have to do it now?

'I don't know what to say,' I said.

Conor grinned, and sat down on the sofa, stretching his legs out in front of him, and linking his hands behind his head.

I walked over to the window and looked out at the street. This was always going to be hard, I thought, there's no point in dragging it out any longer. My stomach churning, I turned around to face him.

He said, 'I guess Amber will be moving out of here, now that she's hooked up with a movie star?'

'Er, yes.' The blood was pounding in my head.

'Do you know when? It'd be good to have an idea of how soon we'll have this place to ourselves.'

'We won't.' To my dismay, it came out much harsher than I intended. 'I – I'm sorry, Conor, but that isn't going to happen.'

Conor frowned. 'We talked about this before you went to

Greece,' he said. 'Amber moving out. You and me living here. The two of us.'

'Yes, we did,' I said, 'but nothing was decided.' I took a deep breath and squared my shoulders. 'There's no easy way to say this, so I'm going to come straight out with it. I did a lot of thinking while I was away, and I know now that I don't want to live with you.'

Conor's eyes widened. Then he shook his head. 'You don't mean that.'

'I do,' I said. 'I'm not in love with you, Conor. I don't want to be with you. I'm sorry, really I am, but you and I are over.'

'You're *breaking up* with me?' He sounded incredulous.

'I'm so sorry—'

'You swan off on location, leaving me here thinking that we're *living together*, and then you come back and tell me that we're *finished*.' He sprang to his feet, and paced back and forth, coming to a halt in front of me. 'Have you been with another guy? You have, haven't you?'

There was, I thought, no sense in denying it. That wouldn't make him feel any better.

'I never meant for it to happen,' I said. 'I never meant to hurt you.' Even as I spoke, I winced at the hideous clichés. In a moment, I'd be telling him that I hoped we could still be friends.

'Who is it?' Conor's eyes narrowed. 'Is it Jason?'

Jason. Who had said goodbye to me at the airport and walked away. My chest constricted. I wasn't about to start discussing Jason with Conor.

'You don't need to know,' I said.

'It's Jason,' Conor said, with cold certainty.

'It doesn't make any difference who it is,' I said. 'I realised that my feelings for you had changed — that you and I were over — before anything happened between me and him.'

'Is that right?' Conor said. 'You might have thought to mention it to *me*.'

'I tried—' I bit back the urge to remind him that he was the one who'd cut off all communication between us.

Conor's mouth curled in a sneer. 'You've been stringing me along the whole time you were in Greece.'

'No, it wasn't like that,' I said, stung by the contempt in his voice.

'You are a piece of work, you know that, right?' he snarled. 'Was Jason the only man you've slept with while you've been with me? What else haven't you told me?'

This from a man who for almost a year had managed to avoid mentioning that he'd slept with my flatmate. Anger flared up inside me.

'You've a nerve,' I said, 'when *you're* the one who'd been living a lie for months.'

'What the hell are you talking about?'

'Amber told me,' I said, my voice rising. 'I *know*, Conor, so don't try and deny it.'

Conor's body went rigid. '*Amber*. But how did she know? She's never even met Ginny—'

'Who?' I said. 'I was talking about you and Amber . . .'

He didn't answer. Suddenly, he couldn't meet my eyes.

'Conor,' I said, 'who is Ginny?'

'She—I—'

'I see,' I said. *Ginny*. A scene began playing in my head, the lighting painfully bright . . .

'Jenny,' he groaned. 'Oh, Jenny.'

I lay beside him, telling myself I'd misheard him, that his calling out another girl's name meant nothing . . .

What I'd *heard* was Jenny. What he'd *said* was Ginny. He'd called *me* by *her* name.

'How long has it been going on?' I demanded. 'Weeks? Months?'

'I don't know. Not exactly.' Abruptly, as though his legs had given way beneath him, he slumped down on the sofa. 'Since March, I think. I was in rehearsal for *Sometime, Never.*'

I thought of all the times he'd told me rehearsals had overrun or he'd come back in the early hours after a night out – supposedly with other members of the cast. What an idiot I'd been.

'She wasn't in the play,' Conor said. 'I met her in a bar . . .'

I thought, her and how many others?

'Laurel?' Conor said. 'I'm explaining to you what happened. You're not listening.'

He was explaining months of cheating on me. The man was unbelievable.

'I want you out of my flat,' I said.

'What?'

'You can't stay here tonight,' I said. 'You must see that. Pack up your flippin' boxes and leave.'

'Oh, come *on*, Laurel. Be reasonable.'

'Didn't you hear what I said?' I crossed the room and opened the door. 'You need to leave. Now.'

'You're throwing me out? Where am I supposed to go?'

'How about Ginny's place?

He flinched at that.

'Just go, Conor,' I said.

For a long moment, he regarded me in silence and then he said, 'We're not coming back from this, are we?'

'Not this time,' I said.

Chapter Forty-one

Conor appeared in the doorway to the living room, holding a suitcase.

'I think I've got everything,' he said.

I got up off the chair where I'd sat while he'd carried his belongings out to his car, and followed him down the stairs to the front door, which he'd left open. He stepped outside.

'I don't expect we'll see each other again,' he said.

'No,' I said.

'You've got my number if you need to contact me.'

I won't, I thought. I resisted the urge to tell him that, and nodded my head. The stiff politeness with which we were conducting this conversation was surreal, but it was preferable to a shouting match.

'I'll go, then,' he said.

He turned away. I shut the front door. He was gone.

All at once, I was trembling all over. I stumbled to the stairs and sank down on the bottom step. So much time I'd wasted feeling guilty about Conor, who even while he was sharing my home, was playing around. He'd betrayed me again and again, and I'd forgiven him, because I'd loved him, and thought he loved me, but he didn't know the meaning of the word. How could I have been so stupid? And why, oh why, had I let a misplaced sense of guilt stop me breaking up with him while I was in Greece?

Jason. The scene at the airport replayed in my head. Jason's expressionless face. The finality with which he'd said goodbye. Jason walking away from me without a backward glance.

No, I thought, Jason and I can't end this way. I can still put things right between us.

I stood up, and on trembling legs walked up the stairs, and back into the living room, where I was immediately assailed by the sickly scent of the roses – they were, I noticed, already wilting. Picking up my mobile, I retreated to my bedroom, pausing on the threshold when it occurred to me to wonder if Conor had brought Ginny here while I was away, if he'd slept with her in my bed. I told myself not even Conor would sink as low as that. I looked around the room. It was as I'd left it, except that Conor's possessions were no longer scattered on every surface. He was my past. I wasn't going to let him wreck my future.

Clutching my phone, I sat down at my writing desk. I didn't have a script for this. I couldn't rewrite the dialogue until it sounded right. All I could do was speak from my heart.

I called Jason's number. The phone rang and rang, but just when I thought he wasn't going to take the call, he answered:

'Laurel. What do you want?'

'I – I had to speak to you,' I stuttered.

'Are you home?'

'I—Yes, I'm in my flat.'

'Is Conor with you?'

'What?' How could he think that? 'No. I told him to go – and he went. It's like I told you, Conor and I are over.'

'After seeing the two of you together at the airport, I find that hard to believe.'

My stomach twisted painfully into a knot. 'I know how that must have looked to you, but I'd no idea he was going to turn up like that. When I saw him, I didn't know what to do, I couldn't think—'

'You cheated on him with me,' Jason said. 'How could I ever trust you when I know that you cheated on your boyfriend?'

'No, that's not what happened,' I said. 'I should have told you about Conor, but—'

'Letting myself become involved with you while we were in Greece was a mistake.'

'Don't say that. What you and I had in Greece was good. We can have that again.'

'No, we can't.' Jason's voice was harsh now. 'Greece – *us* – wasn't real. It was a fantasy – like the films that play in your head. And now it's over.'

'We can get through this.' My breath was coming in short, sharp gasps. 'We have to talk—'

'I've nothing more to say to you. I'm going to ring off now.'

'Jason – please – don't do this—'

'Goodbye, Laurel,' Jason said, and ended the call.

I stared at my phone. He didn't want me. I loved him, and for three sunlit weeks on a Greek island, he'd been mine, but I'd lost him.

That was when I slumped forward on to my desk, burying my head in my hands, my shoulders heaving as I wept.

Chapter Forty-two

'I still think it's probable there was at least one Mycenaean settlement on Kyros,' Jason said. 'I was just looking in the wrong places.' He drained the last of his wine.

'You could go back to the island another time and search again,' Emily said.

'I can't see myself getting funding for a full survey based on a gut feeling.'

'It's not only that,' Emily said. 'We've both seen the Kyros fragment. Archaeologists have made discoveries on the basis of an ancient text before now.'

'A few words on a scrap of papyrus is hardly the same as the *Iliad*,' Jason said. He shrugged his shoulders. 'Besides, I've more than enough work to do here in London.' His phone, which he'd placed beside his plate on Emily's dining table, began vibrating, but he ignored it.

'Your phone's buzzing again,' Emily said, not even bothering to pretend she wasn't looking at the caller ID. 'That's the second time she's called you this evening.'

Jason picked up his mobile and switched it off.

Emily rested her elbows on the table and steepled her fingers. 'So, you've co-written a film script with her, taught her Archaeology 101, lived under the same roof as her on a Greek island, and now you won't answer your phone when she calls?' Her eyes narrowed. 'Did something happen between you and Laurel Martin while you were in Greece?'

Laurel. The sight of her wading out of the sea, her smile as he leant in to kiss her, the scent of her hair, the softness of her body lying next to his . . .

Jason sighed. He hadn't meant to talk about Laurel this evening, but somehow he hadn't been able to stop himself – it hurt to mention her name, but she was so much a part of everything he'd done in Greece. And now that Emily had scented the possibility of a romantic liaison between the two of them, he knew she wouldn't leave it alone. Especially as Philip wasn't there to distract her.

'Laurel and I became close when we were on Kyros,' he said. 'I hoped we'd carry on seeing each other when we got back to London, but it didn't work out.'

'Are you going to tell me why?' Emily said.

Laurel and her boyfriend together at the airport, his hands all over her as they kissed.

'No,' Jason said, his voice sharper than intended. 'That's between me and her.' He raked his hand through his hair. 'Sorry, Emily, I didn't mean to snap.'

Laurel sitting next to him on the plane, her eyes wide with fear. His overwhelming need to protect her. His longing to put his arms around her and hold her close.

I'll never hold her again, Jason thought, and felt as if he'd been punched in the stomach.

What you and I had in Greece was good.

I can't trust her. I have to get her out of my head.

'Jason?' Emily said, her eyes full of concern. 'Are you OK?'

'I'm tired, that's all,' Jason said. Hardly surprising, he thought, as I've barely slept in four days. 'I should head home. I've an early start in the morning.' He pushed back his chair. 'Thanks for dinner, Emily. You and Philip will have to come to mine once he's back from the Sicily excavation.'

They went out into the hall, and said their goodnights, and Jason walked home through the dark empty streets.

Back at his flat, he went straight to bed, as exhausted as if he'd

278

spent all day digging under a hot Mediterranean sun, only to lie awake, Laurel hovering at the edge of his mind, like a tune played on a flute by an unseen musician.

A gap in the curtains showed him it was light outside long before he fell asleep.

Amber's voice came to me from my bedroom doorway. 'You've had a week of wallowing,' she said. 'That's long enough. I'm staging an intervention.'

I twisted around in my chair to face her. 'It's been five days. And I'm not wallowing. I'm working on a pitch.'

'That looks like an empty screen to me,' Amber said, coming to stand beside my writing desk.

I shut my laptop. 'It's not going too well. I can't seem to focus.'

'You can't write because you're thinking about Jason,' Amber said, putting her hands on her hips. 'This may be a stupid question, but have you tried calling him again?'

'Of course I have,' I said. I'd lost count of the number of times I'd tried to contact Jason. 'He rejects my calls. He doesn't reply to my messages—' My words stuck in my throat.

'Are you in love with him?' Amber said.

To my dismay, my eyes filled with tears. I blinked them away. If I let myself cry again, I wasn't sure I'd be able to stop.

'Yes, I love him,' I said, my voice no more than a whisper. 'But he doesn't want me.'

'For goodness' sake, Laurel,' Amber said. 'You need to fix this.'

'I can't,' I said. 'I only wish I could, but our story is over.'

Amber rolled her eyes. 'If it was a screenplay, would you end it this way?'

'N–no,' I said.

'Then rewrite it.'

'And how am I going to do that,' I said. 'When Jason won't answer his phone?'

'For a screenwriter,' Amber said, 'you really are lacking in imagination. Go and see him. Sit on his doorstep if you have to. That way he has to talk to you—'

The doorbell rang, making us both jump.

'That'll be Harry,' Amber said. 'I'm staying at his place this week-end, and going straight from there to the studios on Monday.'

'Off you go, then,' I said. I made myself smile at her. 'Good luck with *Swords and Sandals* next week.'

'I just hope we can get through a day's filming without Drew having a strop,' Amber said. She put her hand on my arm. 'Don't give up on love, Laurel. Go and find Jason. Fight for him the way Lysander fought for Chloe.'

'Chloe and Lysander didn't—' I began, but she was already heading out of the room. I heard her running down the stairs. The front door opened and shut.

Jason. My heart ached for him. He was so angry with me. Should I call him one more time? I couldn't keep hounding him. *Go and see him.* Could I – should I – do that? I loved him, but that didn't mean I got to be with him. Chloe and Lysander hadn't stayed together. I'd hurt him very badly . . .

Cut! Cut! Cut!

I had to go to him. I'd no idea where he lived, but I knew where he worked.

If there was a chance of my writing a happy-ever-after for me and Jason, I had to try.

He'll be there, I told myself, as I stepped out of the lift. He has to be.

On shaking legs, I walked along the corridor to Jason's office and knocked on the door. There was no answer. I knocked again. Silence. I tried the handle, but the door was locked. My heart sank. Having first sought out Jason in the lecture theatres on the ground floor of the Humanities building and found them deserted, I'd gone up to the Archaeology department. Now, I knew of no place else to look for him. Unless . . . My mind went back to the other times I'd come to Aldgate . . . and Jason's friend who thought he worked too hard.

I walked further along the corridor, checking the nameplates on the doors, halting by the one that read *Dr Emily Page*. Please let her be in, I thought. My pulse racing, I raised my hand and knocked.

A female voice called, 'Come in.' A wave of relief broke over me. I opened the door and went inside.

Emily Page's office was very like Jason's, lined with bookshelves, furnished with a desk and chairs, but with plants and photos on the desk and windowsill. Emily herself was sitting at her desk, staring at me over an open laptop.

'Hello, Emily,' I said, not entirely comfortable with the intensity of her scrutiny. 'I don't know if you remember me? Jason Harding introduced us.'

'Laurel Martin,' Emily said. 'You were in Greece with Jason. He told me.'

I wondered what exactly Jason had told her about our time in Greece. The tone of her voice wasn't obviously *un*friendly, but it wasn't particularly friendly either.

'I was hoping you'd know where I might find him,' I said. 'I tried the lecture theatres – and his office, of course.'

'He isn't on campus today,' Emily said.

'D–do you know when he'll be back?'

'Not until the new university term starts in October.'

'Oh, no . . .' My legs felt so weak that I clutched at the edge of Emily's desk to steady myself. Although I suspected I knew the answer, I said, 'I really need to see him. Would you be able to give me his address?'

'I'm afraid I can't give out personal information about my colleagues,' Emily said.

'No, of course not,' I said. 'I wouldn't have asked – but Jason won't take my calls – I may never see him again, and I can't bear it – I don't know what else I can do—' My voice became a sob. My vision blurred, and I stumbled to the door.

'Laurel, wait,' Emily said. 'Please.'

I turned around. To my mortification, tears were running

down my face. Emily jumped up from her desk, guided me to a chair, and sat down beside me.

'I-I'm s-sorry,' I said, rummaging in my bag for a tissue.

Emily waited until I'd got a hold of myself, and then she said, 'I saw Jason a couple of nights ago. He didn't go into detail about what happened between you, but I know that you and he were together in Greece, and now you're not, and he's deeply unhappy. I hope the two of you can work things out, I really do.'

'Will you tell him I came looking for him?' I said.

'I will,' Emily said.

'Thank you, Emily.' Recalling that I'd interrupted her working day, I stood up. 'I should let you get on. I've taken up enough of your time.'

'You're welcome,' Emily said. Going back to her desk and resuming her seat, she added, 'When I saw Jason the other night, he mentioned that while you were in Athens, you'd enjoyed visiting archaeological sites together.'

'Yes, I – we – did,' I said, bemused.

'There's an excavation taking place near Piccadilly Circus right now,' Emily went on. 'Some builders digging the foundations for a new office block uncovered the ruins of a Roman building, and it's currently being investigated by a team of archaeologists from Aldgate University. Anyone who happened to be in that part of London could come across it.'

'Oh?' I said. '*Oh*. Thank you, Emily.'

Chapter Forty-three

I stood on the pavement, the midday sun beating down on my head. A few streets away, in Piccadilly Circus, a bronze winged archer, the Greek god of love and desire, stood silhouetted against a summer sky. If you can spare an arrow, Eros, I thought, I could really do with your help right now.

Opposite me, on the other side of the road, was the construction site – the excavation – a gaping hole between two narrow buildings on either side. Hoardings shielded it from view, but there was a gap through which I could see a guy – one of Jason's fellow archaeologists, I supposed – walking to and fro, a phone pressed to his ear. As I watched, he ended his call, and vanished behind the hoarding. The thought came to me that accosting Jason here in his own world might make him even angrier with me than he was already, but I'd come too far to give up now. My heart hammering in my chest, I crossed over the road. Ignoring a sign proclaiming 'Danger Do Not Enter', I stepped through the gap in the hoardings, and cast my gaze over the dig, searching for the man I loved.

In front of me, I saw a stretch of flat, hard-packed earth, wide enough to accommodate the large white tent that stood in one corner. Beyond the tent, a wooden ramp zigzagged down a steep slope, shored up with metal, to an area of uneven ground, several metres below street level, containing piles of rock, gaping pits, and the remains of what to me looked very much like the broken columns and tumbled walls I'd seen in the Agora in Athens. All over the site, archaeologists wearing bright yellow hard hats knelt scraping at the ground with trowels, taking photographs, sifting earth in large round sieves, or sitting on upturned buckets and writing in notebooks, but I couldn't see Jason. I walked further into the site, pausing at the top of the ramp.

A male voice shouted, 'Hold it right there!'

Spinning around, I saw two men had come out of the tent, and were now striding towards me. One was the archaeologist who I'd seen talking on the phone. The other, a hard hat on his head, his clothes covered in dust, was Jason. My stomach clenched into a knot.

'You can't be here,' the other archaeologist said, as the two of them planted themselves in front of me. 'Didn't you see the sign?'

Jason's blue eyes met mine. I thought, if this was a movie, I'd rush into his arms. Instead, I stayed where I was and looked steadily back at him.

'This dig is closed to the public,' the other guy said.

His gaze still on my face, Jason said, 'It's all right, Ravi, I know her. I'll take it from here.'

Ravi shrugged. 'I'll leave you to it, then.' With a quizzical glance in my direction, he went back inside the tent.

Jason continued to gaze at me in silence, breathing hard, his chest visibly rising and falling. Please, *please,* say something, I thought. Even if it's to tell me to go away.

A winged archer fits an arrow to his bow and lets fire . . .

'I won't let you walk out on me without fighting for what we have,' I said. 'I can't let you give up on us.' Without conscious thought, I placed my hand on my heart.

A female voice said, 'Dr Harding?' Unnoticed by either me or Jason until she spoke, a girl of about twenty, with large round glasses and long blond hair under her hard hat, was standing on the ramp, a few feet below us. Jason tore his gaze away from me.

'Yes, Hannah, what is it?' he said, his voice hoarse.

'I think I've found something,' she said.

'Give me a minute, and I'll come and take a look,' Jason said.

The girl scurried off down the ramp to be met at the bottom by five more archaeologists of around her age.

'My students.' Jason gestured vaguely towards the four boys and two girls who were now heading off towards the far side of the site. 'I should go and see what they've turned up.' He cleared his throat. 'Laurel . . . would you like to take a look at the excavations?'

For a moment all I did was gape at him. Whatever he was thinking or feeling about me right now, he wasn't sending me away.

'I–I'd like that very much,' I said.

'Wait here a sec . . .' He disappeared inside the tent, re-emerging with a hard hat which he gave to me. 'Watch your step,' he said, glancing at my feet. 'Those shoes don't pass my risk assessment for this dig.'

Placing the hat on my head, my legs feeling decidedly weak, I walked down the ramp at his side.

'The deeper we dig,' he said, coming to a halt when we reached the bottom of the ramp, 'the further back we go in time. This level is nearly two thousand years old.'

My gaze roamed over the stumps of columns and a pile of dull red tiles, and came to rest on Jason's face. What, I thought, is going on in his head?

To break the silence, I said, 'What was this building?'

'We're not sure yet,' Jason said, 'but my gut feeling is that it was a *hospitium*, a Roman inn, rather like a motel—' He broke off. 'I have to go and supervise those students of mine. Their enthusiasm for field work isn't yet matched by their skill.'

We made our way through the excavation – several of the archaeologists on the site paused in their digging, scraping, and examination of piles of rock to look at us curiously as we passed – Jason pointing out the ruins of a bath house, and the remains of a mosaic floor. I walked beside him, my heart fluttering and my head all over the place. If he's still angry with me, I thought, surely he wouldn't be giving me this guided tour?

'So what have we got?' Jason said, as we reached Hannah and

the other students who were gathered in a long shallow trench of bare earth. 'Show me, please.'

Kneeling on the ground, Hannah indicated the position of what she'd found. 'I stopped digging as soon as I hit metal.'

Jason crouched beside her. 'I see it,' he said. 'May I have your trowel?' She passed it to him, and he began scraping away at the earth surrounding the buried artefact. From where I was standing, I still couldn't make out what it was, but the students were all craning forward, excitement sparking between them like electricity. I realised I was holding my breath. This, I thought, is what it was like for Chloe when she discovered Lysander's sword.

After about five minutes, Jason sat back on his heels. 'There – I have it,' he said. 'Let's get the rest of the dirt off it. Does anyone have water?'

Immediately, six hands holding water bottles shot towards him. He stood up, and the students clustered around him, effectively blocking my view of whatever it was he'd uncovered, as he poured water over it. I heard Hannah say, 'Oh, my goodness!' and one of the boys say, 'How cool is that?'

'Come and see, Laurel,' Jason said.

The students parted to let me through, and he held out his hand to show me a slender gold ring resting on his palm.

'It's a woman's ring,' he said. 'Third century, I think. Look at it more closely.'

Bending my head over the ring, I saw a pair of clasped hands engraved on the smooth gleaming metal, still visible after centuries under the earth.

'It's beautiful,' I said.

'It is,' Jason said. 'The engraving is a symbol of love.'

'A love token,' Hannah said. 'That's so romantic.'

'Lovers have been exchanging rings for centuries,' Jason said. 'The Romans wore wedding rings on their left hands as we do today. They believed that the *vena amoris* – the vein of love – ran straight from the ring finger to the heart.'

'Is it valuable, Dr Harding?' one of the students asked.

Jason looked down at the ring resting on the palm of his hand. 'I'd say it was valuable for what it represents,' he said. He handed the ring to Hannah. 'Make sure you tag it.'

Hannah nodded vigorously. 'I will, Dr Harding. I'll take it to the finds tent straight away.'

'You do that,' Jason said. 'When you find something as valuable as that ring, you ought to take good care not to lose it.' His blue eyes caught my gaze and held it. 'I once lost a valuable find. Or rather, not knowing what I had, I threw it away.' I felt his hand clasp mine, and my heart started beating very fast. 'I've been such an idiot, Laurel. You and me – I really messed up.'

'I made mistakes too,' I said.

'Not the way I did,' Jason said. 'I was so angry – I refused to listen to you, and walked away, even though I knew deep down that I was making the worst mistake of my life.' He moved closer to me, so that our bodies were almost touching. 'If you could only forgive me, Laurel, I promise you this – I'll never walk away from you again.'

'You want to rewrite our story?' I was trembling all over.

'I want us to write an original screenplay together – and for us to sign it off as a shooting script.' He put his arms around me and bent his head towards mine.

'Oh – Jason—' My heart brimmed. Dimly, I was aware of Hannah gasping, and a couple of the boys nudging each other with their elbows.

'*Sa agapo*,' Jason said. A smile playing about his mouth, he added, 'I'll translate that for you, if you like.'

'I don't need a translation,' I said.

And then he kissed me, and everything else, the excavation, the students, the blue sky above faded away.

Just like in a movie.

Chapter Forty-four

Two Years Later

I am sitting on a sun-baked rock, looking out over the Aegean to the horizon, where the sea merges into the sky in a shimmering heat-haze, when I hear the sound of the jeep. Twisting around, I see Jason getting out of the driver's seat. He sees me at the same moment and waves, before vanishing inside our studio apartment. A minute or so later, he is striding across the beach towards me. I jump up and run to meet him, and he kisses me very thoroughly.

'How was your day?' I say.

'Good,' he says. 'We put in a new trench, and it looks as though the site is even more extensive than I thought.'

We sit down next to each other on the rock and, his eyes shining, he brings me up to date on the progress of the dig in the hills behind the small village of whitewashed houses where we are staying, and the finds made that day by the international team of field archaeologists and archaeology students under his direction. His discovery of the Kyros site, when we were on our island-hopping trip around Greece the previous summer, has caused a sensation in the archaeology world – and beyond. And while Jason was exasperated by the brief flurry of media interest in him personally – 'I don't see what my having blond hair and blue eyes has to do with the discovery of a Mycenaean citadel' – he had to admit that the publicity helped him raise the funding for the excavation.

'They're hard working,' Jason says, now, of his students, 'and eager to learn – although I was rather taken aback when, on the way down the hill, in front of them all, the American boy asked me if it was true that I discovered my wife's wedding ring on a Roman site in London.'

I laugh – it hasn't escaped my notice that there is just as much gossip on a dig as on a film set. I hold up my left hand and the engraved ring on my fourth finger shines in the sunlight. It's a replica, of course – the original is now in the British Museum – but the rumour that, on his wedding day, eminent archaeologist Dr Jason Harding presented his wife with a two-thousand-year-old artefact he'd smuggled off an archaeological site is surprisingly persistent.

'It might not be strictly what happened,' I say, 'but it'd make a great scene in a rom-com.'

'I told the students it's a perfect example of how historical facts become legend – like the Trojan War – but I'm not sure that I convinced them,' Jason says with a wry smile. 'Anyway, what did you get up to today, while I was shovelling dirt under a hot sun?'

'You love all that digging,' I say, and he doesn't contradict me. On the days I've gone with him to the site – I'm a useful washer of potsherds – I've seen the enthusiasm with which he swings a pickaxe, his muscles rippling under his T-shirt. It's as well none of his team can see the movie playing in my head at those moments. 'I had a less strenuous day than you,' I say, having divided my time between writing under the shade of the vine-covered trellis and sunbathing on the beach, 'but I have some good news. I got an email from Marcus.'

'And?' Jason says.

'He loves my screenplay for *The Winged Archer*, and wants to make the picture.' I think how fortunate it was that before I sent my script to Farley Productions, I'd had Jason check it for anachronisms. How was I to know they didn't have potatoes in ancient Greece?

'But that's brilliant news,' Jason says. 'Not that Marcus is ever going to turn down an original screenplay from the writer of *Swords and Sandals*.' He puts his hand over mine. 'I know I've told you this before, but I really didn't understand how huge that film was going to be until I saw the crowds in Leicester Square.'

'That was such an amazing night.' I picture myself a year ago, walking along the red carpet on my new husband's arm, wearing the gold headband I'd bought in Athens, and I can't help smiling. Other scenes from *Swords and Sandals*' premiere, and the days that followed, float into my head in quick succession: Harry signing autographs for the fans, the blinding camera flashes as he and Amber pose together for the press photographers, Marcus twirling a giggling Shannon around the dance-floor at the after-party, Drew Brightman loudly informing everyone that he was flying out to LA for meetings with all the major studios . . . and the subsequent industry gossip that a stand-up row with a top Hollywood exec was the reason why he's not directed a picture since . . . Jason and me reading the ecstatic reviews of *Swords and Sandals* . . . Marcus phoning to tell us that the film had broken both cinema box office and streaming records . . . The two films I've worked on since then, now in production . . .

'I owe so much to Chloe and Lysander,' I say to Jason.

'So do I,' Jason says. 'If it wasn't for them, I'd never have made my greatest discovery. And I don't mean that ruined palace up on the hill.'

'What then?' I say.

'You,' he says. 'The greatest discovery of my life was that I love you, Laurel.'

'I love you, Jason,' I say.

Jason's smile melts my insides. He leans in for another kiss, and then, hand in hand, we walk down the beach, and swim in the blue Aegean Sea.

The Screenwriter and the Archaeologist is the best screenplay I've ever written.

Acknowledgements

Thank you to everyone at Headline who helped to turn *Love on Location* from a manuscript into a book, especially Clare, Sophie and Greg.

Another special thank you must go to my amazingly supportive and encouraging writer friends who are always ready to talk books and writing: Paula Fleming, Alison French, Annette Hannah, Lucinda Lee, Melissa Oliver, Sophie Rodger, Giulia Skye, Kathleen Whyman and Julia Wild.

And last but not least, thank you to Guy, Joanne, David, Sara, Iain, Laura and Marc for the beta-reading, the book-trailer-making, general cheerleading and especially for answering my questions about the film industry – you can use my house as a location any time! And a special mention to Dino – you can now say your name is in a book.